THE NIGHT WINDOW

Dean Koontz is the author of more than a dozen *New York Times* No.1 bestsellers. His books have sold over 500 million copies worldwide, and his work is published in 38 languages.

He was born and raised in Pennsylvania and lives with his wife Gerda and their dog Elsa in southern California.

🐦 @DeanKoontz
ⓕ Facebook.com/deankoontzofficial
www.deankoontz.com

DEAN KOONTZ
THE NIGHT WINDOW

HarperCollins*Publishers*

HarperCollins*Publishers*
1 London Bridge Street,
London SE1 9GF

www.harpercollins.co.uk

Published by HarperCollins*Publishers* 2019
1

First published in the USA in 2019 by Bantam Books,
an imprint of Random House,
A division of Penguin Random House LLC, New York.

A catalogue record for this book
is available from the British Library

ISBN: 978-0-00-829139-6 (HB)
ISBN: 978-0-00-829142-6 (TPB)

Text design by Virginia Norey

Printed and bound in Great Britain by
CPI Group (UK) Ltd, Croydon, CR0 4YY

MIX
Paper from
responsible sources
FSC **FSC® C007454**
www.fsc.org

This book is produced from independently certified FSC™ paper
to ensure responsible forest management.

For more information visit: www.harpercollins.co.uk/green

To Gerda,
who is my Jane

—

In memory of Ruth Ebner,
also known as Pepper, who was not just a faithful reader
but also an advocate of my work and much loved
by her many friends

Creating a neural [brain] lace is the thing that really matters for humanity to achieve symbiosis with machines.

—ELON MUSK

Ain't it strange the way we're ignorant
How we seek out bad advice
How we jigger it and figure it
Mistaking value for the price

—PAUL SIMON, "So Beautiful or So What?"

THE NIGHT WINDOW

PART ONE

Sucker Punch

1

The triple-pane floor-to-ceiling windows of Hollister's study frame the rising plain to the west, the foothills, and the distant Rocky Mountains that were long ago born from the earth in cataclysm, now dark and majestic against a sullen sky. It is a view to match the man who stands at this wall of glass. The word *cataclysm* is a synonym for *disaster* or *upheaval* but also for *revolution,* and he is the leader of the greatest revolution in history. The greatest and the last. The end of history is near, after which his vision of a pacified world will endure forever.

Meanwhile, there are mundane tasks to perform, obligations to address. For one thing, there is someone who needs to be killed.

In a few hours, when a late-season storm descends on these high plains east of Denver, the hunt will begin, and one of two men will die at the hands of the other, a fact Wainwright Warwick Hollister finds neither exhilarating nor frightening. Of profound importance to Hollister is that he avoid the character weaknesses of his father, Orenthal Hollister, and at all times comport himself in a more formidable and responsible manner than had his old man. Among other things, this means that when someone needs to be eliminated, the killing can't always be done by a hireling. If a man is too finicky to get blood on his hands once in a while, or if he lacks the courage to put himself at physical risk, then he can't claim to be a leader in this world of wolves, nor even a member of the pack, but is instead only a sheep in wolf's clothing.

The hunt will occur here, on Crystal Creek Ranch, Hollister's twelve-thousand-acre spread, unto itself a world of pine forests and rolling meadows. The chase will not be fair, because Hollister does not believe in fairness, which exists nowhere either in nature or in the human sphere. Fairness is an illusion of the weak and ignorant; it is the insincere promise made by those who manipulate the masses for gain.

The quarry, however, will have a chance to survive. A very slim one, but a chance. Although Hollister's father, Orenthal, had been a powerful man physically as well as financially, his heart had been that of a coward. If ever he had decided that he couldn't farm out *all* the violence required for the furtherance of his business, if he'd seen the moral need for every prince to be also a warrior, he wouldn't have given the quarry any chance whatsoever. The hunt would have been an empty ritual with only one possible end: the triumph of Orenthal and the death of his prey.

Now the security system, which always knows Hollister's location in this forty-six-thousand-square-foot residence, speaks in a soft, feminine voice. *"Thomas Buckle has arrived in the library."*

Thomas Buckle is a houseguest from L.A. The sole passenger on Hollister's Gulfstream V, he landed two hours earlier, at eleven o'clock this morning, on Crystal Creek's six-thousand-foot airstrip, was driven 1.6 miles from the hangar to the main house in a Rolls-Royce Phantom, and settled in a guest suite on the main floor.

He will most likely be dead by dawn.

The house is a sleek ultramodern masterpiece of native stone, glass, and stainless steel, with floors of limestone on which ornately figured antique Persian carpets float like lush warm islands on a cold pale sea.

The library contains twenty-five thousand volumes that Hollister inherited from his father. The old man was a lifelong reader of novels. But his son has no use for fiction. Wainwright Warwick Hollister is a realist from his epidermis to his marrow. Orenthal also read many works of philosophy, forever searching for the meaning of life. His son has no use for philosophy because he already knows the two words that give life its meaning: *money* and *power*. Only money and power can defend against the chaos of this world and ensure a life of pleasure. Those people whom he can't buy, Hollister can destroy. People are tools, unless they decline to be used, whereupon they become merely obstructions that must be broken and quickly swept aside—or eliminated entirely.

With no need for his father's books, he had considered donating the collection to a charity or university but instead moved them to this place as a reminder of the old man's fatal weakness.

Now, at one o'clock, as Hollister enters the library, Thomas Buckle turns from the shelves and says, "What a magnificent collection. First editions of everything from Ray Bradbury to Tom Wolfe. Hammett and Hemingway. Stark and Steinbeck. Such eclectic taste."

Buckle is twenty-six, handsome enough to be an actor, though he dreams of a career as a famous film director. He has already made two low-budget movies acclaimed by some critics, but box-office success has eluded him. He is at a crucial juncture, an ambitious young man of considerable talent whose philosophy and vision are at odds with the common wisdom that currently prevails in Hollywood, which he has begun to discover will limit his opportunities.

He has come here in response to a personal phone call from Wainwright Hollister, who expressed admiration for the young man's work and a desire to discuss a business proposal involving film production. This is a lie. However, as people are tools, so lies are nothing more than the various grips that one must apply to make them perform as wanted.

Upon the director's arrival, Hollister had briefly greeted him; now there is no need for the formalities of introduction. A smile is all he requires when he says, "Perhaps you would like to select one of these novels that's never been filmed and make it our first project together."

Although he is the least sentimental of men and although he has no capacity for the more tender emotions, Wainwright Hollister is graced with a broad, almost supernaturally pleasant face that can produce a smile with as many charming permutations as that of any courtesan in history, and he can use it to bewitch both women and men. They see compassion when in fact he regards them with icy contempt, see mercy when they should see cruelty, see humility when he views them with condescension. He is universally thought to be a most amiable man with a singular capacity for friendship, though in his heart he views everyone as a stranger too unknowable ever to be a friend. He uses his supple, glorious smile as if it were a farmer's seeding machine, planting kernels of deceit deep in everyone he meets.

Having been flown to Colorado in high style and having been treated like a prodigal son, Thomas Buckle takes seriously the offer to select any book in this library to translate to film. He looks around wonderingly at the shelves of material. "Oh, well, I sure wouldn't want to make that choice lightly, sir. I'd want to have a better idea of what's here."

"You'll have plenty of time to pore through the collection later," Hollister lies. "Let's have lunch. And please dispense with the 'sir.' I haven't been knighted. Just call me Wayne. 'Wainwright' is a mouthful, and 'Warwick' sounds like the villain in some superhero movie."

Thomas Buckle is an honest young man. His father is a tailor, a salaried employee of a dry-cleaning shop, and his mother works as a department store seamstress. Although his parents struggled to contribute to his film school tuition, Thomas paid for most of it, having worked part-time jobs since his freshman year in high school. On his two movies, he cut his fees for writing and directing, in order to increase the budget for actors and scene setups. He's too naïve to realize that his producing partner on those projects cleverly siphoned off some of the studio's money, which Hollister discovered from the exhaustive investigation he commissioned of Buckle's affairs. As the child of honest people, as an earnest artist and a striver in the all-American tradition, the young man has an abundance of hope and determination, but a serious deficit of street smarts; much to learn and no time left to learn it.

As they make their way from the library to the dining room, Tom Buckle can't restrain himself from commenting on the grandeur of the house and the high pedigree of the paintings on the walls—

Jackson Pollock, Jasper Johns, Robert Rauschenberg, Andy Warhol, Damien Hirst. . . . He is a poor boy enchanted by Hollister's great wealth, much as the sorcerer's apprentice might be captivated by the mystery of his master during the first day on the job.

There is no envy in his manner, no evidence of greed. Rather, as a filmmaker, he is besotted with the visuals. The drama of the house appeals to him as a story setting, and he is spinning some private narrative in his mind. Perhaps he imagines a biographical film of his own life, with this scene as the turning point between failure and phenomenal success.

Hollister enjoys answering questions about the architecture and the art, telling anecdotes of construction and acquisition. Only when he senses Tom Buckle has been drawn into his host's orbit, and then with great calculation, does Hollister put one arm around the young director's shoulders in the manner of a doting uncle.

This familiarity is received without the slightest stiffening or surprise. Honest men from honest families are at a disadvantage in this world of lies. The poor fool is as good as dead already.

2

The wisdom of millennia and numerous cultures was stacked on a grid maze of shelves flanking dimly lighted aisles in which no one searched for knowledge, all as quiet as an undiscovered pharaoh's tomb in a pyramid drifted over by a thousand feet of sand.

That first Friday in April, Jane Hawk was ensconced in a library in the San Fernando Valley, north of Los Angeles, using one of the public-access workstations that were nestled in a computer alcove, which currently offered the only action in the building. Because every computer featured a GPS locater, as did smartphones and electronic tablets and laptops, she carried none of those things. Although the authorities searching for her knew she used library computers, on this occasion she avoided websites they might expect to be of interest to her. Consequently, she was relatively secure in the conviction that none of her probes would trigger a track-to-source security program and pinpoint her location.

In her effort to expose a cabal of totalitarians at the highest echelons of government and private industry, she'd repeatedly zeroed in on a person who appeared to be at the point of the pyramid, only to discover each time that the true numero uno was someone else still cloaked in mystery. Recently, she had been urgently working with those names, all wealthy individuals, seeking connections among them. She had found one: a very public commitment to philanthropy, perhaps because being seen to have a charitable nature could be cover for dark intentions.

Although there were tens of thousands of charities they could have chosen, the people she knew to be near the top of this cabal served on the boards of many of the same nonprofits. And the one whose name was most often associated with theirs, Wainwright Warwick Hollister, a new figure to her, happened to be the wealthiest of them all.

In a conspiracy this radical, this bent on transforming America—indeed the world—the supreme leader, the self-appointed intellectual who inspired the loyalty of others, did not necessarily have to be the one with the most money. A fanatical passion for change and dominance might lift a man of modest means to that position.

However, Hollister, a megabillionaire, had a generously funded foundation of his own, and the deeper she probed into it, the more curious and suspicious it seemed.

Wainwright Hollister's foundation, ostensibly formed to support cancer research, had made significant donations to a nonprofit under the control of Dr. Bertold Shenneck, the genius who had conceived of, developed, and refined the nanotech brain implant that made possible the cabal's quest for absolute power. *Bingo.*

Many people using a computer or smartphone became so distracted that they ceased to be aware of what happened in the world around them and were in Condition White, one of the four Cooper Color Codes describing levels of situational awareness. After earning a college degree in forensic psychology in three years, after eighteen weeks of training at Quantico, and after having served as an FBI agent for six years before going rogue, Jane was perpetually in Condition Yellow: relaxed but alert, aware, not in expectation of an attack, but never oblivious of significant events around her.

Continuous situational awareness was necessary to avoid being cast abruptly into Condition Red, with a genuine threat imminent.

Between yellow and red was Condition Orange, when an aware and alert person recognized something strange or wrong in a situation, a potential threat looming. In this case, through peripheral vision, she realized that a man who'd entered after her and settled at one of the other computers was spending considerably more time watching her than the screen before him.

Maybe he was staring at her just because he liked the way she looked. She had considerable experience of men's admiration.

Her own hair concealed by an excellent shaggy-cut ash-blond wig, blue eyes made gray by contact lenses, a fake mole the size of a pea attached to her upper lip with spirit gum, wearing a little too much makeup and Smashbox lipstick, she was deep in her Leslie Anderson identity. Because she looked younger than she was and wore a pair of stage-prop glasses with bright red frames, she could be mistaken for a studious college girl. She never behaved in a furtive or nervous manner, as the most-wanted fugitive on the FBI list might be expected to do, but called attention to herself in subtle ways—yawning, stretching, muttering at the computer screen—and chatted up anyone who spoke to her. She was confident that no average citizen would easily see through Leslie Anderson and recognize the wanted woman whom the media called "the beautiful monster."

However, the guy kept staring at her. Twice when she casually glanced in his direction, he quickly looked away, pretending to be absorbed in the data on his screen.

His genetic roots were in the subcontinent of India. Caramel skin, black hair, large dark eyes. Perhaps thirty pounds overweight. A pleasant, round face. Maybe twenty-five. Dressed in khakis and a yellow pullover.

He didn't fit the profile of someone in law enforcement or that of an intelligence-agency spook. Nevertheless, he made her uneasy. More than uneasy. She never dismissed the still, small voice of intuition that had so often kept her alive.

So, Condition Orange. Two options: engage or evade. The second was nearly always the better choice, as the first was more likely to lead to Condition Red and a violent confrontation.

Jane backed out of the website she had been exploring, wiped the browsing history, clicked off the computer, picked up her tote, and walked out of the alcove.

As she moved toward the front desk, she glanced back. The plump man was standing, holding something in one hand, at his side, so she couldn't identify it, and watching her as he spoke into his phone.

When she opened the door at the main entrance, she saw another man standing by her metallic-gray Ford Explorer Sport in the public parking lot, talking on *his* phone. Tall, lean, dressed all in black, he was too distant for her to see his face. But on this mild sunny day, his knee-length raincoat might have been worn to conceal a sawed-off shotgun or maybe a Taser XREP 12-gauge that could deliver an electronic projectile and a disabling shock from a distance of a hundred feet. He looked as real as death and yet phantasmal, like an assassin who had slipped through a rent in the cosmic fabric between this world and another, on some mystical mission.

The Explorer, a stolen vehicle, had been scrubbed of its former identity in Mexico, given a purpose-built 700-horsepower 502 Chevy engine, and purchased from a reliable black-market dealer in Nogales, Arizona, who didn't keep records. There seemed to be no way it could have been tied to her.

Instead of stepping outside, she closed the door and turned to her right and made her way through the shelves of books. The aisles weren't a maze to her, because she had scouted the place when she arrived, before settling at the computer.

An EXIT sign marked a door to a back hallway that was fragrant with fresh-brewed coffee. Offices. Storerooms. An open refreshments niche with a refrigerator. A short hall intersected the longer one, and at the end, another door opened out to a small staff-parking area with an alleyway beyond.

Three cars and a Chevy Tahoe had occupied this back lot when she'd checked it earlier.

Now, in addition to those vehicles, a white Cadillac Escalade stood in the fifth of seven spaces, to the west of the library's rear door. The woman in the driver's seat of the Caddy had the same caramel complexion and black hair as the man at the computer. She had a phone to her ear and was speaking to someone, which didn't prove complicity in a plot, though her eyes fixed on Jane like a shooter's eyes on a target.

In any crisis situation, the most important thing to do was get off the X, move, because if you weren't moving away from the threat, someone with bad intentions was for damn sure moving closer to you.

Avoiding the Escalade, Jane went east. Along the north side of the alley, shadows of two-, three-, and four-story buildings painted a pattern like castle crenellations on the pavement, and she stayed in that shade for what little cover it provided, moving quickly past Dumpsters standing sentinel. To the south, past the library, there was a park, and beyond the park a kindergarten with a fenced playground.

She was opposite the park, where phoenix palms rustled in a light breeze and swayed their shadows on the grass, when the tall man in the raincoat appeared as if conjured, coming toward her, not running, in no hurry, as though it was ordained that she was his to take at will.

The structures to her left housed businesses, the names of which were emblazoned on the back doors: a gift shop, a restaurant, a stationery store, another restaurant. The buildings in that block shared walls, so there were no service passages between enterprises.

When a sedan pulled into the east end of the alley and angled to a stop, serving as a barricade, Jane didn't bother to look behind herself, because she had no doubt the Escalade had likewise blocked the west end of the alleyway.

As she hurried along, she tried doors, and the third one—CLASSIC PORTRAIT PHOTOGRAPHY—wasn't locked. She went inside, where a series of small windows near the ceiling admitted enough light to reveal a combination receiving area and storage room.

The shelves were empty. When she turned to the alley door to engage the deadbolt, the lock was broken.

She'd been skillfully herded to this place. The previous tenant had moved out. She had walked into a trap.

3

The formal dining room, which seats twenty, isn't intimate enough for the conversation that Wainwright Hollister intends to have with Thomas Buckle. They are served in the breakfast room, which is separated from the immense kitchen by a butler's pantry.

A large Francis Bacon painting of smudges, whorls, and jagged lines is the only painting in the twenty-foot-square chamber, a work of alarming dislocations that hangs opposite the ordered vista of nature—groves of evergreens and undulant meadows—visible beyond the floor-to-ceiling windows.

They sit at the stainless-steel and cast-glass table. Buckle faces the windows, so the immense and lonely nature of the ranch will be impressed upon him by the time he learns that he is to be hunted to the death in that cold vastness. Hollister faces the young director and the painting behind him, for the art of Francis Bacon reflects his view of human society as chaotic, confirms his belief in the need to impose order by brute power and extreme violence.

The chef, Andre, is busy in the kitchen. Lovely Mai-Mai serves them, beginning with an icy glass of pinot grigio and small plates of Andre's Parmesan crisps. She wears a verbena fragrance as subtle as the mere memory of a scent.

Tom Buckle is clearly charmed by the girl's beauty and grace. However, the almost comic awkwardness with which he tries to engage her in conversation as she performs her duties has less to do with sexual attraction than with the fact that he is out of his element, the son of a tailor and a seamstress, abashed by the splendor of the wealth all around him and uncertain how to behave with the staff of such a great house. He chats up Mai-Mai as if she were a waitress in a restaurant.

Because she's well trained, the very ideal of a servant, Mai-Mai is polite but not familiar, at all times smiling but properly distant.

When the two men are alone, Hollister raises his glass in a toast. "To a great adventure together."

He is amused to see that Buckle rises an inch or two off his chair, intending to get up and lean across the table in order to clink glasses with his host. But at once the director realizes that the width of the table will make this maneuver awkward, that he should take his cue from Hollister and remain seated. He pretends to have been merely adjusting his position in the chair as he says, "To a great adventure."

After they taste the superb wine, Wainwright Hollister says, "I am prepared to invest six hundred million in a slate of films, but not in a partnership with a traditional studio, where I'm certain the book-keeping would leave me with a return far under one percent or no return at all." He is lying, but his singular smile could sell ice to Eskimos or apostasy to the pope.

Although Buckle surely knows that he's in the presence of a man who thinks big and is worth twenty billion dollars, he is all but struck speechless by the figure his lunch companion has mentioned. "Well . . . that is . . . you could . . . a very valuable catalog of films could be created for that much money."

Hollister nods agreement. "Exactly—if we avoid the outrageous budgets of the mindless special-effects extravaganzas that Holly-wood churns out these days. What I have in mind, Tom, are exciting and intense and *meaningful* films of the kind you make, with budgets between twenty and sixty million per picture. Timeless stories that will speak to people as powerfully fifty years from now as they will on their initial release."

Hollister raises his glass again in an unexpressed endorsement of his initial toast. Buckle takes the cue, raising his glass as well and then drinking with his host, a vision of cinematic glory shining in his eyes.

Leaning forward in his chair, with a genial warmth that he is able to summon as easily as a man with chronic bronchitis can cough up phlegm, Hollister says, "May I tell you a story, Tom, one that I think will make a wonderful motion picture?"

"Of course. Yes. I'd love to hear it."

"Now, if you find it clichéd or jejune, you must be honest with me. Honesty between partners is essential."

The word *partners* visibly heartens Buckle. "I couldn't agree more, Wayne. But I want to hear it out to the end before I comment. I've got to understand the roundness of the concept."

"Of course you know who Jane Hawk is."

"Everyone knows who she is—top of the news for weeks."

"Indicted for espionage, treason, murder," Hollister recaps.

Buckle nods. "They now say she even murdered her husband, the hero Marine, that he didn't commit suicide."

Leaning forward a little more, cocking his head, Hollister speaks in a stage whisper. "What if it's all lies?"

Buckle looks perplexed. "How can it all be lies? I mean—"

Holding up one hand to stop the young man, Hollister says, "Wait for the roundness of the concept."

He leans back in his chair, pausing to enjoy one of the Parmesan crisps.

Buckle tries one as well. "These are delicious. I've never had anything quite like them. Perfect with this wine."

"Andre, my chef," Hollister says, "is an adjusted person. He is obsessed with food. He lives only to cook."

If the term *adjusted person* strikes Thomas Buckle as odd, he gives no indication of puzzlement.

After a sip of wine, Hollister continues. "According to friends of hers, Jane became obsessed with proving her husband, Nick, didn't commit suicide, that he was murdered, and when she took a leave of absence from the FBI, she devoted herself to investigating Nick's death. On the other hand, authorities and media say she was merely putting up a good front to divert suspicion from her role in his death.

We're told she drugged him and got him into the bathtub and slit his throat, cutting his carotid artery with his Marine Ka-Bar knife in such a way that it looked to the coroner as if he'd taken his own life. *But what if that's all a lie?"*

Buckle is intrigued. *"What if* is the essence of storytelling. So what if?"

Hollister continues with relish. "Jane told friends that in her research she found a fifteen-percent increase in suicides during the past few years, that all of it involved well-liked, stable people successful in their professions, happy in their relationships, none with a history of depression, people like her husband."

"A few nights ago," Tom Buckle says, "on that TV show *Sunday Magazine,* they did an hour about Hawk. They included experts who said the rate of suicide isn't constant. It goes up, goes down. And all this about happy people killing themselves isn't the case."

"Remember my what-if, Tom. What if it's all a lie, and some in the media are part of it? What if Jane Hawk is on to something, and they need to demonize her with false charges, silence her?"

"You see this as a conspiracy story."

"Exactly."

"Well, then, it sure would be a conspiracy of unprecedented proportions."

"Unprecedented," Hollister agrees. "Heroic. Involving thousands of powerful people in government and the private sector. Let's say these conspirators called themselves . . . Techno Arcadians."

"Arcadia. From ancient Greece. A place of peace, innocence, prosperity. Essentially Utopia."

Hollister beams and claps his hands twice. "You are just the young man to understand my story."

"But why 'techno'?"

"Do you know what nanotechnology is, Tom?"

"Very tiny machines made up of a handful of atoms, or maybe molecules. They say it's the future, with unlimited medical and industrial applications."

"You are so cutting-edge," Hollister declares and pushes a call button on the table leg. "When I saw your films, I said, 'This is a guy on the cutting edge.' I'm delighted to see I was right."

In answer to the silent summons, Mai-Mai returns to freshen their wine and remove the empty plates that held the Parmesan crisps.

Thomas Buckle smiles at her and thanks her, but he seems to have intuited that the proper behavior in these circumstances is to treat her with reserve, not as if she were working at Olive Garden.

The entertainment business hasn't coarsened him yet, for though Mai-Mai fascinates and attracts him, he watches her not with evident lust, but with an almost adolescent wistfulness and yearning.

When the two men are alone once more, Hollister says, "Let's suppose these conspirators, these Techno Arcadians, have developed a nanomachine brain implant, a control mechanism, that makes complete puppets of the people in whom it's installed. And the puppets don't know what's been done to them, don't know they're now . . . property."

The director blinks, blinks, and a certain quiet excitement comes over him that has nothing to do with six hundred million dollars, that arises from his passion for filmmaking.

"So . . . central to the story would be the issue of free will. A conspiracy intent on subjugating all humanity, the death of freedom, a sort of technologically imposed slavery."

Hollister grins like an amateur author thrilled that a real writer found merit in his scenario. "You like it so far?"

"I damn well do. I like it more by the minute. Even though Jane Hawk inspired the idea, we can't say this is her story, so we'd have to change the character to maybe a CIA agent or something, make her a little older. Maybe it's even a male lead. But one thing . . . why would anyone submit to having such a brain implant surgically installed?"

Leaning forward again, punctuating his revelation with a wink, Hollister speaks in a stage whisper. *"No surgery required. You drug them or otherwise overpower them when they're alone, and the implant is administered by injection."*

4

Jane Hawk hurried out of the storage room. Milky daylight spilled through a large sales area and curdled to gray in a hallway. Two doors stood open on each side of the hall, a shadowy bath and dark empty offices.

At the front of the store, two frosted-glass show windows each bore the words CLASSIC PORTRAIT PHOTOGRAPHY painted in script, reversed from Jane's perspective. Between the windows stood a door with a frosted inlay, and as she approached it, a man shape loomed beyond like a stalker emerging out of fog in a disturbing dream.

He must be one of them. She'd have to take him down to get to the street and away, but even if he was a mortal threat, she could not risk resorting to gunfire when there were sure to be pedestrians on the sidewalk.

The tall man in the raincoat might already be entering the back of the place from the alleyway.

Jane's attention swung toward an interior door to her right, four panels of solid wood, no glass. If it was only a closet, she was cornered.

Instead, beyond lay stairs ascending into gloom. In nearly blinding darkness, she used the handrail to guard against a fall until she arrived at a landing. Another flight led up to a second landing where pale light issued from an open door.

Perhaps the photographer who had once run a business out of the ground floor had lived above his studio.

Considering that the people closing in on her seemed to have herded her into this building, one of them might be waiting in the second-floor apartment.

Her heart labored but didn't race, for she was in the grip of dread rather than full-blown fright. If these were Arcadians—and who else could they be?—they were not going to kill her here. They were going to corner her, Taser her, chloroform her, and convey her to a secure facility where she could scream herself hoarse without being heard by anyone sympathetic to her plight.

Ultimately they were going to inject her with the neural lace that would web her brain and enslave her. Then they would drain from her the names of everyone who had been of assistance to her in this crusade and would insist upon knowing the whereabouts of her five-year-old son, Travis. When she was their obedient puppet, they would eventually instruct her to kill herself.

But not just herself. She knew these elitist creeps. She knew the icy coldness of their minds, the blackness of their hearts, the pure contempt with which they viewed those who did not share their misanthropic view of humanity and did not endorse their narcissism. They would relish cruel vengeance for the trouble she had caused them, for their comrades who had tried to murder her and had been killed instead. They would instruct her to torture her own child and slaughter him; only when he was brutally ravaged and dead would they tell her to kill herself. In the thrall of the nanoweb, with its filaments wound through her brain, she would be unable to resist even the most horrific of their commands.

Compared to injection, a quick death would be a mercy.

She put her tote beside the open door. Drew the Heckler & Koch Compact .45 from the rig under her sport coat. She hated clearing doorways in such situations, but there was no time to hesitate.

Pistol in a two-hand grip, leading with head and gun, low and fast, she crossed the threshold, stepped to the right, back against the wall, eyes on the Heckler's front sight as she swept the room left to right.

Three windows facing the street. No blinds or drapes. Morning light slanting in under scalloped fabric awnings. No furniture. No carpeting on the hardwood floor. Nothing moved except a few dust balls stirred by the slight draft she'd made on entering.

An archway connected this room to others toward the back of the building, where darkness reigned, and there was a door on the right, ajar.

She held her breath and heard only silence. Both training and intuition argued that if someone was in the apartment with her, he would have made a move by now.

The silence was broken when a sound rose from below, perhaps someone ascending the stairs.

She returned to the apartment entrance to retrieve her tote. Among other things, it contained $90,000, all of which—and more—she had taken from the stashes of wealthy Arcadians who had tried and failed to kill her. She couldn't afford to lose it; she was fighting a quiet war, but a war nonetheless, and wars cost money.

The building was old, and the stairs creaked under the weight of whoever was climbing them.

She closed the door. The deadbolt was intact. She engaged it.

5

Mai-Mai serves a small chopped salad sprinkled with pine nuts and crumbles of feta cheese.

Tom Buckle smiles and thanks her and watches her lithe form as she exits through the butler's pantry.

When the girl is gone, Wainwright Hollister says, "I need to explain how an injectable brain implant might be feasible, Tom. I don't want you to think of this as a science-fiction movie. It's a thoroughly contemporary thriller."

"I know a little about nanotech, Wayne, just enough to accept the premise."

"Good. Very good. Now suppose hundreds of thousands of these microscopic constructs can be suspended in ampules of fluid and stored at temperatures between—oh, let's say—thirty-six and fifty degrees, where they remain in stasis. When injected, the warmth of the blood gradually activates them. They're brain-tropic. The veins conduct them to the heart, then the carotid and vertebral arteries

bring them to the brain. Do you know what the blood-brain barrier is, Tom?"

Buckle evidently finds the salad highly agreeable and pauses to swallow a mouthful before saying, "I've heard of it, but I'm no whiz when it comes to medical matters."

"Nor do you need to be. You're an artist and a damn fine one. Ideas and emotions are the stuff of your work. So . . . the blood-brain barrier is a complex biological mechanism that allows vital substances in the blood to penetrate the walls of the brain's numerous capillaries while keeping out harmful substances such as certain drugs. Let's imagine these amazingly tiny nanoconstructs have been designed to pass through the blood-brain barrier, after which they assemble into a control mechanism in the brain."

"Could they really self-assemble? I mean . . . many, many thousands of them?"

"An excellent question, Tom. We wouldn't have a viable story if I didn't have an answer!" Hollister pauses to enjoy his salad.

"It's snowing." Thomas Buckle points to the windows behind his host.

Hollister turns in his chair to watch the first snowflakes, the size of quarters and half dollars, spiraling out of the low clouds like some jackpot disgorged by a celestial slot machine.

Refocusing his attention on his guest, he says, "The forecast is for twelve inches. Temperature will drop to the low twenties by nightfall. No wind yet, but it's coming. Winter lingers on these plains. Have you experienced a storm in territory such as this?"

"I'm a California boy. My experience of snow is entirely from TV and movies."

Hollister nods. "If a man were on the run from a killer on a night like the one coming, his least concern might be his would-be assassin. The weather itself could be the deadlier foe." Before Buckle might wonder at this odd statement, his host favors him with a beguiling smile. "I've got a story in mind for just such a movie. But before I bore you with a second scenario, let's see if I can make my nano tale convincing to the end. You asked how these tiny constructs could be made to self-assemble in the brain. Have you heard the term 'Brownian movement'?"

6

Jane was at the moment safe behind the locked door of the second-floor apartment, although not safe for long.

This was a two-story building, and like all the buildings on this block—whether two, three, or four stories—it had a flat roof with a low parapet. There would be an exit to the roof somewhere in these rooms, probably by way of a metal spiral staircase tucked into a service closet.

But she didn't want to go up and out that way. If she got to the roof through a trapdoor or through a stairhead shed, she might discover that they had anticipated her and had stationed one of their own up there to greet her. Then she would have nowhere to go.

Even if no sonofabitch with an XREP Taser waited above, Jane didn't fancy a wild flight across rooftops as in a James Bond flick. Although the buildings varied in height, they were contiguous, and she was likely to find service ladders bolted to walls to allow roof-maintenance men easy passage from one elevation to another. However, she'd already counted five agents in this operation, so there might be more. And if they had mounted a force of that size, they might also have a drone at their service.

She'd previously survived an encounter with two weaponized drones in a San Diego park, something similar to a DJI Inspire 1 Pro with a three-axis gimbaled camera. An eight- or ten-pound drone couldn't be fitted with even a miniature belt feed loaded with .22-caliber rounds, because the recoil would destabilize the craft. But those in San Diego featured a low-recoil compressed-air weapon that fired needle-like quarrels perhaps containing a tranquilizer.

The people now closing in on her would not risk using such a drone on a busy suburban street in a commercial district, but they might keep one hovering above the roofs where, if she appeared, she could be at once dropped unconscious without much chance that anyone at street level would see the assault.

The prospect of a machine assailant gave her a deeper chill than did a thug with a Taser XREP 12-gauge, not necessarily for good reason, but because it seemed to herald a new world in which those people not enslaved by nanoweb neural lace would be policed and punished by robots incapable of empathy or mercy.

She went to the front windows of the apartment living room, which faced onto the street and offered her the best—the only—chance of escaping capture.

7

Sitting with his back to the windows, Hollister is so attuned to the moment, so looking forward to Tom Buckle's sudden realization of his dire situation, so enthusiastic about the pending hunt, his senses so heightened that he can almost feel the huge snowflakes spiraling through the windless day behind his back, can almost hear those delicate wheels of crystal lace turning as they descend, can almost smell the blood that will form patterns in brilliant contrast across a canvas of snow.

"Brownian movement," he explains, "is progress by random motion. It's one of nature's primary mechanisms, Tom. The easiest way to explain is with the example of ribosomes, those tiny mitten-shaped organelles that exist in enormous numbers in the cytoplasm of human cells. They manufacture proteins."

When his host pauses for wine, Buckle appears to be dazzled when he says, "Man, you've really worked this story out in detail."

Hollister can feel his blue eyes twinkling with merriment, and he knows his captivating smile has never served him better. "Only because I so very much want you to be part of this, to sign on for this adventure with me. Now, ribosomes. Each one has more than fifty different components. If you break down thousands of ribosomes into their individual components and thoroughly mix them in a suspending fluid, then they ricochet off the molecules of the suspending medium and keep knocking against one another until one by one the fifty-some parts come together like puzzle pieces and, amazingly, assemble into whole ribosomes again. *That* is Brownian movement. It works with Bertold Shenneck's control mechanism because each of the components is designed to fit in only one place, so the puzzle can't assemble incorrectly."

" 'Shenneck'?" Buckle asks.

Hollister should not have mentioned Shenneck, who had in fact invented the nanoweb implant. Now he covers his slip of the tongue. "As I was working this out, I needed to name some characters. That's just what I call the scientist who developed the nanoweb implant."

"It's a good name for the character, but . . ." The director frowns. "It sounds a little familiar. We should check it out, make sure there's not a prominent Bertold Shenneck out there anywhere."

Hollister dismisses the issue with a wave of one hand. "I'm not wedded to the name. Not at all. You're better than I am at this."

Having finished his salad, the director blots his mouth on his napkin. "So how long does it take this brain implant to assemble once it's been injected?"

"Maybe eight or ten hours with the first-generation implant, but the device will be improved, so it might be brought down to, say, four hours. The subject has no memory of being restrained and injected. Once the control mechanism is in place, his mind can be accessed with a key phrase like 'Play Manchurian with me.' Once accessed, he'll do anything he's told to do—and think he's acting of his own volition."

The key phrase delights Buckle. "That great Cold War movie about brainwashing. *The Manchurian Candidate.* John Frankenheimer directed from a Richard Condon novel. Sinatra and Laurence Harvey. Angela Lansbury as Harvey's power-mad mother. About 1962, I think."

"Shenneck liked his little jokes. The scientist character. Whatever we're going to call him."

"My head is swimming, Wayne, but in a good way. I'm really getting into the whole concept. But exactly how does this tie to Jane Hawk, where we started?"

Responding to the call button, Mai-Mai enters to remove the salad plates.

Hollister says, "Just imagine, Tom, that these Techno Arcadians are intent not only on repressing the unruly masses by injecting and controlling selected leaders in politics, religion, business, and the arts. They also want to prevent charismatic individuals with wrong ideas from influencing the culture."

Tom smiles at Mai-Mai and then responds to his host. "What wrong ideas?"

"Any ideas in disagreement with Arcadian philosophy. Let's say it's been decided that controlling these charismatic types isn't enough, that it's necessary to remove their unique genomes from society, prevent them from propagating. So they receive a brain implant and are later directed to commit suicide."

Tom Buckle nods. "Like Jane Hawk's husband. But how would these people be chosen for elimination?"

"A computer model identifies them by their public statements, beliefs, accomplishments. Then they're put on the Hamlet list."

"'Hamlet'? Why Hamlet?"

"The theory is that if someone had killed Hamlet in the first act, a lot more people would have been alive at the end."

Frowning, Tom Buckle says, "For the movie, we'd probably have to call it something other than the Hamlet list. Anyway, how many people would be on this list?"

"Let's imagine the computer model says that, in a country as large as ours, two hundred and ten thousand of the most charismatic potential leaders in each generation would have to be removed at the rate of eight thousand four hundred a year."

"Mass murder. This is a very dark movie, Wayne."

"To the Arcadians, it's not murder. They think of it as culling from the herd any individuals with dangerous potential, a necessary step toward peace and stability."

Mai-Mai returns with the entrée: sea bass, asparagus, and miniature buttered raviolis stuffed with mascarpone and red peppers.

Conversation throughout the main course focuses on what changes to make in the lead character and possible twists and turns in the story line. Hollister mentions the "whispering room," a feature of the brain implants, by which adjusted people are able to communicate with one another via microwave transmission, brain to brain, as Elon Musk, of Tesla and Space X fame, has predicted will eventually be possible. They have the potential of forming a hive mind. The idea delights Buckle. Hollister enjoys this blue-sky session far more than he would if he were actually going to finance a motion picture.

Movies are terrible investments. Perhaps three out of ten make a profit. And there are countless ways that the distribution company can massage the box office numbers and pad the costs, so when there is a profit, much of it disappears.

However, Tom is bright and enthusiastic. Inventing this movie with him is a pleasure. The more the young man talks, the clearer it becomes that the computer model was right to put him on the Hamlet list, and it is good that he will be dead by dawn.

When Mai-Mai returns to remove their plates, Hollister says, "The time has come for you to do as we discussed."

She meets his stare, and though she is submissive, she is also afraid. Her lips part as if she will speak, but instead of words, her voluptuous mouth produces only tremors.

As she stands beside her master's chair, Hollister takes one of her hands in both of his, and he smiles reassuringly. He speaks to her as he might to a daughter. "It's all right, child. It's just a moment of performance art. You have always excelled as an artist. This is what you were born to do."

Her fear abates. The tremor fades. She answers his smile with an affectionate smile of her own. She bends down to kiss his cheek.

Tom Buckle watches with evident perplexity. When Mai-Mai leaves the room with their plates, the filmmaker is at a loss for words and covers his uncertainty by taking a sip of wine and savoring it.

"I see you're curious about Mai-Mai," Hollister says.

"No, not at all," Buckle demurs. "It's none of my business."

"In fact, Tom, it's the essence of your business here. Mai-Mai is twenty-seven, a year older than you, an exceptional woman."

Tom glances toward the swinging door through which Mai-Mai left the room. "She's quite beautiful."

"Quite," Hollister echoes. "She's also supremely talented. Her paintings redefine realism. They're stunning. By the time she was twenty-two, she'd won numerous awards. By the time she was twenty-four, her work was represented by the most prestigious galleries. She broke new ground as well by combining several of her larger paintings with a unique form of performance art that began to draw enthusiastic crowds."

"Does she still paint?"

"Oh, yes. Better than ever. Magnificent images exquisitely rendered."

"Then why . . ."

"Why is she here serving us lunch?"

"I can't help but wonder."

"She creates paintings but doesn't sell them anymore."

"You sure know how to build mystery, Wayne."

Hollister smiles. "I've intrigued you, have I?"

"Greatly. I'd love to see these paintings."

"You can't. After she finishes a new canvas, she destroys it."

Bafflement creases Tom Buckle's brow. "Whyever would she do such a thing?"

"Because she's an adjusted person. She made the list."

This incident with Mai-Mai has disoriented Tom just enough so that the word *list* has no immediate meaning for him.

"The Hamlet list," Hollister explains.

Puzzlement gives way to misunderstanding, and Tom smiles. "You give one hell of a pitch meeting, Wayne. And she's quite an actress."

"She's not an actress," Hollister assures him. "She's just an obedient little bitch. She destroys them because I tell her to."

Just then Tom Buckle's gaze shifts from his host to the wall of glass behind him. "What on earth . . . ?" Tom rises from his chair.

Wainwright Hollister gets to his feet as well and turns to the window.

Mai-Mai stands naked on the terrace, in the swiftly falling snow, facing them and smiling serenely, seeming more mystical than real.

"Her body is as perfect as her face," says Hollister, "but one can grow tired even of such perfection. I've had enough of her."

A scarlet silk scarf drapes Mai-Mai's right hand. It slides to the snow-carpeted terrace, revealing a pistol.

"Performance art," Tom Buckle tells himself, for he is both confused and in denial.

Soundlessly snow falls and falls, cascades of white petals, as Mai-Mai puts the barrel of the gun in her mouth and seems to breathe out the dragon fire of muzzle flash, seems to fold to the terrace in slow motion, the flowerfall of snow settling silently on her silent corpse.

8

Jane raised the lower sash of a double-hung window.

A foot below the windowsill, running nearly the width of the building, a five-foot-wide cantilevered marquee overhung the public sidewalk, the front of it bearing the name of the closed photography studio.

She dropped her tote onto the lid of the marquee and followed it through the window.

The entire block was from the Art Deco period, and each of the shared-wall buildings had its own stylized marquee, each separated from the next by a two-foot-wide gap. Jane hurried eastward, sprang from that first projection onto a second, from the second onto a third.

With the tote slung over her left shoulder, she knelt on the edge of the third marquee, facing the building, gripped the decorative masonry cornice, and slid backward into empty air, hanging by her hands for a moment before dropping to the sidewalk.

She startled an old guy in a tam-o'-shanter and walking with a three-footed cane. "Pretty girls falling from the sky!" he declared. "These are days of miracles and wonder."

In the drop, her tote had slid off her arm. She snared it from the sidewalk.

"If only I were fifty years younger," he said.

Jane said, "If only I were fifty years older," kissed him on the cheek, stepped between two parked cars, and dodged across three lanes of traffic.

From the farther side of the street, she looked back and saw the man in the dark raincoat at the open window through which she had exited the building, and below him another man venturing forth from the recessed entryway to the former photography studio. They both had spotted her.

At the corner, she turned north, out of their sight. Ahead, a thirty-something guy was preparing to climb onto a fully chromed Harley Road King cruiser. His open-face helmet boasted an American flag decal. She hoped it meant something to him.

Breathless, she said, "Give a girl a ride?"

He didn't look her up and down as men usually did, only met her eyes. "Where you going?"

"Anywhere but here. And fast."

"Cops or not cops?"

She had to give him something to win cooperation. "Maybe they carry a badge, but it's bogus."

As he swung aboard the saddle, he said, "Climb on and hold tight."

She sat just forward of the saddlebags, tote straps over one shoulder, arms around him.

The motor was hopped up, with the distinct sound of Screamin' Eagle pistons and cylinders.

Jane glanced over her shoulder. One of her pursuers turned the corner.

The Road King shot away from the curb.

9

The sky unseen behind the raveling white skeins with which it cocooned the world, and on the terrace Mai-Mai's once lovely form stiffening under a crystalline lacework . . .

This side of the windows, Tom Buckle repeats, "Performance art," though the artist is not going to stand up, bloodied and brainless, to take a bow.

Adam, Brad, and Carl, the three most senior members of the ranch's eighteen-man security force, who once had other names and personalities and real lives, enter the breakfast room. They are dressed in black, with the Crystal Creek Ranch logo in white stitching on the breast pockets of their shirts.

Although Tom Buckle still regards the suicide of Mai-Mai with stunned disbelief, he at once responds to these three men with fear and alarm, as well he should. They have the intensity of wolves on the hunt, and though their stares are as sharp as filleting knives, there is a deadness in their eyes that implies, quite accurately, that they are as coldhearted as machines.

"Tom," Hollister says in a tone of voice that suggests nothing out of the ordinary has occurred, "do you remember the name of the brainwashed assassin in *The Manchurian Candidate*?"

Tom eases away from the newcomers. "What is this? What the hell is happening here?"

In answer to his own question, Hollister says, "His name was Raymond Shaw. Specimens like these three"—he gestures toward the security agents—"we call rayshaws. One word. Lowercase *r*. They're adjusted people, injected with a control mechanism. But this nanoweb is different from those administered to Mai-Mai and Nick Hawk and others on the Hamlet list. This version scrubs away their memories, every last one, deconstructs their personalities, and programs them to be bodyguards who, without hesitation, will give their lives for their master. I am their master, Tom, and if I tell them to kill you, they will do so with extreme prejudice."

The film director eases away from the rayshaws until he backs into a sideboard. He is physically rigid, but there is no doubt he's reeling mentally and emotionally.

"Your work has earned you a place on the Hamlet list, Tom, and therefore a death sentence."

The filmmaker dares to look away from the rayshaws and meet his host's eyes. Although he is a screenwriter as well as a director, he is at a loss for words, perhaps struggling to make sense of this bizarre turn of events and plug it into a dramatic structure that promises him a triumphant resolution.

"I could order these men to subdue you and inject you and send you back to California with no knowledge of anything that has occurred here."

Wainwright Hollister rounds the end of the table, approaching Tom Buckle.

"Do you know Roger and Jennifer Boseman?"

As if shell-shocked, Tom says, "What?"

"Roger and Jennifer Boseman?"

"They live next to me, neighbors, next door."

"Their daughter Kaylee, ten years old. She's quite a beautiful child. After you're injected, adjusted, and sent home, if I call you in a few weeks and instruct you to kidnap Kaylee, rape her, torture her, kill her, and then kill yourself . . . you will obey."

He comes face-to-face with his guest.

"After that outrage, the two acclaimed films you've made will be judged the work of a monster, withdrawn from distribution in all formats, never to be seen again. Whatever small effect you've thus far had on the culture will be erased."

The director finally accepts what he desperately doesn't want to believe. "Dear God, it's real. The nanoweb, the injections, the enslavement."

"Yes. But 'enslavement' is the wrong word, Tom. Most human beings are impetuous, imprudent, ignorant, given to superstition and other irrational behavior. They're maladjusted. For their own sake and to preserve this fragile planet, we merely intend to adjust them."

"You're insane."

"No, Tom. I'm the clearest-thinking person you'll ever meet. I have no illusions about the meaning of life."

Hollister favors the younger man with a kindly smile worthy of a country doctor in a painting by Norman Rockwell.

"I'm also a man of profound convictions. I don't always leave the dirty work to others. Sometimes I do the adjusting myself. The adjusting or, as in your case, the extermination. But I am also a fair man, Tom. In the contest to come, you will have a chance to survive."

As though inspired by countless moments of movie heroics, Tom Buckle throws a punch, but as ineptly as a supporting character who is playing a fool. Hollister blocks the blow with a forearm, seizes Buckle's wrist, twists that arm up behind the man's back, and shoves him hard. The director staggers into the window wall and slaps both palms against the glass to stop himself from crashing through.

To the rayshaws, Hollister says, "Mr. Buckle needs to be suited up and instructed as to the rules of the hunt."

Just then the first wind of the storm invades the terrace, and the scarlet silk scarf, which once covered Mai-Mai's pistol, billows off the snow-skinned flagstones and undulates six or seven feet above her corpse, as though it is her very spirit, risen from her hushed and cooling heart.

10

The twin-cam engine, maybe 95ci, gave the bike true zip. The driver worked the five-speed transmission with finesse and took hard corners with the confidence of a *Star Wars* character piloting an antigravity sled.

After an almost twenty-minute ride, he slowed in a residential neighborhood in a part of the valley far enough north that it didn't qualify as a Los Angeles suburb. The houses were old, the properties large, the trees tall and plentiful, live oaks and eucalyptuses and all kinds of palms, some of them long left untrimmed.

He pulled into a driveway that ran alongside a meticulously maintained bungalow with craftsman details. The place was shaded by immense, well-kept phoenix palms.

At the back of the property stood a separate garage with three double-wide doors, one of which rose as the Harley approached. The driver coasted under the up-folding panels, stopped in the garage, killed the engine, and put down the kickstand.

Jane had been expecting him to drop her miles from where they started, but in a public place. Evidently he had brought her home instead. The three garage bays were deep and open to one another, housing a well-equipped machine shop and a number of motorcycles.

Wary not so much because he'd brought her here of all places, but because the world in its dark ways had woven wariness through her bones, she got off the Road King, alert for trouble.

He removed his helmet, put it on the bike seat, stripped off his driving gloves, combed his thick hair with one hand. Wide-set malachite eyes. Clean, strong features. The suggestion that a smile was imminent.

Jane said, "Thanks for the lift."

He cocked his head to study her.

"But where are we, and how far do I have to hike to get a bus?"

A low growl drew her attention. An enormous dog stood at the open garage door. A mastiff with an apricot-fawn coat, black face, and sooted ears.

Mastiffs had a reputation as aggressive, which they weren't—unless trained to be.

Her rescuer finally spoke. "You leaned in all the way, never tensed no matter how radical the rake."

"I've ridden before."

"Ridden or driven?"

"Both."

Indicating the glowering dog, his master said, "Sparky's harmless. No bark, no bite."

"No wag, either."

"Give him time. Maybe old Sparky knows you're carrying a concealed weapon."

"How would he know that?"

"Maybe the cut of your sport coat."

"Your dog has street smarts."

"Also, when you were holding tight and leaning in, I felt it against my back."

She shrugged. "It's a dangerous world. A girl's got to look out for herself."

"Too true. Anyway, I've got a solid bike for you."

"I didn't know I was in the market for one."

"You were on foot, so they must've made your car."

" 'They'?"

"The guys with bogus badges."

"You brought me all the way here to sell me a bike?"

"I didn't say sell."

"I'm not going to *work* for it."

"Stay cool. I'm way married. My wife's in the house right now. She saw us drive up. Anyway, she's all I need."

Jane put down the tote bag to have both hands free. She glanced toward the house. Maybe the wife existed, maybe she didn't. If she existed, perhaps she was insurance against an attempted assault—or maybe she was cool with rape and would even assist her husband. Jane had once taken down a serial killer whose wife charmed his targets into a sense of safety so they could be easily abducted; she cooked elaborate meals for the girls during the weeks that her husband used them, brought fresh flowers to their windowless basement prison, and assisted in the disposal of their broken bodies after hubby wearied of them. She said she did it because she loved him so much.

"Name's Garret. Garret Nolan."

"I'm Leslie Anderson," she lied.

His face finally formed the smile that had been pending. There was a knowing quality to it, which disturbed Jane.

The mastiff had entered the garage. He intently sniffed her shoes as though to map the journey that had brought her here.

Garret Nolan went to a wall switch and clicked on the lights in all six vehicle stalls. "Racers, street cruisers, touring bikes. I break them down, build them better, customize them. If you need to get all the way to the Canadian border, you'll want a bagger."

From the Canadian border reference, she inferred that he had assumed more about her status as a fugitive than she'd given him reason to deduce. She felt the skin crepe on the back of her neck.

"I have two Road Kings," he continued, "rebuilt slick, but I've got too much in them just to give them away. What I *can* give you is this 2012 Big Dog Bulldog Bagger, which I was going to tear down next. It's a righteous bike."

"You don't have to give me anything. I have money. I can pay."

"I won't take your money. The Big Dog has a lot of miles on it, but it's in good shape. I've ridden it myself. You don't need it flashed up with Performance Machine wheels, Kuryakyn mufflers, and all the rest. It's a reliable beast of burden and won't call undue attention. Test ride it around the neighborhood. You like it, take it. There isn't a license plate, but you could maybe go a couple thousand miles before a cop might notice."

She stared at him in silence until his lingering half smile flatlined. Then she said, "I ask for a ride out of a tight spot, and you want to give me a bike. What's this about, Mr. Nolan?"

He shrugged. "I believe you. I want to help."

"Believe me about what?"

"That you're innocent."

"I never said I was innocent. Anyway . . . innocent of what?"

He was a big guy, about six feet two and solid, with an air of rough experience about him, and yet he suddenly seemed as shy as a boy, looking down at his shoes to avoid meeting her eyes.

"Innocent of what?" she pressed.

He gazed through the open door, at the house shaded by phoenix palms, at the still cascades of fronds in the warm, breathless day.

She waited, and when he looked at her again, he said, "That's a bitchin' disguise, but seeing through disguises was part of my job. You're her. You're Jane Hawk."

11

Sparky, the mastiff, sniffed along the zipper of the tote bag, as though trained to locate the banded stacks of hundred-dollar bills that, among other things, it contained.

"If I were Hawk," Jane said, "maybe it wouldn't be smart of you to say so to my face. Half the world hunting her down, she must be one crazy desperate bitch."

Garret Nolan smiled again. "I won't say what service I was in. We did black-ops work in Mexico and Central America, no uniforms, we went native. Our actions targeted MS-13, other gangs, those linked to nests of Iranian operatives in Venezuela, Argentina, Nicaragua."

He turned his back on her and went to a square of perfboard beside a workbench and took a set of keys from one of the pegs.

"We knew who we were looking for—names, faces—but a lot of the time they changed their appearance. This funny thing happens when you use facial-recognition programs to see through disguises. When you do it long enough, often enough, it's as if your brain uploads a little of the software, so you develop an eye for a masquerade, no matter how well it's done."

When he returned to her, he held out the keys, which she didn't at once accept.

"Another problem you have is you're a damn good-looking woman."

"If I were Hawk, what should I do—scar myself?"

"Women as good-looking as you rarely use so much makeup and eye shadow, such bright lipstick. If it can't improve the face, maybe it's meant to obscure it."

"That's all you've got?"

"The mole on the upper lip. Why haven't you had it removed?"

"I'm skittish about doctors and scalpels."

"Fake moles, fake port-wine birthmarks, fake tattoos—they're popular camouflage. I don't need a scalpel. Bet I could remove it with a little spirit-gum solvent."

"Leslie Anderson," she insisted. "Born in Portland, late of Vegas, got myself in trouble when I jacked five thousand credit-card numbers that my hacker boss had stolen, went into business for myself, running a buy-and-fence operation, until he found me."

Nolan still held out the keys. "The color-changing contact lens on your left eye isn't fitted properly. There's a thin crescent of blue above the gray. Jane Hawk has blue eyes."

She remembered how, on first meeting him, he had not looked her up and down, but had stared intently into her eyes.

"The ash-blond wig is the best, tightly fitted for action," he said. "But if the color was natural, your skin would probably be paler. With your complexion, your hair's more likely to be honey blond— like Jane Hawk's."

She took the keys from him. "I don't have to be Jane Hawk to need the bike. But if you're hot on giving it to Leslie Anderson—"

"'—born in Portland, late of Vegas,'" he said. "Another thing is how you move. Spine straight, shoulders back, athletic, quick and confident. That's how she moves in what film they have of her."

"Mama Anderson taught her girl not to slouch."

"Then there's the fact the media says Jane Hawk took part in some terrorist attack in Borrego Springs three days ago, maybe a hundred dead, maybe a lot more than that. They say she's still somewhere in Southern California."

"If I were her," Jane said, "I'd be long gone from the state."

Denied the chance to investigate the tote's contents, the mastiff grumbled with disappointment when Jane picked up the bag.

"I really can pay for this," she said.

"Then what would I have to brag on when you're vindicated?"

She stowed the tote in one of the bike's saddlebags. "Let's say I'm her. Why would you do this?"

"From my days in . . . the service, I know how deeply the enemies of freedom have penetrated this country's institutions, public and private sector. The way they're demonizing you, their viciousness and ferocity, tells me you're right about the plague of suicides, and somehow it's . . . engineered."

"I haven't heard Hawk says it's engineered."

"Maybe because nobody's given her a chance. Digital technology and biotech—somehow they have to be part of this."

"I wouldn't know."

He said, "People are dazzled by high tech, but there's a dark side, dark and darker. What horror isn't possible today . . . it'll be possible tomorrow."

"Or maybe it is, after all, possible today," she said.

12

The three rayshaws were of a physical type, big men with thick necks and broad shoulders and sledgehammer fists, their eyes cold, their stares as impersonal as camera lenses, as if they were not of women born, but instead were immortal archetypes of violence, risen from some infernal realm millennia earlier, having come down the centuries on a mission of barbarity, cruelty, and murder.

They escorted Tom Buckle to the guest suite where he'd left his baggage. Nothing he said could engender a response. They spoke to him only to tell him what he must do. They didn't overtly threaten him; mortal threat was implicit in their every look and action.

Items that didn't belong to him had been placed on the bed: long underwear, a flannel shirt, a Gore-Tex/Thermolite storm suit by Hard Corps, two different kinds of socks, supple-looking gloves. Beside the bed stood a pair of boots.

"Strip naked," one of the men commanded. "Dress in those things."

Tom recognized the futility of appealing to these creatures' common humanity, for there was nothing human about them other than their form. Their faces varied, but their expressions were eerily the same, as neutral as the masks of mannequins. No emotion shaped their features. Their faces lacked evidence of personality, and they seemed as remote and ghastly as the pale whiteness of the moon in daylight.

Wainwright Hollister's movie was in fact reality, and Tom Buckle was the doomed lead in a noir thriller where the theme was meant to be the hopelessness of hoping. He was Edmond O'Brien in *D.O.A.* Robert Mitchum in *Out of the Past*.

Watching him undress, the three men said nothing.

He obeyed them. He could do nothing but obey. He believed Hollister's assertion that they were killing machines.

For twenty-six years, he had lived a relatively charmed life, on a glide path into film directing. He'd never known terror until now. He was terrified not only of these creatures and of Hollister, but also by a sudden sense that a sinkhole might open in his psyche, a sucking black madness from which there could be no escape.

As Tom dressed in the storm suit, Mai-Mai's suicide played in his memory so vividly that the room around him seemed to darkle like a theater where all the light was contained within the screen: her exquisite face, her beautiful body, she a symbol of mystical power, as if she were a goddess who stepped down from a heretofore unknown pantheon, the scene remembered in black-white-gray, as though from a movie made in the 1930s, but for the scarlet silk scarf that slid off her hand and the muzzle flash of the pistol, her collapsing with an awful grace, her seeming power revealed as an illusion, removed from this world with as little concern as Hollister might give to a cockroach before stamping on it.

The room was warm, but Tom felt as cold as the snow-swept world beyond the windows. His heart drummed with fear, but there was anger in it, too, an icy rage that scared him. He had never been an angry man. He worried that his fury might compel him to do something that would diminish his already slim chance of survival.

When he was suited and booted, with the hood snug around his face, the three men led him into the vast garage, where Hollister maintained a collection of expensive, exotic vehicles: a Lamborghini Huracán, a Rolls-Royce Phantom, a Bugatti Chiron, an armored Gurkha by Terradyne, and maybe twenty others. A showroom-tile floor. A pin spot highlighting each set of wheels.

They took him to a Hennessey VelociRaptor 6 × 6, which was a bespoke version of a Ford F-150 Raptor, a jacked-up six-wheel crew-cab truck with numerous upgrades. The driver sat alone in the front. The other two rayshaws flanked their prisoner in the backseat, so that Tom felt wedged between the jaws of a vise.

As they drove into the gray light and spiraling snow showers of the late afternoon, the hulk to Tom's right recited the simple rules of the hunt. The quarry would be given a two-hour lead. On foot, he could head in any direction that he wished—except that he must not attempt to return to the residence. Security sensors would be aware of his approach well before he drew near the house, and he would be cut down by Crystal Creek Ranch personnel with Uzis.

"Adjusted people," Tom said, still struggling to believe what ample evidence proved to be true.

His instructor's facial features remained as graven as cemetery granite, his stare chisel sharp but shallow. "The quarry will be armed with a nine-millimeter Glock featuring a ten-round magazine." Neither he nor the other men used Tom's name or even once referred to him with the pronoun *you*.

The rayshaw produced the gun, sans ammunition, and briefly explained its features.

Tom owned a pistol with which he practiced, at most, once a year.

The other three hundred and sixty-four days, the weapon was in the back of his nightstand drawer. He had no illusions about being a good marksman.

His instructor gave him the Glock. "The magazine and ammunition will be provided upon arrival at the starting position of the hunt. The quarry will also receive six PowerBars for energy, as well as a tactical flashlight."

"A map," Tom said. "A map and a compass."

None of the three men responded.

Snow raveled now in countless skeins through the loom of the day and formed a pristine fabric on the land.

"Hollister said I'd have a fair chance." There was no evidence that they had heard him. Nevertheless, he said. "What's fair about this? Nothing. Nothing's fair about it."

His own voice embarrassed him, sounded like the whining of a coddled child. He fell silent.

The VelociRaptor grumbled into the growing storm and the slowly dimming day, flakes like midget moths swarming through the beams of the headlights. They had turned off the blacktop that linked the residence to the distant airplane hangar housing the Gulfstream V, and seemed to be following a dirt track difficult to discern under thin shifting scarves of snow.

Fifteen or twenty minutes from the house, the truck came to a stop. The men flanking Tom opened the back doors and got out.

When he hesitated to follow, one of them said, *"Now,"* putting such menace into one word that Tom at once obeyed.

13

In Garret Nolan's garage, Jane straddled the motorcycle, flexed her hands around the grips, looking it over—speedometer/ tachometer, clutch lever, brake lever, throttle—getting the feel of the machine before putting up the kickstand.

Nolan said, "One more thing you should know. They say Jane Hawk avoids bus stations, train stations, and airports because facial-recognition programs scan travelers for known terrorists and wanted criminals. But that's not good enough anymore."

Jane was curious, but Leslie Anderson was on the run only from her former boss, not from the feds, so neither of them expressed interest in what Nolan had said.

"About a year ago," he continued, "the Chinese government began deploying among their police departments these freaky damn eyeglass-mounted cameras equipped with face-rec tech. Now some of my buddies still in U.S. spec ops recently received the same gear."

Six months earlier, Jane would have taken such a claim with the entire contents of a salt shaker. Fixed-camera recognition systems were connected to remote facial databases stored in the cloud, so vast they—along with artificial-intelligence analytics—couldn't be loaded onto the front end of a wearable camera. But technology was advancing at a remarkable pace, especially the tech that could be used for population control and oppression.

"These sunglasses are wired to a handheld device with an offline facial database of up to ten thousand faces," Nolan said. "The AI is good enough to match a suspect's face to one in the d-base in just six hundred milliseconds. Fixed cameras have limited lines of sight, but someone wearing these can look *everywhere*."

She couldn't restrain herself from saying, "That sucks."

Nolan said, "If this gear is being issued to some in the military, you can bet your ass security agencies on the domestic side also have them. So maybe if you ever happen to run into Jane Hawk someday, tell her the one face currently sure to be in that portable d-base is hers. Nowhere is safe."

"Has anywhere ever been?"

From the seat of a nearby Harley, he picked up a pearl-white Shoei X-9 Air helmet with a dark-smoke shield. "Too bad you can't wear this everywhere."

Accepting the helmet, Jane said, "What if they nail me and trace this bike back to you?"

"They can't."

"Why not?"

"Ever since I left the military, I've been doing business in ways that move me step by step toward the edge of the grid."

"Gonna go all the way off?"

"Sooner than later, we'll sell the house and head so far up-country you'd think it was the nineteenth century."

"Sorry to hear that," she said. "The more people like you and your wife who get out of the game, the more likely the bastards will win in the end."

He shrugged. "We've got one life, and we don't want to live any part of it on our knees, which is likely if we stay here."

14

The two rayshaws walked Tom to the front of the Veloci-Raptor and about another forty feet through the vehicle's lances of light before halting. One of them gave him the unloaded pistol. The other put a plastic sack with a drawstring closure on the ground at his feet.

They returned to the truck and boarded it. The vehicle hung a U-turn and drove away, taillights tinting the snow with a suggestion of blood as it dwindled into the white cascades.

Although Tom stood shaking, he was warm enough in his storm suit.

He stooped to open the bag with the drawstrings. It contained the promised PowerBars and a knitted ski mask that he could wear under the storm-suit hood, with holes only for his eyes and mouth. There were also the promised tactical flashlight, the magazine for the Glock, and ten bullets.

He inserted the ammunition into the magazine, the magazine into the pistol, the pistol into a zippered pocket on the thigh of the storm suit's right leg. He distributed the knitwear and six PowerBars in other pockets.

Maybe the drawstring bag would come in handy. He'd keep it and, until nightfall, carry the flashlight in it.

As he closed the bag, the Bell and Howell Tac Light clinked against something he hadn't noticed. He fished inside and came up with a microcassette recorder.

When Tom pressed PLAY, Wainwright Hollister spoke to him. *"You will die in this lonely place, Tom Buckle. If you'd been injected, adjusted, and sent back to California, at least you'd have had the pleasure of a fleeting orgasm when you raped ten-year-old Kaylee at my command. But although there will be no pleasure for you in the hours ahead, you'll be blamed for Kaylee's kidnapping a few days from now, because when her body is found in your home, it will bear your semen and your blood, which we will harvest from you after your death. The world will know you as a monster, Tom, and everyone will despise your films. You will be sought by police but, of course, never found. Who can say how many rapes and murders of other little girls will be attributed to Tom Buckle, the phantom pedophile, in years to come? Please don't use the nine-millimeter Glock to kill yourself. I'm so looking forward to the hunt and the moment when I remove the threat to a stable future posed by your dangerous ideas and undeniable talent. Get moving, Tom. You have only a two-hour lead."*

Whether the recording was intended to be a psychological weapon that would unnerve Tom and make him easier prey or signified nothing more than the billionaire's narcissism and cruelty, Hollister had provided his quarry with precious evidence of the murder that he intended to commit and of the Arcadian conspiracy in which he was a key player. Instead of depressing or unnerving Tom, the recording brought the light of hope into his heart and warmed him with the realization that Hollister wasn't as prudent or smart as he had seemed in the context of his magnificent house and the company of his zombie guards.

He rewound the message and pressed PLAY again, intending to listen only to the threat of the first sentence, so that it might inspire him to escape or put up a hell of a fight if confrontation proved unavoidable. The recorder hissed slightly louder than the descending flakes that softly sheered the air, hissed and hissed, but the words it had conveyed had been erased, evidently even as they had first issued from the speaker.

The meadows were clotted with old snow and silvered with fresh, but he felt as if he stood on a burnt plain, in a world scourged by an apocalyptic fire, the pine woods in the distance as black as columns of char, the current storm an ashfall, the incinerated sky in slow collapse, the unseen sun not merely in decline but dying in the wake of a nova flare.

He could almost believe he was asleep, all this a dreamscape of a world in the wake of judgment. The insanity of the Arcadian scheme and the suddenness with which he'd been plunged into mortal peril merely because his talent put him on a list of undesirables seemed too fantastic to be other than a nightmare that would dissolve when he thrust up from his pillow and threw back the covers and switched on a bedside lamp.

Although he'd never known such cold as this, the day abruptly grew colder when the early stillness of the storm was swept away by a sudden wind out of the northwest. The snowflakes that had kissed his face now nipped. Wind stung his eyes, and tears blurred his vision.

15

Because she was riding a bike much different from the one on which she had sped away with Garret Nolan, Jane risked cruising to the motel, a one-star enterprise trying to pass for a two, where she had left her luggage the previous night.

Her locked suitcases contained nothing irreplaceable. However, because of the urgency of the investigation she'd undertaken and the ever-growing intensity of the search for her, she didn't have time to go clothes shopping or visit the source in Reseda from whom she obtained guns, driver's licenses in multiple identities, license plates, color-changing contact lenses, wigs, and other items that were essential to the chameleon changes that kept her free and alive.

They had apparently tied the Ford Explorer Sport to her; but that didn't mean they knew where her lodgings were. In fact, if they knew, they wouldn't have come after her in the library, but would have been lying in wait in the motel room when she returned.

If she could safely retrieve her bags, so much the better.

The entire San Fernando Valley had once been a thriving part of the California dream; but some communities were now in decline. The almost third-world shabbiness of this neighborhood belied the Golden State's image of high style and glamour that was barely sustained by the grace and beauty of the better coastal towns. Potholed streets, littered and unkempt parks, used hypodermic needles glittering in the gutters, graffiti, public urination, and homeless people camped in the doorways of vacant buildings were testament to corrupt and incompetent governance.

The Counting Sheep Motel was a mom-and-pop operation, cracked white stucco with blue trim, sixteen units on two levels encircling a courtyard with a swimming pool. The pool was small, its coping fissured and stained; a mermaid and her adoring entourage of cartoon fish were painted on the bottom, shimmering under water that seemed not quite as clear as it ought to be.

Jane's room—number three—was on the ground floor, at the front of the building. There was no sign of unusual activity.

She rode to the end of the block, turned right, curbed the Big Dog, and fed coins to the parking meter.

After taking the tote from one of the saddlebags, she walked back to a bar and grill called Lucky O'Hara's, across the street from the motel. She took her helmet off only as she reached the entrance. In addition to the name of the establishment, the sign above the door featured a pot of gold and a leprechaun.

Assuming Lucky O'Hara had earlier enjoyed a lunchtime rush, now at three thirty-five the crowd had gone. Two retirees sat at the horseshoe bar, each alone, one of them in low conversation with the bartender. A young couple engaged in an intense discussion in one of the booths that lined both side walls. The tables at the front of the room were not occupied. Jane sat at a window table for two, with a clear view of the motel that stood across the street and somewhat west of her position.

If the owner and staff and primary clientele of Lucky O'Hara's had once been Irish Americans, that seemed no longer the case. The waitress who took Jane's order—two hamburger steaks, one atop the other, hold the hash brown potatoes, add extra vegetables, a side of pepper slaw, a bottle of Corona—was a pretty blond-haired black-eyed girl with a Bosnian accent.

The pilsner glass was frosted, the Corona ice cold. Properly chilled beer was one of the humble pleasures that kept her in a positive frame of mind during this ordeal of threat and violence. A hot shower, a piece of favorite music, the fragrance of a flowering jasmine vine growing on a trellis, and countless other little graces reminded her of how sweet life had once been and could be again. As motivation, a desire to live well and freely again was second only to her fierce determination to keep her child safe and to give him a future from which those who would enslave him had been eradicated.

She watched the motel during lunch. Red curb restricted parking to the farther side of the street. There were no paneled vans that suggested surveillance. No obvious sentry slouched in any of the cars or SUVs.

A few doors south of the motel, overdressed for the mild day in layers of ragged sweaters and a black-and-green tartan scarf, masses of hair and beard bristling as if fossilized in that configuration following an electric shock, a vagrant sat on the sidewalk, his back against the wall of a vacant storefront. Beside him stood a shopping cart in which were heaped large green trash bags bulging with whatever eccentric collection constituted his treasure.

Such a disguise was within the repertoire of a true stakeout artist. The vagrant was the sole subject of Jane's suspicion—until he got to his feet, stepped to the recessed entry of the building, dropped his

trousers, and defecated. Although a federal agent on such an assignment would take pride in the exactitude of the details of his costume
and behavior, he would not feel obliged to take a dump in public for
the sake of authenticity.

Glittering in the sunlight, traffic passed in riotous variety. Jane
could not detect any vehicles repeatedly circling the block in a rolling
surveillance of the motel.

The appearance of normalcy at Counting Sheep concerned her.
When nothing whatsoever in a scene looked suspicious, when it
seemed picture-postcard serene and downright churchy, it was at
such high contrast with everyplace else in this fallen world that you
had to wonder if it was a setup. She had developed measured paranoia as a survival trait not just since going on the run, but from her
years in law enforcement.

She spooned ice from her water tumbler into the pilsner glass to
chill the remaining beer, finished lunch, eyed her watch—4:33—
ordered another Corona in a chilled glass, and asked for the check.

She paid and tipped 30 percent as soon as the beer arrived, so that
when she took another hour, the waitress wouldn't worry that maybe
she would skip out on the check. She said, "The bastard was supposed to be here when I arrived. I'll give him another hour to hang
himself."

Whether she had acquired her cynicism in Bosnia or California,
the waitress bluntly said, "Dump him."

"I keep saying I will, but I don't."

"Girl like you has options."

"So far none better than him."

"They play too much video game."

"Who does?" Jane asked.

"This generation men. Video game, porn, Internet—they don't
know how to be real anymore."

"Prince Charming is dead," Jane agreed.

"Not dead. Just lost. We need to find. You can't find when you
won't look."

"Maybe you're right. Do *you* keep looking for him?"

"I look, I hope, I date—but always with knife in purse."

"Really? A knife in your purse?"

The waitress shrugged. "Is L.A. A girl can't take chances these days."

Jane nursed the second beer through another hour, watching the motel while pretending to be waiting for Mr. Wrong. The homeless man with the shopping cart moved on to defecate elsewhere. The elastic shadows stretched eastward. The traffic quarreled in greater volume through the street, as if there were no other avenue in all the world, every traveler bound frantically for the same and perhaps terrible place. Counting Sheep continued to represent itself as innocent and safe.

Excessive hesitation was the mother of failure. Winning required considered action. Get off the X. Move.

She returned to the motorcycle parked on the side street. She cruised around the block, pulled into the motel lot, and parked in front of Room 5, two doors north of the unit in which she'd left her luggage.

No one was currently in the immediate vicinity. If she was a figure of interest to someone, he might be watching her from behind a window, through parted draperies.

She took off her helmet, left it on the seat of the Big Dog, and went boldly to Room 3.

High situational awareness. In Condition Yellow. No eyes in the back of her head, but alert for any sound that didn't belong in the basketweave of street noise.

She keyed the door and pushed, and it swung into a coolness of shadows, revealing the furniture as colorless shapes in the gloom.

Before crossing the threshold, she slid her right hand under her sport coat, to the grip of the pistol in her shoulder rig.

Warily, she glanced back at the parking lot, at the street, at the motel office to the south. Nothing.

A single-file succession of fat crows, eerily silent for their raucous kind, passed low overhead. Crisply defined shadows, blacker against the pavement than the birds were black against the sky, glided past her feet, as if to encourage her to flee with them.

She was not Jane Hawk. She was Leslie Anderson. If her pursuers knew about the Anderson ID and this motel, they would have come for her in this place rather than at the library. Somehow they knew about the car, but only the car.

She entered, closed the door, switched on lights. A housekeeper had been here. The bed was made. The fragrance of an orange-scented aerosol freshened the room, though under it lay the faint lingering staleness of marijuana smoke from some previous guest. The door to the small bathroom stood open wide, and a frosted window admitted enough light to reveal that no one waited in there.

All seemed the same as when she had checked in the previous afternoon. Nonetheless, she sensed a wrongness in the room that she could not define.

Two sliding mirrored doors served the closet. As she approached them, she looked not at her image, but at the reflection of the room behind her, which seemed somehow strange and not an exact likeness, as if a threat thus far invisible might materialize from some dark dimension suddenly folding into this one.

Engine noise swelled as a vehicle pulled off the street and into the motel lot. She focused on the room door reflected in the mirror before her. The engine died. A car door slammed. She waited. Nothing.

Sometimes in the deep of night, when the sleeper's fantasy is benign—a golden meadow, an enchanting forest—anxiety arises with no apparent cause, just before the dream is invaded by men without faces, whose fingers are razor-sharp knives. Her disquiet now was akin to the dreamer's apprehension, the cause intuited rather than perceived.

As she slid the left-hand closet door to the right, it stuttered slightly in its corroded tracks. Her two suitcases were gone. She pushed both doors to the left. The other half of the closet also proved to be empty.

She drew the Heckler & Koch Compact .45 and turned to the room, which had taken unto itself the strangeness that she had previously perceived only in the mirror, so that every mundane object seemed to have an alien aspect, malevolent purpose.

The bathroom window was too small to serve as an exit. The room door offered the only way out.

Draperies with blackout linings covered the window to the left of the door. She would gain nothing by parting those greasy panels of fabric to see what awaited her outside. Whatever it might be, she had no choice other than to go to it.

Pistol in hand but held under her sport coat, she opened the door. After the lamplit room, the sun-shot world made her squint. She stepped outside.

The Big Dog Bulldog Bagger had disappeared. To her left, in front of Room 1, under an ill-kept phoenix palm, stood the metallic-gray Ford Explorer Sport that she had abandoned at the library several towns from here.

Neither of the exits from the motel parking lot was blockaded. No cops. No plainclothes agents.

All seemed counterfeit, as if the street were only a movie set on a studio backlot.

In the new world aborning, reality seemed frequently displaced by virtual reality.

Most people were so enchanted by high technology, they didn't see its potential for oppression, but Jane was aware of the darkness at the core of the machine. The current culture deviated radically from previous human experience, ruthlessly reducing each woman and man to mere political units to be manipulated, balkanizing them into communities according to their likes and dislikes, so everything from cars to candy bars could be more effectively marketed, robbing them of their privacy, denying them both a real community of diverse views and the possibility of personal evolution by censoring the world they saw through the Internet to make it conform to the preferred beliefs of their self-appointed betters.

In such a world, there were daily moments like this one at the Counting Sheep Motel, across the street from Lucky O'Hara's Bar and Grille with its smiling leprechaun and pot of gold, situations that felt unreal, that suggested the world had come unmoored from reason.

A man sat in the front passenger seat of her Explorer. In the shade of the big tree, with patterns of palm fronds reflected on the windshield, little of him could be seen.

As Jane approached the driver's door, she held the pistol at her side, against her leg.

The window in the driver's door was down, allowing her a better view of the guy who waited for her. She knew him. Vikram Rangnekar of the FBI.

PART TWO

Bad Weather

1

The wind did not shriek, but moaned as if Nature had fallen into despair, and the snow slanted out of the northwest with none of the softness that the scene suggested, so that Tom Buckle turned his back to the icy teeth of the blizzard.

His vision cleared as the tears that the wind stung from his eyes briefly warmed his cheeks. In the gray spectral light of the hidden and fast-declining sun, the vast plain seemed not to fade into the storm, but to be dissolving at its farthest edges, crumbling away into some white void.

He looked southwest toward the great house. The lights were not entirely screened by the snow, but there weren't even vague window shapes or identifiable lampposts, only a low hazy amber glow to mark the location of the distant residence. Tom yearned for the warmth within Wainwright Hollister's walls. He briefly fantasized about returning to steal a vehicle—something big like the VelociRaptor or the armored Gurkha—and escaping overland or battering through some formidable gate at the entrance to the ranch. However, he believed what he'd been told about the security system's ability to detect his approach and about the ruthlessness with which he would be machine-gunned.

For precious minutes, with his two hours of lead time ticking away, he stood in indecision, unable to set out in one of the directions that were not forbidden to him. He had no paths to follow. And in the arc of escape allowed him, each of those two hundred seventy degrees appeared to be a direct route to certain death. He was not an outdoorsman. His survival skills were limited to the savvy that kept his film career alive, and that had not yet proved to be enough to put him on even the B list of directors. As the child of a tailor and a seamstress, having spent thousands of hours watching uncounted movies, his experience of the natural world was limited to city parks, public beaches, and documentaries. In this immense, unpopulated snow-swept tract of land, he simply didn't know the first thing to do any more than if he had just stepped out of a starship onto the surface of a planet at the farther end of the galaxy.

He felt small and vulnerable, as he hadn't felt since childhood. His breath plumed from him in pale ghostly vapors, as if with each exhalation he were shedding a fraction of the spirit that inhabited his too-mortal flesh.

If he didn't know how to survive, one thing he *did* know was that Hollister would never mount the fair pursuit he promised, that the crazy sonofabitch wouldn't come on foot, but in an all-wheel-drive vehicle. And the billionaire would be tracking his quarry by means far more sophisticated than reading footprints and sifting spoor from the masking snow.

Before leaving California, Tom had checked out Crystal Creek Ranch on the Internet. Google Street offered no images, but Google Earth provided extensive satellite photographs. He had been dazzled by the size of the main residence and its associated buildings, enchanted by the verdant vastness of these twelve thousand acres.

Now he remembered the watercourse for which the ranch was named. Less of a creek than a small river, it spilled out of the western highlands and flowed past the house, southeast through various woods and meadows, continuing far beyond Hollister's property and eventually passing under Interstate 70.

Using the glow of the distant residence as a reference point, Tom tried to call to mind the satellite images of the ranch and remember the route by which the interstate proceeded somewhat south and then more directly east toward Kansas. His recollection was at best hazy.

He had no idea how many miles he would have to walk in order to reach the highway. Thirty? Fifty? It was so distant that even on a clear night the headlights of the traffic could probably not be seen from here. Yet the interstate offered his only hope of finding help.

The Hollister property was surrounded by other enormous—and lonely—ranches, as well as by unpopulated federal territory. He might wander for days and never encounter a neighbor or a single government land manager.

Carrying the drawstring bag containing the tactical flashlight, he set out south-southeast. He wondered how he would maintain that course when distance and the bleak deluge screened from him the lights of the house, which were his only reference point.

Perhaps a hundred and fifty yards ahead lay a pine woods expressed like vertical strokes of an artist's charcoal on white paper, robbed of detail by the waning light and waxing weather. The river ran through some but not all of the ranch's woodlands. If he got lucky and found it among these nearest trees, he could make his way along its banks to the interstate without fear of becoming disoriented and lost in the blizzard. If nothing else, the woods seemed to offer cover.

Tom didn't bother to check the wristwatch they had allowed him to keep. It didn't matter whether fifty-five or fifty-six minutes of the promised two-hour lead remained. He surely did not have that much time. Not really.

Hollister was a murderer. Murder was not merely a crime but also a lie, for it made a claim that some lives had no value. If the billionaire could deny the fundamental truth of the profound meaning of every life, he was a liar's liar, a font of falsehood. He might already be on the hunt.

With fresh powder pluming from his boots, the rotten drifts of other days and tangled masses of frozen grass crunching underfoot, Tom crossed the meadow, leaving a trail that would not quickly be filled in his wake. Erratic wind not only drove the falling flakes but also fashioned them into pale shapes, phantoms in graveclothes, that hastened across the plain in the weak and dimming light. The land seemed haunted. The world had become so strange that he would not have been surprised if a figure more solid than the apparitions of snow had suddenly loomed before him, a naked beauty with her ruined face concealed by a shimmering mask of scarlet silk.

2

The Counting Sheep Motel in its slow disintegration. The hive hum and swarm buzz of traffic, the amplified serpent hiss as a bus air-braked for passengers waiting on a bench, in the distance the hard *tat-tat-tat-tat-tat* of what might be either a jackhammer or an automatic weapon. Bright orange sun, ink spill of purple shadows seeping eastward.

In the front passenger seat of Jane's Explorer Sport, warming the moment with his smile, Vikram Rangnekar said, "Hello, Jane."

Jane stood at the open window in the driver's door, pistol drawn, muzzle pointed at the pavement. "What is this?"

"I've missed you."

"Been busy."

"I lie awake at night worrying about you."

"I'm okay."

"You look okay. You look fabulous."

"So . . . what is this?" she asked again.

"The disguise is optimal cool. It's good."

"Maybe not good enough."

"May I say, you're prettier without it."

"Looking hot isn't my main objective these days."

"I have no gun. I mean you no harm."

"Puts you in a damn small minority."

"If you don't shoot me, I can be of great help to you."

"You're FBI."

"Not an agent. Never was. Just a computer buccaneer who *used to work* for the FBI. I resigned two weeks ago."

Vikram was a white-hat hacker of great talent. Occasionally the

Department of Justice had poached him from the Bureau and put him to work on what would have been criminal black-hat projects if they had not been conducted under the auspices of the nation's primary law-enforcement agency. He'd had an innocent crush on her even when Nick had been alive, though he knew that she was—and always would be—a one-man woman, and he'd liked to impress her with his mastery at the keyboard. As an agent, before going rogue, Jane had always operated by the book, never resorting to illegal methods. But she had wanted to know what the corrupt inner circle at Justice might be doing, and she had encouraged Vikram to show off. He had developed back doors—"my wicked little babies"—to the computer systems of major telecom companies, alarm-company central stations, and others, and he had instructed Jane in their use. Once she had gone rogue, the ability to ghost through those systems without being detected had more than once gotten her out of a tight corner.

"If I weren't your friend," he said, "there would be like a hundred agents here, a SWAT team, helicopters, dogs, bomb robots. But it's just me."

"Not only the government wants to wring my neck."

"Yeah, there's some freaky group calling themselves Techno Arcadians, but I don't know what they're all about."

Surprised by his knowledge, even as limited as it was, she surveyed her surroundings. Nothing amiss. She looked at Vikram again. "How do you know about the Arcadians? They don't advertise."

"Get in. Take us for a drive. I'll explain."

"Who were those people at the library?"

"Family. A brother. An uncle. Cousins. You look wonderful."

"Where are my suitcases?"

"In the back. Take us for a drive. I'll explain."

"I don't want to kill you, Vikram."

"Good. I don't want to be killed."

"So don't make it necessary."

She holstered the pistol and climbed behind the wheel of the Explorer and pulled the driver's door shut.

3

For three days, Charles Douglas Weatherwax waits in a luxurious suite in the Peninsula Hotel in Beverly Hills, anticipating his next assignment. He is a tall, strong, graceful man with a face of such clean, stylized lines that it looks like an Art Deco work worthy of being the hood ornament on a high-end automobile in the days when cars had hood ornaments and didn't all look alike. He follows a high-protein low-carb diet, takes eighty vitamin pills a day, every twelve hours drinks a health product called Clean Green, and never fails to apply a number-fifty sunscreen after shaving. Each day before dinner, he sets out from his hotel on a long walk, which in part takes him through the park across the street.

During these strolls, as at all other times, he is looking for something that will justify his existence. There are people, sad cases, who never find their purpose in life. Charlie is not one of them. He has long known the meaning of his life, and he finds his mission deeply fulfilling.

During his first tour of the park, on Wednesday afternoon, he encounters a blind man sitting on a bench, in the shade of a trio of palm trees. The guy is fiftysomething. Shaved head. Neatly trimmed salt-and-pepper beard. An MP3 player rests on the bench beside him. Without an earpiece, he listens to Jeremy Irons read T. S. Eliot's "Burnt Norton," the first of the poet's *Four Quartets.*

The listener's blindness is suggested by dark glasses worn in the shade, implied by a white cane propped at the side of the bench, and confirmed by a beautiful German shepherd lying at its master's feet. The grip of the leash lies untended on the bench, testament to the seeing-eye dog's obedience and dedication.

"Time past and time future / What might have been and what has been / Point to one end, which is always present . . ."

Jeremy Irons reads the lines without artifice. His straightforward presentation speaks powerfully to Charlie Weatherwax.

Charlie doesn't interrupt the poem but continues on his way without a word to the blind man.

From childhood—he is now thirty-four—he was taught the importance of committing random acts of kindness. His father was a community organizer with a genius for winning grants to improve the quality of life in less fortunate neighborhoods, and his mother was a high school principal, later a district superintendent. Both are now retired. He has often heard them speak of the rewards of a life of service; random kindness is key to their self-image.

The following afternoon, Thursday, he discovers the blind man on the same bench, in different clothing but listening now to "The Dry Salvages," the third of Eliot's *Four Quartets*. On this second encounter, Charlie realizes that he must act. But by doing what?

"There is no end of it, the voiceless wailing / No end to the withering of withered flowers . . ."

Charlie passes the blind man and his dog, the voice of Jeremy Irons propelling him as if he is a leaf on the surface of a swift stream.

He says nothing, does nothing—and throughout the remainder of the day regrets his inaction. By dinnertime, his regret has grown into remorse, a sharp-toothed guilt gnawing at his heart. His sleep is troubled. There is little chance that he will encounter the blind man again and be able to make things right.

Yet now, later Friday afternoon, at the same hour as before, Charlie comes upon the sightless listener in the park. Fortunately, he has prepared for this most unlikely third chance.

"Beautiful dog," he says, and scratches the shepherd under the chin and sits on the bench. "What's his name?"

Clicking off the audiobook, the man says, "Argus. He's a treasure."

"Unusual name for a dog."

The guy looks toward the sound of Charlie's voice rather than directly at his face. "In Greek mythology, Argus was a giant with a hundred eyes."

"Ah. Unusual but apt. You were listening to T. S. Eliot."

"Yes, the *Four Quartets*. I never tire of it. So allusive and layered, words as music. It's a kind of meditation for me."

"Beautiful," Charlie agrees. "However, its meaning has always stumped me, I'm afraid, too complex for my feeble brain. His cat poems are more my speed."

The blind man smiles. *"Old Possum's Book of Practical Cats.* Amazing that he could write works of great depth *and* some of the most charming light verse ever put to paper."

Charlie quotes, " 'Jellicle cats come out tonight / Jellicle cats come one come all . . . ' "

Argus's master recites, " 'The Jellicle moon is shining bright / Jellicles come to the Jellicle ball.' "

Hoping for the chance to rectify his previous failure to engage the blind man, Charlie has brought with him a hamburger patty spiced and cooked to perfection by the Peninsula Hotel's room-service chef.

Approaching the bench, he'd taken it from a small plastic bag. Now he drops the meat on the park path in front of the dog.

Quoting the four opening lines from "Macavity: The Mystery Cat" louder and with less grace than Jeremy Irons might have performed it, Charlie covers the sound of the shepherd quickly consuming the patty and then says, "Name's Harvey Hemingway, no relation. Friends call me Harv."

"John Duncan," says the bald and bearded fan of Eliot. "Pleased to meet an admirer of Old Possum."

Charlie chats him up for a few minutes and then, when no one is close to them, no one approaching along the path, he says, "I gave Argus some hamburger—"

"Oh, I wish you wouldn't have," says Duncan.

"—laced with a fast-acting sedative," Charlie says.

Alarmed, the blind man stiffens and calls the dog's name. When there is no response, he fumbles for and locates the grip loop of the leash where it lies on the bench. He tugs, but Argus is deep in dreamland.

"He'll be out for maybe two hours and groggy for an hour after that," Charlie says, "but no permanent damage."

"What the hell is this?" Duncan demands, putting some steel in his voice, as if he is capable of following through on a threat, as if he is

Samson, eyeless in Gaza, but still possessing the strength to defeat his enemies.

Charlie puts a hand on his companion's shoulder. "Listen to me, shithead, and listen close. There's no one near us in the park. Lots of traffic out there on Santa Monica Boulevard, but all they see is two friends on a bench. They call L.A. the City of Angels, but there are angels in Hell, too, and they're not the kind would do you any kindness. You call for help, you make a sound, no one will hear or care—and I'll blind your dog. I have a sharp penknife. I can do it easy."

John Duncan is as still as if he were a bronze figure of a man installed on the bench as a sculpture.

"What I'm going to do," Charlie explains, "is shock you hard with a handheld Taser. I'll do it three times. Each time longer than the one before. It's going to hurt like hell. If you scream or cry out, I blind Argus and leave. In fact, you do any more than whimper like a baby, the dog will need a seeing-eye dog of his own. You hear me? You understand?"

"Why?" Duncan asks.

"You've heard about people who want to make the world a better place by doing random acts of kindness? Well, they're a bunch of phonies. They live a lie and love it. There's nothing real about them. *I'm* the real deal. I'm what the world is truly about—acts of random cruelty."

As Charlie reaches under his sport coat and withdraws the Taser from a holster, Duncan leans forward, hands clasping his thighs, and pleads, "Please don't. For God's sake—"

Jamming the poles of the Taser against the blind man's neck, Charlie pulls the trigger.

To John Duncan, a five-second shock probably feels as if a hive of wasps has come alive inside him, swarming and stinging through bone and flesh in an angry search for an exit. His teeth chatter like one of those old novelty sets of wind-up dentures, and then they stop clacking against one another when his jaws clench tight. He shudders, writhes in place, as if tortured by clonic seizures, which continue for a moment after his tormentor lets up on the trigger; his body jerks, arms flail, and then semiparalysis locks him in his corner of the bench. He is pale and glistening with perspiration. A thread of drool unravels from one corner of his mouth. Faithful to his dog, he neither calls out for help nor screams in pain.

If Duncan makes a scene, Charlie won't follow through on his promise to cut the eyes of the shepherd. He likes dogs. He isn't a monster. He hates people, but he likes dogs. The threat to harm Argus is just a tool to control the blind man, to ensure that he will be submissive.

The second Tasering lasts ten seconds.

Traffic slows and then surges on Santa Monica Boulevard, each motorist in his own world as surely as he is isolate in his vehicle, oblivious of the drama on the park bench as he is also abstracted from the lives of the other citizens of the city. John Donne wrote, *No man is an island, entire of itself*, which Charlie Weatherwax knows to be the ripest bullshit. The human species is an infinite archipelago of islands with rough seas separating them. All men and women are vortexes of pure self-interest, their self-love whirling at such velocity that true concern for others can never escape the centrifugal force of their narcissism.

To see his victim's vacant stare, Charlie plucks off John Duncan's sunglasses and throws them aside before Tasering him yet again, this time for fifteen seconds. Throughout Duncan's body, every fascicle of nerve fibers short-circuits. The sightless orbs roll back in the man's head as he is once more gripped by seizures, so that his gaze is without irises, blank and white, a stare as pitiless as nature itself.

Charlie puts away the Taser and rolls the half-paralyzed blind man onto his right side, against an arm of the bench, just long enough to extract the wallet from his right hip pocket. He finds a photo ID and memorizes Duncan's street address. He returns the ID and leaves the wallet on the bench.

Hardly more than a minute has passed since Charlie administered the first shock.

They still have the park to themselves, though a woman pushing a stroller is entering from Wilshire Boulevard.

Propping Duncan in a corner of the bench, Charlie says, "Do you hear me, Johnny?" The blind man makes a wordless sound of distress, and Charlie amps the menace in his voice. *"Do you hear me, Johnny?"*

Duncan's words are slurred, but his eyes roll back into place, like symbols on the wheels in the windows of a slot machine, bright blue but oblivious. "Yeah, I hear."

"I looked in your wallet. I know where you live. You ever tell anyone about this, describe me to anyone, I'll pay you a visit."

"No. I won't. I swear."

Charlie rises to his feet. "Random acts of cruelty, Johnny. That's what the world's about. That's the sum of it. Get ready for the next one. It'll be coming. They're always coming."

The woman with the stroller has stopped at a distant bench. If she eventually continues in this direction, she will not find the blind man while Charlie is still in sight.

He continues on his way. When he glances back, he sees John Duncan leaning forward on the bench, vomiting on his shoes.

In a couple of hours, the dog will wake. An hour after that, it will be alert and stable enough to lead its master home in the early dark.

The pain John Duncan has experienced is nothing compared to the profound humiliation that he now endures and that will seethe in him for days to come. Perhaps he will fall into despair, which is not necessarily a bad thing. If it does not destroy you, despair can be a fire that burns away the erroneous understanding of the world by which so many people live. If all of the blind man's illusions can be reduced to ashes, if he can come to understand the truth of the world, that it was not shapen except by chance and that it has no meaning, that nothing matters but power, its acquisition and its use, that power is won by the infliction of pain and humiliation on others, then he will be free for the first time in his life. Even with the limitations of his disability, he might more often avoid being a victim.

Serving as a missionary of pain and humiliation, committing random acts of cruelty, is not work suitable for a common street thug or a crooked politician. Both drug-pushing gangbangers and corrupt senators lie to themselves and to others, claiming to act for the benefit of the clan, for the common good and social justice, in response to oppression, when in fact they seek power for power's sake. Liars and those who live a lie cannot remake the world for the better. A missionary, like Charlie Weatherwax, must embrace no lies, must live by no illusions, bleak as that might be, for power is the only truth, and truth is the source of power.

4

With its thousands of blacktop rivers and millions of metal currents, the Los Angeles evening rush lasted not one hour, but three or four. The Valley streets overflowed with vehicles surging-slackening-surging to and from the dysfunctional freeways. Vikram gave Jane an address, but the flood of traffic didn't frustrate her. There were many questions to be answered, explanations to be made, and an understanding to be arrived at before they reached their destination.

She said, "You could have confronted me in the library."

Vikram shook his head. "Not safely, I think. When you see me suddenly show up, you don't see a lean but sinewy dark-eyed black-haired young man who might have been a Bollywood star. Instead you see FBI, and you think you're trapped. So logically, an unfortunate confrontation ensues."

" 'Lean but sinewy'?"

Vikram shrugged. "When describing myself to various online matchmaking services, the word 'slim' can be interpreted as meaning skinny or worse. Anyway, say I show up in the library and say just maybe you don't shoot me, there's still bound to be a scene that people are witness to. They call the police, they post it on YouTube, and we are toast."

"Your relatives herded me into that vacant photography studio.

Why weren't you waiting for me in that place, where there weren't any witnesses?"

Vikram raised his right hand, pointing at the roof of the SUV with his forefinger, as if to say, *One important point to consider.* "Remember, the chase had only just begun, and you were virtually sweating adrenaline."

"I don't sweat virtually."

"Nevertheless, the math said the risk of my being shot on sight was still too high at that time."

"'Math'?"

"I have my formulas. It was wiser to lead you through a few twists and turns, give you time to understand this wasn't a standard law-enforcement operation. Then I show up alone, no backup, and you realize I am harmless."

"Who is Garret Nolan?"

"Mr. Motorcycle? He's not one of us. He was just a hiccup. There are always hiccups. Some say that life is one long series of hiccups, although personally I'm not so pessimistic. Farther along that street from Mr. Nolan, a Honda waited at the curb, its engine running. A bright red Honda. Studies show that, in a crisis, the eye is drawn to red things. My brother, wearing a flamboyant red shirt, was prepared to leap out of the red Honda and dash into a Chinese restaurant, ostensibly to pick up an order of takeout, but in fact giving you a chance to steal his wheels, which of course we could track by its GPS. However, you found Mr. Nolan first. Beware, the traffic light is about to turn red."

Jane braked to a stop. She looked at her passenger.

Smiling into her silence, Vikram said, "What?"

"You scripted it like some chase scene in a movie?"

"When I build a back door into the computer system of a major telecom provider, I don't just wing it, you know. To get away with it, I have to be meticulous. Being meticulous is what makes me Vikram Rangnekar."

"If Garret Nolan was a hiccup, unexpected, how did you track me from the time he gave me a ride?"

"Just in case, my cousin Ganesh tagged you earlier in the library."

She recalled the plump guy in khakis and a yellow pullover, at a workstation near her in the computer alcove. " 'Tagged'?"

"As you were leaving, Ganesh fired a little device loaded with an adhesive microminiature transponder. Hit you in the back."

When she had glanced at Ganesh, he'd been holding something in his left hand, down at his side. "I didn't feel it happen."

"You wouldn't," Vikram said. "It's low-velocity. The soft projectile weighs three-quarters of an ounce. It partially unravels and weaves itself into the fabric of your coat. Lithium battery the size of a pea. It's trackable by satellite, just like any vehicle with a GPS."

She said, "*Jhav.*"

Vikram's eyebrows arched. "That is a Hindi word."

"But appropriate."

"Wherever did you learn that word?"

"From you."

"Not possible. I would never use that word in the presence of a woman."

"You use it all the time when you're at a computer, backdooring your way into one place or another."

"Is that really true? I was unaware. I hope you don't know what it means."

"It means 'fuck.' "

"I am mortified."

"It's me who should be mortified, being tagged and not even aware of it. *Jhav!*"

A horn blared behind them. The light had changed.

Vikram again pointed at the roof with one finger. "The light has changed."

"No shit?" she said as she took her foot off the brake.

"I sense you're perturbed at me."

"No shit?"

"Why are you perturbed at me?"

"You played me. I don't like being played."

"The math said it was necessary."

"Math isn't everything. Trust is important."

"I trust the math."

"I remembered you as a sweet man. I forgot the annoying part."

Vikram grinned. "Is that really true?"

"Yes. You can be über-annoying."

"I meant the 'sweet man' part."

Rather than encourage him, she said, "So you knew what motel I was staying in."

"Yes. But I expected you to return there in the red Honda, not on the motorcycle. Nevertheless, it worked out."

"How the *jhav* did you find me in the first place?"

"Just so you know, I am not one who is turned on by women talking dirty."

"Don't make me have to shoot you, Vikram. How did you find me?"

"Now *that*," he said, "is quite a story."

5

Charlie Weatherwax leaves the blind man in the park, crosses the boulevard, and walks through the public spaces around city hall, into a residential neighborhood of tree-lined streets, and from there into the fabled shopping district of Beverly Hills, north of Wilshire. The sidewalks are crowded with moneyed locals bearing shopping bags, also with gaping tourists dazzled by the gleaming shops as well as by the countless Mercedes, Bentleys, and Rolls-Royces. They see one another and interact, but they do not know one another, these islanders of the human archipelago, and they would have it no other way, though if asked they would lay claim to all manner of communal values.

As the sky gradually darkles and the lighted windows of the closing shops radiate glamour and romance into the evening streets, he makes his way to a fine restaurant at which he has a reservation. A choice table awaits him in a corner of the elegant Art Deco bar, the design of which seems to have been inspired by the clean, highly stylized features of his face.

He is not halfway through his martini when he receives an encrypted call on his smartphone. In spite of all its vast resources in both the public and private sectors, the Arcadian revolution has taken two weeks to get a lead on Vikram Rangnekar, but at last they are ready to provide Charlie with an address. His team will be awaiting him at the Peninsula in an hour.

He must be satisfied with a less leisurely dinner than he anticipated, and a single martini instead of two. But the evening will be a lively one, with hard truths taught to the revolution's enemies.

6

Riding shotgun without benefit of a shotgun, Vikram Rangnekar thought, *I have never been happier*. Which was amazing, considering that he had been happy for all his thirty years. According to his mother, Kanta, he had never once been cranky as a baby, and indeed had greeted the obstetrician and delivery-room nurses not with a cry of distress at being expelled from the womb, but with a sound that seemed to be part sigh, part giggle, and with a smile. His father, Aadil, called him *chotti batasha*, which meant "little sugar candy," because he was always so good-natured and cheerful. There were those who resented being exposed to his unrelenting sunniness, and a few who even despised him for it; he repaid their hostility with neither anger nor pity, but with indifference, for he was not inclined to let other people annoy him.

Of course bad things had happened to Vikram. No one got a free ride in this troubled world. There were times when he was sad, but those spells were transient and almost always related to the death of someone he loved or admired. For as long as he could remember, he'd understood that happiness was a choice, that there were people who didn't realize it was theirs to choose or who, for whatever reason, preferred to be perpetually discontented, even angry, even despairing. Most of that type were very political, which Vikram was not. Or they were consumed by envy, which Vikram was not. Or they loved themselves too much, so that they never felt the world was treating them well enough, or they liked themselves too little and wished they were someone else. Vikram liked who he was, although he didn't think he was God's gift either to the world or to women.

He'd had his share of romance. He wasn't a virgin at thirty. There were some women who liked lean and sinewy guys who were gentle and treated them with respect. Of his few paramours, however, none had been fated to be with him forever. One turned out to be waiting to meet a slab of muscle named Curt, who would abuse and disrespect her, and she went off with him. Another, in her second year of graduate school, having learned that men were unnecessary social constructs, vowed to have relations henceforth only with a battery-powered device. The third, an idealistic girl named Larisa, pursuing a career in broadcast journalism, to her dismay concluded that her chosen profession was largely populated by "narcissistic, ill-educated phonies," and left Washington, where Vikram lived in those days, to return to her hometown—Cedar Rapids, Iowa—where she hoped "to find something real."

Fortunately, Vikram's happiness did not depend on the condition of his romantic life.

He thought again, *I have never been happier,* and of course his current extreme good cheer had everything to do with his driver, Jane Hawk, with whom he'd been infatuated for more than five years. His was largely a platonic infatuation, though not entirely. He was a man, after all, and Jane was too beautiful and too desirable for any straight man to yearn to be only her friend. However, he knew there would never be any romance between them. The sadness of that realization was but a droplet compared to the great warm welling of happiness that he felt just being in her company. When Nick had been alive, no man on Earth could have stolen Jane's heart, for she had loved him—and he'd loved her—with an intensity that nineteenth-century novelists had described convincingly, but that was seldom found in contemporary arts because such love alluded to a higher love that inspired only contempt in the artists of this era—well, contempt and fear. In death, Nick haunted his lovely widow, not by his spirit's choice but by her insistent invitation; even if Jane thoroughly avenged her husband's murder, Vikram suspected that Nick might always be in the doorway of her heart, barring entrance to all other men.

Unrequited love was reward enough for him, which had better be the case, considering that, by coming to this woman's aid, he put his life at risk and might not survive long enough to earn even a kiss on the cheek.

"How did you find me?" she repeated as she piloted the Explorer Sport through a Pamplona of wheeled bulls all charging southward on Interstate 405 into a sudden inexplicable absence of congestion, the light of the setting sun flickering off brightwork and window glass.

"It's known that you've been driving off-market vehicles with forged plates," Vikram said. "You had to abandon a black Ford Escape in Texas when the highway patrol pulled you over for some reason, not realizing who you were. You left the trooper handcuffed to your Ford and split in his cruiser. The FBI took your car apart, trying to track its history, but they got epsilon out of it, nothing, nada. I remembered something you told me after you closed the Marcus Paul Headsman case, about this cash-only car dealer in Nogales, Arizona."

Marcus Paul Headsman had been a serial killer who tried to live up to his surname by collecting the heads of his victims and storing them in a freezer. He said he would have liked to keep their bodies as well, but he would have had to buy several new freezers, for which he lacked the funds.

Headsman had stolen a vehicle from Enrique de Soto, who ran a black-market operation out of a series of barns on a property outside of Nogales. Enrique paid boosters for hijacked cars and trucks. He ferried the hot merchandise directly across the border to Nogales, Mexico, where his people stripped out the GPS and all identifiers.

They rebuilt the engine of each vehicle to ensure it would be faster than anything a cop would be driving and returned it to Arizona. Enrique provided forged registration papers and license plates for every customer, which in spite of being bogus had been inserted in Department of Motor Vehicles digital records and would allay the suspicions of any officer of the law. When Headsman was caught, he gave up Enrique, hoping to buy a little leniency.

"I remembered," said Vikram. "I remember so much of what you told me over the years. Probably all of it. So I backdoored Bureau case files to see what had happened to Enrique de Soto."

"Nothing happened to him," Jane said. "We were after Marcus Paul Headsman, and we got him. No time for small fish like Enrique."

Even when the Bureau was well managed, when it wasn't being weaponized and used against domestic political enemies, it was nonetheless overwhelmed with cases and needed to practice triage, focusing its manpower on the most egregious crimes that were urgently in need of being addressed. When lesser scofflaws were found wriggling under the rocks that had been overturned in the pursuit of more dangerous and consequential felons, they were either referred to local authorities or added to a collateral-crimes file for later investigation, which is what happened to Enrique de Soto's case. *Later investigation* usually translated as *the day after never*, because there was always bigger game to hunt.

Vikram said, "I remember you wanted to go after de Soto, but if you pushed the issue, your superiors would see you as a quarterback for lost causes. You had to conform to the Bureau Way if you were to have a future in it."

"And look how well that turned out."

"So I figured maybe you were getting vehicles from de Soto. I deleted him from the collateral-crimes file, so that no one else in the Bureau would make a connection between him and the Headsman case, and I went down to Nogales to talk with him."

They were coming toward an exit to a place they didn't want to go. Jane changed lanes, took the ramp, descended the banked curve at what felt like two Gs, and shot into a neighborhood of industrial buildings that loomed in dark and threatening configurations against the crimson western sky.

She pulled to the curb, put the Explorer in park, switched off the headlights, and turned to Vikram. *"Are you freakin' crazy?"*

"What? What'd I do?"

"Ricky de Soto isn't just some half-assed chop-shop dirtbag. He deals weapons, he's in human trafficking, he's a stone-cold killer when he has to be."

"Well, *you* deal with him."

"I don't have any choice but to deal with him, I know *how* to deal with him, I can hand him his balls on a plate if I have to, but I still watch my back every damn second I'm near him. But *you*! You weren't trained at Quantico. If you carried a gun you'd be no danger to anyone but yourself. When you walk into Ricky's operation, you're a bunny rabbit stepping into a wolf's den."

"I'm no bunny rabbit," Vikram protested.

She punched his arm.

"Ow!"

"You're a sweet, naïve damn bunny rabbit," she insisted, and she punched him again to emphasize her assertion.

7

On the freeway high above, headlights drilled the descendent night as traffic rocketed toward Long Beach and points south. Of the surrounding factories and warehouses and storage yards, some were eerily lighted and engaged in seemingly infernal industry, others perhaps abandoned, dark walls bearing spray-painted Day-Glo gang symbols like the runes of an off-planet civilization. The streets were vaguely lighted by lampposts, some having been shot out for sport. As the last sunlight bled from the sky, the only vehicles on the move nearby were large trucks that resembled military transports embarked on a clandestine mission in a world at perpetual war.

Jane's heart pounded as though she'd just boarded the Explorer after a hundred-yard dash. She had lost people who were dear to her, who were dead because they tried to help her, and their deaths weighed on her more painfully every day. Others were even now at risk, not least of all the people who had taken her son, Travis, into their home in Scottsdale, to hide him there for the duration. She could kill any bloody-minded Arcadian who came at her with murderous intent and suffer no enduring anguish, but the guiltless who died because of her were a stain on her soul. She hoped, perhaps irrationally, that she'd be able to conclude this crusade without inducing other innocents to join the resistance only then to forfeit their lives.

And now here was Vikram.

"What'd you hit me for?"

"I don't want you dead."

"Don't worry about me. I've got winnitude."

" 'Winnitude'?"

"Winnitude. I land on my feet like a cat."

"Like a kitten. Ricky de Soto is a viper. You're not in his league."

"Obviously he didn't kill me."

"Which is astounding. You just walk in on him, wanting to know did he sell me some off-market wheels—*me*, the most-wanted fugitive in the country."

"I knew it was tricky—"

" 'Tricky'?"

"So I didn't go alone."

She closed her eyes. "Whatever you're about to say isn't going to make it better."

"There were five of us. My brother. An uncle. Two cousins, including Judy, the one who was driving the Escalade at the library earlier. There's safety in numbers."

"There's no safety in numbers," Jane disagreed.

"What's he going to do—kill us all?"

"Yes. Exactly. He'd likely kill you all, have his guys dig a mass grave with a backhoe, dump you in it, cover you up, and go out for a nice lunch."

"First thing, I explained about the Bureau's collateral-crimes file, how I'd done him the big favor of deleting him from it."

"I want to hit you again. Damn it, Vikram, at that moment he realized *only you* know about him and only you could one day insert him in the file again or tell the FBI about him."

Massaging his arm where she'd hit him, Vikram thought about what he'd done. After a silence, he said, "I guess it could have gotten ugly at that point."

"Ugly. Oh, you don't *know* ugly."

"But it didn't." He grinned and said, "You know why it didn't get ugly? Because Enrique is hot for you."

"That's not exactly news to me, Vikram. If I didn't have the widow-in-mourning excuse, I'd have had to pull a gun on Ricky more than once."

"I explained to him how I could help you if I could find you, how I could almost surely find you if I knew what you were driving. I gave him a demonstration on his computer, how I can backdoor everyone from the FBI to the National Security Agency to Homeland Security. He was mega impressed. He offered me a position with his company."

"It's not a company, Vikram. It's a criminal operation."

"Anyway, he was excited to think you might survive all this and then you'd owe him and maybe think of him as Sir Gilligan."

"Who?"

"I realized he meant Galahad, from the knights of the Round Table, but I didn't think it would be smart to correct him."

"That's why you still have a tongue."

"Anyway," Vikram said, pointing at the roof again with his right index finger, "the important thing is he believed me. He told me what he'd last sold you and what license plates he put on it."

Nationwide, most police cruisers and many government vehicles were equipped with 360-degree license-plate-scanning systems that automatically recorded the numbers from all the vehicles around them. They continuously transmitted the data to regional archives but also to the National Security Agency's million-square-foot data center in Utah.

Three years ago, at the instruction of corrupt officials high in the Department of Justice, Vikram had installed a rootkit in the NSA's system. This powerful malware program functioned at such a low level that he could swim through their data troves without risk of drawing the attention of IT security sharks.

Although he had delighted in demonstrating his genius—his wicked little babies—to Jane, although he had taught her how to backdoor telecom companies, the Department of Motor Vehicles in any of the fifty states, and numerous other entities, he had carefully avoided exposing her to charges of espionage. He had never shown her how to access the NSA or any other intelligence service.

So after making a new best friend in Enrique de Soto, he had back-doored the NSA to search the archives of license-plate scans for the number that Ricky had provided when he'd sold the Ford Explorer Sport to Jane.

"In the less than two weeks you've had the vehicle," Vikram said, "the plates have been scanned on twelve occasions. Twice in Arizona. Otherwise in various places in Southern California. The most recent was Wednesday, in the San Fernando Valley, on Roscoe Boulevard, by a scanner-equipped car belonging to the Environmental Protection Agency."

The NSA also retained vast video files from key public-building security cameras and from tens of thousands of traffic cams in major metropolitan areas. Using the date and time—12:09 P.M.—of the EPA automatic recording of the Explorer license plate, Vikram accessed those video archives to review the intersections of Roscoe Boulevard and other streets in the vicinity of the sighting.

"It was Wednesday evening when I was tooling this, using my lap-top in a hipster hotel in Santa Monica. I found your Explorer on video in ten minutes and followed it nine blocks to the Counting Sheep, where it seemed you'd taken a room early that afternoon. So then I got in my car and drove there for real, and sure enough your SUV was parked right in front of Room Three. Before you hit me again, consider that if it was the black hats who had that license number, you'd already be in their custody or dead."

Jane grimaced. "I'm not going to hit you again."

"But I'll understand if you do. Totally. Unequivocally. I now understand your point of view. Enrique. Viper. Out of my league."

"If you were at the motel two nights ago, why didn't you contact me then?"

"The math was still way bad. High probability that you would've shot me on sight, at least to wound."

"What—your formulas are based on the assumption I'm trigger-happy?"

"No, no, no. But math is math. I went back to my hotel and cooked up my little scenario in about an hour and got my cast together, and it worked out great."

Although he was thirty, there was a part of Vikram that would be forever an ebullient teenager.

"Sweetie," Jane said affectionately, to be sure that she had his complete attention, "do you understand how deep the shit is that you're in now?"

"Up to my chin," he said with a smile. "But you need help. You need a friend. I am your friend."

"How do you know I'm not as evil as they claim?"

"Don't be ridiculous."

"Maybe I did kill Nick, just like they say. Maybe I sold national security secrets. Maybe you don't know me at all."

"I know you. My heart tells me who you really are."

"Your heart, huh?"

"Heart and brain and intuition. You are good to the bone."

She sighed and shook her head. "No one is good to the bone. The things I've done, had to do—you don't know. Do you also realize, if you become a target of these people, your family will be targeted, too, everyone you drew into your 'little scenario'?"

"I've taken care of my relatives. They're deeply hidden. Deeply, deeply. The black hats know nothing about them."

"Wrong. This is Google World, Facebook World, Big Brother masquerading as Big Friend, so they know *everything* about your family, including what underwear they buy."

"They have vanished in the mists," Vikram insisted. "They can't be found."

"Anyone can be found."

"They haven't found you."

"More than once they have. It's been so close I just about had to shed my skin to slip away."

"Anyway, they don't have to stay hidden for long. Just until we vindicate you and destroy your enemies."

In the interest of keeping him real, she gave him some snark. "This is Friday evening. Do you figure to finish the job by Sunday?"

A huge flatbed eighteen-wheeler with tires as large as those on a supersized earthmover came off the interstate. Like prison-yard searchlights, the headlamp beams washed through the Explorer. The truck driver, high in his cab, wore sunglasses at night and looked as hard-faced as a robot. An enormous construct of some kind was chained to the flatbed and concealed by canvas tarps. It was all quite ordinary, surely, but lately even the most mundane things often seemed strange and menacing.

When the truck passed and the sound of it faded, Vikram said, "For every back door I built into a computer system, at the order of someone at Justice—and even twice for the FBI director himself—I also built a second back door for my personal use. They weren't wise to that. The old guard is enthusiastic about the power that technology can give them but at the same time ignorant about it. They knew epsilon about what I was doing for myself."

Weariness had pulled Jane down in her seat. Now she sat up straight behind the wheel.

Vikram spoke fast, as if afraid she wouldn't give him time to win her over. "So now I can ghost through any intelligence-service, law-enforcement, or government computer system of consequence. I can read the encrypted internal emails of every warped agent of every gone-to-the-dark-side agency searching for you. It's all archived, this history of evil scheming. I'd already been phantom reading, which is how I caught sly passing references to Arcadians now and then. I didn't know what it meant, but it seemed like they must be some kind of secret society. So then what I did is I scanned a humongous amount of text messages of anyone who mentioned Arcadians, searching for other unusual words that maybe were dog whistles, you know, that meant something special to them. And I found terms they shared like 'adjusted people' and 'brain-screwed' and something called the 'Hamlet list,' though I haven't been able to figure out what any of it means. I also kept seeing these weird references to a central committee, regional commanders, cell leaders, as if they're some crazy nest of total revolutionaries. And then what I did is I developed this algorithm, an app to scan all archived messages by the tens of thousands per hour and identify as many people as possible who are using these terms."

When Vikram ran out of breath, Jane took a moment to find her voice. "You . . . you've got names?"

"Lots of names."

"How many? A hundred? Two hundred?"

"More than three thousand eight hundred."

"Holy shit."

"Some of them are real pooh-bahs, top of the food chain in government, industry, the media."

Jane had killed several Arcadians who had given her no choice but to cut them down, and she had identified others, perhaps a score of them, maybe two score. "I've been collecting evidence, but . . . but you put together a whole damn membership directory."

"I'm sure it's nowhere near complete, but it will be in a few days. What exactly are they up to? Why do all these people want you dead? Did they kill Nick? Why did they kill him?"

Hope thrilled through her, a positive expectation more intense than anything she had felt in weeks. A prickling sensation traced the ladder of her spine, and her heart beat faster, and something akin to joy induced a deep pleasurable shudder. "Vikram, you're a genius."

"Yes, I know. But you're a genius, too. I've reviewed your Bureau file. Your IQ is one-sixty-five."

"I couldn't have done what you've done," she said.

"Well, I can't do the things you do. You're right—I would be a danger to myself with a gun."

"I'm sorry I called you a bunny rabbit."

He shrugged. "There's some truth in the description. Though I would die for you."

"Don't say that. Don't even think it."

"Well, but I would." He looked away from her, gazed into the cloistered realm of the aged industrial district, where the shadows seemed sentient and sinister, where the inadequate lights distorted and concealed more than they revealed. In a voice softened by the particular modesty that is a sensitive shrinking from any indelicate subject, he said, "I've admired you for a long time. I won't call it more than admiration. It can't lead to anything more. I understand that. I don't mean to embarrass you, and you must not respond, there is no possible response, but I just needed to say it."

She reached out and took his hand and brought it to her lips and kissed it once.

Having difficulty swallowing, her chest tight with emotion, she switched on the headlights, pulled away from the curb, and returned to the interstate.

8

The false twilight of the storm gave way to the true twilight. Darkness came down through the stately pines with the wind-driven crystalfall, and the fragrant trees arrayed themselves in the blizzard's ermine, so that little of the snow accumulated on the floor of the woods. On sunny days, not much sunlight penetrated the layered vaults of needled branches, and there was little underbrush to inhibit progress.

Tom Buckle was able to move surely if not swiftly among the evergreens. However, the progress that the terrain allowed didn't build his confidence. Until he found the river, Crystal Creek, he couldn't know whether he was heading in the right direction, and the river eluded him. He seemed to be moving southeast in a straight line toward the interstate, but in truth he had no references by which he could determine direction. Maybe, in these parts, moss grew only on the north face of the trees or perhaps the pines inclined toward the eastern sun because the mountains to the west shortened the afternoon, but he was no Daniel Boone, and he was likely to be wrong about everything he imagined from moss to inclination. He was half-afraid that he might not be making any headway at all, that in his disorientation, he might be circling through the woods and, were he to switch on the Tac Light, would find himself tramping across tracks he had made earlier.

In this forest of the night, Tom was not blind, but his dark-adapted eyes left him half-sighted. The architecture of nature was rendered in shades of gray and shapes without detail, and at the farther limits of vision, the woods seemed amorphous, changing. The trees were marshaled like the ranks of an army of silent giants in a dream, awaiting violent action. He wanted to cover as much ground as possible before using the Tac Light, for fear that Wayne Hollister might be nearer than he knew. But then he arrived at a shape that nature hadn't made, a looming irregularity in the sameness of pines. He heard a low rhythmic sound distinct from the steady drone of the wind and the hiss of the needled boughs that combed it.

He dared the flashlight at its least intense setting. Before him stood a square, windowless structure of tightly mortared native stone, about eight feet on a side, too small to be inhabited. The four slopes of the roof met at a pinnacle that featured a finial like a large ice pick encircled by an eggbeater. Mounted on each slope, aimed into its quadrant of the forest, a bowl-like object about three feet in diameter had sloped walls funneling to a depth of perhaps eighteen inches, from the center of which protruded a finely textured cone.

Tom's gut fluttered as if cocooned within it were some winged thing eager to fly free, and the chill that climbed his spine had nothing to do with the cold against which he was outfitted.

The rhythmic, muffled thumping seemed to come from under the small building. He doubted that it could be anything other than the leaden chugging of a propane-fueled generator supplying power to whatever the structure contained.

The bowl-like objects on the roof were reminiscent of high-gain antennas. In fact, they could be nothing else.

He thought he understood what he had come upon, but he needed to be certain about the purpose of this place. He put the Tac Light on the ground, tilted it to illuminate the door, and withdrew the gun from the zippered pocket on the right leg of his insulated storm suit. He had only ten rounds, but he couldn't conceive of needing more than two or three in any confrontation with Hollister; if he didn't kill the man with the first few shots, he would be cut down himself. Heedless of ricochets and shrapnel, he aimed at the door and fired three rounds into the wood between the metal escutcheon and the jamb, the crack of pistol fire echoing loudly through the dark and frosted woods.

Bullet-split wood splintered the air, and the muzzle smoked, and the guts of the lock rattled when he kicked the door, rattled louder on the second kick. The door burst open when he kicked it a third time.

Warm air breathed over him. Like the tiny green, red, and white eyes of some exotic vermin, scores of indicator lights regarded him from the darkness within. He felt for a wall switch to the left of the door, found it. Banks of arcane equipment were revealed along three walls of the hut.

Wainwright Warwick Hollister was one of the world's wealthiest men, and as such he had enemies. Indeed, he evidently thought the entire free society in which he lived was a threat to him. He seemed to be in the grip of profound paranoia. Tom intuited the purpose of this building. The billionaire feared that if a hit team somehow got onto this vast property undetected, they would first marshal their forces in the cover of timberland and then make their way within striking distance of the main house by staying as much as possible within one swath of forest after another. This hut was an automated listening post, of which there were no doubt more situated in other isolate woods. Computers running sound-analysis programs would seine from the common chorus of nature any noises that implied a human presence and would alert the security detail at the main residence.

Hollister didn't need to track bootprints in the snow or search the storm-shrouded night for the flicker of a flashlight. He need not have the knowledge of an Indian scout of another era. He was at this moment being informed telemetrically that Tom Buckle was transiting these particular acres of pines.

In fact, the moment the door of the hut had been breached, an alarm—silent to Tom—surely would have alerted those at the house. No doubt Hollister, whether on foot or in a vehicle, had likewise been informed by way of whatever communications device he carried.

The hunter was even now venturing through this island of trees or approaching its shores, and he knew *precisely* where his quarry could be found.

Gripping the pistol in his right hand, Tom Buckle snatched the Tac Light off the ground with his left, turned from the hut, and ran the gauntlet of evergreens. His eyes were not dark-adapted anymore. And he could no longer presume that darkness would avail him more than speed. He kept the Tac Light on its broadest, palest setting, the better to see optional pathways through the pines, but also because its narrowest, brightest beam was so intense that, on a clear night, it could be seen two miles away. The density of the woods precluded detection at such a distance, but Hollister was likely to be much nearer than that and perhaps closing fast.

The thick-growing woods, seeming to condense around him as he ran, made it unlikely that he would be shot in flight, even if the billionaire was armed with a fully automatic carbine. Scattered patches of the dirty crusted snows of other days and a thick carpet of pine needles provided treacherous footing. However, the greatest danger came from low-hanging branches, of which there were few in this mature woods, though not few enough.

He had lost all sense of direction. He wanted only to flee from the hut and find a meadow, where the faint phosphorous glow of the snowfield would make the flashlight unnecessary. Perhaps there would be no high-tech listening stations in the open land, where Hollister need not fear that assassins might gather undetected.

The billionaire's voice played in memory as Tom ran: *I am also a fair man, Tom. In the contest to come, you will have a chance to survive.*

Perhaps a fragile thread of truth wove through Hollister's tapestry of lies, but the devil was in the definitions of *fair* and *chance*. He was as fair as certain poisonous spiders are fair when they paralyze their prey with venom that leaves them feeling no pain while later they are eaten alive. And one chance in a thousand is still a chance, as is one in ten thousand.

9

Traffic congealed again, and during the rushless last hour of their journey to Newport Beach, Jane told Vikram Rangnekar about Bertold Shenneck's nanoweb implants, the Hamlet list, the adjusted people, the brain-scrubbed rayshaws shorn of memory and personality, reprogrammed as stoic and obedient killing machines. She explained the degree to which the cabal could influence—maybe even control—the majority of media outlets, as well as the extent of their infiltration into the FBI, Homeland Security, NSA, and other national security and law-enforcement agencies. She skimmed through the high points of her actions in recent weeks, quickly describing what evidence she had gathered.

Although Jane's story sounded like a fever dream even to her, Vikram listened with just a few interruptions, and his silence signified neither disbelief nor even skepticism. What he had learned on his own were pieces of a puzzle that clicked into place with each of her revelations, forming a dire picture that was as logical and convincing as it was dark and strange. Each time she glanced at him, his sweet face hardened further from disquiet to dismay to dread. Once when he met her glance, she saw a horror of the future in his large, expressive eyes.

Nearing Newport, as Jane transitioned from Interstate 405 to State Highway 73, Vikram said, "If we could capture one of these adjusted people and put him through an MRI, would we see proof of this brain implant?"

"I guess so. I don't really know. I don't think we could get one of them to cooperate, and even if we saw proof, I'm not sure we could drill through the media blackout on all of this."

"The Arcadians have it locked down that tight?"

"I don't know how many journalists, publishers, and other media types are true believers in the cause and how many might be adjusted people, brain-screwed, being controlled by Techno Arcadians. But, yeah, they seem able to block all reportage of this."

The congestion relented again, and traffic was moving fluidly.

As they descended to the new freeway via an elevated connector, Jane saw a patrol car below, snugged against the right-hand shoulder of the roadway, waiting for an unsuspecting motorist to enter the down ramp faster than the posted speed allowed. She looked at the speedometer. She was all right.

"A few weeks ago," she continued, "I spoke to a forensic pathologist, Dr. Emily Rossman, who had worked in the Los Angeles medical examiner's office. When she trephined the skull of a woman who committed suicide, she saw the nanoweb."

They swept past the cruiser and merged one lane to the left, heading south on State Highway 73. In the rearview mirror, she saw the patrol car's headlights bloom. Its roof-mounted lightbar suddenly blazed and began flashing with authority.

"Dr. Rossman saw a gossamer fairylike structure of intricately designed circuits netting all four lobes of the brain, disappearing into various sulci, with a concentration on the corpus callosum. She was scared shitless. She thought she was looking at evidence of an extra-terrestrial invasion."

The patrol car was coming up fast behind them, but no siren wailed yet.

"Shortly after Dr. Rossman opened the cadaver's skull, maybe as a reaction to contact with the air, the nanoweb dissolved. She said it was 'like the way certain salts absorb moisture from the air and just *deliquesce.'"

Still without a siren, the cruiser moved one lane to the left of the Explorer and sped past, dwindling in the night as if it, too, were a construct of deliquescent salts.

"There was residue?" Vikram asked.

"Some. Dr. Rossman sent it to the lab. She never got the report be-cause the next day she was told to leave and accept severance pay or be fired. They had trumped up a charge against her."

"Don't they videotape autopsies?"

"As I recall, the video disappeared."

Vikram pointed to a sign that listed upcoming exits. "We're close now. Get off at MacArthur Boulevard."

The patrol car was nearing the top of the exit ramp as Jane drove onto the bottom of it.

Halfway up the ramp, she glanced in the rearview mirror to see if another black-and-white might be tailing her. Nothing.

She said, "I feel boxed in even when I'm not."

"Which is why you've survived this long."

From MacArthur Boulevard, they turned onto Bison—and saw a cluster of four police vehicles in front of a store in an upscale strip mall to the right.

"Tell me that's not where we're going," Jane said.

"It's not. Turn right at the next corner."

He pointed to a self-storage facility on the north side of the street. "There's a package waiting for us. A ladder to the stars."

10

The clear heavens of the day have slipped behind blankets heavy with unspent rain to bed down for the night. In the southeast, as the sea of clouds rolls across the last quadrant of the sky, the moon is drowning.

La Cañada Flintridge, in the foothills of the San Gabriel Mountains, north and east of Los Angeles, offers a high-quality suburban lifestyle, neighborhoods of well-kept homes on tree-lined avenues. Strangely, the pavement is in need of considerable repair and the lampposts provide no light on the street where Ashok Rangnekar lives with his wife, Doris.

Charlie Weatherwax, missionary for the truth of random cruelty, is being driven by the second-in-command of his four-member crew, Mustafa al-Yamani. Because they are valued members of the Arcadian revolution, they have been assigned a luxury SUV, a Mercedes-Benz G550 Squared with a 4.0-liter 416-horsepower biturbo V8, which will go from zero to sixty miles per hour in 5.8 seconds, provided at the expense of the Department of Homeland Security, which is one of the agencies for which they hold valid credentials.

Mustafa is an ambitious thirty-two-year-old who intends one day to live in a mansion on Long Island Sound, in East Egg village, and be warmly welcomed by old-money society as one of their own. In the interest of remaking himself to fulfill his dream, he has petitioned Homeland Security to allow him to proceed in court to have his name changed to Tom Buchanan, but permission has not been granted, as the department is currently short of the number of employees with Arabic names that it needs to meet its multicultural quotas.

Charlie and Mustafa are adamantly not two of a kind, and yet they get along well. Charlie's high-protein low-carb diet, augmented with eighty vitamin pills a day and regular drinks of Clean Green, is a Spartan regimen compared to Mustafa's fondness for the richest French cuisine and his tendency to order two desserts with dinner.

Charlie is six feet three and lean as a wolf, while Mustafa is five feet eight and as solid as a pit bull. Mustafa pursues only icy blue-eyed blondes, while Charlie will bed any good-looking woman as long as she likes a little pain and/or humiliation with her sex, which he is able to deliver in a most refined manner.

"What kind of deplorable neighborhood is this?" Mustafa asks with evident distaste. Although English is his second language, he has diligently bleached every trace of an accent from his speech. "They don't remove the dead trees, and that lamppost looks as though it fell over months ago."

Charlie says, "We're at the extreme northern end of the valley, on the very edge of La Cañada. People who live here aren't looking for downtown action."

"Yes, well, if this Vikram fellow hacked millions of dollars from nine different government agencies, whatever is he doing in a place like this?"

"Perhaps," Charlie said, "he thinks it's the last place we'd ever look."

"With all the money he tweaked out of the system, why would he choose to live with an uncle and aunt?"

"Maybe because he likes them."

"They must be a wildly entertaining couple if he's willing to settle in a backwater like this."

Long in preparation for his ascendancy to the social heights of East Egg, Mustafa carries a cordless razor with which he freshens his shave every three or four hours, wears a cologne so subtle that one is not consciously aware of its scent, and sleeps every other night with whitening strips affixed to his teeth. A cosmetic surgeon has refashioned his proud Arabic nose into something Mustafa thinks British and suggestive of English blood in his family tree dating to the age of colonialism. The hair between the knuckles of his fingers has been removed by electrolysis, and his nails are at all times so well manicured that his hands resemble those of an exquisitely detailed mannequin.

Now those hands suddenly tighten on the steering wheel. Mustafa brakes almost to a full stop, so that behind them the headlights of the Cadillac Escalade, which carries three other agents on Charlie's four-man team, flare brightly in the tailgate window of the G550. He points to a large white sign with black lettering. "What do you make of that?"

DANGER
PROCEED AT RISK
PAVEMENT FAULTS
SLIDE ZONE

"There were wildfires last summer and heavy rains this winter," says Charlie. "Always a bad combination. Let's have a look."

Here and there a swath of pavement is missing, as if it's been sloughed away by torrents of racing water, and in its place is a temporary rampart of compacted soil topped with gravel. At each of these points, the hillside to the right is a steep slope of raw earth perhaps inadequately restrained by a makeshift retaining wall of portable concrete barricades. Otherwise the pavement is either in decent condition or only fissured and potholed.

Some streetlamps are missing, others are fallen over, and all are dark. For the last few blocks, the residences have been only on the left side of the street, many with lights aglow. Now the houses are dark and without landscape lighting. Some are surrounded by recently erected chain-link fences bearing signs sternly warning against trespassing.

The seventh and last of the dark structures is the address at which they expect to find Ashok, Doris, and Vikram Rangnekar—aunt, uncle, and the nephew who is a fugitive from the law. It is an enormous residence on at least an acre, standing among live oaks, the style of its architecture not definable in the gloom. This property is also fenced with chain-link unsuitable to an upscale neighborhood. Beyond the gate, a Mercury Mountaineer is parked in the driveway.

When Charlie and Mustafa get out of the bespoke G550 Squared, soft sheet lightning flutters through the rumpled clouds, as though a bright winged legion above the pending storm is hastening to the Apocalypse. There is no thunder flowing in the wake of the flying flame, and the night is uncannily still, all wind deep in a pocket of the storm, waiting to be spent.

The three men from the Cadillac precede Charlie and Mustafa to the gate in the fence: Pete Abelard, Hans Holbein, Andy Serrano. Pete and Hans have cleared their sport coats from belt holsters, and each has a hand on the grip of his weapon, ready to draw and fire, although Vikram Rangnekar is not considered likely to be violent.

By the time Charlie follows the trio, a man has exited the Mountaineer in the driveway. He has come to the farther side of the gate, through which he is speaking to Andy Serrano, who has flashed his FBI badge rather than Homeland ID, because in spite of several unfortunate recent directors, the Bureau is still held in higher regard by the public than is Homeland. Andy is shining a flashlight on this fortysomething Latino, who seems neither in awe nor afraid, his stance relaxed and his face composed.

Because this Latino—Jesus Mendoza—appears unarmed and cooperative, Charlie moves to the gate and shows his badge and takes charge of the scene. As Mendoza swings open the barrier at Charlie's demand, he denies knowing anyone named Rangnekar and insists that the owners of the property are Norman and Dodie Stein, who have been his employers for nearly twenty years. He is a full-time gardener and jack-of-all-trades.

On his smartphone, Charlie has photos of Ashok, Doris, and Vikram, which he shows to Mendoza.

"No, sir. Not him. Not her. No, sir, not him, either. I haven't ever seen these people."

According to Bureau investigators, Vikram Rangnekar formed a limited liability company, Smooth Operator Development, twenty-six months earlier. Two months thereafter, Smooth Operator formed a limited partnership called Chacha Ashok. *Chacha* is Hindi for *uncle*, specifically for an uncle who is your father's brother. Sixteen months ago, Chacha Ashok, L.P., had purchased this residence in La Cañada Flintridge.

"This house," Charlie assures Mendoza, "is on the property-tax rolls as owned by a limited partnership controlled by Vikram and Ashok Rangnekar. Ashok and Doris Rangnekar are also registered to vote in this district."

"There is some terrible mistake, sir. I am sad to say you have been misled. But then I know nothing of taxes and voting. To me, politics seems like a sickness, and I own no house. Until two months ago, I lived here, in an apartment above the garage."

Mendoza is polite, self-effacing, but he lacks one quality that Charlie most appreciates in citizens with whom he must interact in situations like this. Although Mendoza is humble, he is not meek. Humility is good; Charlie Weatherwax *expects* any subject of an interrogation to be no less than humble, but humility is not enough. In urgent cases like this, he never trusts an interrogee until he has reduced him all the way to meek submission.

He puts away his smartphone and looms over Jesus Mendoza, who is even two inches shorter than Mustafa al-Yamani. He makes a point of exaggerating the Spanish pronunciation of the man's name, calling him *Hey-Seuss*, emphasis loud on the first syllable, as if he is calling out to the author who wrote *How the Grinch Stole Christmas.* "Hey-Seuss, is it? Listen to me, Hey-Seuss, and listen good. If you're covering for Vikram Rangnekar, Hey-Seuss, I'll bust your skinny ass and put you away in some shithole of a federal prison for ten years. We're going to search this place from top to bottom, Hey-Seuss, and you will assist us without delay."

Mendoza smiles and shrugs. "Of course. We know that the law is good, if a man use it lawfully."

As sheet lightning fluoroscopes the body of the impending storm and shadows like revealed malignancies briefly caper around Charlie, he senses that he has been rebuked. "Exactly what's that supposed to mean?"

Instead of answering the question, Mendoza says, "Because of recent mudslides, the city has condemned the property. Mr. and Mrs. Stein are contesting the condemnation in court. Deep caissons can be installed, retaining walls built, the home saved. If the law will allow. Meanwhile, no one is permitted to live in the house."

"So what are you doing here?" Charlie asks.

"Sir, you see, I can no longer garden or make repairs. I work the night to keep out vandals who might damage the house before it can be saved."

"Do you think we will vandalize the place, Hey-Seuss?"

"No, sir. Of course not. You are the law. Come with me. I will show you there is no Rangnekar and never was."

11

A flurry of light fanning through enfolded clouds. No thunder in the mute throat of the imminent storm. In the hard glare of the security lamps, row after row of identical storage units stood like sleek mausoleums in an automated graveyard for antiquated robots in a machine civilization with pretensions to an immortal soul.

The facility was quiet on this Friday night. An owl urgently queried them from some roost unseen.

When Vikram unlocked the door to his unit and rolled it up, the clatter echoed along the serviceway, suggesting to the owl that silence was safer.

Vikram switched on the light. Several cardboard cartons occupied a small portion of the storage space, with a hand truck to move them.

"A satellite dish 1.1 meters in diameter," he said. "Transmitter, receiver, satellite modem, plus all the cables and gimcracks to install a VSAT system."

"For what purpose?" Jane asked.

"To connect with the Internet via satellites through a series of Internet service providers, so we can go online from any point on the road, weather permitting, and switch then from one ISP account to another at the first indication someone is tracking our signal."

"You can do that?"

"I can do that from a mobile platform."

"What mobile platform?"

"I'm thinking a motor home."

Jane indicated the cartons. "What did all this cost you?"

"Nada. Used my personal back doors. This gear was ostensibly ordered by the Department of Education, through its Office of Educational Research and Improvement, and express-shipped by the manufacturer to an elementary school in Las Vegas. The school has been closed for two years. My cousin Harshad camped out on its doorstep, waiting for the FedEx delivery, and then he brought this equipment here, as we prearranged."

The care Vikram had taken to acquire the equipment and his talk of using multiple Internet service providers began to suggest to Jane the shape of his intentions. "Have you already set up several accounts with satellite ISPs?"

"More than several. Thirty-six. One is held by the Bureau of Indian Affairs, another by the Fish and Wildlife Service, another by the United States Mint, another—"

"I get it," she said. "No one in these agencies is aware of these ISP accounts."

"They're shadow-booked. And only I have the password that'll activate them."

During the weeks that she'd been consumed by this crusade, Jane had endured many moments when ultimate triumph seemed impossible, but she'd never grown despondent. Despondency drained your energy, made every effort seem useless; it led to despair, and those who surrendered to despair were committing themselves to failure and perhaps to death. Her precious child was a lamp in this dark world, and she owed him confidence, energy, determination; she owed him everything. For all the times that triumph had felt beyond her grasp, there had been comparatively few moments when hope had been more than a pilot light, when it had burned at full flame in her heart. But now, for the second time in an hour, she felt as if the world was bright with promise; belief and trust unified within her mind and heart, so she knew that special purity of hope called faith— faith that she'd succeed, that her enemies would fail.

She said, "Those thirty-eight hundred names you mentioned, the suspected Arcadians—you're going to drill in hard, verify them, and prove they're part of the conspiracy."

"Verify them, find any others, the full directory. They seem to be organized into cells, classic revolution structure. That structure is stupidly predigital, vulnerable to algorithmic cross-referencing of micro details."

"What about the names on the Hamlet list? Those who've been murdered and those who're still alive but condemned?"

"I'll find them, too. Plus everyone who's been injected with a control mechanism. They'll have records somewhere, everyone they control, their secret slaves."

She didn't believe in fate, but her voice was hushed, as if she feared tempting the very power whose existence she denied. "We could blow it wide open."

"We *will*," Vikram promised.

"My God, when they realize what you're doing, they're going to go nuclear. Maybe literally."

"Which is why we use back doors as much as possible, why we keep jackrabbiting from one ISP to another."

Indicating the cartons, she said, "Are we moving this stuff tonight?"

"Yeah."

"Where to?"

"Casa Grande, Arizona."

"Tell me about it on the way," she said and hurried to the Explorer to raise the tailgate.

12

Charlie Weatherwax badly wants the condemned house to belong to Chacha Ashok, L.P., with a direct link to Vikram Rangnekar, and if the fugitive and his uncle can't be found here, Charlie hopes to turn up at least a clue as to where they have gone.

However, as he and Mustafa al-Yamani, in the company of Jesus Mendoza, tour the rambling residence with flashlights, his hopes fade. The place has been stripped of all belongings. Their voices sound hollow in these barren musty-smelling spaces, echoing back from adjacent rooms like the muffled pleas of spirits speaking through the veil between worlds.

Outside, part of the backyard has slid into the deep canyon behind the property. The fractured swimming pool can no longer hold water. Two large oaks have fallen over as the shifting earth has withdrawn from their roots.

Inside the house, as well, are signs that the structure is under stress. Spiderweb fissures in ceiling plaster. Here and there a buckled seam between panels of drywall. An occasional narrow crack in the limestone floors, as jagged as a Richter graph line depicting the energy released by an earthquake.

As though he thinks Charlie and Mustafa are lying about being FBI and are sinister inspectors from the city's building department, intent on enforcing condemnation, Mendoza continues to insist that the property can be stabilized with caissons and retaining walls, that the damage can be repaired, that the house can be made as safe as any place in the world.

"That's the problem," Charlie says. "There is no safe place anywhere in the world."

This statement either mystifies Mendoza, which means he's dimwitted and delusional, or he feigns mystification, which means he's deceitful, engaged in a pretense of wide-eyed innocence. In either case, room by room, Charlie is increasingly offended by this small man's eagerness to speak on behalf of his employers' interests as ardently as if the property to be saved were his own.

Three sharp flashlight beams scale the shadows from the rooms. Charlie's and Mustafa's lights are at all times coordinated. Jesus Mendoza's beam, however, insistently probes elsewhere from theirs, as though he means to misdirect them, to distract them from subtle clues that will prove Vikram Rangnekar has indeed been here.

In an upstairs hallway, a sectioned ladder is half unfolded from an open trapdoor in the ceiling.

"What's up there?" Charlie asks, spearing the overhead darkness with his flashlight.

"Just the attic," Mendoza says. "The trapdoor was closed last time I was here. Movement in the structure must've sprung the latch. We *need* those deep caissons and retaining walls."

Mustafa al-Yamani pulls the ladder down and locks it and leads the way into the upper chamber. With mild protests that there is nothing of interest in the attic, Mendoza follows Mustafa. Charlie ascends last.

The attic features a finished floor and is high enough to allow even Charlie to stand erect with plenty of headroom. The requisite spiders creep along the radials and spirals of their crafting, and dead pill bugs litter the white melamine underfoot.

But there is also a sturdy six-by-three-foot folding table on which stand a computer, keyboard, mouse, and printer.

Pretending surprise, Mendoza says, "Where did those come from?"

"Where, oh where, indeed?" Charlie snarks.

Mustafa drops to one knee to examine the dismantled logic unit that is tucked under the table. "The hard drive has been taken out. It's gone."

Beside the table stands a paper shredder. The floor around it is littered with confetti, but there are also a few crumpled pages that escaped the scissoring maw of the machine. Mustafa smooths out these papers and examines them. With an expression as solemn as that on the face of the sphinx, he hands one of his discoveries to Charlie.

Produced by the color printer, it is a photograph of Jane Hawk.

13

Like a dreamscape fogged and forbidding. Clothed with snow, the wind is white, and the land lies in virginal dress. Only the woods are dark, but they hold neither threats nor secrets for Wainwright Hollister, whose listening stations have told him where Tom Buckle has been and where he has gone.

Under the hood of his storm suit, he wears an earpiece with mic, through which he can communicate with members of the security team at the main house, who provide a running report of Buckle's whereabouts, to the extent this can be known. Using a frequency below the commercial band that serves radio stations, with sufficient wattage to reach anywhere on Crystal Creek Ranch, they transmit to a special FM receiver in his vehicle.

He is riding a state-of-the-art snowmobile powered not by a gasoline engine, but by lithium batteries. Given the weight of the vehicle, which is light compared to an automobile, a full charge provides a range of between 140 and 200 miles, depending on the difficulty of the terrain. Even at the lower end of that mileage spectrum, he has more than enough power to run down the film director before this machine dies on him.

He is immensely enjoying this. He needs a break, a brief escape from the pressures of the revolution that he is leading. A recent event in Borrego Valley, California, has put him under tremendous stress. Fortunately he thrives on stress. He is energized by stress. The earth will crack in two before Wainwright Hollister will bend to stress. All he needs is this brief respite, this lark with Tom Buckle, and then he will resume his historic march toward Utopia.

The events in Borrego Valley, during the intense search for Jane Hawk's son, have spooked some members of the Arcadian central committee. A seventeen-year-old man named Ramsey Corrigan, injected with a control mechanism, suffered a catastrophic and unprecedented psychological collapse as the nanoweb formed over and within his brain. His memory was obliterated. He lost all identity. His ego dissolved, leaving nothing but the id, which is the cold, reptilian, ravenous aspect of the mind that seeks pleasure at any cost and is normally restrained by the ego. For such a fearsome creature, primal pleasures are the *only* pleasures, and extreme violence is far more thrilling than even sex. Ramsey Corrigan slaughtered his mother, father, brother, and an Arcadian agent—bit, tore, and savaged them with inhuman ferocity, all in just two minutes. Then he broadcast his psychological disintegration by way of the whispering room to other adjusted people throughout Borrego Valley—fortunately no farther—a crazed but nonetheless compelling rhythmic rant that infected *them* with catastrophic psychological collapse. A hundred and eighty-six people perished in the ensuing animal violence, necessitating a cover-up that paints events as a terrorist attack involving Jane Hawk.

If Hollister doesn't rule the Arcadian central committee with an iron fist, they will order the reprogramming of the adjusted people, removing the whispering room function from them. But one glitch does not equal Armageddon. For all their revolutionary zeal, some on the committee are gutless. The invaluable whispering room allows the community of the adjusted to be controlled as one in a crisis, and it will make them a formidable force as the revolution progresses. Anyway, there are nearly seventeen thousand people with nanoweb implants, and reprogramming them is not a small matter that can be accomplished in an afternoon.

Ramsey Corrigan is a one-off. No other like him will be seen. Hollister is certain of this. He is certain because his faith in the technology and the revolution is deep and unshakable. There is one god, and its name is Power, and no one can fail who worships Power to the exclusion of all else.

The snowmobile is a remarkable thing, a fabulous toy. The great benefit of battery power is quiet. The machine makes but two sounds: the soft *click* of the slide-rail cleats being pulled along by the suspension wheels; the even softer *shush* of the front skis gliding over the snow.

Hollister is not using the headlamp, relying instead on the ghostly glow of the dead-white snowfields, which appear to produce illumination much as a night sea sometimes brightens with the cold candescence of millions of luminous plankton. The only light produced by the snowmobile is from the digital instrument panel between the handlebars, and that is partially screened by the low, tinted windshield.

However, after traveling around the long woods where Buckle violated the listening station, arriving at the open fields into which the fugitive now progresses, Hollister comes to a full stop and pulls on a pair of night-vision goggles. This gear amplifies the meager existing light eighty thousand times and renders the world in eerie shades of green, seeming to transform the snow into a melted plain of glass left radiant and radioactive in the wake of a nuclear armageddon.

The advantage provided by the snowmobile has reduced Buckle's two-hour head start to perhaps ten minutes. He is now relatively nearby.

Although there are no listening stations in the open meadows, Hollister has other ways of finding his quarry, beginning with the night-vision goggles. He scans the green snowscape before him, the falling flakes like emerald embers, searching for a shambling man who is perhaps already stumbling with exhaustion.

He can't with certainty know which way Buckle might have gone. The fugitive possesses no compass or other means of determining one direction from another, and he might therefore wander in helpless confusion. Aboard Hollister's Gulfstream V, during the flight from Los Angeles, Buckle told the stewardess that he'd used Google Earth to study the ranch; he said he couldn't wait to see if the property was as stunning from ground level as it was from orbit. If he has any survival skills whatsoever, he'll realize that he can avoid walking in circles only if he finds the watercourse for which the ranch is named and follows it southeast to the distant interstate. A soft denizen of Hollywood, Buckle doesn't have the stamina to reach the highway, but if he remembers the river, and if Hollister gets ahead of him to lie in wait, the filmmaker might hike directly to his death.

No man shape materializes out of the wind-blown green veils, nor any slouching prairie wolves, which will have retreated to their dens for the duration of the blizzard.

The least desirable outcome is for Buckle to wander without strategy, become hopelessly lost, and be finished by the forces of nature before his host can look him in the eyes and put a bullet in his head. As a predator, Hollister has no interest in carrion.

14

In this high redoubt of spiders and conspirators, Mendoza's flashlight brightens the photograph with which Charlie Weatherwax confronts him. The jack-of-all-trades studies the picture as if it is not a simple portrait but is instead as abstract and profoundly puzzling as any Jackson Pollock painting.

"You know who she is," Charlie says.

Mendoza frowns. "I don't think I've ever seen her."

"You've seen her, all right."

"Maybe a movie actress. I don't go to the movies much. All the noise, the violence, the silly superhero stories. I read instead. Tell me who she is."

Mustafa says, "Everyone knows who she is."

Mendoza shrugs and returns the photo to Charlie.

"Jane Hawk," Mustafa says. "That's Jane Hawk."

Mendoza frowns. "I hear the name sometimes, some lady in the news. I don't watch news. Hurricanes, tornadoes, shootings, sex, fires, bombs, scandals, all the time end-of-world stories. Like some kind of pornography. I don't like sick pornography."

The man's pretense of ignorance and virtue irritates Charlie. "Vikram Rangnekar is believed to have assisted Jane Hawk in the commission of numerous felonies early in her crime spree, *Hey-Seuss*. It's now thought he's dropped out of sight to join forces with her. So stop shoveling shit at us, peckerhead, or I'll bust your balls."

"The law shouldn't talk like you," says Mendoza as he withdraws a smartphone from a pocket of his zippered khaki jacket. The phone is already unlocked.

"Put that away," Charlie commands.

"I'm calling Mr. Norman Stein, my employer. I can't talk to you the way you are. This is his house. He'll have to talk to you."

"Don't," Charlie says, dropping his flashlight on the table as he draws the pistol from his belt holster. Stein, if there is a Stein, will likely warn Rangnekar.

Mustafa says, "Drop the phone, Mr. Mendoza."

"Get smart, Hey-Seuss. We need to question your employers now."

"They are not criminals. They won't run and hide."

"Drop the damn phone, asshole."

Mendoza presses a name in his directory and puts the iPhone to his ear as it speed-dials.

Charlie steps toward him, intending to knock the phone out of his hand.

Mendoza quickly backs away. "I'm not armed. This is only a phone. You can see it is only a phone." Then to Stein or whomever, he says, "Hello, Mr.—"

Charlie shoots him once in the head, and spiders thrash across their webs, startled by the crimson spray.

As the dead man collapses, Mustafa says, "I suppose you felt that was necessary."

"Shit happens," Charlie says.

"It happens frequently around you."

"He shouldn't have pulled a gun on us." Using the black-and-white patterned display handkerchief from the breast pocket of his Tom Ford suit, Charlie withdraws a snub-nose .38 revolver from the belt holster in the small of his back, crouches, and presses the weapon into Jesus Mendoza's right hand.

Mustafa says, "Cool handkerchief. Is that Dolce and Gabbana?"

"No. Tom Ford."

"A Tom Ford display hankie with a Tom Ford suit? You don't think that's too . . . pat?"

"If you want to move with the crowd in East Egg village one day, subtle elegance and consistency of style is the right choice."

"I understand flamboyance isn't good. But now and then an outfit needs a little punch of something."

Plucking the dead man's smartphone off the floor and rising to his full considerable height, Charlie says, "Maybe you shouldn't set your sights on East Egg. You might be more comfortable in Miami, down in South Beach."

Mustafa winces. "You have a cruel streak."

"It's my mission," Charlie says.

15

Bobby Deacon enjoyed a net worth of more than five million dollars, but when he wasn't bedding down in three-star chain motels that offered Wi-Fi, he lived in his Mercedes-Benz Sprinter, which he had once called "the luxurious bastard child of a torrid shack-up involving an ultra-high-end motor home and a small-business delivery van." On the rare occasion when a metaphor occurred to Bobby, it was nearly always sexual in nature, whether appropriate or not.

The passenger compartment of the customized Sprinter had been extended by three feet and separated from the driver's cockpit by a partition paneled in high-gloss bird's-eye maple with an inlaid plasma TV and hidden DVD player. Amenities included a Bose sound system, power shades on the side windows, and a refrigeration unit that held twenty-four beverage containers. High-fiber-count golden-

wheat wool carpet. Two immensely comfortable recliners upholstered in cream-colored leather. Behind a door at the back was a toilet
with holding tank and a sink offering hot and cold water. The walls
and ceiling were upholstered in cream-colored leather with inlaid
panels of more bird's-eye maple.

A sextet of superbly efficient batteries allowed the passenger compartment to be powered and temperature-controlled for as long as
four days without the need to start the Sprinter's gasoline engine.

Although Bobby thought that a Sprinter looked best in black, this
one had a snow-white exterior. The psychology of color was such that
a white vehicle rarely struck anyone as suspicious. Likewise, the
Mercedes name and emblem shouted respectability. On seeing a
white Mercedes Sprinter parked on a quiet residential street, no one
would wonder if criminal activities were being planned behind the
shade-covered windows of its passenger compartment.

Bobby committed crimes—mostly burglary, occasionally a rape
when an opportunity arose, murder only twice—but he didn't consider himself to be a criminal. He was an agent of justice. In fact, if he
were ever required to fill out a form on which he had to state his oc-
cupation, he would capitalize that title: Agent of Justice. Now and
then in dreams, he wore a T-shirt emblazoned with those words in
all caps: AGENT OF JUSTICE. If the dream involved violence, the caps
were bold: **AGENT OF JUSTICE**. Bobby's dreams were more often than
not violent.

Bobby was twenty-nine years old. He stood six feet one and
weighed just a hundred thirty-nine pounds. He thought of himself as
a whippet, one of those sleek dogs narrower than greyhounds, elegant and fast and agile and stronger than they looked.

When he was twenty, during a burglary, he discovered this major-
hot housewife home alone, and he was all over her for a few hours, as
only Bobby Deacon can be all over a woman. Her name was Meredith. When he finished with Meredith, she was shaking with terror,
but she was even angrier than terrified. She called him disgusting,
said he was like a pale spider, a hideous white spider. He said whippet, but she said spider and kept repeating it. She was so crazed in

her anger that she had no regard for either his feelings or her safety, as if she had nothing more to lose, though of course she did. Bobby always carried a pistol, but he didn't want to kill her. He wanted her to live with the knowledge that an agent of justice had visited her in her fancy house and had extracted from her a price for her arrogance and unearned privilege. He always carried knives in addition to his gun. He left Meredith with a new face, one that she would never want to see in mirrors.

Now he sat in a cream-leather recliner, watching TV, though he wasn't running a movie. The image on the screen was of the house across the street. Cameras were concealed in the Sprinter's exterior trim, allowing Bobby wide-screen views to the front, back, and both sides. He could zoom in on whatever subject interested him and study it as if from arm's length.

This wealthy neighborhood in Scottsdale, Arizona, had many fine properties, but he was focused on the Cantor residence. Standing on two large lots, the house belonged to Segev and Nasia Cantor, who were successful entrepreneurs, fifty-two and fifty respectively. Segev's hobby was coin collecting. He and his wife greatly admired Art Deco–period sculpture and painting, and had acquired a lot of it.

Even when people were circumspect about what they revealed on Facebook and other social sites, as were the Cantors, the Internet provided a thousand windows into their lives, of which they were often unaware. Bobby Deacon knew everything he needed to know about Segev and Nasia. He was confident that burglarizing their home would be hugely rewarding and that they deserved to be hit and hit hard.

He'd never known anyone of their class who *didn't* deserve being hit. They were who they were, just asking for it, and Bobby Deacon was justice.

In spite of the house alarm, Bobby expected to slip into the residence with ease. There were techniques by which to foil even the most sophisticated security systems, and Bobby knew them all. In addition to valuable Art Deco sculptures and period jewelry, he expected to steal maybe half a million dollars' worth of rare coins. The

Cantors stored the collection in a safe, but no safe ever built could withstand an assault by Bobby Deacon, who could crack them like walnuts.

But something was wrong.

The previous day, Segev and Nasia had left on a long-planned two-week vacation to England. The house should be vacant. Nasia's widower father, Bernie Riggowitz, was a peripatetic geezer who, in spite of being eighty-one, regularly took long road trips, driving all over the country, revisiting places he and his late wife, Miriam, once enjoyed together. By now, Bernie was supposed to be halfway to Florida.

Bobby knew all this because, a week earlier, long before parking the Sprinter here yesterday and beginning surveillance, he approached the house at night and, to certain windows, he affixed stick-in-place microphones the size of a quarter and half an inch thick. Because these devices were semi-transparent and placed in the corner of the glazing, they weren't easily noticed. They could pick up voices to a distance of thirty feet. They didn't transmit what they heard, but each included a tiny chip with significant storage capacity served by a forty-eight-hour microbattery. Two nights later, he returned and harvested the audio-rich mics, downloaded their contents, and listened to all manner of conversations among Segev, Nasia, and Bernie.

Bobby felt almost as if he and these three individuals were family. He despised them no less for having gotten to know them better, but then families largely comprised people who despised one another secretly if not openly. There were no loving sitcom families anymore; in fact, there never had been. The closer that people lived to one another and the more they knew about one another, the more reasons they had to hate one another, for there was much injustice among them and little equity. Bobby Deacon had profound experience of this truth.

Anyway, Bernie hadn't left for Florida.

But that wasn't the only thing wrong with this situation.

First, there were the dogs. There had been no dogs in this house, and now there were two German shepherds. When old Bernie walked them, they behaved well on their leashes, calm and obedient.

Bobby didn't dislike dogs, but he didn't trust them. Cats and burglars had more in common than burglars and dogs. If he might still be able to knock over the Cantor place, then he must sedate the dogs. He would have shot them dead, except that in such a quiet neighborhood, using a gun even with a sound suppressor seemed too risky.

Old Bernie was not the worst of it and neither were the dogs. The big problem was the little kid.

The boy was maybe five years old. He neither went on walks with the dogs nor came out to play, at least not that Bobby had seen. Sometimes the boy stood at a window, staring at the street.

Segev and Nasia had two daughters, but they were grown and married and gone away to lives of their own. Neither daughter had yet given her parents a grandchild. Bobby had seen photographs of them on Facebook. He was willing to impregnate either of them—or both—and freshen the genetics of the family.

So the boy was a mystery.

Bobby could sedate the dogs with a tranquilizer gun. In respect of the quiet neighborhood, he could slit the throats of the old man and the boy as they slept. He was swift and silent.

However, he didn't like kids, didn't like dealing with them even to slit their throats. They hadn't reached the age of reason. They were unpredictable. You never knew what a bratty kid might do. Little kids were packages of craziness. Besides, a twerp like this one could scream as loud as a fire-truck siren and be even quicker than a whippet; Bobby Deacon had profound experience of that truth.

The previous night, in spite of the addition of the dogs, Bobby risked venturing onto the Cantor property again, this time planting a stick-in-place microphone only on a kitchen window at the back of the residence. If there might be one room where the boy and the old man were likely to have conversations, the kitchen was the place. Later this night, he will return to retrieve the mic, download its contents, and see if anything they said might clarify the current situation.

At the moment, the TV screen offered a medium close-up shot of the target house, where lights glowed only in ground-floor rooms. Alerted by sudden movement at a front window, Bobby zoomed in to the max.

The boy gazed out at the street. He was a good-looking kid. No one would ever compare him to a hideous spider. Good looks were the ultimate injustice, worse than a high IQ, worse even than wealth. Why should one person be born pretty and another not? Pretty people had a great unearned advantage. Of all the reasons that agents of justice were necessary to balance the scales, exacting a toll from pretty people was the most important if equality was eventually to be assured.

16

The ruins of the disintegrating sky were channeled by the wind and settled on the land, white onto white, moment by moment erasing reality from the night. In this bleak realm between life and death, uncountable ghosts chased one another across the spectral plain, from nowhere to nowhere.

In spite of his knitted ski mask, Tom Buckle's face was cold. The wind pasted snow to the fabric, which was at first melted by his body heat. But then fresh barrages assaulted him and the temperature fell and the exterior of the mask became crusted with ice, to which fresh snow adhered, until he felt as if he were wearing a knight's metal helmet with visor. Only the mouth hole remained soft at its edges, kept flexible by his smoking breath. He scraped at the mask with one gloved hand. The knitwork remained rigid, and what snow came loose from it stuck to the glove, in which he could feel his fingers stiffening.

Although the storm suit kept him alive in this fierce weather, it also promoted an ambulatory claustrophobia. He felt as though he were wound in graveclothes, being mummified by wind and cold. The in-

creasing awkwardness with which he moved filled him with a growing horror of being rendered helpless, which was quite apart from his
fear of Hollister.

When he came to the river—Crystal Creek—he didn't at first understand what he was seeing. A wide ragged-edged band of blackness slithered snakelike through the virgin meadow, bearing on its
back random patterns of white scales. Then he realized that the black
was water, too deep and swift to freeze over, and the white scales
were plaques of ice or ice-crusted flotsam being carried downstream.

If he'd found the watercourse sooner, the discovery would have
exhilarated him. But already he was too tired and too daunted by the
storm to be convinced that the river offered a certain path to help and
salvation. Nevertheless, wearily he followed the flow, for it would in
time lead him to the trafficked interstate, if he could stay upright long
enough.

He thought that he had been afoot about three hours, although it
could have been an hour less or an hour longer. He had lost all sense
of time. He didn't strip open the storm cuff on his sleeve and check
his wristwatch, because whatever the truth, there was a better than
even chance that it would be so different from his perception that it
would unnerve him.

The threadbare reality of the snow-blinded night recovered a measure of substance when trees appeared on an elevated portion of the
riverbank. Not a forest this time. A mere copse of eight or ten pines.
He made his way among them, grateful for a brief reprieve from the
wind.

The last of the trees stood damaged, perhaps by a recent gale that
had been much greater than the current one. An enormous bough,
cracked and sagging away from the trunk, swayed back and forth,
brooming the earth.

This sight inspired Tom to search for a manageable branch that he
could break off from the larger mass. When he continued into the
next stretch of meadow, he moved backward, sweeping the snow
with the thickly needled branch, obscuring his footprints in the inches
of new powder. He couldn't entirely erase his trail, but he was able to

soften his tracks sufficiently that the storm might obliterate what remained in just a few minutes.

Progressing in this fashion slowed him considerably. But being
able to do something, however feeble, to foil his pursuer also gave
him a welcome sense of empowerment, somewhat knitting up his
badly raveled confidence.

Tom didn't know whether he reversed a hundred yards or three
hundred along the riverbank before, gasping and nearly exhausted,
he came to the crossing. He hadn't expected a bridge. But the moment he glimpsed the span, he knew there must be others like it,
mending the divide that the river scored through the ranch.

The sturdy post-and-plank construction—one lane wide, with a
balustrade and handrail on each side—looked more like a pier than a
bridge, because in forty feet or so, it faded into the blizzard, as did the
river below. He was reminded of winter days on the beaches of Southern California, when piers seemed to wither away into the fog-
shrouded sea.

The structure began on an elevated section of the bank, eight or ten
feet from the river's edge, and was raised about six feet above the
racing water, ensuring its survival during a flood. Carrying the pine
branch, Tom descended the bank, slipped under the bridge, and sat
sheltered from the wind, the water surging past in front of him. He
needed to catch his breath and eat a PowerBar.

He was able to extract one from a zippered pocket in which he had
stowed it, but his gloved hands were too clumsy to strip off the wrap-
per. He pulled up his ski mask and tore at the package with his teeth.
For hours, consumed by fear and fighting off despair, he hadn't
thought about anything but escape and death. With his first mouthful
of the high-protein bar, he realized how hungry he was, and when he
finished the first, he tore open a second.

The monotonous moan-and-whistle of the wind had become like
tinnitus, a sound so consistent that he wasn't always consciously
aware of it. When a faint but rhythmic sound arose, it was in such
high contrast to the windsong of sameness that he became at once
alert. He sat forward, loosened his chinstrap, pulled back his hood.

The soft mechanical clicking noise grew less rapid as it grew louder and nearer. When very near indeed, it abruptly stopped. No source of light brightened the night beyond the bridge, nothing to suggest what had made the sound, but Tom intuited a malevolent presence that froze him in a troll crouch of apprehension.

He strained to hear anything else within the wind's monotony. After half a minute or so, the noise arose again, in a slower meter this time but then quickening. Suddenly the mysterious thing was overhead, on the bridge, its presence certified not merely by the rhythmic *click-click-click*, but also by the creaking of the plank floor under a substantial weight and by the clatter of something being propelled across the span. It seemed to be a mechanical construct, but it produced no engine noise.

As the racket passed overhead and continued toward the farther bank of the river, Tom scrambled out from under the bridge and rose cautiously beside it, his head at the level of the deck. He saw a snowmobile receding toward the north shore, a figure seated upon it. He could only suppose that the vehicle was battery-powered and that the rider must be Wainwright Hollister.

17

South to San Diego. Satellite dish and associated equipment on board, Vikram in the passenger seat with his feet on the dashboard, Arthur Rubinstein on the music system—Chopin: Piano Concerto in E Minor, op. 35—the windshield wipers sliding back and forth in conflicting tempo with the music, the night awash, the sky depleted of sheet lightning but swollen with rain.

He listened intently to the great pianist, accompanied in this case by the Los Angeles Philharmonic, maybe because the performance enchanted him, maybe because he wanted to understand why Rubinstein meant so much to Jane.

Partway through Piano Concerto No. 2 in F Minor, op. 21, he said, "You, too, are a great pianist."

"Good enough. Not great."

"So you say. But I've heard you play."

"Then you don't have an ear developed well enough to know the difference between good and better."

"They say your father is a great pianist. Martin Duroc. They fill the concert halls where he plays. You've long been estranged from him."

"A great, homicidal pianist," she said.

"Which means?"

If she and Vikram were going to travel the Valley of the Shadow together, they should have no secrets. "He murdered my mother."

He took his feet off the dashboard and sat up straight. "They say she committed suicide when you were eight. You found the body."

After a long darkness, sheet lightning opened the skull of the sky, revealing clouds fissured like the surface of the brain and black with malignancies.

"He was supposed to be five hundred miles away," Jane said, "preparing for a performance the following day. But he was home that night. I heard the argument. I saw. I thought no one would believe me. I was afraid of him. He is a totally intimidating sonofabitch. Let's not talk over Rubinstein."

They listened to the rest of the Piano Concerto in F Minor.

When it was finished, she switched off the system.

After a mutual silence, Vikram said, "You once had a full music scholarship to Oberlin. You turned it down."

"I was more interested in forensic psychology."

He said, "Sanity and insanity, the why of criminality. You got your degree—then the FBI."

"That's the story."

"He stole your music from you."

"Like hell he did. He stole my mother and my innocence. No one can steal my music."

She reached out to restart Rubinstein.

"Wait," Vikram said.

She drove the rain-slick highway, the reflection of headlights in the wet blacktop seeming to pull her like tractor beams toward some destiny she didn't want to contemplate.

He said, "I'm so sorry."

"You've nothing to be sorry for."

"I knew about the estrangement, but I didn't know you came from such a . . . dysfunctional family."

A dark laugh escaped her. " 'Dysfunctional' is one word for it."

"My mother, Kanta, said I was born giggling. My father, Aadil, called me *chotti batasha*, which means 'little sugar candy.' My family was not to any degree dysfunctional—and yet both my mother and my father are long dead."

18

At the sight of his would-be killer on the snowmobile, Tom Buckle turned to flee, but he was halted by the realization that Hollister was tracking him in the dark, without using the vehicle's headlamp. If he didn't need light to see, he had night-vision gear.

The billionaire's promise to give his quarry a fair chance did not preclude him from using all manner of technological advantages—night-vision goggles, a mostly quiet snowmobile, listening stations, and perhaps much more. Considering the distance to the interstate, the impediment of the storm, and Tom's diminishing stamina, there was little likelihood that determined flight would keep him alive. In fact, there was no chance whatsoever.

He thought of climbing onto the bridge and chasing after the snowmobile and shooting Hollister. In the back. But he wasn't sure he could do it. Not in the back. He was the only child of a humble tailor and a gentle seamstress whose exceptional workmanship was matched by their decency and honesty. He hadn't been raised to shoot anyone in the back—or even to speak ill of anyone behind his back. His parents' lives were as superbly cut and stitched as the clothing on which they labored. If Tom wanted anything more than he wanted to be a successful director, it was to be worthy of his mom and dad, to honor them by living as they had taught him to live, for he loved them more than life.

And suddenly he knew that trying to shoot his enemy in the back would be as fruitless as it would be cowardly. Because Hollister didn't play fair, had never been taught fairness, and didn't take chances. Under his storm suit, his torso would be wrapped in Kevlar. Bet on it. Even his hood was likely to be lined with a bulletproof material, something tougher than Kevlar.

For Tom Buckle, only one course of action offered a slim hope of survival. In recognition of it, he returned to the space under the bridge and settled in the darkness on the riverbank. He must shelter from the flensing wind and driven snow. Stay warm. He must not exhaust himself in an impossible trek to the distant interstate. He had four more PowerBars. He could melt snow for drinking water.

If a day passed without Hollister finding him, two days, they would probably assume he'd lost his way in the storm and perished. Maybe he had been injured in a fall. Or blundered into the river. Or been set upon by prairie wolves. If his body lay under drifted snow, they wouldn't expect it to be found until circling carrion birds marked its position following the spring thaw.

When Hollister might be convinced that his prey had proved unequal to the elements and died at Nature's hand, Tom could then set out under the cover of darkness, avoiding the woods, with the hope that no listening stations were positioned in the open fields. Without the blizzard to impede him, he would make much better time and would have greater stamina.

Although this seemed his best—his only wise—choice, Tom Buckle didn't feel good about it. He felt like a small, weak animal cowering in its burrow.

These lunatics had blacklisted him, Hamlet-listed him, as a threat to the culture, as if he could make an already decadent and death-obsessed culture worse with his little movies, which in fact celebrated courage, freedom, hope. *That* was the burr prickling his conscience.

He told stories of courage and fortitude, stories of ordinary people who refused to be crushed by the system or dictated to by self-appointed elites. Yet here he was, quailing in this dark funk hole, beaten down without ever having been beaten up, afraid and on the run from people who couldn't tolerate diverse opinions, who demonized all dissent from the received wisdom of their class and kind, who despised those not in their club, totalitarians costumed as champions of Utopia. If he cowered from them and did not stand boldly against them, they wouldn't need to kill him to render his work meaningless; he would have done that himself, proving his movies were lies, false art in the service of self-deception.

He thought of Jane Hawk, of the vituperation directed at her, the false accusations, the blackest hatred ginned up in the media, the legions wanting to kill her on sight or, worse, inject her with a nanomachine control mechanism, so that the meaning of her life would be theirs to determine, her body theirs to ravage, her mind theirs to oppress. Once in a while, a movie qualified as art because it was about truth. Art was art only if it honored enduring truths; otherwise it was pulp or propaganda. It seemed to him now that Jane Hawk was living art, her commitment to truth so profound that she risked her life in the pursuit of it.

Tom was twenty-six, not yet of an age to have experienced a satori, a moment of sudden enlightenment so consequential that it changed him forever, but now a satori shook him to his core. Art made life in a dark world tolerable, but when a declining culture arrived at a critical depth, art alone was insufficient either to restore that culture to health or to prevent its further descent into an abyss. He could make a hundred films that moved the mind and heart, but at this perilous moment in history, the only art that mattered was life lived in service to absolute truth, as Hawk was living hers. Having retreated from confrontation with Hollister, cowering here beneath the bridge, Tom Buckle was neither a man nor an artist, nor truly alive. He was shape without form, as stuffed with straw as a scarecrow of which even crows were not afraid, and if he were ever to like himself again, he had to *act*.

Just then he heard it. The *click-click-click* of the snowmobile. On the bridge. Returning from the north side of the river.

19

Vikram Rangnekar was not one to dwell on loss, because to dwell on it was to disrespect the gift of life and risk becoming obsessed with the fact that all the losses throughout the years eventually lead to the loss of life itself.

As they raced south into the rain, he did not dramatize his losses with tears or quaking voice, but merely said, "My mother and father died the same day, a week after my twelfth birthday. This was in Mumbai. They went to the market. It was a time of demonstrations, as is often the case. Marxists were demonstrating and Maoists and anarchists. Also maybe two hundred animal-rights activists who cared nothing for animal rights, but were paid by Waheed Ahmed Abdulla, a notorious Muslim gangster, to cause chaos at a courthouse, so that Waheed's favorite hit man could kill a certain honorable judge and escape into the crowd. At first unaware of one another, the Marxists and Maoists and anarchists arrived in the same square by different routes. They became enraged by one another, and all three factions were infuriated by the animal-rights activists, whom they considered to be shallow political thinkers. There was as well an elephant that became dangerously agitated by all the chanting and the shouting. Exactly how it happened, no one could say. But someone fired shots, the elephant stampeded, and the various angry elements in the crowd flung themselves at one another with great fervor, trapping among them innocents who just wanted to go to the marketplace. In the end, many were injured and six died. It tells you much about the tenor of those times that the Marxists, the Maoists, the anarchists, and the fake animal-rights activists proudly claimed responsibility for the deaths and dared authorities to prosecute them. Only the elephant did not acknowledge blame."

" 'Elephant.' "

"Yes, elephant."

Jane glanced away from the rain-beaten highway. Her eyes were gray in the instrument-panel light. He wished she weren't wearing contacts. The true color of her blue eyes was quite remarkable.

She said, "You made all that up."

"Not a word. Life is a tapestry of tragedy and comedy, terror and fortitude, despair and joy, and it's routinely more colorful and crazy than anything I—or anyone—could invent."

"How did you get to America?"

"My father's brother, Ashok, had emigrated years earlier, long before the riots and the elephant. He had attained citizenship. He brought my brother and me to this country. I was naturalized in time, became to the computer what you are to the piano, took a job with the Department of Justice, served my country by doing lawful work, but also unlawful work when ordered to do it. I didn't like making my wicked little babies, even for the boss. When I became convinced you were being persecuted for discovering some truth, I decided to make amends for my wicked babies by helping you. So I stole fifteen million dollars from various government agencies to finance this operation, and I am now a fugitive like yourself."

Her smile was uncertain. "Fifteen million bucks? What's the punch line?"

"It's not a joke."

"It's not a joke, huh? So how do you steal fifteen million?"

"Lots of government agencies have lax budget controls. Money disappears all the time. Some call it 'spillage.' I found it easy to back-door various accounting departments, issue a contract payment for a company I called Spearpoint Consulting, and specify immediate wire transfer to an established bank account, so basically a robot comptroller sent me the money. Three hundred thousand here, five hundred thousand there. It adds up."

He seemed to have rendered her speechless, which tickled him.

At last she said, "You actually stole fifteen million? To help me? Are you out of your mind?"

"I do not believe so."

"You do not believe so?"

"I do not believe I am out of my mind."

"Damn it, you've ruined your life, Vikram."

"Together we will prove the cold hard truth, and you will be vindicated, and I will be totally exonerated because my motive was pure."

"'Pure'?"

"You keep repeating things I say."

"Because I can't believe you said them."

"But I did."

"Vikram, nobody steals fifteen million and is exonerated."

"Then I will be the first."

When working at a computer, Vikram was an obsessive planner, cautious and meticulous. However, in his personal life, he could often be impulsive. He thought this was a good thing, because one needed balance. All three of his lovers had been charmed by his boyish impulsiveness. Stealing fifteen million dollars was by far the most impulsive thing he'd done, and he was pleased with himself.

Jane said, "I didn't ask you to do this. I never would."

"You didn't need to ask. I knew it was the right thing."

"Damn."

"I sense that you want to hit me again."

"You sense correctly."

"Hit me if it will make you feel better."

She did not hit him. "What the hell did you need fifteen million for?"

"Equipment. And the motor home that will be delivered to us in Casa Grande by an employee of Enrique de Soto."

"Oh, my God."

"And then there was the considerable expense of secreting my relatives—Uncle Ashok, Aunt Doris, my brother, and four cousins—where they can't be found for the duration. All in all, I've spent nearly one million. The other fourteen is for contingencies."

"'Contingencies.'"

"Yes."

"What contingencies?"

"Any that arise. It's difficult to know what contingencies might arise while conducting a counterrevolution against such vicious people as these Arcadians. It would be so sad if we came within an inch of triumph and ran out of funds, failed, and died horribly."

"Vikram . . ."

"Yes, Jane?"

She shook her head.

"Is something wrong?" he asked.

"I'm afraid for you."

"I'm not afraid for me."

"That's part of why I'm afraid for you."

She switched on the music as though to put a period to their conversation.

On the pavement, in the headlights, shatters of hard rain glittered and danced as if the heavens were unleashing a storm of glass needles, and the civilized communities of the coast, to both sides of the highway, seemed to have collapsed into a dark void that the interstate bridged at the peril of all who traveled on it.

"Beautiful," he said of the music. "More Chopin?"

"Yes. Twenty-one nocturnes."

"A lot of nocturnes."

"When you've listened to them, you'll want twenty-one more."

"Chopin is your favorite composer?"

"One of them. I like his music for its brilliance, but also because it's the one thing my father can't play well. Chopin wrote with great tenderness. My father is a stranger to tenderness."

After a few minutes, he said, "Are you sure you're not mad at me?"

"Vikram, I am not mad at you. I am *terrified* for you, and I will continue to be terrified for you until you have the good sense to be afraid for yourself. Now let's not talk over Rubinstein. It's like shouting curses in church."

In truth, he was a little bit afraid. But he didn't want Jane to know. He could only love her from afar, and his love must always be platonic, and perhaps it would be forever unrequited even in its platonic form, but it was nonetheless love, and a guy did not want the object of his love to know that he was scared.

20

It's a goblin night: eerie green snowfields, the falling flakes like luminous citrine scales shed by some gathering of dragons in the sky.

On the north side of the river, Wainwright Hollister scans the wintry and otherworldly landscape, but there is no sign of Thomas Buckle struggling through the blizzard. On the south side of the river, there were vague footprints for a while, but they vanished a few hundred yards before the bridge. There are none here in the northern fields.

He swings the snowmobile around and returns to the bridge. When he is almost to the south side of the structure, he suddenly wonders if the filmmaker, physically unequal to the challenge of the storm, has taken refuge under the plank-floored span.

After traversing the remainder of the bridge, Hollister drives about thirty yards farther and pulls to a stop. He takes off his night-vision goggles, dismounts, and leaves the snowmobile silently idling. He draws his pistol—fully automatic, with a twenty-round magazine—and returns on foot along the tracks left by his vehicle, relying on the phosphorous glow of the snowfield that seems to produce this spectral luminescence of itself.

The groaning, keening wind will mask his approach. Arriving at the south pier, he won't announce himself with a flashlight but will crouch and fire a burst of ten or twelve rounds into the darkness under the bridge. If Tom Buckle is sheltering there, he'll be taken by surprise and either killed or mortally wounded.

21

The frozen riverbank his floor, the plank bridge his ceiling, this niche of darkness all but blinding, the click and clatter of the returning snowmobile like the centipedal approach of a hungry stalker in a nightmare about grossly enlarged insects.

When the vehicle seemed about to pass overhead, Tom Buckle scrambled from under the east side of the bridge. Gloves tucked in a pocket, pistol in a two-hand grip, he rose to his feet and saw that he'd misjudged the snowmobile's speed and position. It was already beyond him, gliding off the bridge.

He started up the slope, intent on shooting Hollister as the man motored past, this demon of untruth, this relentless enemy of all meaning and freedom, who meant to erase the past in its splendor and craft a disenchanted future where power was the only truth and slavery was renamed public service. But Tom slipped, stumbled, fell. By the time he thrust to his feet and reached the crest of the riverbank, the snowmobile was about ten yards away, heading south, fading into the falling snow.

Tom hurried forward through the vehicle's tracks but quickly realized that the distance, the strong wind, and his inexperience with firearms made a successful hit nearly impossible. He staggered to a halt.

Out there at the limits of visibility, the snowmobile seemed to slow. It stopped. Seen through driven skeins, in the witchy light of the snowfield, barely revealed by the eerie instrument-panel light from his vehicle, Hollister appeared to be dismounting. Either he'd had sudden trouble with the vehicle—or perhaps he meant to approach the bridge on foot after establishing that he had driven away.

Tom didn't know if it might be intuition or survival instinct or inspiration of a higher nature that seized him and flung him into sudden, frantic motion. He sprinted back toward the bridge until, glancing over his shoulder, he saw that the storm masked him and

Hollister from each other. Then he turned east and hurried along the riverbank for more than ten yards. He dropped to the ground and, as much as possible, made himself as one with the snow that was drifted against a low palisade of brush.

He could no longer see the snowmobile. But then a hunched and bearish figure materialized from that direction and proceeded toward the bridge, fading in and out of the blowing torrents as if it were an apparition haunting a dead world fallen into perpetual winter.

Tom's first intention had been to circle behind his would-be killer and take him by surprise, but he kept thinking about the eerie glow of the snowmobile. Wouldn't Hollister have switched off the motor before he dismounted, and wouldn't the instrument panel have gone dark? Unless . . . unless the battery-powered nature of the vehicle required that it run continuously in cold weather as bitter as this, lest it be difficult to start.

When the phantom figure shambled past his quarry at a distance of maybe forty feet, Tom hesitated and then got up from the ground. He pocketed the pistol but didn't take time to pull on his gloves before he hurried toward where he thought the snowmobile would be found.

Bent forward, squinting, wishing he could dare the Tac Light, he almost missed the vehicle's tracks. He followed them away from the river. As the faint radiance of the snowmobile's instrument panel first caught his attention, a burst of gunfire rattled through the night behind him.

22

As one who is reinventing the world, raising civilization out of a sordid past of superstition and rampant self-deception, forcing humanity to become as efficient as a superbly engineered machine, Wainwright Warwick Hollister often feels a fullness of self that suggests a destiny even greater than what he can thus far imagine. A fullness of mind, as though he knows all that needs to be known and is too wise ever to be dethroned. A fullness of body, so that he believes he could physically crush any opponent. At times like this, in the urgency of the hunt, when he senses that he's closing on his hapless prey, his manhood is fiercely swollen, throbbing against his abdomen. Nothing enlivens the libido like murder, because it is the ultimate act of resistance to the pathetic fiction that every life has intrinsic value, which everyone of the master class and every *honest* slave well knows to be a lie.

He moves with stealth in the carpet of snow, crouches at the southern pier of the bridge, and hesitates only a few seconds, to savor the moment. Then he leans around the base that supports the bridge and squeezes off a barrage of pistol fire.

No shout of surprise or scream of pain erupts from that dark redoubt. Hollister jukes backward when he takes his finger off the trigger, but there is no return fire.

When he switches on his Tac Light and sweeps the beam across the sloped riverbank, he finds no dead man. However, the thin skiff of snow blown under the span has been disturbed, as though Buckle might have rested there and then shuffled out the farther side. Far more intriguing is a pine branch with a broken stem, the needles crusted with snow.

Before his pupils can iris down to pinpoints, while his eyes are still somewhat dark-adapted, he clicks off the light and turns away from that bolt-hole. Still in a crouch, he presses his back to the bridge pier. Having made a target of himself, he scans the night not with fear—he will never fear an effete specimen like Thomas Buckle—but with the keen observational skills of a warrior.

Every moment of the day, he is a man-at-arms able to destroy other men financially and emotionally in acts of corporate warfare or destroy them literally during a hunt like this. Not for him the thousands of novels, the fictions, in which his father, Orenthal, found refuge from the world. Wainwright Warwick Hollister wants no refuge; he wants *the world*, and he will have the world, because absolute power and the ruthless wielding of it cannot be resisted.

Now he scans the duotone kaleidoscope of the churning storm, white flakes and gray drear, certain that his exceptional mind and superlative senses will detect the slightest purposeful movement in the whirling chaos, that if Buckle is circling on him, then Buckle is as good as dead, for Thomas Buckle is neither a chameleon nor a warrior nor—

Then Hollister remembers the snowmobile and realizes there is a one in a thousand chance that his quarry is just barely smart enough to have screwed him over.

He scrambles to his feet, crests the riverbank, and hurries along the snowmobile tracks that the wind is diligently smoothing away.

23

Earlier Tom had pulled up his ski mask to eat the Power-Bars, had drawn back his hood to listen to the snowmobile, and stripped off his gloves to better handle the pistol, which he hadn't needed. The stinging cold tattooed his face, made his ears ache. His hands were stiff. He had time only for the gloves, and he had difficulty working his hands into them as he sat astride the snowmobile.

He was familiar with motorcycles, and the controls of this machine were similar to those of the hogs he'd ridden, though not exactly the same. Hand throttle but no brake on the handlebars. When the tracks stopped moving, the vehicle would stop without need of a brake. He anxiously scanned the instrument panel, afraid of making a mistake and stalling out and not being able to restart.

The first shot must have gone wide, but it shattered his indecision. As he did what he thought he needed to do, the second shot sang a wasp song past his right ear, and the snowmobile lurched forward as the third bullet cracked off the tail section or the snow spoiler behind him. Wherever the fourth round went, it didn't kill or wound him. The vehicle's suspension wheels turned, clicking over the cleats, and the slide rail slid, and the tracks churned fast forward into the storm.

24

Hollister thinks he has eight or ten rounds left, but he must have fired more than ten or twelve when he hosed the dark space under the bridge, because only four shots remain. Three other twenty-round magazines are distributed in the pockets of his storm suit, but he has no time to extract one and put it to use.

As the snowmobile surges forward, Hollister doubles his effort, running as full-tilt as the terrain allows. He can sprint faster than any man he knows, because he is in fabulous shape—an Olympian, really—but he understands that he can't leap on Buckle and drag him off the seat. He wants just to stay close to the snowmobile for a few seconds, because the earpiece-microphone unit that he's wearing will remain functional only within a thirty-foot radius of the receiver-transmitter aboard the vehicle.

He alerts the security team at the main residence. *"Buckle's got the snowmobile! Find him, kill him!"*

As the lucky sonofabitch filmmaker powers away into the night and storm, Hollister comes to a halt, gasping for breath. He ejects the depleted magazine from the pistol, extracts a loaded magazine from a zippered pocket, and squeezes off a burst of automatic fire. The snowmobile is out of sight and the wind howls like a wolf pack, and there seems to be little chance that he can score a hit. He fires a second burst. He's a first-rank pistoleer, truly a master marksman. Even firing blindly, he might bring down the fugitive. With his superior skills, his uncanny intuition, and the instincts of a born warrior, there is at least an outside chance that he can achieve what would be impossible for other men. He fires the third and final burst, emptying the magazine.

He stands in expectation that he gradually realizes will be unfulfilled.

He ejects the spent magazine from the pistol. He inserts a fresh one. He holsters the weapon.

The rayshaws are coming. They'll find their master, Hollister, because there is a battery-powered GPS sewn into his storm suit.

As insurance against just such an unlikely turn of events as this, a GPS is included in Thomas Buckle's suit as well. Because this has been a fair contest, Hollister has not tracked his quarry by the signal the man emits. Now, however, even if Buckle abandons the snowmobile, they will at all times know his whereabouts.

Thus far Hollister has given the filmmaker a fighting chance, in a game with equitable rules sincerely observed. This has been strictly mano a mano, a war of two conducted on a level battlefield, in a may-the-best-man-win spirit. But that is over. When he has the opportunity, Thomas Buckle doesn't step forward to fight like a man, even though he is armed with a pistol. Instead he hides in a hole as any rat would hide, and when his hole is found, he runs just like a frightened rat would run. He steals what isn't his, only so that he can flee faster than he could have fled on foot. There is no reason to respect such a gutless specimen. Tom Buckle has proved that he doesn't deserve fair play, that he deserves only contempt and quick extermination.

The flexibility of Wainwright Hollister's gloves allows him to use his pistol without taking them off, but they are less warming than the thicker gloves that have been issued to the filmmaker. He zippers open pockets in his insulated pants and slips his aching hands into them.

The icy wind is sharp. It cuts at his face even through the knitted ski mask. He turns his back to it.

The rayshaws have been standing by for just such an unlikely emergency as this. They will be here in ten minutes.

He stands with head bowed, the gale striking hard blows against his back.

Even though the rayshaws will be here in perhaps nine minutes, it makes sense to take shelter until they arrive. Bent into the wind, he follows his own dissolving bootprints toward the bridge.

In the cheerless gloom of the empty winter-beaten plains, in the ceaseless turbulence of the crystaled air, the night is crowded with the shapes of things rather than with things themselves, vague mirages of strange pale structures shimmering into existence only to evanesce in an instant. Both fantastic chimeras and phantoms in human form are conjured out of the interplay of the swirling snow and the eerie moonless moonlight of the snowfield, as real as Hollister himself, there in his peripheral vision, but not there when he turns his head to look directly.

He is perhaps halfway to the bridge when an apparition of a different character manifests off to his left, a ripple of color in the storm-bleached night, a silken scarlet something. When he turns his head, the thing doesn't disappear, but flutters like a flame, no more than ten feet from him, lit not by the snowshine, which would have robbed it of most of its color, but luminous of itself, as if woven of some unearthly silk. It is the precise shade of the scarf with which naked Mai-Mai had covered the pistol in her hand before biting on the barrel and emptying her pretty head onto the flagstone terrace.

This sight transfixes Hollister, who at first doesn't realize that he has halted in his trek toward the shelter of the bridge. If Mai-Mai's scarf hasn't been recovered with her body, if it has blown away into the vast reaches of Crystal Creek Ranch, the odds that it would appear in this place, at this time, are infinitesimally small, one in a billion, one in a trillion. Having capered through the storm, it should be tangled and encrusted with snow, pasted to a tree in one woods or another, or buried in a drift.

Yet it is as pristine as when it slid from Mai-Mai's hand. It should blow away into the blustery night; but it flutters in midair like a flame tethered to a wick and candle, quivering as if in a feeble draft, the storm without effect on it.

He stands agape.

Abruptly the scarf—or whatever it might be—ripples to the ground and billows toward Hollister, at cross-purpose to the wind. It is like some exotic sea creature fluttering across the floor of an ocean, a scarlet manta ray or dazzling jellyfish, and he steps back to avoid it. The thing undulates past him, seemingly as much under its own power as he is, and it vanishes eastward through a southward-wailing wind.

For a moment, Hollister is unable to move. The scarf seems to have scored a line through the snow before him, a line he can't see but that he dare not cross.

He isn't superstitious. There is no such thing as a ghost, no spirits that might linger after death to haunt a place or person, for there is no such thing as a soul, of which a ghost might be a manifestation. Human beings are brain and body, mind and meat, and nothing else whatsoever. Superstition is the toxin produced by weak minds infected by fantasy and philosophy; and Wainwright Hollister will have none of it. Whether one in a billion or one in a trillion, the timely appearance of the scarlet scarf is but an example of logical synchronicity in a universe full of infinite possibilities.

He feels the cold again and hears the wind that for a moment had seemed to be silent even as it continued to blow. He crosses the unseen line drawn by the vanished silk, hurrying toward the shelter of the bridge.

25

Wet legions march across the roof. A veil of water glisters past the kitchen window, overspill from a clogged rain gutter.

At the breakfast table in the kitchen sits Norman Stein. He is fifty-two years old, five feet six, too thin except for a little potbelly, with a face that would be suitable for one of those tasteless lawn-gnome statues. Most people probably think that he has a sweet quality, but Charlie Weatherwax regards him with disdain, for Stein looks weak, wears thick glasses, and dresses indifferently.

He can't fathom why a woman as attractive as Dodie Stein, who is also at the table, would hitch herself to such a man. She is forty-nine, looks at least ten years younger, and is an inch taller than her husband. With raven hair and green eyes, she has the face of a Ralph Lauren model, the perfect skin of a woman in an Estée Lauder ad, and a body that is pornographic even when she's dressed demurely, as now, in tan slacks and a white blouse.

Inexplicably, she is *not* Norman's second, trophy wife. They have been married for twenty-eight years. Together they have achieved their success in retail jewelry.

Because Jesus Mendoza's smartphone was in use when the jack-of-all-trades died and dropped it on that attic floor, Charlie didn't need a fingerprint or password to access the contacts and find both the phone number and the address for the Steins. While they fight the city to be allowed to stabilize and save their home, they are renting a house in another upscale neighborhood of La Cañada Flintridge.

Although the Steins have been easy to find, getting them to acknowledge their relationship with Vikram Rangnekar has been difficult. As it now seems that Rangnekar is associated with Jane Hawk, the Steins are possible collaborators with the most-wanted fugitive in America, whom a grand jury has charged with treason and multiple murders. The Steins pretend ignorance and innocence. They express outrage at Charlie's insinuations. They call his suspicions absurd, bizarre, ludicrous, utter bullshit, and they insist that his intrusion into their home, with his team of four agents, is illegal.

They want an attorney.

They are not going to get one.

Even the shrimp husband with the face of a gnome appears not to be afraid. "We don't know anyone named Vikram anything, and all we know about Jane Hawk is what we see on TV. So stop this good cop, bad cop routine. We have the right to call our attorney."

Charlie and Mustafa have not been playing good cop, bad cop. They have been playing bad cop, worse cop, and they are about to squash this mismatched pair.

Hans Holbein enters the kitchen with a Medexpress kit that contains ampules of an amber solution in which are suspended the many thousands of tiny parts of nanomachine control mechanisms; it also contains hypodermic syringes and everything else needed to brain-screw this uncooperative pair. A little more than four hours from now, when they are adjusted people, they will do what they are told and will reveal everything they know about Vikram Rangnekar.

Although the Steins have no idea what the Medexpress carrier contains, Norman views it with grave concern and rises to his feet. "Damn you, I'm calling a lawyer."

Mustafa al-Yamani is standing near the jeweler, and he doesn't hesitate to strike out. "Get real, Normie," he suggests, and slaps the man hard across the face with the obvious intention of not just subduing him but also humiliating him. Norman staggers backward, nearly falls over his chair, and collapses into it.

Dodie bolts to her feet, a tigress, and reaches for the Medexpress carrier, perhaps intending to sling it at Mustafa.

Pulling his gun, giving her a point-blank view of the muzzle, Charlie says, "Back off, bitch, or I'll put a bullet between your pretty tits."

For Norman and Dodie Stein, the threat and the crudity of it are the equivalent of sudden immersion in ice-cold water. They are shocked into silence, and she drops into her chair. Even if these invading men *are* what their Bureau ID claims, it's now clear to the Steins that the intruders must be something more than FBI, something worse, something terrible.

Charlie's smartphone rings, and when he checks the caller ID, he discovers that it's the leader of his Arcadian cell. He steps out of the kitchen for the conversation.

The leader reports that during a review of the property-tax records, it's been found that Chacha Ashok, a limited partnership, is no longer listed as owner of the house in the slide zone. It is now shown to be owned by the Norman and Dodie Stein Living Trust. Likewise, the voter roles no longer show Ashok and Doris Rangnekar at that address, but instead Norman and Dodie Stein. Appended to the records in each instance are the words YOU HAVE BEEN VIKRAMIZED.

The cell leader says, "The little piece of shit hoaxed the data so that it read what he wanted until the third time we accessed it for verification. Then the little scumbag had programmed the records to self-correct automatically, and his snarky little gotcha message popped up."

Evidently, Rangnekar had chosen the house expressly because it was condemned and uninhabited. Then he had put together the tableau in the attic: computer, printer, paper shredder, photo of Jane

Hawk. He couldn't have known Jesus Mendoza would be there when Arcadians showed up, or that Mendoza would anger Charlie Weatherwax, a man on a mission.

The leader says, "The little piece of shit is in the process of pulling one stunt too many. NSA hacker chasers think he's inside the computer system of the ATF right this minute, up to something big."

"The Bureau of Alcohol, Tobacco, and Firearms? Something big? What something?"

"We'll know soon. The creep is spoofing his way into the ATF, ricocheting through an exchange in Canada and pinballing through half a dozen cities in the U.S., but we're tracking to source now and will get his real location any minute."

After the cell leader terminates the call, Charlie returns to the kitchen, where Mustafa and Hans are holding the husband and wife at gunpoint.

Norman and Dodie have moved their chairs closer together. They are holding hands. They are focused on each other rather than on their guards. She is smiling at her husband.

The Steins are innocent, and Charlie has no reason to continue tormenting them. However, they have offended him with their arrogant insistence on their rights.

He instructs Hans, Pete, and Andy to remain here, inject the Steins, and stay with them until they are adjusted people. "After the webs have formed, if the bitch appeals to you, do with her what you want—and make sure that Mr. I'm-calling-a-lawyer sits like a good boy and watches all of it."

26

Ten miles east of Alpine, California, Jane drove out of the rain, though the moon and stars remained sunken in a sea of clouds.

At 9:10 they left the interstate at El Centro, in the Imperial Valley, which offered some of the richest farmland in the world. She found a likely restaurant, and Vikram, clearly wanting to assume the role of protector as much as she might allow, insisted it would be safer for him to go inside and place their order, since the entire law-enforcement apparatus of the United States wasn't on the lookout for a beautiful monster named Vikram.

He returned with large Cokes and bags containing thick roast beef sandwiches with Nueske's bacon, provolone, Havarti, and peppered tomatoes, in a hero bun spread with basil oil.

On the way to Arizona, Jane drove while he ate, and he drove while she ate, and the dinner music was not Rubinstein playing Chopin, but Dean Martin singing his long-ago pop hits.

When she finished her sandwich, Jane wiped her hands on paper napkins and switched off the music. "Facial recognition capability is no longer limited to transportation hubs. I've been told it's gone mobile. There's now this handheld device linked to camera-equipped eyeglasses. It can hold up to ten thousand faces and recognize a match in six hundred milliseconds. Some federal agents already have them. Before long so will an increasing number of state and local cops."

"Cool."

"Not cool. Soon the kind of light disguises I've been using won't be enough to stay safe. Maybe they already aren't. And you aren't disguised at all."

"I don't need a disguise."

"Really? In national security circles, you're more famous than any Bollywood star."

"If they're fans now, just wait till they see my dance moves."

She sighed in frustration and for a moment buried her face in her hands. Then she looked at him and said, *"Chotti batasha."*

He grinned. "You remembered."

"Being a little sugar candy now will only get you killed."

He shook his head. "No, no. We'll wreck these Arcadians in two or three days, Jane. We'll soon vindicate ourselves."

"I need you to understand the risk."

"I understand. Your life is on the line. So is mine. So what?"

" 'So what'?"

"So what?" he said. "From the day we're born, our lives are on the line. You never know when an enraged elephant is going to charge through the marketplace."

27

It was only 10:15 P.M. when the last of the lights went out in the Cantor house. Bobby Deacon watched the residence on his TV, from the comfort of the Mercedes-Benz Sprinter parked across the street.

Scottsdale was a quiet city. Many of its residents were early-to-bed types, either because they were overachievers who wanted to get to work early or because they were retirees. Retirees came from all over the country to live in the sunshine of Scottsdale. Bobby despised retirees and overachievers with equal venom, because most of the retirees had once been overachievers but were now, in his estimation, living unproductive lives for years and years, for decades, greedily sucking up more than their share of resources.

When he wasn't setting up a burglary or committing one, Bobby Deacon didn't want the company of retirees; he wanted action: loud music, good drugs, fast women. He didn't like fast women; he merely wanted them. In fact, he despised fast women, slow women, short women, tall women, quiet women and loud women, rich women, poor women, women of every kind, because he needed them. The way women took advantage of a man's need for them—the way they teased and manipulated and controlled and mocked—made them all queens of injustice. As an agent of justice, Bobby felt a special duty to balance the scales between women and men at every opportunity.

Not that he liked men any better than he liked women. Men who were more muscular than whippet-thin Bobby Deacon had bullied him bluntly or subtly, sneered at him openly or covertly. Weak men assumed he was a loser like them. Smart men looked at his narrow face and receding brow, and thought him stupid. Stupid men insulted him by assuming he, too, was stupid.

Bobby liked people in theory but not in practice, which was their fault, not his. He thought of himself as a champion of the oppressed multitudes, the suffering masses, and outsiders of every kind. He only wished he liked a few of them as individuals. So many held wrong opinions, ignorant beliefs; they were insufferable. But serving as the champion of deserving victims whom he despised was the burden that he must bear.

At eleven o'clock, Bobby left the Sprinter and went for a walk in the warm desert night. He was all but incapable of sauntering or strolling. He had the metabolism of a roadrunner, the impatience of a hyperactive cat, and his most casual pace was a few steps slower than racewalking. Therefore, he wore a T-shirt and shorts and running shoes, so that he might appear to be dedicated to exercise, which in fact he loathed. Eventually he arrived at the Cantor house across the street from his Sprinter. He went around to the back of the residence. He didn't fear the dogs, even though they were big. Except when they were taken for a walk, the German shepherds were kept in the house. Bobby removed the half-inch-thick quarter-size semi-transparent microphone that he'd placed in one corner of a kitchen window, and continued his pretend constitutional, in time returning to the Sprinter.

He drove away from the Cantor neighborhood and returned to the motel where he had been staying under the name Max Schreck, for which he had credible ID and a working credit card. He showered and put on black silk pajamas with a cool pattern of little red grinning skulls.

After snorting two generous lines of coke, a stimulant, he poured a double shot of Jack Daniel's, a depressant, seeking the balance in his life that he also sought for society as a dedicated agent of justice. Then he set up his laptop and support equipment on the motel room desk. He downloaded the contents of the microphone chip to a CD and labeled it for the historical record because he was confident that the justice he imposed on those from whom he stole would, in years to come, secure for him a reputation as a modern-day Robin Hood.

He discovered that he'd captured three lengthy conversations between Bernie Riggowitz and the boy. He didn't like retirees, and children were uniquely unsettling because their brains weren't fully developed and they were unpredictable. The prospect of listening to a geezer and a little brat yammering at each other made Bobby want to reach for more drugs, but this was work, and a lot of money was involved, so he had to keep a clear head.

Partway through the first recording, a third person joined in the conversation. The unknown speaker's voice was of a deeper timbre than old Bernie's, but it was mellifluous and sweet, as though this mystery person was a child who had grown big but somehow remained a child. The kid with a child's voice was called Travis, and the other childlike person was called Cornell, which meant there were *three* people in the house with the two dogs.

"Well, this sucks," Bobby said.

He was so agitated by this complication that he couldn't sit still at the computer. He got up and went into the bathroom and used the Sonicare to brush his teeth.

Bobby Deacon brushed his teeth on average twelve times a day. If he had used a regular toothbrush, he probably would have brushed his gums away and would have seen a periodontist for transplants years ago. He approached dental hygiene with great seriousness, for his smile was his best feature. Women had never complimented him on his good looks or his hair or his lean body, but many had told him that he had a nice smile. His teeth were as white as the whitest quartz, aligned in perfect rows.

He took considerable pride in his teeth. In addition to all the usual uses for them, Bobby's choppers were both an extension of his highly erotic persona and an instrument of intimidation. In the heat of a sexual encounter, he sometimes liked to bite the woman he was with, not always, just now and then. And on those occasions when his partner proved resistant, one bite—and the threat of more—could usually subdue her. Some people were more freaked out by being bitten than they were by the threat of a knife or a gun; Bobby found this amusing.

He returned to the motel room desk and continued to listen to the three-way conversation, and no more than a minute passed before he discovered that the little kid, Travis, was the son of Jane Hawk. Stunned, he replayed the revelatory passage three times, four, five.

Then he paused the audio.

He stood up, wildly energized.

He went to the mirrored closet door and stared admiringly at himself in his black silk pajamas with tiny red skulls in rows as even as his teeth.

He said, "Jackpot."

28

In Arizona, the sky was as dry as the land below, salted with stars, the moon like a bitten Communion wafer.

They arrived in Casa Grande at ten minutes past midnight. Jane used her Leslie Anderson ID to book two units at a three-star motor inn and paid cash.

After they quietly unloaded the Explorer and stowed everything in their rooms, she hugged him. "Goodnight, Vikram. Sleep well."

"You, too."

"No elephants."

"No elephants," he agreed.

She retreated to her room and into a weariness as deep as any she'd known. This had been a long and eventful day, but it was also emotionally exhausting because of the anticipation of triumph that Vikram had brought with him. The flame of hope that always burned within Jane was low but steady, and it could not be extinguished. However, the hope inspired by Vikram's plan was immediate and bright and exacting. Faith in the eternal demanded no effort, took no toll; but any plan of human conception that inspired hope also required a constant expenditure of energy to sustain it, especially when it was a hope for success against great odds.

She removed the shaggy-cut ash-blond wig, took out the contact lenses that made her blue eyes gray, peeled off the spirit-gummed mole on her upper lip, and traded Leslie Anderson for Jane Hawk. After a shower as hot as she could tolerate, she put on a T-shirt and underpants, went to bed, tucked her Heckler & Koch Compact .45 under the pillow next to hers, and turned off the lights. Recently she had often needed a vodka-and-Coke or two in order to sleep, but on this night sleep came without inducement.

So did the dream. The last few nights, since certain horrific events in Borrego Springs, sleep had taken her on a tour of places from her past and ultimately to a portent of her future.

She dreamed of the bedroom in the house of her childhood, each detail as it had been, except that she wasn't a child in this visit, but an adult, not of the same scale as the furniture. Of all the things that might have fascinated her, she was drawn to a window, beyond which waited a night of the strangest character. No slightest fragment of a moon, no stars, no uplight from the suburb in which the house stood. The darkness had distilled into perfect blackness. However, what lay before her wasn't merely the absence of light. The gloom lacked another essential quality that she could not at once name. In the fluid manner of dreams, the bedroom became her dorm room at university, then morphed into her dorm room at the academy at Quantico, then became her and Nick's bedroom in the house they had owned in Alexandria, before his death. In each place she moved inexorably toward a window, in the grip of a chilling but unspecific presentiment. She drew open a bamboo curtain in one instance, raised a pleated shade in another, pressed aside a drapery in Virginia. Window by window, she became more sensitive to the cold truth of the absolute blackness beyond the glass. The blinding dark wasn't empty. Unseen structures and a maze of streets lay unmapped within it, and teeming multitudes surged through whatever metropolis, engaged in business unknowable. When next she found herself in a familiar hotel suite, the one in which she and Nick had honeymooned in the heart of Manhattan, she raised the lower sash of the operative window, for it was a glorious building erected before the age of glass monoliths. Out of the lightless void wafted the scent of the city, a mélange of odors both appealing and vaguely offensive. Sounds came to her as well, though not the rumble of traffic, nor the ceaseless sirens that had once been a motif of the city's lullaby, nor spirited voices in conversation, nor a single cry of argument, nor laughter. There were instead the footfalls and rhythmic breathing of legions, the susurration of multitudes in motion, engaged in evidently urgent but unimaginable tasks, surging through the blinding dark. As she listened and strained to see some lesser darkness in this eclipse of all radiance, her disquiet swelled into fear, and her heart raced. The room changed once more, though it was the same hotel and the same window in some future time when the interior design had been re-done. The barren walls were without art, and the furniture without character, everything sleek, functional, lacking even the slightest adornment; and if this might be an age when minimalism was in style, it was also an age when cleanliness was not considered impor-tant, for the walls were stained, the floors soiled. As she leaned into the open window, she at last understood what essential quality, in addition to light, was missing from this strange city, and her fear be-came terror. Frenetic life existed in this darkness, people in the grip of quiet desperation, harried on some mission, in the throes of fulfilling some bleak agenda—but there was no freedom in the busy throng, no freedom and hence no worthwhile purpose to this endless bustling. The darkness was not an absence of light, but an absence of meaning, for meaning arose only from the exercise of free will. The life in this darkness lacked all merit and significance. This utter lightlessness was of the mind and soul, for it was the world of the Singularity, the long-anticipated merging of humanity and artificial intelligence, brains threaded through with the neural lace of nanotechnology. When she tried to retreat from the window, she found herself in the grip of a dual gravity that wedded her to the earth at the same time that it pulled her toward the window, into the window, outward into a life of enslavement in the hive.

She woke in an icy sweat and sat up in bed and threw back the covers and said, *"Travis."*

PART THREE

Storm Troopers

1

The wind seemed to have seceded into factions and gone to war with itself, cannonading volleys of snow from multiple directions at once, the plain like a battlefield smoky with ceaseless explosions and the fumes of ruination.

Frantic to escape Wainwright Hollister's gunfire, Tom Buckle squeezed the throttle hard, and the snowmobile shot forward so fast that his inexperience with the controls almost resulted in disaster. The land lay in treacherous folds, and the vehicle careened across corrugations of hillocks and furrows. He felt as if he were astride a mechanical bull in a faux rodeo, bouncing on the seat, nearly bucked overboard. Then the machine launched off a crest and went airborne before dropping perhaps ten feet. It didn't roll, landed flat on its skis and tracks, but he might have been sent tumbling if his legs hadn't been clamped tight to the seat. When the handlebars jerked free of his grip, he also lost his hold on the throttle, so he came at once to a stop.

Through the turmoil, he'd unintentionally changed directions more than once. He didn't believe that he was any longer headed south. The only thing he felt sure about was that he hadn't turned 180 degrees; Hollister was still behind him and not directly ahead. Therefore, he proceeded at a more judicious speed for a few minutes until he felt that he had put sufficient distance between himself and his nemesis before coming to a halt.

Although hours old, the storm gathered power even as the wind blustered more erratically. The blizzard no longer merely whistled or groaned, but shrieked as though he had crossed the border from Colorado into some netherworld banshee nation.

In escaping Hollister, Tom hadn't dared the headlamp. Now when he switched it on, he was only marginally less blind in the swirling chaos of a near whiteout than he had been in the dark.

The softly glowing instrument panel was a digital display that offered choices: MAIN, MAP & TRAILS, DIAGNOSTICS. . . . As the wind defeated the windshield, whipping white currents across the touch screen, Tom scrolled down, investigating options, until he came to GPS SETTINGS.

He should have realized that the snowmobile might be equipped with a GPS, but the discovery unnerved him. If it offered guidance, it also pinpointed his location for the ranch's security team, those expressionless dead-eyed rayshaws.

When he tried to engage the GPS by entering INTERSTATE 70 as his destination, the screen responded with INADEQUATE DATA. He tried again with INTERSTATE HIGHWAY 70, but this also was deemed inadequate. As he tried to think of another way to identify a desired end point for this trip, the GPS keyboard disappeared, replaced by the words SERVICE UNAVAILABLE.

The storm suit kept him warm enough, yet he shivered within it. And his breath seemed to plume from him in less volume of vapor than before, as though his body must be cooling, his exhalations carrying less heat than they should have.

The cessation of GPS service might be a consequence of the extreme weather. Or it might mean the Crystal Creek Ranch security force could disable that function at a distance. The latter seemed more likely.

But if they could deny him GPS guidance, they might still be able to track him with the same technology. *Count on it.* They would be on his tail soon—if they weren't already—on snowmobiles and possibly by other transport.

He scrolled up and tapped MAIN. An arc—0 to 9—spanned the upper portion of the screen, labeled RPM x 1000. Under that a speedometer window currently registered zero. The batteries were only 32 percent depleted.

The display included a compass. He was currently facing due west, toward the distant Hollister residence. Interstate 70 lay to the south/southeast. If the compass could be trusted, Tom no longer needed to find the river and follow it to the highway.

He eased the snowmobile forward into the cold churning murk, wishing he could make better time, reminding himself that a blind man dared not run. The killers would be coming somewhat faster in his wake; others would probably attempt to get ahead of him and intercept him before he could reach the interstate and the promise of help that it represented.

His memory of the rayshaws—flat voices, expressionless faces, dead eyes—adrenalized him, and his heart rate spiked. Scrubbed of all memories of their past, their original personalities erased, pro-grammed to be obedient killing machines with no regard for their own lives, they were more chilling than the robots of the Terminator movies. At one time they were creatures of free will, his brethren in the drama of humanity, and the transformation forced upon them lowered them beneath the beasts of fields and forests; their souls had not been bargained away in deals with the devil, but had been robbed from them by other men, power-mad men who were in rebellion against their own nature and against all the limitations of the natural order. The rayshaws didn't eat human flesh, and they didn't shamble through their days in various states of decay, but they were no less the walking dead than were the zombies of countless films and TV programs. If they didn't kill him, they could transform him into one of them, not with a bite, but merely with a few injections, for this new world of radical technology cleaned up the gory horrors of old, made them clean, clinical, and efficient.

Gliding through the darkness, through the storm, through this liv-ing nightmare of ultimate evil, Tom no longer yearned for a career as a director, no longer wanted acclaim or wealth or the recognition of his filmmaking peers. He wanted only a life and a chance to live it well.

2

Wainwright Warwick Hollister under the bridge, huddled in fury, his pride bruised, seething with indignation. This man of a thousand winning smiles isn't able to summon one now. He isn't meant for this humiliation, to have been outfoxed by the son of a mere tailor and a seamstress, by a Honda-driving nobody who wears off-the-rack suits and has directed just two low-budget films with quaint themes and insipid values. Buckle has earned worse than the death that is the reward for being named to the Hamlet list. His fate is now this: to be injected with the nanoweb control mechanism and transformed into an adjusted person, and then to have his testicles cut off without benefit of anesthesia, rendering him twice a eunuch. Hollister will do the surgery himself.

As one who has suffered since childhood to achieve his current position in life, Hollister believes he has earned the authority to teach others the truth that nothing worthwhile is achieved without pain.

When he was but ten years old, his mother schemed to divorce Hollister's father, Orenthal, and take her son with her. Wanting an heir molded in his image, not in hers, the old man hired a battalion of attorneys and private detectives to defend his parental rights. Nevertheless, there was an intolerable risk that Mother might in the end prevail. Intolerable because, though she would be a rich woman post-divorce, she would have but a tiny fraction of the great wealth of Orenthal, who was even then a billionaire.

Young Wainwright stole a pack of cigarettes from his mother's supply and a butane lighter from his father's study. Over several days in his room, biting on a rubber ball to stifle his cries, he embellished his fair arms with cigarette burns, treated them with Bactine and Neosporin to prevent infection, and wore long-sleeve shirts to hide the damage. When his arms were proof of horrific abuse, he applied lit cigarettes to his tender prepubescent groin.

Father's estate at that time, in Connecticut, had a staff of twenty-eight. The head housekeeper, Mrs. Ripley, a widow, was a bit of a sadist, although Wainwright didn't yet know that word. What he *did* know was that Mrs. Ripley took too much pleasure in boiling live lobsters for dinner, grinning fiercely into the enormous pot as the creatures convulsed, that she was hell on the occasional feral cat that wandered onto the property, that she tormented the younger girls on the household staff until at times she made them cry, and that when she pinched him with apparent affection, she pinched too hard and long, her eyes spooky-witchy as she did so.

Even at ten, Wainwright Hollister had a talent for reading the truth of people, and he approached Mrs. Ripley with little fear that she would decline to conspire with him to ruin his mother or that she would reveal his treachery to anyone. What he wanted of her was to whip his back with a leather belt hard enough to scar, treat the wounds to prevent infection, and acquire for him the painkillers that would allow him to endure such an ordeal. In return, after she confirmed his testimony against his mother, he would champion her to his father, refer to her as his guardian angel, and pressure the old man to reward her generously. Furthermore, he promised to pay her a hundred thousand dollars from the first—and smallest—installment of his inheritance, which he would receive when he turned eighteen.

Whether or not Mrs. Ripley believed he could be trusted to pay off eight years hence, the numerous burns on his arms and groin were proof of his fortitude and commitment. He secured her agreement to the plot. Even back then, he suspected that the reward to be paid by his father and the hundred grand nearly a decade later were of less importance to her than the opportunity to whip him with a leather belt and destroy his mother's reputation, if not her life.

The estate manager, the head housekeeper, and the butler—with his wife, who served as Mother's personal assistant—lived in three private cottages, each surrounded by a charming garden at the back of the estate. In Mrs. Ripley's private quarters, she whipped young Wainwright with somewhat more fervor than he anticipated, but she proved to be a diligent nurse, especially when treating wounds required the application of a stinging salve.

When those wounds scabbed and when the last of the scabs crumbled away, when the cigarette burns had aged enough to suggest not just recent violence but a history of abuse, the complex divorce proceedings had reached a courtroom. Mother's accusations of serial adultery were countered by Father's trumped-up but quite cunningly documented charges of her rapacious embezzlement of funds from family accounts.

At that time, Mrs. Ripley approached Orenthal to say that young Wainwright had long adored her and called her Auntie Edna, that they had a special relationship, she and this dear child, that he came to her with all his hopes and dreams and fears. This was the first that Father had heard of such adoration, but he listened with interest as Mrs. Ripley told him of the boy's terror of being remanded to the custody of his mother. She said he'd visited her at her cottage in the predawn hours and revealed a dreadful secret that he had kept from her, from everyone: Since learning of Orenthal's infidelities two years earlier, Mother had punished the child for the father's sins and had so intimidated him that he dared tell no one until now.

After Father's physician examined Wainwright and photographed his scars, the boy was interviewed by the judge in chambers, with no one else present except his father's and mother's chief attorneys. Wainwright had rehearsed his testimony for days, spent hours in his room, delivering his lines with varying degrees of intensity and inflection. In front of the judge, he didn't overplay his role. He spoke quietly of fearing his mother but also, movingly, of loving her, of wondering why she didn't love him. He was not angry, only bereft and confused and beaten-down by his experience. When he wept, he did so quietly, sitting with head bowed and shoulders slumped, hands in his pants pockets. With a concealed pin, he penetrated the lining of a pocket and cruelly pierced his thigh. This minor wound produced too little blood to show against his black slacks, but it was sufficiently painful to ensure tears—not just his own but those of the woman who was his mother's attorney.

It was not true that he loved his mother, and it wasn't true that he feared her. He feared only living with her in reduced circumstances, of going from a fifty-two-thousand-square-foot mansion on a twenty-acre estate to a house perhaps a third that size on a measly acre. Father would remain a billionaire, and Mother might be worth only fifty million, which didn't augur well for the boy's future if his father, embittered about losing custody, reduced Wainwright's ultimate inheritance. Even though he was only ten, the boy had an adult's understanding of finances and a sybarite's appreciation for the pleasures and uses of great wealth.

For surrendering custody without a fight, Mother accepted a more generous settlement than she had any right to expect. Father doubled Mrs. Ripley's salary, and Wainwright called her Auntie Edna for the rest of her life. He paid her the promised hundred thousand dollars from the first installment of his inheritance, and at the age of sixty-one she died in her sleep in her private cottage, surrounded by her charming garden. Her death was from natural causes, not at Wainwright's hand. At her funeral, he wept without resorting to a pin in his pocket, because over the years he'd learned to crank up any emotion as he might turn on a faucet.

Now, under the bridge, the indignation and rage that have held him in their grip begin to relent a little only because disquiet claims a place in his mind and heart. The rayshaws seem to be taking longer than they should to rescue him. He cautions himself not to be impatient. The weather is terrible. Security can't reach him as quickly as on a sunny day. The battery-powered GPS sewn into his storm suit is insurance against disaster. His rescue is inevitable.

The space under the bridge offers protection from the skirling wind, but it is as dark as the far side of the moon. He holds his hand inches from his face but isn't able to see it.

Never before has any degree of darkness intimidated Hollister. He does not suffer from nyctophobia. He is not weak like his father. A man who, at the age of ten, burned his penis with a cigarette, if only once, is not a man who fears anything.

The quiver of disquiet that troubles him might better be called misgiving, a sense that he has made a mistake, miscalculated. Losing the snowmobile to Buckle is his first mistake in longer than he can recall.

It's unlikely that he will make another anytime soon. He is not a man who commits errors with regularity.

Indeed, what he feels now is not either disquiet or misgiving, but a vague suspicion, of what he can't at first explain. Slowly he comes to realize intuition is telling him that he is not alone under the bridge, that he shares the darkness with . . . With what?

After decades of absence, true wolves have returned to this part of the plains. However, even in weather as foul as this, it isn't likely that a wolf would take shelter under a structure ripe with the scent of the men who built and frequently use it, rather than in a wildland den.

Nevertheless, a worm of foreboding squirms in his mind, and he isn't able to cast it out. To allay his concern, he needs only to scan the space with his Tac Light—which is when he realizes that he has lost it.

3

With two lines of cocaine and two shots of Jack Daniel's working in his bloodstream, Bobby Deacon was as balanced as the scales of justice and ready to roll. He would not be spending the night in his motel room, after all. He had already changed out of his black-and-red silk pajamas into a white T-shirt bearing the words AGENT OF JUSTICE in red block letters under a red skull, pale-green hospital scrubs that concealed the radical T-shirt, and white rubber-soled shoes.

After stopping at an all-night supermarket, he drove his Mercedes Sprinter to the neighborhood in which the Cantors lived. He parked about half a block away from the place, on the same side of the street as their house instead of directly across from it.

His pale-green shirt had three-quarter sleeves and hung long to cover the 9 mm Sig Sauer P-226 in the belt holster on his right hip.

In the back of the Sprinter, he withdrew a Rambo III knife from a storage drawer. Makassar-ebony handle. Twelve-inch-long two-and-a-quarter-inch-wide blade of 440c stainless steel. Seventeen and a quarter inches long overall. Two pounds five ounces. Keenly pointed to pierce, stropped to slice, as pretty a death-dealer as ever was made. He inserted it in a custom leather sheath and attached it to his belt, at his left hip. The hospital scrubs hid this weapon, too.

Carrying a large white-canvas tote bag containing everything else he needed, Bobby got out of the Sprinter and locked it. Your average TV and movie burglar usually dressed head to foot in black, supposedly to blend with the night and slink like a cat through the shadows. Any guy wearing black and slinking through a high-end neighborhood of Scottsdale would be a cop magnet and would end up facedown on the ground, hands cuffed behind his back. A guy in white wanted to be seen, and people who wanted to be seen were considered as innocent as a white Mercedes van. Bobby looked like he was an intern or an orderly coming home from the swing shift, a dedicated and exhausted caregiver.

All but one of the houses on the block were dark, the occupants either parasitic retirees dreaming of yet another round of golf in the morning or greedy overachievers who would be up before dawn and grubbing for the almighty dollar; there was little chance that anyone would be at a window and find Bobby suspicious. Anyway, he needed less than a minute to reach the Cantor driveway, and during that time, no traffic passed in the street.

At this hour, timers had turned off the landscape lights. Palm trees and olive trees graced the property, casting moonshadows, but with full confidence in his right to be here as an agent of justice, Bobby moved boldly to the back of the house.

On the flagstone patio, by the kitchen door, he put down the tote. From it he withdrew an automatic lock-picking device, called a police lock-release gun, that he had purchased on the Dark Web, and he set it aside. In respect of the two dogs, he took a tranquilizer-dart pistol from the bag and put it beside the lock-release gun.

ATN PVS7–3 night-vision goggles, MIL-SPEC Generation 4 gear used by all branches of the military, would make it possible for him to ghost through the house without turning on lights. He strapped on the goggles, but with the lenses tipped up on his forehead for the moment.

The last item he extracted from the tote was an illegal radio-wave jammer that had been manufactured in Uzbekistan. He had purchased it from a couple in Reseda, California, who supplied a wide variety of useful gear and weapons obtained through their contacts in eastern Europe and Russia, as well as superb counterfeit ID and documents that they created themselves.

He had deeply researched the home security package installed by Vigilant Eagle, and had in fact hacked into the company's computer system without being detected. Theirs was a well-engineered but traditional alarm featuring sensors on doors and operable windows. After the alarm was set, if a door or window was opened, the affected sensor notified the home-base computer somewhere in the house, usually in a closet, and a call went out on a dedicated phone loop, alerting the alarm company's central station, which in turn notified the police.

The greatest weakness in the system was that the sensors communicated via radio waves. Having learned the frequency on which Vigilant Eagle operated, Bobby was able to jam it and prevent the sensor from alerting the home base. Recognizing this flaw, a lot of alarm companies had added anti-jamming software to their systems, but thus far most of it was garbage that didn't defeat the jamming, that only lit a ZONE FAULT indicator that no one would notice, without an accompanying audio alert.

He slipped the thin pick of the lock-release gun into the keyway on the back door and pulled the trigger four times until all the pin tumblers lodged at the shear line. He withdrew the pick and put the device aside.

Bobby pulled down the night-vision goggles and seated them over his eyes. The gear rendered the world in greens because the human eye was most sensitive to those wavelengths of light nearest 550 nanometers, the green portion on the spectrum. This allowed for a dimmer display that didn't quickly deplete the battery.

If the security system included motion detectors, Bobby had no fear of them. They would not have been engaged with two dogs roaming the house.

From the tote, he removed the deli sausages he had bought at the all-night supermarket and stripped away the packaging.

When he opened the door, no alarm sounded.

He tossed the eight sausages into the kitchen and crossed the threshold with the tranquilizer pistol in his right hand.

Most German shepherds were by nature diligent protectors of the family. They tended not to sleep continuously through the night, but periodically patrolled the perimeter of the house before returning to bed. In Bobby's experience, upon the discovery of an intruder, they rarely barked or attacked at once, but growled low in their throats as they took a moment to assess the situation.

The gift of sausages wouldn't convince a trained attack dog of Bobby's benign intentions, but ordinary house pets were usually at least confused by this ploy long enough for him to pop them with the sleepy-time pistol.

As he eased the door shut behind him, two growling dog shapes with radiant-green eyes padded into the kitchen. The scent of the sausages elicited a canine double take that would have been amusing if they hadn't had such wicked teeth.

The meat distracted them just long enough for Bobby to squeeze off two point-blank shots. The pistol employed compressed air and made the thinnest whisper of sound. The potency of the tranquilizer was such that the dogs did not have the time or the clarity of mind to address this affront with either a howl or a feeble assault. They mewled and staggered and slumped onto their hindquarters. They slid flat to the floor and whimpered and sighed and settled into sleep.

Bobby stood listening to the house. Quiet.

The alarm was still engaged, but no call had gone out to the central station.

Having successfully entered the house, with the pistol on one hip and the massive Rambo III knife on the other, with the two big dogs prostrate before him, Bobby Deacon experienced a thrill of power, of extreme potency, and is ready to be all over a woman, as only he can be all over one. As far as he knows, there is no woman here at the moment; therefore, that desire will go unfulfilled for a while. However, there are people to kill and a boy who must be worth millions to the right buyer—a lot of fun to be had in the interim—so sexual gratification delayed will only be sweeter when he can have it.

4

By twenty minutes past midnight Pacific time, Saturday, Charles Douglas Weatherwax is back in Beverly Hills, in his suite in the Peninsula Hotel, this time in the company of Mustafa al-Yamani.

Their cell leader assures them it is indeed Vikram Rangnekar who has for hours been inside the computer system of the Bureau of Alcohol, Tobacco, and Firearms, via a back door of his own design. He has spoofed his way there through a Canadian exchange, a Mexican exchange, a Grand Cayman exchange, and an intricate series of U.S. exchanges that has made tracking him to source difficult. However, the best hacker chasers in the National Security Agency are hot on his trail, and soon they will locate him.

Because there is every reason to believe that Rangnekar will be found somewhere in Southern California, Charlie and Mustafa are told to be ready to move out at a moment's notice. To pass the time, they sit at a game table in the living room of Charlie's suite, drinking black coffee and playing 500 rummy for ten dollars a point.

Charlie places an assortment of sixteen vitamin pills beside his coffee and occasionally washes down one of them. By the time he has taken all the pills, Mustafa owes him $3,345.

Laying the two, three, and four of spades on the table, Mustafa says, "In East Egg village during the summer, where I will stay in a hotel until I have my own estate, there will be much sunshine. One will need sunglasses. Which will be the most appropriate frames—those by Giorgio Armani or Gucci?"

"For Long Island, I once would have said Prada, but no more. Tom Ford."

"Tom Ford frames? Not perhaps Garrett Leight?"

"Tom Ford," Charlie insists as he draws a card from the stack.

"Maybe Dior Homme?"

"Perhaps in a few years. Now, Tom Ford."

"I've worried a lot lately about swim trunks," says Mustafa.

"For East Egg."

"That is correct. For the beach and pool parties."

"There won't be pool parties of the kind you mean. Déclassé."

"But there will be the beach."

"You'll want Missoni swim trunks."

"I thought perhaps Neil Barrett."

"Not the worst choice, but not the same statement as you'll make wearing Missoni."

When Charlie places four aces on the table, Mustafa expresses his consternation by saying, "Your mother kisses little girls on their pee-pee."

"No doubt true. All those years she was a school principal, then superintendent, she had many opportunities to do as you say."

Drawing a card from the stack, Mustafa says, "If someone were to insult my mother, I would slit his throat."

"They wouldn't approve of that in East Egg village."

"Charles, may I ask, what is your problem with your parents?"

"By their actions they taught me to despise phonies, which they are. Every random act of kindness they committed was meant to shine their apple so that no one would suspect they were siphoning federal grants into their own pockets. They made me into a forty-year-old Holden Caulfield."

"That is a reference to the lead character in *The Catcher in the Rye*, is it not?"

"Yes."

Mustafa adds the five of spades to the two, three, and four that he previously laid down.

Charlie draws a card, a joker. Everything he holds will play, and he goes out.

Caught with thirty points in his hand, Mustafa says, "Your father has sex with diseased goats."

Charlie's smartphone rings. The cell leader is calling. The NSA has tracked to source the computer with which Vikram Rangnekar is buccaneering through the most top-secret data at the ATF.

5

The Cantor residence was like some weird haunted house in an amusement park, rendered in shades of Day-Glo green, Bobby Deacon the lethal spirit that prowled its rooms.

In the laundry off the kitchen, he found the door between the house and garage. He dared to open it because the radio-wave jammer remained operative. Somewhere on a zone display within the system, another red light appeared, a silent indicator.

Quietly he dragged one of the German shepherds into the garage and then the other, being careful not to knock their heads against anything. A large water bowl for the animals stood in a corner of the kitchen, elevated in a wire rack for easier access. He carried it into the garage and put it near the sleeping duo. He also placed near them the sausages they hadn't time to eat. He left a light on for them. He didn't find dogs as repellent as he found most people.

After closing the interior door to the garage, he returned to the kitchen and stood listening. The two Sub-Zero refrigerators made no noise whatsoever. On the ovens, the digital clocks changed their blazing numbers without a tick. A clatter startled him and made him reach for the knife in its sheath before he realized the noise came from the icemaker as it spat fresh cubes into its storage bin.

With the enormous knife in his right hand, he explored the spacious ground floor, room by room. When magnified eighty thousand times and processed by image-enhancement technology, even the faint inflow of light from distant streetlamps and ambient infrared were enough to ensure that he wouldn't knock anything over.

For a task like this, he preferred the knife because his Sig Sauer 9 mm, even with its sound suppressor, was not perfectly silent.

His whippet form served him well as he swiftly climbed the stairs. Not one tread creaked underfoot.

On the upper floor, a door stood open. Beyond, the master suite. The bed neatly made. No one there.

Farther along the hallway, he eased open a door and entered a room and saw the boy fast asleep.

He went to the double bed and stood looking down at the kid, who was sleeping on his belly, snoring softly. Bobby put the knife on a nearby chair and drew the tranquilizer pistol from under the waistband of his pants.

He needed to move the boy without waking him. Natural sleep was not deep enough to allow such a maneuver. Travis weighed probably fifty pounds less than one of the dogs, so Bobby hoped that the dose of sedative in the hypodermic dart wasn't large enough to kill him. Jane Hawk's brat might be worth millions alive, but he wasn't worth beans if dead.

He squeezed the trigger.

The kid let out a thin cry of surprise or pain. He raised his head from the pillow and seemed to blink in bewilderment and said, "Wha—?" Then he collapsed and began to snore again.

The moment was like something in one of those fairy tales that Bobby found so putrid when he was a kid: the beautiful young prince, heir to the throne, dreaming peaceably in the witchy light; the intruder come to steal the brat for the king of the trolls in return for having a curse lifted from himself. Bobby always imagined his own versions of such stupid stories: like, it's a beautiful little sleeping princess, not a prince, and the intruder rapes her, kills her, and then finds the queen in her bedchamber, rapes and kills her as well, then beheads and guts the king of the trolls for daring to put a curse on him in the first place.

Now he jammed the tranquilizer pistol under his waistband. He retrieved the knife from the chair and returned it to its sheath.

He pulled the covers back from the boy and lifted him off the bed and carried him to the open door.

Quiet pooled in the house.

As silent as any sneak thief in a fairy tale, Bobby carried the boy downstairs.

6

Under the bridge, Hollister remains convinced that he is not alone. Having lost his Tac Light, he has only logical deduction and imagination with which to explore the palpable darkness and identify what might be sharing it with him.

Logic doesn't take him very far. He has already ruled out the possibility of a wolf. The only other man abroad in this gruesome weather is Buckle, and Buckle is off on the snowmobile.

Hollister hasn't much exercised his imagination over the years. The novels that enchanted his father seem to be a waste of time to him. He finds movies frivolous, theater tedious. Most music strains to inspire with idiot chords and jejune melodies. The only art he likes is that of painters who furiously assault the viewer with the hard truths of life—Pollock, Rauschenberg, Joan Miró, the marvelous Marcel Duchamp, Edvard Munch—who celebrate the truth of nihilism and who know that there is only one sensible response to the void over which life is lived: power, power, brute power, exercised in one's self-interest, with no limits and no mercy.

Because he never indulges in fantasy, he can't be imagining another presence looming near. Impossible. He is not a child given to seeing bogeymen under the bed. This awareness of a threat arises from his singular survival instinct, which he believes to be equal to that of any predatory beast on the earth and far superior to that of other men. The threat is real. Imminent. Ironically, however, because his powers of imagination have atrophied, he isn't able to conceive of what menace might be nearby in this blinding dark.

He sits with his back pressed to the south pier of the bridge, his head mere inches below the plank flooring, his pistol in both hands, peering toward the river that can't be seen, listening for the sounds of a stalker who can't be heard above the wind.

Something has gone wrong with the security team. They should be here by now. They aren't coming on a snowmobile; that would take too long in a storm of this intensity. They're coming in two Sno-Cats, big four-passenger machines on steel treads. No amount of snow or even steep slopes of ice can defeat a Tucker Terra Sno-Cat. One Sno-Cat should be fast on Tom Buckle's trail, and the other should be here now, brightly lighted, with three rayshaws to help him into the warm cabin.

The Sno-Cat is not here.

He is unable to imagine what happened. Rayshaws are as reliable as Sno-Cats. Rayshaws do what they're programmed to do, endure pain that would disable an ordinary man, overcome any obstacle, because they are meat machines, without fear, without doubt, without concern for their lives.

The strangest aroma penetrates the fabric of his ski mask: a lemony fragrance, but not exactly with the zest of lemon . . . more like verbena. It is an impossible scent in this place, at this time. Yet it lingers for five seconds, ten, before fading, to be replaced by the smell of the damp wool of the ski mask and Hollister's fish-scented halitosis.

The song of the storm has changed to a threnody, a lamentation, sorrowing through the night as if Nature is grieving over some loss. And then a whisper so soft, so intimate, comes to Hollister through the warp and weft of the weaving wind: *"Master . . . master . . ."*

The voice is so faint that it can't be real, not when he's wearing the tightly secured hood that muffles even the storm. He will not credit it. He tunes it out, and in fact it goes away.

But then it returns. *"Master . . . master . . . master . . ."*

When he unfastens his hood and pulls it off his head, the mourning wind grows louder, but it does not drown out the whisper. Faint as the voice is, he nevertheless recognizes it, and again he smells a trace of the verbena fragrance that she often wore.

He had instructed Mai-Mai to call him "Master" only when she came to his bedroom to do whatever might please him. Unfailing deference and total submission during sex always thrilled Hollister.

The whisper and the verbena can't be real. She is dead.

But it's also true that this can't be his imagination running amok. He does not allow himself the weakness of fantasy, and such visitations as this are the worst kind of imagination—superstition.

Therefore, he must be hallucinating. Good. He is back in the realm of logic.

There are medical conditions of which hallucinations might be a symptom, including Parkinson's disease, but Hollister is in perfect health. He is an exemplary physical specimen. Olympian, really. Hallucinations might also be related to the adverse effects of a medication, but he's on no medications. They can also be a result of substance abuse, but he uses no drugs. He needs no drugs. Power is his only drug. Logic leads to one inescapable conclusion: Someone has slipped a hallucinogenic substance into something that he has eaten or drunk.

Everyone on the Crystal Creek Ranch staff is either an adjusted person or a totally brain-scrubbed rayshaw. None is capable of such treachery against the supreme master of the Arcadian revolution.

Logic leaves him nowhere to go but to the realization that the deceitful film director, Thomas Buckle, is the sole suspect. Buckle began his counterrevolution not when he captured the snowmobile, but much earlier, at some point before or during dinner, when by some cunning trick he must have contaminated Hollister's food or drink.

This is no shock to him. For most of his life, he's been aware that no one can be trusted. When one is only ten years old and one's mother selfishly takes steps to end her marriage in spite of the potential to reduce your ultimate inheritance from more than a billion to perhaps a few million, when she would move you from a sprawling first-class estate with a staff of twenty-eight to a mere McMansion with at most two maids and a semi-butler—*your own mother*—then you must regard humanity not as a clan of which you are a member, but as a nest squirming with a unique species of viper that has no capacity for loyalty even to its own kind. Thomas Buckle has proven to be a particularly vicious snake, coming from California with the belief that Hollister is going to fund his pathetic films with millions of dollars—and yet he doses his benefactor with a hallucinogenic substance.

Hollister's anger at this treachery and at the helplessness that has been imposed upon him grows until it is as intense as any rage he has ever known. It is worse than what he felt toward his mother when she raised the issue of divorce. Indeed, it is as bad as the even greater fury he had felt, a year prior to the prospect of divorce, when she had given birth to Hollister's brother, Diederick Deodatus Hollister.

Even before Mother had schemed to reduce her first son's inheritance by leaving his father, she'd plotted to *halve* his future prospects by bringing his sibling into the world. That first threat to his wealth was more easily dealt with than the second: a private moment with the two-month-old baby at three o'clock in the morning, the gentle application of a pillow to his face. A while later, the night nanny discovered Diederick lifeless, a tragic case of sudden infant death syndrome, which takes the lives of fewer than two infants per thousand.

As furious as Hollister was the night he entered that nursery, he is even more furious now. Like Diederick, Tom Buckle has earned his death.

Again he experiences the olfactory hallucination of the verbena fragrance followed by Mai-Mai's voice, as though her lips are mere inches from his right ear. *"Master . . . master . . . master . . ."*

Where is the damn Sno-Cat?

7

The four-billion-year-old moon in a slow, silent descent. The million-year-old desert—once a sea, once a swamp—where now coyotes prowl in sacred silence over Indian graves older than history, where snakes lie with lidless eyes in anticipation of the morning sun. The town of Casa Grande, less than 150 years old, seeming abandoned in the light of its streetlamps . . .

After the dream of the night window, Jane Hawk had been unable to get back to sleep. She dressed and moved a straight-backed chair to the window. She opened the draperies partway and sat in the rented dark, watching the hotel parking lot in expectation of one kind of trouble or another.

As she had awakened from the nightmare, she'd spoken her child's name. She couldn't shake the feeling that Travis was in jeopardy. She had no good reason to believe such a thing, and she cautioned herself not to act precipitously.

Travis was tucked away in Scottsdale, safe in the Cantor house, under the protection of Bernie Riggowitz, who was as responsible as any man she knew, assisted by sweet Cornell Jasperson, a singular package of personality disorders who would no doubt nevertheless die for the boy, watched over as well by two dogs that adored him. Jane was unable to think of any way the Arcadians could have located him.

Often the voice of intuition was clear, its warning specific. At other times, however, it spoke in a murmur, more an uneasiness than a call to action. In such cases, she was well advised to ponder her situation carefully before risking a wrong step, as might a woman who found herself on a ledge, forty stories above the street, with no idea how she got there.

Just because she had spoken Travis's name as she woke from the dream didn't mean the anxiety gripping her arose from a presentiment that the boy was in danger. It might instead mean that she feared never seeing him again because, intuitively, she was aware that somehow *she* was in imminent peril.

At 3:20 mountain time, she opened the connecting door between units and went into Vikram's room. He slept in the glow of a bedside lamp with a hand towel draped over the shade to soften the light.

When she sat on the edge of the bed, he didn't stir. Although thirty, he might have been a boy sleeping as deeply as only boys sleep before they learn the unsettling truths of the world. She spoke his name twice and shook him gently by the shoulder.

Upon waking, he appeared briefly bewildered. He spoke several words in Hindi, then smiled at her.

She said, "Earlier you said the motor home is being delivered at ten o'clock?"

"Yeah." He yawned. "They're bringing it straight from Enrique's shop in Nogales, about a two-hour drive."

"Where are we meeting them? Not here."

"No. In the parking lot at the Holiday Inn."

"He doesn't know we're staying here?"

"No. He doesn't think we're getting to Casa Grande until morning, just before the meet."

"Was the Holiday Inn your idea or Enrique's?"

"His. He said you'd want it to be somewhere public."

"He said that, did he?"

"Don't you want it someplace public?"

"How big is this Holiday Inn?"

"I scoped it out when I passed through here on the way back from Nogales last week. It's maybe a hundred and eighty units. Semi-humongous, with a large parking lot."

She thought about that and then said, "Get up, get dressed, we're out of here."

"Well, but I can't do that just now."

"Why not?"

"I'm terribly swollen."

"Swollen? From what? You don't look swollen."

"But I am," he said sheepishly. "I am immensely swollen. You must leave the room before I throw aside the sheets."

"Oh. Yeah. I understand." Jane rose from the edge of the bed, moved toward the connecting door, and glanced back at him. "You're quite the gentleman, Vikram."

He smiled shyly and spoke in Hindi again.

"That sounds like what you said when you first woke up."

"It is. *'Yeh shaam mastani madhosh kiye jaye.'*"

"What does it mean?"

" 'This most beautiful night intoxicates me.' It is a line from a song."

She smiled, then grimaced. "This isn't an adventure, Vikram."

"It feels like an adventure."

"It's a war. Mistake a war for an adventure, you won't live long."

"If it makes you more comfortable, I'll do my best to stop thinking of it as an adventure."

"Good. Ten minutes. We'll load the Explorer but leave do-not-disturb signs on the room doors. We'll walk over to the Holiday Inn, get a room there, have breakfast in their restaurant. It's not even two blocks."

8

The rain passes, but the night glistens and drips. The lights of the L.A. metroplex glimmer across valleys and foothills as if to infinity.

Charlie Weatherwax and Mustafa al-Yamani are en route to a warehouse in an industrial area near Ontario, California, where they—and two agents coming from San Bernardino—will take down the hacker whom Mustafa now calls the "bad boy from Mumbai."

According to the National Security Agency, the back door into the computer system of the Bureau of Alcohol, Tobacco, and Firearms was created by Vikram Rangnekar, formerly of the FBI, and was only discovered the previous afternoon. For the past several hours, the fox has been raiding that chicken coop, sucking sensitive data out of egg after egg, looking for failed and even illegal operations that, if made public, will embarrass the ATF and result in several of its higher-level bureaucrats winding up in jail.

They have allowed Rangnekar to continue his thievery, so that they might have time to track to source the computer he is using. This has proved to be a monumental task, as he has entered the ATF system by way of the most elaborate spoofing exercise anyone has ever seen, not just ricocheting through a long series of telephone exchanges but also in the process pausing to use back doors that he has previously established in certain telecom companies, setting ticking-clock system failures that shut down those organizations in his wake. He is responsible for telephone-service interruptions in seven smaller U.S. cities—from Buffalo to Nashville to Sacramento—lasting as little as forty minutes and as long as two hours. This is the equivalent of James Bond in his ultracool spy car, foiling his pursuers by spreading clouds of smoke, superslick oil, and a carpet of nails on the highway behind him.

The corrugated metal walls of the large warehouse stand on a concrete foundation. Small windows are set high under the eaves, and pale light rises to them from a source deep in that cavernous space.

A chain-link fence surrounds the property. In contradiction to the light inside, a FOR LEASE sign on the gate indicates the building is between tenants.

Mustafa parks across the street from the target, in front of what might be a factory of some kind that calls itself QUIK QWAK, where thirty or forty vehicles suggest a night shift at work. Here they will await the arrival of the agents from San Bernardino.

Having settled the issue of swimsuits over a game of cards at the hotel, they have en route had a discussion of the proper beach blanket, sun umbrella, and insulated cooler with which to outfit that portion of the exclusive East Egg beach to which one has staked claim, and Mustafa now raises the most difficult issue of sandals.

"If one wants to be seen as from an old-wealth family, one would not wear brightly colored flip-flops among such sophisticated beachgoers. But there are so many designer sandals to choose from. It is bewildering. What do you think of Opening Ceremony?"

Charlie considers before saying, "It's a good sandal, if you don't mind being seen in something that costs just a hundred bucks."

"Valentino Garavani offers exquisite Italian craftsmanship at about three hundred fifty."

Charlie grimaces. "In my opinion, that sandal makes you look like a gigolo. There's a Dan Ward design at about three hundred that's the definition of elegant simplicity—just three double loops of bungee straps to hold your foot to the basic-black sole."

"I am embarrassed to say that I'm unfamiliar with that sandal. Really, Charles, you're an invaluable source of information and advice in these matters."

"Early on, I learned from my parents what's most important in life, and I've kept my head on straight ever since."

The agents from San Bernardino arrive in a black Dodge Charger, a basic vehicle that indicates they are young, relatively new to the revolution, and have not yet earned much in the way of perks. That is good. Hungry for success, they will take instructions dutifully and be as ruthless as the situation requires.

The Dodge parks in front of the Mercedes G550. Charlie and Mustafa confer with the new agents between vehicles.

Verna Amboy is dressed in a black suit and white blouse. She's attractive in spite of a Cleopatra haircut with thick black bangs that squares her face and gives it a robotic quality. Verna's lips are ripe enough to be the sole graphic element in a poster for a porn flick, but Charlie isn't hot for her, because he suspects that, in the bedroom, she deals out pain while refusing to endure any.

In black suit, white shirt, black tie, black porkpie hat, and black-and-white high-tops, Eldon Clocker looks as though he went to an alternate-universe FBI Academy that doubled as a school for blues musicians. But he stands maybe six feet four and has a neck like an oak-tree trunk. When it comes to backup, Charlie favors big. Eldon also proves to be articulate and intense. Regarding backup, Charlie values intelligence almost as much as he does size.

The four of them cross the street. The chain-link gate was once secured with a large padlock. Someone has severed the thick shackle of the lock with a bolt cutter. The gate rolls aside smoothly.

The warehouse has several entrances. The lock has been drilled out of one man-size door.

Vikram Rangnekar has no history of violence. Nevertheless, the four draw their guns.

Charlie orders Verna to be the first to clear the doorway. She'll make the smallest target. "We want him alive," he reminds her, because when he'd first issued that instruction on the other side of the street, she had seemed to frown with disappointment.

9

At four o'clock in the morning, Jane as Leslie Anderson and Vikram as Vikram were seated in a booth, in the quietest corner of the restaurant in the Holiday Inn, among only six or eight people having breakfast at that hour.

Thus far they had received no food, just coffee. After sleeping maybe two hours, Jane needed the brew black and in quantity.

She took a small bottle from her purse, a pill from the bottle, and washed the pill down with coffee.

"What's that?" he asked.

"Acid reducer. If I'm lucky, I can avoid a bleeding ulcer until I'm thirty. Listen, when Enrique's guys get here, it isn't going to be what it looks like. They'll have the motor home, and they'll take the second half of the payment for it, but they won't just go away."

"Well, but that's the deal."

"Enrique de Soto is a vicious snake. When you showed up in Nogales with your relatives, you spooked him, and he wanted to kill all of you. He only does business by the recommendation of people he trusts."

Vikram shrugged. "We've been over that. Your name carried a lot of weight with him."

"I didn't recommend you. The only reason he didn't kill you right then is because you struck him as too naïve to be anything but what you claimed to be. He rolled the dice, did a deal, but not for the money."

"He didn't make a gift of the Southwind, you know. He took the cash, a lot of it."

"And he'll take the rest. But if he has his way, he'll go back to No-gales with the money *and* the motor home."

Pointing to the ceiling with his index finger, Vikram said, "One problem with that scenario. Why would I pay the rest of the money for nothing?"

She sipped her coffee and stared at him over the rim of the cup, confident that, even as innocent as he was about these things, he would eventually answer his own question.

After a silence, he said, "Oh. You mean he'll take the money and tell me to go pound sand."

"Not quite."

The waitress arrived to pour more coffee and report that their orders would be ready in a few minutes.

When Jane and Vikram were alone once more, she pointed to the ceiling with both index fingers and said, "Two things," before folding her hands around the warm cup. "First, he considers you and your relatives a major loose end. A risk worth taking, but a loose end none-theless. Along with your money, he'll take you and torture you till you tell him where to find your brother, uncle, cousins. Then he'll kill all of you."

Vikram looked dubious. "That seems extreme."

"Not to Enrique."

"Maybe you misjudge him."

"And maybe I'm a purple possum."

"You said—'two things.'"

"He's going to take me out along with you. He's overdue for trying it. He doesn't want business as high-profile as mine."

Vikram shook his head. "He likes you."

"He's hot for me. Not the same thing as liking me. I doubt Enrique likes any women for other than one reason."

"He spoke so admiringly of . . . of not just how you look but of what he called your 'take-no-prisoners kick-ass spirit.'"

"Women don't say no to Ricky. Not twice, anyway. I've said no to him several times, with attitude. I hoped I'd never have to go to him again for anything. He's a super-macho thin-skinned sociopath, eager to put me in my place, which he thinks is tied spread-eagle to a bed, naked, under him. He'll use me for weeks, then kill me or figure how to get a big payday by giving me to the Arcadians."

Vikram was adamant. "No, no, no. Impossible. You don't truly believe such a thing can happen. That can't happen."

"Why can't it?"

"Well, because you're . . . you're who you are."

"I'm no superhero, sweetie. If Ricky comes here with enough of his men, and if we don't play this smart all the way, we'll be in that Southwind and on our way to Nogales shortly after ten o'clock."

"But we're meeting in a public place. He knew you'd want it in a public place."

"The moment you said he made an issue of that, I was sure he's going to jack us. He's trying to make me think he knows the rules he has to play by and he's cool with them. Did he also make a point of introducing you to the men who'll make the delivery?"

"This guy named Tio will drive the motor home."

"Short dude, about the size of a jockey," Jane said, "with a welt of scar tissue across his throat."

"Yeah, that's him. And this other guy named Diablo will follow in a Porsche 911 Turbo S, so he can take Tio back to Nogales. That's it. Just the two, and if you think Diablo's some Terminator type, he's hardly any bigger than Tio."

Jane smiled thinly. "A mongoose is a small animal, but in a fight, it'll kill a poisonous snake every time. Anyway, the fact that Ricky told you there would be two and introduced you to the smallest guys on his crew means there'll be more than two, maybe four, most likely five, and the others will be head-buster types."

"But it's a busy parking lot, people coming and going right next to a busy street. A lot of people would see."

"All they need is a distraction."

"What distraction?"

"Maybe something blows up."

" 'Blows up'?"

The waitress arrived with their orders. A cheese omelet for Jane, no potatoes, no toast; a cheeseburger with no bun. For Vikram, two eggs over easy with bacon and home fries.

"What could blow up?" Vikram asked.

"A car, maybe part of the hotel."

"You're serious."

"Or maybe one of Ricky's guys steals a truck, plows it into some cars in the intersection, gets out, shoots a few people, and fades away in the chaos."

Vikram gaped at her as she forked up a mouthful of the omelet. "I understand the tactic of distraction. But shooting people just for that purpose?"

"Ricky's guys aren't exactly human-rights activists."

"But . . . but then, what're we gonna do?"

"The only thing we can do now that it's come to this—be very careful."

He lowered his gaze to his food. "I've lost my appetite."

She said, "When I'm done with this, I'll take your plate. But not the home fries. They'd go straight to my hips."

10

The main room of the warehouse is cold and damp and dark but for one bank of fluorescent fixtures suspended on chains.

A search has confirmed that whoever was here earlier is gone. Although the building has the feel of a haunt, if spirits linger in this place, they do so with utmost discretion.

In the fall of hard white light is a folding table, and on the table stands an operative computer, the power cord trailing away to a distant outlet. On the screen are the words YOU HAVE BEEN VIKRAMIZED.

"I hate this guy," Charlie says.

In a voice silken but not seductive, Verna Amboy declares, "I'd like to spend an hour cutting his nuts off with a dull knife."

Mustafa regards her with interest, as though he might ask what brand of cutlery would be suitable if the act were committed in East Egg village, but he says nothing.

Eldon Clocker merely nods solemnly, as if in agreement with the lovely Verna.

The four words on the screen blink off. A series of letters, numbers, and symbols begins to appear from left to right. A link to a YouTube video. And here it is.

The scene is familiar. Another table, another computer. The attic of the condemned house that belongs to Norman and Dodie Stein. The camera is shooting from above, at an angle that happens to capture both Jesus Mendoza and Charlie, with Mustafa off to one side but also clearly visible.

Jesus has a smartphone in hand as he says, "I can't talk to you the way you are. This is his house. He'll have to talk to you."

"Don't," Charlie says, drawing his pistol.

Mustafa says, "Drop the phone, Mr. Mendoza."

"Get smart, Hey-Seuss. We need to question your employers now."

"They are not criminals. They won't run and hide."

"Drop the damn phone, asshole."

Mendoza puts the phone to his ear as it speed-dials.

Charlie steps forward, and Mendoza backs away, saying, "I'm not armed. This is only a phone. You can see it is only a phone." And then into the phone he says, "Hello, Mr.—"

Whereupon Charlie shoots him in the head.

The image freezes, and words scroll up the screen like a list of credits at the end of a movie:

VICTIM   JESUS MENDOZA

KILLER   CHARLES DOUGLAS WEATHERWAX

ACCOMPLICE   MUSTAFA AL-YAMANI

Alarmed, Charlie turns away from the screen and peers up into the raftered darkness of the warehouse, where perhaps another camera observes them.

"Say nothing," he warns his team. "Nothing."

11

Vikram decided to eat his breakfast, after all, but he'd taken only two bites when his phone rang. It was a disposable, a burner, purchased at a Walmart, and the only people who possessed the number were his brother, uncle, and cousins.

The call was from Cousin Ganesh, who had tagged Jane in the library the previous morning, and who was now using another burner to report on developments. Taught how to employ all of Vikram's wicked little babies, Ganesh was the one who had spoofed his way through a back door at the Bureau of Alcohol, Tobacco, and Firearms, had complicated the search for him by temporarily crashing telecom systems in his wake, and had thereby misdirected those who were searching so diligently for his cousin Vikram.

"I have kept from you a terrible, terrible thing," Ganesh revealed, "until I could follow it with good news. These bastards went to the Stein house and found the setup in the attic, but a man was there, Jesus Mendoza, providing security for the property at night."

Vikram shook his head. "No, no. It's condemned. No one lives in the place. There aren't any contents to steal."

"He was protecting it from vandals. He took the agents on a tour, and in the attic, when Mendoza tried to call the owner of the house, one of these twisted freaks shot him dead."

Vikram went weak with shock and guilt, the fork slipping out of his fingers and clattering against his plate. "No one was supposed to be there. I didn't know."

Across the table, Jane stopped eating, sat staring at Vikram.

"You *couldn't* have known," Ganesh agreed. "Don't torture yourself, *baba*. Who could imagine anyone doing such a thing?"

"Killed him for trying to make a phone call? Why?"

Jane put a finger to her lips, warning Vikram to speak softly.

Ganesh said, "Only the devil knows the true why of such things.

This freak, the shooter, he's a real *maderchod*. He's evil. But I knee-capped him, screwed him good." With the exuberance that was so characteristic of him but absent from his voice until now, he declared, "I took this shitty situation and turned it into *cham-cham*."

Cham-cham was a sweet cheese-based dessert.

With his eyes fixed on Jane's, Vikram said, "What do you mean by 'screwed him good,' Ganesh-ji?"

"The camera in the Stein attic got him and his partner clear enough. I used the NSA's best facial recognition software to match them in the government-employee files."

In disbelief, Vikram said, "You backdoored the National Security Agency system for this?"

"Like you taught me so well. Then I edited a little video of the murder, identified everyone in it, and uploaded it to YouTube."

Vikram felt as if his heart were a clockwork, its spring being wound tighter by the second, until it might destruct. In the attic setup, they had included a tiny broadcasting camera activated by a motion detector, only so that they would know that the Arcadians had taken the bait and been misdirected there.

"How? How did you post it?"

"Through a phantom account, of course. Don't worry. No one can trace me."

"Ganesh-ji, *baba*, the back doors to lesser bureaucracies were to be used like we planned. But those to major intelligence and law-enforcement agencies—you were to stay away from those except in the worst crisis."

"The *maderchod* blew Jesus Mendoza's brains out for making a phone call."

"That's a horror, a tragedy, an outrage," Vikram said, striving to keep his voice calm, "but it's not a crisis. Only I decide when we're in a crisis. Remember? Only me."

Ganesh sounded chagrined when he asked, "Then I have not made shit into *cham-cham*?"

"Where are you now?"

"In the parking lot at Quik Qwak."

Vikram's clock-spring heart could not be wound tighter. *"Across the street from the warehouse?"*

"Most of the employees drive SUVs, so I'm virtually invisible in this Escalade."

Ganesh was in that parking lot to make use of the spillover zone of Quik Qwak's Wi-Fi service. The moment he saw, through the warehouse camera, that the searchers had found the computer with YOU HAVE BEEN VIKRAMIZED on the screen, he ought to have left the area.

"You should have split by now," Vikram said.

"I wanted to see their reaction to the video. It was awesome. The freak who shot Mendoza might have to change his underpants."

"If they come out of there and see you leaving—it's not time for a shift change, and Quik Qwak's workers don't drive Cadillacs."

"It's an SUV, and most of them drive SUVs."

In an intense whisper, Vikram said, "Not Escalades, *baba*! Abandon it now. Leave on foot with just your laptop, not by the street, out the back, and don't let them see you. Get far away before you call Uncle Ashok and have him pick you up. Then throw away the phone. Go, Ganesh. Damn it, *go, go, go!*"

He terminated the call and switched off the burner phone.

His hands were shaking.

Jane said, "You see why I take an acid reducer?"

12

Charlie Weatherwax leaves Verna and Eldon to collect the laptop on the folding table, although he doubts it will contain anything of value to assist in the search for their quarry. Vikram Rangnekar is as slick as a lubricated condom.

As he steps out of the warehouse with Mustafa, Charlie says, "For all I know, maybe your Mumbai bad boy can watch the interior of this place from Alaska, sitting in front of a screen for hours on end, in order not to miss the very minute when we come through the door, so he can stick it to us with that video before we pull the plug on the computer. But I get the feeling this crap he's throwing at us is more down-and-dirty street tactics than it is the kind of operations the supervillains in James Bond movies put together from their remote castles."

The stars are reclaiming the night from the clouds, and a bearded moon gazes down like a radiant prophet, its glow quivering in a few shallow puddles of rainwater on the blacktop.

As he and Charlie cross the empty parking lot, Mustafa says, "I'm worried about that video."

"Don't be. Our friends in the private sector are taking it down already. You heard me make the call."

"But some people will already have seen it and saved it."

"The Internet is awash in fake news. The crazies believe everything they see, and everyone else believes nothing. Any comments about the video, on Twitter or wherever, will be purged. Anyone who gets fixated on it and keeps tweeting will be shadow-banned, so nobody will ever see their posts and they'll think they're the only one who cares."

As they pass through the gate they opened earlier, Mustafa says, "What does that mean—'street tactics'?"

"Could be that someone was watching the place when we arrived, old-fashioned surveillance, and operated the warehouse computer not from a thousand miles away but from across the street."

As they approach their Mercedes, Mustafa looks past it to the parking lot of Quik Qwak. "Maybe we better have a look over there."

13

As the night slowly waned in Scottsdale, Bobby Deacon sat at the Cantors' glass-topped kitchen table with Travis Hawk.

The boy's wrists were duct-taped to the arms of his chair. He was still out cold, sleeping off the sedative delivered by the dart pistol. His head hung low, chin on his chest.

Bobby had no fear that the other two residents would pose a problem. He used the pistol to sedate them while they slept; they were bound and gagged in their bedrooms. Lost in propofol dreams, they did not yet know that Bobby existed or that he had taken control of the house.

He had found a bottle of excellent Scotch in the Cantors' bar and poured a few ounces over ice. He sipped it while considering exactly what he would say when, in a few minutes, he made what might prove to be the most important phone call of his life.

While he enjoyed the whisky, he also studied the sleeping boy, deeply resentful of the kid's good looks. The mother was seriously gorgeous, which was why the media couldn't get enough of her face—the beautiful monster—and the father had been a handsome guy, so the boy lucked into all that beauty. Everyone who saw him probably told him he was cute. It would no doubt take him hours and hours to name all the people who loved him. As long as he lived, hot girls would throw themselves at him. Beautiful people had so many unearned advantages, privileges, that there ought to be camps where they were sent to be made plain or even hideous. As an agent of justice in this raw-deal world of countless injustices, Bobby Deacon wanted to draw his knife and balance the scales by carving a little ugliness into the kid's flawless face. He restrained himself because Travis Hawk was a valuable asset and might decline in value if he looked like a junior version of Frankenstein's monster.

At last, using a burner phone, Bobby entered the Las Vegas number for Carmine Vestiglia, through whom he fenced such stolen merchandise as high-end jewelry and a variety of rare collectibles. A Viagra addict, Carmine slept from noon till six and spent the rest of the day doing business and hookers, whom he called *showgirls*.

Apparently between showgirls, Carmine took the call. "Yeah?"

They didn't use names on the phone for the same reason they didn't advertise their occupations in the Yellow Pages.

Bobby said, "You know who this is?"

"Am I a mind reader? Give me a little more to go on."

Because he took pride in his voice, which he believed to be mellifluous enough to have made him a recording star if he'd had the looks to match his pipes, Bobby took offense at Carmine's failure to identify him from just five words. This had happened before, so it might mean only that Carmine had a tin ear, but it was nonetheless annoying. Bobby sang the first three lines of "Bridge Over Troubled Water."

Carmine said, "Hey, how ya doin', pal?"

"As good as anyone can in such an unjust world."

"Ain't that the truth."

"Listen, I got a delicate thing here."

"Put it back in your pants," Carmine said.

"You're about as funny as diarrhea. Let's play a name game."

"Hit me with it."

"You remember that showgirl you were so hot for you thought maybe you'd ask her to marry you?"

"Come to my senses just in time. You oughta see the bitch lately. She blew up like the Michelin tire man."

"I'm thinking of her first name," Bobby said, because the name had been Jane.

"Got it," Carmine said.

"Now you remember we were talking Western movies that time and the one that was your favorite was my number two?"

"You almost got good taste."

"The director of your number one, you take the s off it and put it with your Michelin tire bitch, and you got a major name."

The movie had been *Red River*, directed by Howard Hawks.

Carmine said, "You got my attention. Now do somethin' with it."

"Easter's coming in a few weeks," Bobby said.

"So? You wanna color eggs together or somethin'?"

"When you were a kid, did your folks buy you Easter candy?"

"They didn't like buyin' what they could find a way to get for nothin'."

"Well, what was your favorite Easter candy? Chocolate bunnies, chocolate eggs full of coconut cream?"

Carmine said, "Shit, I don't know. I guess maybe them eggs but with peanut butter inside. Coconut gives me hives."

"My favorite Easter candy was those little yellow marshmallow chicks. You know what I mean?"

"I'm not some Jersey bozo, pal. I know what little marshmallow Easter chicks are."

"I already got myself one this year. It's cute as hell. If it had a mama, she'd really be missing it."

Carmine sighed. "Ain't its mama just a big yellow marshmallow chicken? We've wandered deep in the weeds, pal. You're makin' no damn sense."

Bobby said patiently, "Remember the Michelin tire showgirl director without the s."

After a thoughtful silence, Carmine said, "No shit?"

"No shit."

"This ain't Easter candy, pal. This here's an Easter miracle."

Bobby said, "I think we should maybe go into the little yellow marshmallow chick business. That is, if you think you can find some financier to back us."

Carmine had another thoughtful silence in him. Then he said, "I ain't never imagined I'd be in the candy business."

"You think there's a big market for this?"

"Yeah, but it's got some risk. Go to the wrong buyer, they want candy for nothin'. They use the law like a sledgehammer, bust you up with it till they get their way. I need to think on it."

"Don't think on it too long. I can't spend my life here."

"An hour or two. So where are you?"

"Where I am," Bobby said, "is where no one can find me. I'll be back to you in an hour."

He terminated the call and sipped his Scotch and watched the sleeping boy.

The Rambo III knife lay on the table beside the 9 mm Sig Sauer.

Bobby wanted to celebrate a job well done. However, he warned himself not to drink too much. Sometimes when he drank, his impulse control suffered grievously. It could happen suddenly, between one sip of whisky and the next, whereupon he went from whippet to wild dog. Too much was at stake here to allow that to happen.

He looked from the boy to the knife to the boy, and he dreamily considered the possibilities, all the many ways that a measure of justice might be meted out. He didn't actually need to *do* anything. Imagining patterns of disfigurement was sufficiently satisfying.

14

In the manner of twenty-first-century American corporations, the name is cute hip while conveying little or nothing about what product or service the company might provide. And the spelling—Quik Qwak—strikes a blow against the oppressive tradition of clarity in language. Although the first word is almost surely pronounced *quick*, Charlie Weatherwax doesn't know if the second is *quack* or *quake*, or if it rhymes with *squawk*. This does not annoy him. On the contrary, as a missionary for random acts of cruelty, he approves of anything that, in however small a way, contributes to societal chaos.

Hondas, Toyotas, Chevys, and Fords fill the parking lot at Quik Qwak. Therefore, the one Cadillac Escalade is an object of interest.

Mustafa notices that affixed to the lower right-hand corner of each vehicle's windshield is a decal—a pair of linked Qs—that evidently signifies the right to park in the employee portion of the lot. The Cadillac has no such decal.

The vehicle is unlocked.

Charlie opens the driver's door, leans inside, and says, "What's that smell?"

At the opposite door, Mustafa peers into an open takeout food container on the passenger seat. "Not much left and rather common fare, I'm afraid. Judging by the vinegar smell, I'd say it's beef vindaloo."

"What restaurant?"

Mustafa shuts the hinged lid of the container and reads what is printed on it. "Pride of India."

Standing erect beside the open driver's door, like an Art Deco masterpiece by the sculptor Paul Manship, after whose work he styles himself, Charlie surveys the parking lot. He speaks one word as if it is a synonym for Satan: *"Rangnekar."*

15

As if Earth had deviated from its historic orbit and swung beyond the warmth of the sun, the night grew colder and the wind more bitter even as dawn was near, the falling snow hardening from flakes to spicules. Infinite white veils conferred upon the once simple plains a new mystique, so that through the billowing layers, the eye glimpsed—or the mind imagined—a realm of strangeness and menace that might at any moment manifest in the fullness of its terror.

Tom Buckle's ice-crusted ski mask was as solid as a plaster death mask. A chill crept across his face, though it didn't yet press a numbness into his features. Hollister had not provided him with goggles. The air stung tears from his eyes, and in spite of the salt content, they crusted into frost on his lashes.

Purblind and blinking ceaselessly, he navigated through the blizzard by the instrument-panel compass alone, unable to make good time because the plains, for all their flatness, were treacherous enough to wreck a fast-moving machine and leave him stranded. He thought not at all about his career or about his future, not even about survival, but only about his past. Memory resurrected so many moments with his beloved mom and dad. And there had been a woman named Jennifer, whom he had dated and with whom he'd broken up. She had seemed too far removed from the film business to be the right fit for him, a young director on his way up. But now he recognized what he'd been blind to then: that she would have been a faithful lover and a stalwart friend, that she would have steadied him, that with her he would have found greater intellectual and emotional depths in himself than he would ever discover alone. He dared hope for another chance.

When pale shimmers of light rippled left to right through the sea of snow ahead, like schooling lantern fish quivering radiantly through oceanic depths, he was so exhausted and disoriented that he thought he must be hallucinating. The storm drowned the light for a minute, but then it came again, this time slightly brighter than before.

He was perhaps as little as one mile from the highway. The slow-moving westward-shimmering headlights of traffic in the nearer lanes suggested that Interstate 70 remained open but allowed travel only at a much reduced speed.

For an hour or more, in spite of every effort to remain upbeat, Tom had allowed a gray despondency to color his thoughts, and though he held on to hope, his grip had grown feeble. Now his spirits rose, but not so fast and high that he felt sure of escape. Whether guided by a lingering thread of discouragement or intuition, he turned to look behind the snowmobile—and saw the high-set floodlights of some tall vehicle coming overland, maybe a mile or two away, approaching at a speed that seemed impossible in weather as bad as this and over terrain drifted deep with snow.

16

The crisp scent of verbena in the dark beneath the bridge. The voice of dead Mai-Mai beseeching: *"Master . . . master . . ."* A sense of something fluttering against the eye and mouth holes of his mask, a supple silken something that is not there when he raises a gloved hand to strip it away. Yet it returns, soft against his lips, and though he can see nothing in the gloom, he knows that this insistent veil is scarlet.

He curses Tom Buckle for slipping LSD or some similar drug to him, and he squeezes off half a dozen shots, swinging his pistol in an arc as he fires, in case the phantom lover has more substance than is usually the case with hallucinations.

Impacted by at least two of the rounds, something reverberates like a large gong, a distinctly metallic sound, which at once rings away Hollister's fear of an ambulatory dead woman and engages his keenly analytic mind. He is long accustomed to thinking of the bridge as a wooden construct standing on concrete piers, but now he remembers that the plank flooring is bolted to a substructure that is essentially a steel pan.

His capacity for logical thinking had made him the star of his university debate team, had enabled him to take his father's mere billion and turn it into thirty billion, had allowed him to grasp at once the utopian promise of the brain implants developed by Bertold Shenneck, and had inspired him to fund the scientist as well as establish the Techno Arcadian network with a group of like-minded people. He knows that he is unique, with an unmatched capacity for logical deduction. A modern-day Einstein, really, though with other interests than physics. Remembering the steel pan supporting the planks, he leaps with lightning speed from link to link in a chain of deductions arriving at the conclusion that, because of the steel span overhead, the security team searching for him has been unable to detect the signal from the GPS sewn into his storm suit.

Hollister banishes hallucinations by a sheer act of will and trollwalks out from under the bridge. As the faintest suggestion of morning waxes beyond the deep, dark overcast, he stands erect in the storm, ramrod straight with righteous indignation and with a fulsome sense of triumph that is nothing new to him. A lesser man, drugged with a near lethal cocktail of hallucinogens, his snowmobile stolen by a sinister Hollywood sleazeball, left to die in a blizzard, would have perished under the damn bridge. Not Wainwright Hollister. He is programmed for survival as surely as he is programmed for massive success, an indefatigable *machine*, as many business competitors have discovered to their dismay, as numerous women have learned to their pleasure. In celebration and defiance, he stands screaming curses into the wind, joyfully vilifying his father, his selfish mother, his weakling brother who died in the crib, and Thomas Buckle until, as logic assures must happen, the second Sno-Cat, manned by three rayshaws, arrives to take him aboard and convey him back into the hunt for the miserable filmmaker.

17

A paleness in the eastern sky, the long and eventful night draining over the western horizon . . .

Maybe Vikram Rangnekar had not expected them to park across the street from the target warehouse and perhaps he had been spooked by how close their vehicles were to the entry lane to Quik Qwak. Maybe he delayed too long while mocking them with the You-Tube video, saw them exiting the warehouse, and decided to abandon the Cadillac in favor of escaping on foot. If so, he has gone behind the factory and out by way of the back of the property.

Charlie Weatherwax places an encrypted call to an Arcadian in the National Security Agency, gives his precise location, and asks for an emergency real-time search of the surrounding area.

This is an industrial quarter stretching for a few miles in every direction. Because the theft of manufactured goods in bulk is ever increasing in such neighborhoods, and because at least a few enterprises in any district of this kind have connections with national defense efforts and are therefore potential espionage and terrorist targets, there will be four-way traffic cameras at every intersection, their video automatically fed to NSA archives 24/7. A lone man on foot, carrying a laptop and moving fast as dawn breaks, should be relatively easy to spot.

By the time Charlie terminates the call, agents at NSA's Utah Data Center and elsewhere are scanning traffic-cam video both from the past ten minutes and from real-time feed.

18

Under the name Chacka Mol, using a forged driver's license that would pass a DMV check, Vikram Rangnekar had booked a room in the Holiday Inn and paid cash before he and Jane ordered breakfast in the restaurant. He had specified a room facing North French Street, which would be much quieter than one overlooking either the busier West Gila Bend Highway or North Pinal Avenue. They were scheduled to meet Enrique de Soto's crew at ten o'clock, in the wider section of the hotel parking lot along North French.

At 5:54 A.M., they stood at a third-floor window, studying the scene below, where the action would occur.

Vikram said, "I wonder if matadors go to the bull ring hours before a fight, to study the stage."

"We're not matadors," Jane said firmly but patiently. "It's not a bull ring; it's a parking lot, and whatever happens down there, it won't be glamorous."

In the early light, as would be the case in the glare of ten o'clock, there wasn't much to see: an expanse of blacktop with rows of demarcated spaces that could accommodate between eighty and one hundred vehicles; ragged, bent, stunted palm trees struggling in desertscape planter beds of yellow-brown pea gravel, like abstract representations of tormented souls in Hell; and to the south, a narrow strip of real grass.

Currently, there were thirty vehicles in this portion of the lot, perhaps some belonging to staff. The number would likely drop as the morning waned and guests began to check out.

She said, "They expect us to come in from the street on wheels. We'll walk out from the hotel instead."

"You'll be relieved to hear," Vikram said, "I have a gun in my luggage."

"Leave it there."

"Well, but I know how to use it."

"Yeah? Where did you learn?"

"From Mike himself," he said with evident pride.

"Mike Himself? Never heard of Mike Himself."

"Mike at Mike Bernall's Gun Shop and Shooting Range."

Scanning the parking lot, thinking about how it would go, she said, "Leave it in your luggage."

"But you said there'll be at least four of them, maybe five."

"If I had a partner trained at Quantico, I'd like the backup. Otherwise, it's a distraction. You'll get yourself killed—and me."

She closed the draperies and crossed the room to an armchair and settled in it and turned off the floor lamp.

Vikram sat on the edge of the bed, in the light of a nightstand lamp. "Mike says I'm one of the best marksmen he's ever trained."

"The way this is going to go down, marksmanship isn't the most important skill."

"You already know how it's going to go down?"

"Ninety percent. You can never be a hundred percent sure."

"So how will it go down? What will they do, what will you do, what should I do?"

Succinctly, she told him.

He was silent for a minute before he said, "That's some scary shit."

"You still want in?"

"I'm already in."

"You can get out."

"Not and leave you. You need my hacking skills."

"Okay then. I'm going to sleep awhile."

He got to his feet. "You can have the bed."

"The chair is fine."

"I won't lie on the bed with you," he promised.

"I prefer the chair, sweetie. If I lie flat, that breakfast is going to reflux on me. You take the bed."

He went to the window and parted the draperies. "My *golis* have retracted, and I stand here as a frightened prepubescent boy."

"You'll be a man again at ten o'clock," she assured him. "I have full faith in you."

She slept.

19

Although Tom Buckle was unable to see anything more than the lights of the tall vehicle racing through the snowswept morning in his wake, it could only be a Sno-Cat riding high on articulated tracks like those on a tank, each of its four tracks independently sprung and separately powered. No terrain in this part of the world could defeat it. By comparison, the snowmobile was a toy.

By now, he surely had escaped Crystal Creek Ranch and must be on property not owned by Hollister. Nevertheless, the occupants of the Sno-Cat were either the billionaire and a few of his demonic brain-scrubbed security men, or only the dead-eyed rayshaws.

Since Tom could see nothing more than the vehicle's lights, he assumed the driver was not able to discern anything of him in the deeply overcast dawn, not yet, because he traveled without the headlight. Therefore, the direct bead they drew on him meant the snowmobile's GPS pinpointed it for them.

Turning the snowmobile northeast, away from the interstate, he let up on the throttle. The tracks ceased moving, and the brakeless machine came to a stop. He quickly got off the vehicle.

He had saved the drawstring plastic bag they'd given him at the start of the hunt, which once contained the PowerBars as well as the magazine and ammo for the pistol. He knotted it loosely around the throttle. When he cinched the knot tight, the snowmobile took off on its own.

Running hard toward the highway, Tom dared glance back and saw the Sno-Cat alter course to pursue the riderless vehicle, giving him a reprieve. But they wouldn't be fooled for long.

20

Carmine Vestiglia owned five legitimate businesses in Las Vegas, including a pawn-it-or-sell-it shop that occupied half a city block and dealt in everything from rock-'n'-roll memorabilia to rare coins and stamps. A third of the basement was walled off from the rest and accessible only through a concealed door. In that secret space, he received stolen goods from the likes of Bobby Deacon. He stored the items there till he could sell them to one of the many passionate collectors on his list of top customers nationwide or, in the case of jewelry, until he broke the necklaces and bracelets down to sell the untraceable stones. Or he waited until enough time passed for hot merchandise to cool; Carmine was a very patient man.

In the first hour of light, Saturday morning, Carmine met with Sutcliff "Sutty" Sutherland not at the pawnshop or any of his other businesses, but in Carmine's sixteen-room apartment, which occupied half of the eighteenth floor of a luxury high-rise. The space was a wonder of golden marble and polished black granite and stainless steel, with carpets by Tufenkian, sleek modern furniture by the likes of Roche Bobois and Fendi and Visionnaire, and heroic-size stainless-steel sinuous abstract sculptures by Gino Miles.

Frameless, insulated sliding-glass doors formed an entire wall that rolled aside at the touch of a button, allowing a seamless continuity between the vast living room and a deep wraparound deck. Although the apartment's state-of-the-art electronics included an automatic daily sweep for listening devices, Carmine preferred to have this conversation outside.

High above the street, they were not in danger of having a directional microphone aimed at them from a standard surveillance van. Hotels and other high-rises rose in their line of sight, but some stood at too great a distance to concern Carmine. As for the few buildings from which a high-gain shotgun mic might pick up incriminating words, he had friends among the bellmen and security staffs who, for a few hundred cash now and then, would let him know at once if the kind of people who had subpoena power started setting up a listening station there, with his apartment as the target.

He and Sutty Sutherland faced each other across a lacquered-metal table with a glass top on which the housekeeper had set a breakfast of fresh fruit and crusty, sugared morning rolls with rich veins of cinnamon paste. A pot of coffee stood on a warming plate.

A light, warm breeze sighed off the Mojave, and already the grumble of weekend traffic rose from the streets of the world's busiest resort, background noises that would screen and distort their conversation if anyone tried to listen by way of a stealth drone hovering in the vicinity. In addition, on the table stood an iPod and Bose speakers, which brought forth the voices of singers from a Las Vegas that was before Carmine's time but for which he longed, the Vegas that had glamour as well as glitter.

Carmine was a big man with the face of a boxer who too often had failed to keep his gloves up, beefy round shoulders, a barrel chest, and hands that looked strong enough to strangle a horse. Sutty was an even bigger man with a face suitable for heroic statuary, a bodybuilder's physique, and long-fingered, well-manicured hands. Carmine wore slacks with an elastic waist and a Hawaiian shirt with a pattern of palm trees and flamingos. Sutty wore a three-piece gray suit cut for concealed carry, a white shirt, and a blue tie held in place with a pearl tie tack. In spite of their appearances, they had more in common than not. Carmine was Carmine, and Sutty was chief personal bodyguard for United States senator Joseph Ford Kargrew; therefore, both Carmine and Sutty were engaged in criminal enterprises.

They ate with the appetite of gladiators, drank coffee, and reminisced a little before Carmine said, "There's this situation—it sounds like bullshit, but I got no reason to distrust the guy who brought it to me."

"So tell me," Sutty said. "I didn't come for the morning rolls, though they're almost better than sex."

"My mother's recipe. Anyway, it's a what-if situation. What if some guy—not just any dumb dick, but a smart guy, a switchblade in shoes, tough and street-taught—what if maybe he stumbles across the people hidin' Jane Hawk's kid?"

Sutty said nothing, just stared at Carmine and chewed.

"So then say this guy, seein' a payday, he grabs the kid."

"What guy is this?"

"I ain't goin' there. What he wants is he wants to fence the boy."

" 'Fence' him?" Sutty said, as though repeating a word in a foreign language that he didn't understand.

"This guy, he can get in any house he wants, slick as a snake swimmin' up a sewer line, comin' out in the toilet. He don't smash no window, don't bust no lock. Takes what he wants and slips out like a spider through a keyhole."

"Can he also make himself invisible anytime he wants?"

"You disappoint me, Sutty."

"You sound like my ex-wives."

"He always fences what he boosts, so he figures to fence the boy. Your boss don't want to be a hero?"

"He already thinks he's God. Hero's a step down. Where is this toilet snake of yours?"

"I don't know. I really don't. He works California, Arizona. So he ain't on the moon. A swap could happen today if maybe the price is right."

The rising sun ascended one more floor, sliding pale light across the terrace, and shadows emerged from all the previously shadowless items on the table.

Sutty said, "Carmine, if this turns out to be a scam, but even if it turns out to be true, either damn way—it could be a shit bomb that neither of us would survive if it blew up in our faces."

"It ain't a scam. And as for shit bombs . . . you think I got where I got without riskin' it all sometimes?"

A large blackbird flew under the terrace of the apartment above and hovered nearby on a warm thermal. Both men stared at it until they were sure it was a real bird; and even though it seemed to be only what it appeared to be, they waited until it flew away before they continued their conversation.

"How much money are we talking about?" Sutty asked.

"Whatever's true about Jane Hawk," Carmine said, "it's sure not what's in the news. It's somethin' bigger than all the shit in the news. A lot of you people have such a crazy hate-on for the bitch, you must be pissin' blood. Twenty million cash."

"The senator is going to say we don't pay ransom."

"Think of it as a reward."

"It's too much, Carmine. Where would we get that much on short notice?"

"It's the damn government, not you and Senator Kargrew. Some years back, the president, he flew one and a half billion in cash off to Iran to get some hostage freed. One and a half *billion*. At least me and my client, we ain't gonna give *none* of our money to crazy terrorists or build a nuke with it."

Sutty pushed his chair back from the table. "This will take time to put together, if it can be done at all."

"You don't got time, Sutty. Say you come back here with some law, or just some muscle, figurin' to cut outta me where my client is. All you'll get is his name—or what name he goes by with me. I don't know his location."

Sutty took the linen napkin from his lap and threw it on the table.

Carmine said, "One more thing. This guy who has the kid, he's high strung, and he has this thing about pretty people."

"What thing?"

"He don't like them. And that boy . . . he's about as pretty in his own way as his mom. You stretch this out, you try to sweat my client, he's liable to go off on the kid and then just split. When he's on the job, he's used to slidin' in and slidin' out. He don't know how to bide his time. This has to be fast."

As Sutty got to his feet, so did his host.

Coldly, the senator's man said, "But twenty freaking million, Carmine."

"Government must be spendin' that much every week just tryin'
to find the bitch. Relax, Sutty. I done a lot for the senator over the
years. We done a lot for each other. You get this boy, you put it on TV
that you got him, and his mother she's gonna melt. She's gonna know
what you can do to him, and all the fight is gonna go right out of her."

"Maybe not," Sutty said. "Maybe there's no fight that can go out of
her. Maybe she *is* fight."

21

Overweight, out of shape, carrying a laptop, on the run,
wishing he hadn't eaten the beef vindaloo . . .

Ganesh Rangnekar, son of Ashok and Doris, knew he was smart,
very smart, but he also knew that he wasn't as intelligent as his cousin
Vikram, and furthermore he understood that in spite of being smart,
he sometimes lacked common sense, a fault that he attributed to the
thousands of hours he had wasted playing video games. The more
you played a game, the more the world of the game seemed real, but
it was the furthest thing from reality. Game worlds rewarded magical
thinking; although the real world was deeply mysterious and riddled
with strange coincidences, magical thinking in this one true life led to
disaster sooner or later.

Sitting in the Escalade, in the Wi-Fi overspill of Quik Qwak, watching events in the warehouse on his laptop, Ganesh had felt like a wizard, and the government agents had seemed to be just a squad of
clueless orcs—until they weren't. He had been getting out of the Cadillac SUV when he saw Weatherwax and al-Yamani exit the building
on the farther side of the street.

With the sun below the horizon and the faint glow of the coming
day fanning softly over the crests of the dark eastern hills, Ganesh ran
behind the factory. Chain-link fencing enclosed a storage yard. A vehicle gate stood open. He hurried into a wide alleyway, sprinted
north, splashing through puddles, until he realized that a running

man carrying a laptop looked like a thief and invited attention. He slowed to a walk. There were night shifts at some enterprises, but others were quiet. A Peterbilt at a loading dock, men driving forklifts, operating hand trucks. Farther along, three men taking a cigarette break behind a building. The alleyway led to a street without sidewalks, the street to an intersection, where he turned left onto a major thoroughfare with walkways. But he felt naked on this wider avenue, in the blazing searchlight of the ascending sun just then painting a first fiery arc above the hills. He darted into another alley, mazing his way through this industrial district with its assembly lines and machine shops, boilerworks and gasworks and ironworks, with its forges and foundries, all of it mysterious and much of it suggesting malevolent forces bent on wicked tasks.

Even the shadowed alleyways with structures hulking to both sides soon ceased to feel like adequate cover. A pair of early crows were pecking at the carcass of a rat with such intensity that they ignored Ganesh as he approached. One protuberant eye of the rodent, swollen from its socket and glazed red by sunlight, regarded him as if with recognition, as if the rat, though dead and beak-torn, were possessed by some unclean spirit dispatched to track him through the eyes of whatever creatures it could inhabit.

At the end of the alleyway, Ganesh crossed a littered street and entered a vacant lot bristling with weeds, strewn with empty beverage cans, chunks of shattered concrete blocks, broken boards. When he came to a railroad spur line, he decided to abandon streets entirely, where the four agents—and by now backup—were no doubt cruising in search of him. He followed the steel tracks that for a while paralleled a concrete-lined watercourse where two or three feet of runoff from the night's storm surged brown, clotted with debris, like the devil's own bathwater. And then the tracks passed some kind of solar farm, acres of barren land outfitted with rank on rank of tilted dark-plastic panels liberally splattered with white Rorschach blots of bird shit.

At last he came to another street, a hoved and potholed two-lane, across from an automobile junkyard where numerous species of motor vehicles had come to their end, in places stacked atop one another like fertile beasts enjoying intercourse in a nightmare about self-reproducing machines. The junkyard's name and address were emblazoned above its gated entrance, and nearby stood a cellphone tower, supporting Ganesh's conviction that he'd found the right place from which to call his father and arrange to be collected.

Gasping for breath, his heart pounding as if it were drumming the rhythm for a dance band's tarantella, Ganesh put down the laptop and took a burner phone from his pants pocket. He sat holding the disposable phone in both hands, waiting for his explosive breathing to subside so he could talk clearly.

He was sweating copiously. The salty perspiration stung his eyes and blurred his vision. He used the sleeves of his pullover to wipe his face.

As he switched on the phone, he heard an approaching vehicle. He looked left. An SUV was speeding in his direction, traveling much too fast for the crumbling two-lane, veering back and forth across the center line as the pavement tested the driver. Another similar sound drew his attention to the right, where a car raced toward him with equal recklessness. For a moment, Ganesh thought the two motorists were engaged in a game of chicken and might collide with deadly force. Instead, almost simultaneously, the vehicles braked hard and, with the full intention of the drivers, fishtailed to a halt, blocking the roadway.

The SUV was a bespoke Mercedes G550 Squared, from which stepped Charles Douglas Weatherwax and Mustafa al-Yamani, stars of the YouTube short film that Ganesh had earlier posted. To Ganesh's right, from the Dodge Charger emerged the woman in black and the tall black man with the porkpie hat who had accompanied Weatherwax and al-Yamani into the warehouse.

Although he was exhausted, Ganesh sprang up, certain that he must flee no matter how poor his chances of escape, that his and his family's very survival depended on giving these people the slip. He turned back the way he had come and ran perhaps twenty yards before the helicopter clattered fast out of the west, flying so low that it seemed the pilot meant to decapitate him with one of the craft's skids. Ganesh threw himself facedown, and the downblast of the aircraft's rotary wing churned a cloud of dust, chaff, and litter that started him coughing.

As the dust settled, Ganesh rose and turned, and came face-to-face with Weatherwax, who said, "You're not Vikram."

"Neither are you," said Ganesh.

Weatherwax backhanded him so hard across the face that Ganesh nearly dropped to his knees. The other three arrived with guns drawn as the helicopter carved an arc in the sky and returned at higher altitude to hover at the ready.

22

The blizzard appeared to be diminishing, or maybe the dismal gray light of the morning, filtered through the pregnant clouds, returned dimension to the world, so that Tom Buckle's mind, numbed by his long ordeal, woke to the truth that there was more to existence than snow.

Fifty yards from Interstate 70, in snow to his knees, he halted and looked north. Visibility remained poor, although he was able to see not merely the lights of the Sno-Cat but also the vague shape of it churning away from him in pursuit of the riderless snowmobile. Then the vehicle turned. From perhaps half a mile, its headlights and roof-mounted floodlights seemed to focus on Tom as if they were the arrayed eyes of some monstrous mutant insect.

At that distance, in this weather, he was a small figure to them, if they could see him at all, which most likely they couldn't, considering that his storm suit was mostly white, with blue design elements. When the Sno-Cat began to move again, however, it came straight toward him.

If the snowmobile emitted a signal by which it could be traced, why not Tom himself? Could a battery-powered transmitter have been sewn into the outfit they'd given him?

Maybe they had gotten close enough to the snowmobile to see that it carried no one, or maybe they had begun to wonder why he was racing away from the highway that offered his best—his only—hope. Whatever the case, they must have realized that they needed to be tracking him instead of the machine.

He turned away from them and frantically slogged forward, to-ward Interstate 70. At this point, the road rose only a foot or two above the plain, and there were no guardrails. The westbound lanes were nearer, the traffic passing much slower than usual, at maybe thirty miles an hour, fitted with tire chains, headlights blazing even now in daylight.

As though harking back to childhood when the thing under the bed would not harm him as long as he didn't lift the overhanging covers and come eye-to-eye with it, he dared not look north again.

He reached the shoulder of the interstate and pulled back his hood and stripped off his ski mask. If some kind of locater had been hidden in the storm suit, it was probably in the jacket. He zippered it open, shrugged out of it, and felt a suspicious shape, small but hard, sewn in the lining of the collar pouch into which the hood could be stowed when not needed. He rolled the jacket in a ball, used the sleeves to cinch it tight, and threw it into the open bed of a slat-sided truck that poked past at about twenty miles an hour.

Standing in a flannel shirt and storm-suit pants, he began shiver-ing violently in spite of his long underwear. He waved at the ap-proaching traffic, scissoring his arms over his head, being highly dramatic about it, trying to convey desperation and urgency. As a director of small movies with intimate stories, he'd frequently coun-seled actors to pare down their gestures, soften their voices, and rely on subtle facial expressions. Now he waved wildly and shouted and felt his face contorting as if he were the last survivor in a horror movie with a chainsaw body count north of ten.

Although this was not weather in which an evil hitchhiker would likely be trying to lure an unwary motorist to his death, several vehicles passed him without slowing, tire chains clicking, drivers and passengers either pretending to be unaware of him or gazing out from the warm comfort of their conveyances with indifference or curiosity or smug amusement, but never with evident pity. Tom was about to lose it, about to plunge from the shoulder of the highway directly into the westbound lanes, dangerously close to glancing northward and, by that act, ensuring that the Sno-Cat would crash into him and pull him under its steel tracks and grind his legs to meat paste in the sausage casing that was his storm-suit pants.

Just then a black Ford crew-cab pickup slowed as it passed him, angled to the shoulder of the highway, and stopped. Tom ran to the front passenger door and opened it and looked in at the driver, who was the only occupant. A block of a guy. Fiftyish. A wide face turned to leather and pleated by the sun. Walrus mustache. Sapphire-blue eyes. Jeans, plaid flannel shirt, cowboy hat. His features were so bold and his presence so dynamic that he seemed familiar, famous, like a country-music star, but he also looked a little dangerous, as though he had often used his fists for something more serious than gripping a golf club. When he spoke he had a whiskey-soaked bass voice reminiscent of Trace Adkins. "You want a ride, son, or you just passin' out pamphlets for Jesus?"

Overcoming his wariness, Tom said, "A ride, yes, thank you." He got in the truck and pulled the door shut. "I'm freezing, this feels wonderful, thank you."

Swinging into traffic and accelerating to the extent that the road conditions would allow, the driver said, "What happened to your car?"

"It slid off the road."

"I didn't see any car."

"It happened a ways back, maybe a mile from where you picked me up. I thought I could walk to an exit, get help."

"You walked a mile an' no damn body give you a ride till me?"

"Maybe I spooked them, I don't know."

"You look about as spooky as a cheese sandwich. Problem is, we're livin' in a time without much kindness."

"Sad but true."

"Name's Porter Crockett."

"Nat. Nathanael West," Tom lied, because this time without kindness was also a time without trust.

Adjusting the heater, Porter said, "You're shakin' like a Pentecostal full up with the holy spirit."

"I've never been so cold."

"Weren't there a jacket to go with those ski pants?"

"Wasn't wearing it when I went off the road. The car rolled. When I crawled out, I was rattled, dazed. Walked away without the jacket."

"They got a service station a couple exits up ahead, Nat. I can drop you there."

"Won't do me any good. The car is racked up bad. Anyway, it's a rental. I'll call the company, tell them where to find it. If you're going farther, like to Denver, that would be great."

"Well, I'm goin' only the two exits. Comin' home. Been over to Kansas to see my daughter and find out if her new hubby is treatin' her like she deserves."

Tom made the grave mistake of looking at the passenger sideview mirror, whereupon of course the bogeyman jumped out from under the bed, figuratively speaking: the big Sno-Cat, at least a hundred yards back in the murk but identifiable by its three over-the-cab floodlights that were higher than the roofs of intervening vehicles.

Although it seemed unlikely that the searchers had been near enough to see what vehicle had given Tom a lift, he said, "Can't we go any faster?"

Porter smiled and shook his head. "You young folks, you're always in a giddyup to get somewhere. You got to learn, nowhere is somewhere worth dyin' to get there. Weren't a plow through here in maybe an hour, maybe two, snow driftin' over in places, compactin' into ice. It's half a miracle traffic's still movin' at all."

The sideview mirror again. Back there in the swirling mists, the Sno-Cat swung out of the extreme right lane to pass another vehicle. On its steel tracks, it was making better speed than Porter.

"You got family in Denver, Nat?"

When with some effort he tore his attention from the mirror and looked at Porter Crockett, who in a most responsible fashion fixed *his* gaze unwaveringly on the treacherous roadway ahead, Tom saw a good man, a caring father. He no longer had any sense that Crockett might be dangerous. With his white walrus mustache and face hammered by experience, he resembled that wonderful character actor Wilford Brimley, or the late great novelist Jim Harrison. *What am I doing, what have I done?* Tom knew the answer to that question, knew *exactly* what he had done; in his terror, in his desperate need to escape, he had put at risk an innocent man, a father, maybe a grandfather, maybe a widower, certainly a Good Samaritan. He'd put Porter Crockett's life in danger, and he'd done so with lies.

"Family in Denver?" Tom said. "No. No one in Denver. I'm from California. My dad's a tailor in a dry-cleaning shop. My mom's a seamstress in a department store. I should've married a wonderful girl, Jennifer, Jenny, just a wonderful woman, but she wasn't in the business, she was real-estate sales, but going to *build* houses one day as well as sell them. I thought I should be with someone in the business. I'm a film director or was, and my name isn't Nathanael West, he wrote *The Day of the Locust,* my name is Tom Buckle, and I'm in deep shit. I can't jive you anymore, it's not right to use you without telling you what the stakes are. These freaking insane people are after me, fanatics, they kill people, lots of people, they're behind us even now in a big damn Sno-Cat, whether they know where I am or not, I can't say, I don't know, but they're behind us. They even zombify people and make them *kill themselves* with brain implants, nanomachine brain implants, it's like Jane Hawk's husband, *it's the whole Jane Hawk thing,* but not the way we've been told to think about it, about her." He ran out of breath.

At last Porter Crockett looked at Tom but only for two seconds, just a beat, during which their eyes met. He returned his attention to the highway beyond the whisking windshield wipers, but then he glanced at the rearview mirror and at the driver's sideview mirror—at the steadily gaining Sno-Cat—before focusing on the road again. He didn't say anything for a moment, as though he might be assessing the mental stability of his passenger, deciding whether to put him out right away or risk taking him as far as the next exit.

He said, "Never saw any Sno-Cat on the interstate before. Never knew any man to say he lied without him first bein' called out on what he said, but you plain up and volunteered the truth, crazy as it sounds. Always thought the Jane Hawk thing was more bullshit than gospel, but never thought I'd pick up a hitchhikin' moviemaker who'd say as much. Looks like it's a day for firsts, and not done yet." Traffic slowed, and Porter let the pickup's speed drop. "What's this now?"

Tom glanced from the sideview mirror to the road ahead and saw a *second* Sno-Cat coming east in the westbound lanes, all its lights ablaze. Maybe seventy yards ahead of them, it rammed a slow-moving vehicle in the extreme right lane, forcing it off the pavement, and every motorist approaching the collision braked in reaction. Some braked too hard, too abruptly, so even tire chains didn't prevent them from sliding. Suddenly half a dozen cars and SUVs were angled to a stop everywhichway across the westbound lanes.

The vehicle that had been rammed off the interstate was the open-bed slat-sided truck into which Tom had previously tossed his storm-suit jacket.

23

Charlie Weatherwax decides that the easiest thing to do is take Ganesh Rangnekar to the deserted warehouse in which he'd set up the computer that had greeted them with the on-screen taunt YOU HAVE BEEN VIKRAMIZED and on which they had been shown the You-Tube video of the murder of Jesus Mendoza. While Mustafa drives, Charlie sits in the backseat with the fat little Ganesh bastard, holding the muzzle of a pistol to his neck. The prisoner has lost his snark; his mouth is pressed tightly shut, as though to assure them that the whereabouts of Vikram cannot be pried from him. His face, designed for sunny smiles, is grim, as though he knows what horrors await him.

But he doesn't know. He can't imagine. He will soon learn.

Mustafa drives through the open gate and stops near the warehouse door through which they entered earlier.

Verna Amboy parks the Dodge Charger at the gate and leaves Eldon Clocker to flash his FBI or DHS or NSA credentials at anyone who might feel they have a right to enter the property. The morning is splashed with sunlight that's drying up the last of the previous night's rain. In her black suit, face framed by raven-black hair, eyes as black as collapsed stars, Verna strides toward the warehouse with head up and shoulders back, as if she is Queen Nefertiti and has, by the exercise of some occult power, stepped out of fourteenth-century Egypt and halfway around the planet, ditching her husband, Amenhotep, for a new life as a Techno Arcadian ruler of the world. She brings with her a temperature-controlled Medexpress carrier containing, among other paraphernalia, twelve ampules of an amber fluid in which are suspended the nanoparts of four brain implants.

Charlie shoves Ganesh into the only chair at the table on which the computer stands, its screen now blank.

He presses the muzzle of the pistol against the back of the prisoner's neck. "Give me a reason to pull the trigger. I'd like nothing better."

Verna puts the Medexpress carrier on the table and opens it. Cold vapor plumes from the interior. With her long, nimble fingers, she sets out three large ampules. She produces a hypodermic syringe, a cannula, a length of rubber tubing to be used as a tourniquet, and an antibacterial wipe in a foil packet, with which to sterilize the injection site.

Watching this with evident alarm, Ganesh says, "Truth serums don't really work. Not well. The accuracy of information obtained with their use is notoriously poor."

No one bothers to tell him that this is not a truth serum.

Mustafa works the right sleeve of Ganesh's pullover up his arm to reveal the crook of his elbow.

"I don't know anything anyway," Ganesh says. "I don't know where Vikram can be found."

No one bothers to tell him that he does not lie convincingly.

Mustafa ties on the tourniquet. He extracts the wet wipe from the foil packet and scrubs the skin on Ganesh's arm, directly over the most prominent vein.

As far as Charlie is concerned, they can skip the antibacterial wipe. He doesn't care if Ganesh dies a few days hence from a blood infection. As soon as they have the information they need, they'll kill him anyway.

Verna finds the vein and begins administering the first of the ampules.

In less than five minutes, all three will have been infused into Ganesh's bloodstream, and the nanoparticles will be making their way to his brain. In approximately four hours, the control mechanism will be active, and he will be their slave, his mind theirs to peel, his secrets readily revealed.

Charlie Weatherwax does not intend to wait four hours to begin the interrogation. If Vikram Rangnekar is, as they believe, making common cause with Jane Hawk, if he knows how to find her and might even now be in her company, time is of the essence. Subjecting the prisoner to extreme torture will not interfere whatsoever with the installation of the control mechanism. If they can learn Vikram's whereabouts in an hour instead of four, or in two hours, or even three, everything that Charlie does to Ganesh will be justifiable.

Not that he needs justification. He has the power and the desire, and that's all he needs in this case. It's all he ever needs.

24

Cornell Jasperson woke to find his ankles duct-taped to each other, loop after loop binding him knee to knee in his pale-blue pajamas, his wrists duct-taped together, some kind of rag in his mouth, a piece of duct tape over his lips. He was confused. He went back to sleep.

When he woke the second time, he was in the same perplexing condition. He didn't want to go to sleep again. He wanted to figure out how this happened to him, but he fell asleep once more.

Waking a third time, he realized he'd been drugged, and his anxiety soared like a bottle rocket. He went a little nuts for a while, though not because he'd been drugged and not because he was restrained hand and foot.

Cornell didn't look like a man who would be afraid of anything. Six foot nine, long-boned, knob-jointed, with misshapen shoulder blades that reminded him of certain versions of Godzilla, with large hands that appeared strong enough to crush a human skull, he had frightened more than a few people who'd come upon him unexpectedly, though he had never intended to scare anyone.

Oh, some people said his milk-chocolate-brown face was as sweet as that of any baby Jesus in a Christmas crèche, but he figured they were just being kind. When he looked in a mirror, he never knew what to think, except that he certainly never thought, *Look, it's Jesus.* Whether his face was sweet or just ordinary, it was not charming enough to win friends easily or attract women.

Which was just as well, because of all the things that Cornell feared—the collapse of civilization, loud noises, crowds, cities, being too sad, being too happy, onions, just to name a few—the worst was being touched. He'd been diagnosed with Asperger's and various forms of autism, which might or might not be the case. Whatever the definition of his condition, when another person touched him, it was like being wounded. A psychic wound. Blood didn't erupt from where he had been touched, but he felt as though the contact sucked from him a portion of his mind and soul. He feared that by one touch and another, people would drain Cornell Jasperson out of himself, leaving a body that was only a mindless husk, and he would be no more.

That was why, lying in bed, he went nuts for a little while when he realized he'd been bound and gagged in his sleep, because that meant *whoever had done it had touched him.* He lay breathing like a marathon runner, each inhalation and exhalation whistling through his nose, the gag now sodden in his mouth, trembling, sweating. He felt vampiric parasites swimming through his blood, hairy spiders and centipedes crawling through his bones and eating his marrow. He might have remained on the bed, in a condition of collapse, for hours if he hadn't remembered the boy.

Travis. What happened to Travis?

For a few days Travis and his two dogs had sheltered with Cornell in Borrego Valley, California, in Cornell's library for the end of the world, above an off-the-grid end-times bunker into which Cornell had expected to retreat the moment civilization began to fall apart. How the boy had gotten there and how the two of them had ended up here in the Cantor house in Scottsdale—well, that was quite a story in itself, one that Cornell found hard to believe, even though he had lived through it.

The dogs. What has happened to the dogs?

When the boy had first come to Cornell's secret retreat, he brought two big German shepherds, Duke and Queenie. The dogs had belonged to Cornell's cousin Gavin and Gavin's wife, Jessie, who had been hiding the boy for Jane Hawk. Something bad had happened to Gavin and Jessie. Cornell still didn't know what had become of them, except he assumed they were dead at the hands of some wicked people.

At first, he had been afraid of the dogs, fearful that maybe they would bite him, but mainly that they would touch him. You could tell people not to touch you, that it made you crazy, and nearly all of them would respect your wishes. But dogs wanted to touch you and be touched all the time, and they didn't know about personality disorders. Cornell had expected the shepherds to touch-touch-touch him into a permanent state of complete collapse.

Except it didn't happen. He discovered that being touched by a dog didn't affect him the same as being touched by another person. The dogs liked him. And he liked the dogs. No, by now, he loved the dogs. He loved the boy and loved the dogs, and that was the biggest surprise of his life, because he couldn't say that he had truly loved anyone before them. He hadn't known that he had the *capacity*. He'd liked some people well enough. But as it turned out, liking and loving were different feelings. And he liked the feeling of love.

Maybe someone has taken the boy. Maybe he's gone forever.

Maybe the dogs are dead.

Maybe the boy *is dead.*

Cornell was bleeding from psychic wounds, while imaginary pestilential hordes crawled over him and within him, spinning webs and laying eggs and eating his flesh, all because he'd been touched in his sleep by a stranger. But at the thought of the boy dead, such self-disgust overcame him that he screamed into the duct-taped wad of soggy cloth that filled his mouth.

Damn you, Cornell, the boy needs your help!

When he had learned he could love, he had also learned that with love came a sense of responsibility for the people he cared about so deeply. People and dogs. Love could hurt as much as hate when you thought you might lose who you loved.

In Borrego Valley, when it'd been just him and Travis and the dogs, Cornell feared that something he might do or something he failed to do would get the boy killed. That terrible fear had made it possible for him to overcome one of his attacks of the heebie-jeebies, to stop thinking about flukes swimming in his blood and spiders weaving webs inside his bones, to settle his nerves and get off the floor and get on with taking care of the boy. If he had done it before, he could do it again. After thirty-two years of living with himself, Cornell still did not understand himself, *but he knew he could do this again.*

In spite of his condition, he had the tools to take care of people. He was highly intelligent. He had money. He'd gotten very rich by sitting alone in a room, developing apps that millions of people found beneficial. He had *capacity*, all kinds of capacity—to love, to make money, to think his way out of tight places like this one. The only thing keeping him from finding the boy and helping him was fear. But there was nothing here to fear: no one who might touch him, no loud noises, no crowds, no onions. His fears were nothing more than excuses, and to hell with them.

Maybe whoever had drugged and taped Cornell was still in the house. He needed to be quiet. He was clumsy; he couldn't help it; clumsiness was built into his misshapen body.

He rolled onto his side, swung his legs off the mattress, and sat on the edge of the bed. Because of the tape around his knees, he couldn't bend them. He sat with his legs thrust out in front of him.

In expectation of a national or even planetary catastrophe, he hadn't merely designed and financed an elaborate secret bunker on the edge of the Anza-Borrego Desert. He had also researched and learned all kinds of survival techniques that might help him live through the chaos between one civilization and the next—including two ways to free himself in the event that someone restrained him with duct tape.

25

Struck by the big Sno-Cat, the slat-sided truck slid sideways across the highway, and the right rear fender slammed into one of two poles supporting a large highway sign. The impact spun the truck perhaps 120 degrees before it skidded off the road and rolled almost in slow motion onto its port side, as if it were a tired beast lying down for the night in mounded pillows of snow.

"I threw my jacket in the back of that truck," Tom told Porter Crockett. "Some kind of locater was sewn into the lining. They were following me by its signal."

"Son, your story becomes a bigger mess of strangeness with each new detail."

"But you still believe me?" Tom worried.

"I'm a believin' kind of fella."

Having entered the interstate going the wrong way, the Sno-Cat now came to a stop astride the extreme right lane, as though the driver operated on the highest authority or didn't give a damn about traffic laws. Two men in storm suits jumped down from the vehicle and hurried to the overturned truck. At this distance, Tom couldn't be sure, but they appeared to be carrying guns.

"If they're law, they're the lawless kind," Porter said. He reached under his seat, withdrew a pistol, put it in his lap, and drove forward. "I been licensed most of my life. You got yourself a pacifier?"

Tom zippered open the pocket on the right leg of his pants and withdrew the 9 mm Glock. "*Not* licensed to carry. It's a long story."

"Be nice if we live for me to hear it."

Porter threaded the pickup among the several whipsawed vehicles littering the highway, moving into the extreme left lane to pass as far as possible behind the Sno-Cat and the overturned truck.

Other drivers began to swing toward the west and find their way forward in the ill-defined lanes. No one seemed of a mind to help the people in the battered truck. This was a new America, in which going to the aid of a stranger was less likely to be rewarded with a thank-you than with a lawsuit or even a bullet in the head.

A third man got out of the Sno-Cat. He was one of the rayshaws who had escorted Tom from the Hollister residence to the starting point of the hunt.

Holding the Glock between his knees, muzzle aimed at the floor, Tom bowed his head and averted his face.

After less than a minute, Porter Crockett said, "Gone past them now."

Peering at the sideview mirror, Tom saw the Sno-Cat that had been in their wake now angling to rendezvous with the one that had rammed the truck. "Let's step on it before they find the jacket instead of me."

"Bein' too fast makes us look like a getaway. Let a couple other folks move out ahead, so we just seem to be dawdlin' along with the herd."

Maybe two inches of well-worked snow, accumulated since the

most recent plowing, groaned softly under the tires, as though the fallen body of the storm suffered their passage.

In the mirrors, the Sno-Cats dwindled, fading into the wind-whipped whiteness, as if they were machines in a dream from which Tom was waking.

Two minutes. Four. Five. No pursuit was mounted.

They topped a gradual incline as the falling snow abruptly thinned. Perhaps a mile away, beacons pulsed in the morning: the lightbars of police vehicles parked across the westbound lanes.

"Roadblock," said Porter, easing up on the accelerator.

Tom said, "Maybe they'll look like police, but they won't be."

"An ever bigger mess of strangeness," Porter muttered, though he expressed no doubt about his passenger's veracity. "Don't have an exit here, but we're goin' off road just a bit."

Fifty or sixty yards past the crest, he piloted the big pickup off the highway, down an embankment, out of sight of the roadblock.

"I know things hereabouts. Nice little state route just ahead."

They came to a highway, two lanes better plowed than the higher road they'd departed. Porter turned left. They passed under I-70, heading south. Flanking the road were leafless cottonwoods, tall and dark and funereal in this last whiteness of a late winter.

"Best we hole up for some breakfast," Porter said. "Let them run their roadblock till they decide there's no fun in it anymore."

"I'm sorry I got you into this," Tom said.

"Weren't you got me in it. Done the deed myself. Anyway, nothin's been this interestin' since 'ghanistan, back in the long ago."

"Afghanistan?"

"Never a dull moment in 'ghanistan."

"How long were you there?"

"Long enough to be ready for home."

26

Cornell sat on the edge of the bed, his long legs sticking straight out, taped at ankles and knees as if he were some half-wrapped mummy. He stared at his large hands, which were bound firmly at the wrists. Whoever had secured him had done so with his forearms pressed together, most likely with the notion that this further restricted him, though in fact it helped facilitate escape.

The tedious way to free himself from duct tape was to find something with a ninety-degree angle—the leading edge of a wall, the corner of a piece of furniture, such as the top of the nearby nightstand—and work it with a sawing motion until the tape finally parted. This could take fifteen minutes, half an hour, even longer depending on the quality of the tape. Cornell felt too great an urgency to try this approach, and he hoped the other technique he had learned would work as well as when, in the past, he'd practiced it after being repeatedly taped by a survivalist trainer who was careful not to touch him.

Even the strongest of men, finding themselves bound in this manner, were helpless for two reasons. First, they strained against their bonds, confident in the power of their muscles, but it wasn't strength that could defeat duct tape. When pulling hard had zero effect, they became psychologically drained, and defeatism set in.

When using a roll of duct tape, it was possible to rip off a piece without scissors by tearing it on the bias, at the angle that took advantage of the weak diagonal in the ply. He could tear it like paper if he got the angle right.

Raising his long arms as high above his head as he could reach, he heard his misshapen shoulder blades crackle like a string of pop beads coming apart. He sat like that for a moment, as if holding a yoga pose. Then in a single, sudden, smooth, swift motion, he pulled his arms simultaneously down and out to his sides, like a Wild West gunfighter going for the weapons holstered on his hips. He had to make two more attempts, but on the third try, the tape split, and his wrists were freed from each other.

He peeled off the broken tape and wadded it and set it in a neat ball on the nightstand. He stripped the tape off his face. He extracted a sodden washcloth—*yuck*—from his mouth and almost set it on the nightstand, but he decided it would mar the finish, so he put it on a pillow instead.

Just then he realized that whoever had bound him had not merely touched him but had touched *his face*, possibly even *his mouth*. This was such a terrible violation of his privacy that Cornell started to go full-on fruitcake again.

A few years earlier, in preparation for the sudden collapse of civilization that would make it hard to find a first-rate dentist, Cornell had had all his teeth extracted and replaced with implants on titanium posts that were embedded in his jaw bones. Although the anesthesiologist wore nitrile gloves, her touch had nevertheless been nearly intolerable; fortunately, she'd been able to put him into a deep twilight sleep quickly. The periodontist promised to wear nitrile gloves as well; whether he did or not, he had worked while Cornell slept, so Cornell had not been consciously aware of whatever horror had been perpetrated on him.

Likewise, he had been asleep during this latest face-touching mouth-touching outrage, which made it possible for him to control his fear now, before it overwhelmed him and forced him to curl into a ball, like an armadillo, in defense against a threatening world.

He found the end of the duct tape that wound repeatedly around his knees. As he stripped it off his pajamas, he surveyed the room for something that could be used as a weapon.

The bedroom was a pretty space. On rosewood Japanese chests used as nightstands stood a pair of figured porcelain lamps with pleated golden-silk shades. The draperies were also golden, and a gold-and-blue armchair was served by an ornate little table with an intricately inlaid marble top. It was not the kind of room where you found shotguns or swords or even baseball bats.

Cornell unwound the last of the tape from his knees and then freed his ankles and rose from the edge of the bed.

Next he needed to locate Mr. Riggowitz, and together they needed to find the boy and rescue him, if he remained to be found and rescued. The task ahead was daunting, with the chance of being touched multiple times and even of having to touch someone else, if just to knock him flat.

As often in his troubled life, Cornell Jasperson took comfort in the music of Mr. Paul Simon, who had sung, *Before you learn to fly, learn how to fall.*

Cornell had been falling through life almost since the day that his mother, a drug-addicted prostitute, had given birth to him. For a long time, he'd fallen like a rock bouncing down the side of a bottomless canyon wall until he learned how to control himself. He had survived a lot of falling, and he was ready to fly.

27

Bobby Deacon was getting worried that the dart-pistol dose was indeed too much for the kid and that the little brat, still sleeping soundly in the kitchen chair, was comatose or something.

He grabbed a fistful of the kid's hair and lifted his head. He peeled back the left eyelid and the pupil of the eye looked maybe too small, a tiny dot. He checked out the right eye, and that pupil seemed larger, though he couldn't be sure. Anyway, Bobby didn't know a damn thing about medicine; he could have spent an hour studying the boy's eyes without learning anything other than their color.

With concern, he took the kid's pulse. Maybe it was much too slow for the heartbeat of a sleeping child, maybe not, but at least it seemed steady.

Well, if the punk was brain-damaged, he remained valuable. He could still be used to lure Jane Hawk. The powers that be, whoever they were, wanted her no less intensely than Gollum wanted the One

Ring of Power with which to rule Middle Earth. Bobby Deacon totally understood Gollum. Totally. Understood him better than Tolkien did. Gollum should have been the one real hero of *The Lord of the Rings* movies, not pretty boy Frodo. Gollum had his head on straight. In a way, this boy was the One Ring, and Bobby would deliver him to the rulers of Mordor for a kingly ransom.

Jane Hawk didn't have to know if now maybe her kid had the IQ of a turnip. He still looked like a cute little hobbit.

Bobby let go of the twisted hair, and the kid's head fell forward again, his chin on his chest.

28

The low gray sky no longer foaming, instead spitting flecks of crystal spittle. The wind now merely a breeze, but as cold as the ancient bones of a mammoth buried deep in arctic ice. The lightbars of the police SUVs cast fleeting swaths of color through the snow-bleached landscape, and every vehicle that arrives at the roadblock raises the hope in Wainwright Hollister that he will get his hands on the treacherous Thomas Buckle.

The two Sno-Cats are positioned miles to the east, to block fresh traffic until such a time that all the drivers who might possibly have picked up the film director can be questioned and their vehicles inspected.

Two rayshaws are present, and all of the sheriff's deputies manning the roadblock are adjusted people bearing nanoweb brain implants. At the very start of the revolution, Hollister made the county his personal kingdom, not merely by the expenditure of tens of millions in largesse, but also by seeing to the injection of every local, county, state, and federal law-enforcement officer in this territory, as well as every elected official. Those currently at this roadblock have control mechanisms that have been accessed with these words: *Do you see the red queen?* They are ready to do what they are told. If anything occurs here about which the outside world should not be informed, these deputies will be ordered to forget that it happened, whereupon their programs will erase every memory of the event.

With a rayshaw to his left and a uniformed deputy to his right, Hollister personally questions each driver. Another deputy opens car trunks and inspects the cargo spaces in trucks and vans.

One by one, the vehicles are cleared, and the search progresses uneventfully—until two strange occurrences, the first hair-raising, the second more so.

They let a Mercury Mountaineer pass through the blockade, and behind it a Porsche Cayenne rolls up to the stop line. The window purrs down. A male driver, a woman passenger. Although Hollister isn't wearing a uniform, the man behind the wheel asks, "What's the hubbub all about, Officer?"

Tom Buckle isn't in the SUV, and Hollister is about to ask if the driver has seen a man in snowsuit pants and a flannel shirt being taken aboard another vehicle. Then he looks again at the woman in the front passenger seat and sees that, with one breast exposed, she is nursing a baby in her arms.

Rather curtly, the woman says, "There's a draft from the open window. Don't you see I have a baby here?"

Hollister looks up from the breast to her face, and he knows her. She is his own mother, she who twice tried to deny him a portion of his inheritance, first by getting pregnant with a second heir, and then by divorcing his father with the intention of taking young Wainwright from the grand estate to a lesser dwelling. Their eyes lock, and her stare has a familiar imperial arrogance, a dark gleam of accusation and contempt. Hollister lowers his gaze to the suckling infant once more. Although the countenances of babies had always before seemed alike to him, undifferentiated blobs, he sees in this one his brother, Diederick Deodatus, the very face over which he held a suffocating pillow so many years earlier.

A fear unlike any he's ever experienced before overcomes him—a shrinking and anxious dread—a sense that some horror will shortly befall him.

She says something more. Whatever words she might have spoken, he hears, *You'll rot in Hell with Mrs. Ripley,* which refers to the head housekeeper who lied under oath, testifying that Mother had tortured young Hollister, burned and flayed him.

Even in the grip of the apparition, Hollister realizes that this woman in the Porsche is not his mother, only vaguely resembles her. She is far too young to be Mother. And Diederick Deodatus is safely dead, by now mere bones in a box, no threat to him anymore. He chokes back a cry of fright and waves the Porsche through the blockade.

He attributes this brief delusion not to frustration and stress and fear of failure, but instead to the residual effect of whatever hallucinogen Thomas Buckle slipped into his food or drink hours previously.

Six vehicles later, a white Mercedes SUV cruises to the stop line, and brings with it a second confrontation far stranger than the first.

29

At eighty-one, Bernie Riggowitz could no longer rely on eight hours per night of uninterrupted sleep. He was routinely obliged to make two trips to the bathroom to take a pee, the consequence of a prostate the size of a cantaloupe.

Sometimes he was awakened by acid reflux because he'd forgotten to take a Pepcid AC before dinner. On those occasions, he chewed two antacid tablets from an economy-size jar he kept on the nightstand, and he sat in the armchair until they had worked.

Occasionally he fell asleep in the chair and dreamed. Lately he'd been dreaming of cheese kreplach and his late wife, Miriam. Often Miriam was making kreplach, and at other times they were eating it together, or they were feeding them to their grandchildren, who in reality were now adults, but who were still little children in the dreams. He didn't know why he dreamed as much about kreplach as about Miriam, whom he'd loved infinitely more than cheese. Maybe it was because, at his age, the time for kreplach was running out; he doubted very much that kreplach were served after death.

Anyway, he had fallen asleep in the chair again, in the pool of light from a floor lamp.

Never before, however, had he awakened to find a thin metal dart protruding from a throbbing pain in his shoulder. Nor had he ever been dizzy in quite the same way, or bound at the ankles and wrists with duct tape, with his arms strapped to the chair arms and loop after loop of duct tape encircling his chest and the backrest of the chair, as if some cockamamie spider, spinning tape instead of web silk, had secured him to be eaten later.

He was gagged, too, and his lips sealed with yet more tape. When he tried to cry out for help, he sounded like a kitten stuck far, far down in a drain pipe.

If something terrible had happened to the *boychik,* Travis, who he was supposed to be sheltering, protecting . . . Well, better he should have been shot in the head in his sleep than this. The room was warm, but the thought that Travis might have been taken away chilled Bernie to the bone.

He struggled against his bonds to no avail, and then the door eased open and Cornell Jasperson stepped into the room. The big man was barefoot in pajamas and a robe, and he seemed to have his right hand stuck in a bronze vase.

Cornell quietly closed the door and came to the armchair. He peered down at Bernie from his great height and then raised one finger to his lips. "Ssshhhh."

Bernie nodded to indicate he understood the need to be quiet.

As if it were a glove, Cornell took the bronze vase off his hand and set it on the table beside the chair. He bent forward and studied the length of duct tape sealing Bernie's mouth. With thumb and forefinger, he reached for a corner of the tape, but then he shuddered as if with revulsion and withdrew his hand.

From a pocket of his robe, he removed a pair of tweezers. He lowered his face close to Bernie again, and with an expression of disgust, he used the tweezers to pinch a corner of the tape. Slowly he peeled it up until he had a sufficient length that he could pull with his fingers, without risking any contact with Bernie's face. He ripped the tape off and folded it and put it on the table.

As Bernie used his tongue to work the sodden washcloth out of his mouth, Cornell said in the softest whisper, "Travis isn't in his room. But he's probably okay. He's okay. He has to be okay. They're in the kitchen, I think. I saw light, heard noises."

The washcloth fell into Bernie's lap. "Who are they?"

"Maybe he. Or she," whispered Cornell. "I use the pronoun *they* only speculatively."

From a pocket of his bathrobe, he withdrew a small pair of scissors and worked the blades.

He said, "Umm, umm, umm," and seemed to be embarrassed.

"What's the matter?" Bernie hissed.

"I trim my nose hairs with these," the giant whispered. "Will it sicken you if I use them to cut you loose?"

"A person could think you're pulling my leg here."

Cornell blinked at him in confusion.

Bernie glanced at the door, expecting it to be thrown open at any moment. "Begin already, before I *plotz*."

With his tongue pinched between his teeth in concentration, Cornell began to cut away the duct tape.

30

Ninety-two minutes after he left Carmine Vestiglia's sixteenth-floor apartment, Sutcliff "Sutty" Sutherland returned with a guy whom he introduced as "John Jones, a friend of Joe." The Joe would be Senator Joseph Ford Kargrew.

Whatever his real name might be, John Jones was a tall, slim, handsome Latino in mirror-polished black shoes and a crisply pressed five-thousand-dollar suit.

Each man pulled a large wheeled suitcase, and Sutty also carried a valise.

John Jones asked if they could put the suitcases on one of the Roche Bobois sofas, and Carmine said yes, and the two men opened the huge bags, which were packed full of banded stacks of hundred-dollar bills. Carmine didn't bother to count it, because they were all gentlemen, and Jones closed the bags and left them on the sofa.

The three went outside, onto the expansive deck. They sat at the lacquered-metal table with the glass top. Street noise ascended somewhat louder than it had earlier, but Carmine nevertheless switched on the iPod, giving them the cover of Sinatra.

Jones said, "My client is pleased to be able to provide the venture capital for this enterprise."

Carmine figured Jones for an attorney.

"If this business is successful, my client will receive certain . . . regulatory relief."

His client was most likely a Central American drug lord. Men in that business could produce twenty million in cash considerably faster than even a crooked senator.

"If the business should fail," Jones continued, "my client will expect the return of his full investment, to the penny."

"*My* client," Carmine said, "he only deals in Tiffany-quality merchandise and always delivers."

Sutty Sutherland leaned forward in his chair. "Maybe it's time we had his name."

"Like I already told you, I ain't got his real name. Calls himself Max Schreck. I once happened to know a hotel where he was stayin', so I had him checked out. He registered there as Conrad Veidt."

"That won't be his name, either," Sutty said.

"No, it won't."

"What number do you have for him?"

"I ain't got no number. He uses burner phones. He calls me, never the other way around." Carmine consulted his wristwatch. "Should be ringin' me soon."

Sutty put his valise on the table and opened it, revealing a mystification of electronics. "Give me your cell."

After a hesitation, Carmine presented his iPhone.

Sutty unspooled a cord from the valise and plugged it into the charging port of Carmine's phone and returned it to him.

Appalled, Carmine said, "You ain't gonna record this?"

"Do I look like an idiot?"

"Right now, yeah."

"We're not recording. We need to get a location on him."

"You can trace a burner phone?"

"With a setup like this, yeah."

Carmine pulled the jack out of his phone. "Soon as you know where he is, the swap ain't on his terms. You'll just go in and snatch the kid."

Sutty looked at John Jones, and the attorney said, "Mr. Vestiglia, I mean this as no reflection on the sterling reputation for trustworthiness that you enjoy in your business."

"Don't go blowin' smoke up my ass."

The attorney continued: "I imagine you and your client have agreed to something like a twenty-five-percent fee for facilitating this deal."

Carmine said nothing.

"But you're a practical man, as we all are here, and you should know that as long as this business concludes successfully, my client doesn't care who gets what from those suitcases."

"And neither does Joe," Sutty said, referring to his boss, the senator.

"As far as we're concerned," the attorney said, "you're the one who found the little yellow marshmallow Easter-basket chicken, and the proceeds are yours. But I leave the decision entirely to you, because you're a practical man with much more common sense than we see in most people these days."

Carmine was deeply offended that they assumed his principles were as flexible as boiled linguini. He brooded for a minute on the sharpest response that would scorn them and establish his virtue beyond question. In the end, he said nothing, but plugged the jack into the charging port of his phone.

31

In the dream, she stood in an unfamiliar room, at a casement window that she had cranked open. Beyond the sill lay that palpable darkness devoid of even the faintest glimmer of light, in which she sensed elaborate structures and a vast labyrinth of unseen streets through which multitudes hurried on urgent missions, revealed only by their footsteps and desperate breathing. A man spoke behind her. *What did you see, Janey?* In turning toward him, she transformed into a child, and before her stood her father, Martin Duroc, mortally close and gazing down with a gargoyle expression. *What did you see?* His hands were at his sides, clenched into fists, not the hands of a world-famous pianist, but those of a murderer. She said that she'd seen nothing. *What did you hear, Janey?* His fists looked as hard as stone, and his eyes were sharp. She thought he could cut her with just his stare. *What did you hear, girl?* She said that she'd heard nothing, nothing, nothing. Just then a voice came from the hateful hive beyond the night window. *Mommy? Where are you? Where are you, Mommy?* In turning away from her father, Jane grew from a child into a woman. The voice from the realm of the enslaved was that of her precious child. Travis. *I'm afraid. I'm so afraid. Where are you, Mommy?* She called to the boy and reached out the open window, her hand disappearing, as though it had been cut off at the wrist. She told him to follow her voice, to reach out, to find her hand, but Travis couldn't find her. The more urgently that she called to him and the farther she reached into the amputating blackness, the farther away his voice grew, until from a great distance he ceased to speak, but screamed instead.

Jane sat up straight in the armchair in the room at the Holiday Inn. After a moment, she realized that the fist knocking on a door was a sound internal to her, the pumping of her heart rampant with terror. She wiped a hand down her face to slough off the lingering web of sleep.

Vikram Rangnekar was working with his laptop at the small writing desk.

As Jane got to her feet, she said, "Getting it done?"

"Almost finished."

She consulted her watch. "They'll be here in twenty minutes."

"Bring 'em on."

After she used the bathroom and washed her hands, she stared into the mirror, wondering how fear could coil in her heart without being visible in her face. The instruction she received at Quantico had little or nothing to do with this tightly controlled demeanor. Maybe it was a consequence of a childhood during which she'd had to conceal her fear of Martin Duroc; for had he suspected what she'd seen and heard the night her mother died, he would have engineered some tragic accident to eliminate the threat she posed. Surviving her father might have been essential training for the task before her in this dark time of unprecedented terror.

When she returned to the hotel room, Vikram had closed his laptop. He stood at the window overlooking the parking lot.

She went to him and put a hand on his shoulder and stared out at North French Street baking in the desert sun. "How're you doing?"

"I'm okay. I'm ready."

"No matter what happens, just drive."

"I'm with the program. But I'm worried about Ganesh. I should have known, smart as he is, he's still like a big kid."

"You can't worry about him right now. You have to worry about yourself, stay sharp."

From some high gyre, a red-tailed hawk plunged into the parking lot, snatched something off the blacktop, stabbed the thing several times with its killing beak, and soared past their window, away. Jane glimpsed a half-dead snake clutched in the talons, wriggling feebly, its mouth fixed on one of the bird's feet. The moment seemed to be an omen—but of what?

32

"Sit very still, please and thank you," Cornell whispered to Bernie. "I don't want to cut you instead of the tape. Don't want to cut you. Don't want to cut you."

Two weeks earlier, in a desperate moment in Texas, Jane Hawk had been in need of wheels, and she had taken Bernie Riggowitz's Mercedes E350 with him in it. She needed not just a car but also someone who could give her cover, because the highway patrol was looking for a woman alone. Neither of them could have foreseen that they would spend twelve eventful hours together, that he would come to love her like a daughter, and that when the previous guardians of Travis were murdered, he would help her rescue the boy and would bring him here to live in Nasia and Segev's house.

Bernie had also not foreseen that he might fail Jane and the boy, because he had spent his life taking care of others, mostly because he wanted to, sometimes because it just turned out that way. He wasn't a *shlemiel*. He'd built a business, raised a family, loved a wife faithfully. Yes, he could make like a faucet sometimes, get all emotional, tear up at a *shmaltzy* movie to such an extent that Miriam had teased him about it. He had watched *Love Story* and *Terms of Endearment* and *Steel Magnolias* maybe ten times each, trying to inoculate himself against sentimentality, but it was hopeless.

The only thing keeping his tears at bay now was that Cornell thought someone was in the kitchen, which meant maybe Travis might not yet have been taken away.

"Hurry already," he whispered to Cornell. "Better you should cut me than let them make off with the boy."

"I'm doing my worst," Cornell whispered, because his condition sometimes caused him to use the wrong word. "I mean breast. I'm doing my breast."

Bernie did not have a good feeling about this.

33

Bobby Deacon called Carmine Vestiglia in Las Vegas. When the fence answered—"Yeah?"—Bobby said, "You know who this is?"

"The twenty-million-dollar man," said Carmine.

Staring at the sleeping boy, Bobby considered the fence's statement. "Did I win the lottery and don't know it?"

"Minus twenty-five-percent finder's fee."

On the phone, in the background, Sinatra was singing "Strangers in the Night."

Bobby had thought maybe three million, two and a quarter after Carmine's take. This bigger number scared him more than it pleased him. He knew this was a big deal, Jane Hawk and all, but twenty million rather than five meant it was a lot damn bigger than he'd understood. Maybe too big. Did anyone really pay twenty million for something like this and just let you walk away?

Into Bobby's silence, Carmine said, "I got it right here, pal. So how you wanna make the trade?"

"You have it that fast?"

"You got a hot commodity, pal. Buyer's anxious, don't wanna bargain, just do the deal."

"I have to think how to do it."

"So think. I'll hold."

"Call you back," Bobby said, and he pressed END.

34

The cold is unearthly, as if Hollister has been transported to a frozen planet far from its sun. He is sweating inside his storm suit, but he isn't warm. His face is slick with sweat, and he feels his features stiffening as though the bitter air is turning that salty film to ice. Although he frequently rubs his face with a gloved hand, there is no ice, yet his features remain stiff. He grows colder, shivering violently.

After the Porsche Cayenne that carried the breast-feeding woman who wasn't Hollister's mother, five drivers present their vehicles for inspection without incident. Then comes the Mercedes SUV.

The window in the driver's door powers down, and behind the wheel sits a young Asian woman in a black suit and scarlet scarf. At first the scarf doesn't seem to be of silk, but then it is, and at first the driver isn't Mai-Mai, but then she becomes Mai-Mai.

When Hollister looks past the driver, he sees another young Asian woman in the passenger seat. She isn't wearing a red scarf, but she also becomes Mai-Mai. Driver and passenger are identical twins.

The rear window on the driver's side opens, and a third Mai-Mai peers out at Hollister.

The power that flows from a multibillion-dollar fortune is intoxicating. As an only child of a billionaire and eventually a far wealthier man than his father, Hollister has led a life of economic inebriation. Long ago he found there is a limit to the exhilaration that comes with buying things, even extravagantly expensive items. A time arrives when, after one acquires everything one can ever want, boredom sets in, a creeping sense that life is meaningless. He's been drunk on money for so many years, he needs that high no less than a heroin addict needs his next injection. He can't live happily without it. Another man in such a condition might seek purpose in philanthropy, but Wainwright Hollister is no more likely to give away his fortune than he is to donate his eyes to a blind man. Having suffocated his infant brother to get a full inheritance, he intends to keep it. Although buying things no longer gives him a money high, he still has one source of inebriation: wielding power over others. Year by year, preserving his image as everyone's best friend, he destroys his rivals, as well as people with whom he just fiercely disagrees, through surrogates, always surrogates, so his targets never know the true agent of their ruination. Eventually, however, even breaking others financially, emotionally, and mentally begins to seem like warm beer. Which is when Dr. Bertold Shenneck's spectacular research into nanotech-programmed behavior control comes along. What power could be more intoxicating than the power to physically and mentally *possess* others and, through possession of them, change the world—the entire world!—to one's liking? It is better than the finest cognac, better than sixty-year-old port; it is the wine of the gods. And the Hamlet list provides Hollister with the occasional opportunity to dispense with the usual surrogates—whether secret business partners or attorneys or rayshaws—and deal death directly, using his own hands. This inspires the highest high. During the past year and a half, he has ordered the destruction of many people, but he has also hunted down and killed four men and two women on the Hamlet list, which has been an eighteen-month-long, nonalcoholic bender. Wainwright Warwick Hollister is the culmination of human history, the ultimate emperor for whom the multitudes have yearned for thousands of years, and no one can win against him.

Except perhaps Thomas Buckle.

Hollister is crashing from lifelong economic inebriation into desperately unwanted sobriety, exhausted and confused and, for the moment, powerless against the clever filmmaker. The opposite of absolute power is total impotence, an intolerable fate; he isn't there yet, but he is falling, falling, falling from the heights.

He seems even to be experiencing the equivalent of the delirium tremens that alcoholics endure when they are denied the poison to which they have become habituated: herewith, three Mai-Mais in a Mercedes SUV. He tries to see them as three young Asian women, each a unique person, but they insist on being Mai-Mai in triplicate.

This is something more than delirium, not a mere hallucination.

The bitch won't stay dead. Her resurrection must have something to do with the fact that Thomas Buckle, *a moviemaker,* witnessed her suicide. In the movies, people frequently return from the dead. Dracula is staked through the heart, subsides into dust—but then appears in a sequel. That is not magic, of course, only fiction. However, maybe Buckle is on the Hamlet list not only because of the films he makes, but also because he has some otherworldly power.

Only two vehicles remain in the lineup behind the Mercedes. Hollister orders the driver in the red scarf to pull through the barricade of police cars and then to the shoulder of the highway.

Three vehicles still wait to be inspected, but they can't see what happens beyond the barricade.

Earlier Hollister inserted a fresh magazine in his pistol. He returns now to the Mercedes, in which Mai-Mai watches solemnly with six eyes. If he can make her stay dead, he will prove that his power is still greater than that of Thomas Buckle. As the deputies and rayshaws watch without objection or shock, Hollister blows out the windows of the SUV, killing the women. He pulls open the doors and riddles their bodies, killing them again.

They have put off their Mai-Mai masks and look nothing like her anymore.

Thomas Buckle must be found.

35

The sun ascending cast shadow on the sixteenth-floor deck where Carmine Vestiglia cursed Max Schreck and Conrad Veidt and whoever else the weird skinny bastard might be. The geek had hung up too quickly.

"But he'll be calling back," said the stylish Latino attorney whose name was so phony it ought to have quotation marks around it every time it was spoken: *My name is quotation marks John Jones quotation marks.*

Studying the readouts in the open valise that was crammed with electronics beyond Carmine's comprehension, Sutty Sutherland said, "We got the number of his burner and a partial location. The call was carried through an exchange in Scottsdale, Arizona. But the satellite didn't have time to get a full GPS position on him. It needed like another thirty seconds."

The three of them stared at Carmine's iPhone.

36

Cornell couldn't understand why the villain, whoever the villain might be, had virtually cocooned Mr. Riggowitz in duct tape, but had restrained Cornell so much less thoroughly. Mr. Riggowitz was bound to the chair as if the villain intended him to die there and be unable to escape until he turned to dust.

"I'm getting you loose, almost there," Cornell whispered.

"Gevalt!" Mr. Riggowitz whispered when the last of the tape was torn from him. He at once sprang up from the armchair as if he were eight instead of eighty-one. "I have a loaded gun in the nightstand drawer."

37

The clocks in the kitchen ovens and the one in the microwave were all digital, but Bobby Deacon could nevertheless hear them ticking. He could hear the planet rotating ominously through yet another hour. He could hear the universe expanding outward in all directions, fourteen billion years and counting, as surely as he could hear his heart pumping away the minutes of his life.

The twenty million dollars so scared Bobby that he didn't want it anymore. He was worth five million, and he had taken ten years to steal that much—a hundred thousand here, fifty thousand there, two hundred thousand. Scoring a cool fifteen million in one day was for sure jumping the shark.

As a dedicated agent of justice, he knew too well how many unjust sonsofbitches were lurking around every corner; this world was infested with the vermin. He stole in the name of the people, even though the people didn't appreciate it and though they often weren't worth having a champion like him. Anytime you stood up for the people and spoke truth to the powerful by swiping their stuff, you risked putting your neck on the chopping block. Bobby was a hero. He allowed himself no doubt that he was a hero; but there never had been a hero born who didn't die.

He speed-dialed Carmine Vestiglia's number, and the fence picked it up on the first ring.

"You know who this is?" Bobby asked.

"No," Carmine said irritably. "Who the hell is this, the queen of England, callin' to talk about tea?"

"I don't want it," said Bobby.

"Don't want what?"

"I don't want to be the twenty-million-dollar man."

"What'cha do, snort a kilo, you're so coked-up you forgot what money's for?"

"I'm grateful and all, but it's too big for me."

"Wait, wait, wait," Carmine said. "Don't go leavin' me here hangin' out to dry in front of these people who come through so good for us."

"That's the problem. I'm scared of those people."

"You ain't even met 'em. These bastards are salt of the earth. Gimme a minute to talk some sense into you."

"Sorry," Bobby said, and he terminated the call.

38

Bernie Riggowitz had founded a company to make and sell wigs up and down the East Coast, and he'd done well over the years, he and Miriam. Bernie knew how to succeed in business, and he was a pretty good father, and he was a better husband than father because not for a moment did he ever fall out of love during sixty-one years of marriage, but he didn't claim to be a man of action. At five feet seven, weighing about 140 pounds, with a little potbelly, he was not a butt-kicking head-busting tough guy. But he knew how to shoot.

During their retirement years, he and Miriam had driven to every corner of this gorgeous country, seeing the sights. America was as big as it was beautiful, and in all the bigness, there were long stretches of dauntingly lonely highway. Once in a while, some hard-boiled types would pull up alongside them, match their speed, and look them over, like contemporary pirates calculating whether the potential booty was worth committing homicide. If glaring back at the thugs failed to convince them that they would be met with resistance, then whoever was riding shotgun—Bernie or Miriam—would reach under the seat and pull a pistol and hold it in clear sight of the scoundrels, which always convinced them to drive on. There never was a need to fire the gun—except during monthly target practice at whatever shooting range might be near them in their travels.

These days, Bernie's weapon of choice was a Springfield TRP-Pro chambered for .45 ACP. It had some kick, but he could control it. He hoped never to use it other than on a shooting range, but if he had to pull the trigger to defend the boy, he wouldn't hesitate.

The pistol wasn't in the nightstand drawer where he'd left it. Bernie knew he didn't suffer from early dementia. He was as sharp as every point on the Shield of David. He still possessed a wigmaker's attention to detail. He never misplaced things, especially things as important as guns. No reason to search the other nightstand or under a pillow or beneath the bed. The *momzer* who had darted and taped him had found the gun and taken it.

39

The kid woke and looked around, but his eyes were heavy, and he slipped into sleep again.

Bobby Deacon got up from the kitchen table and stood looking at the smug little pretty boy, the sleeping brat with the oh-so-sweet face that advertisers would love if he had popped out of some other bitch besides Jane Hawk. It was a face that could sell a gazillion of anything. How many times had this kid been told he was cute or adorable or handsome? Perfect hair, perfect skin, perfect features, blue eyes as dazzling as his mother's. Such a little darling. And now he was the twenty-million-dollar punk. Nobody would have coughed up even twenty bucks to ransom Bobby Deacon when he was five years old. The fact is, they would have paid the kidnappers to *keep* him.

Bobby took off the blouse of his medical scrubs, revealing the white T-shirt with the red skull and the words AGENT OF JUSTICE. He was ready to act in the name of equality, for all the unpretty people who suffered because of the unearned privileges that pretty boys and pretty girls enjoyed at their expense. He picked up the Rambo III knife, two pounds five ounces of sweet justice, pointed to pierce and stropped to slice. If Travis had been a girl, Bobby would have raped her before disfiguring her, but he wasn't hot for little boys that way. Because the punk wasn't a girl, because he denied Bobby an orgasm, the cutting would have to be extensive. If one pleasure was to be withheld, then in the name of justice, the other would have to be enhanced.

40

Sutty Sutherland looked up from the data displays in the valise. "We have an address in Scottsdale."

"I ever see that asshole again," Carmine said, "that freak Max, he ever brings me business again, I'll cut his nuts off and call him Maxine."

"I have to phone the senator with this," Sutty said. "He wants to give the information to the director of the FBI personally."

As Sutty stepped away from the table with his smartphone and turned his back to them, the attorney who could have been a *GQ* model said, "I regret that things didn't work out as planned."

Carmine switched off Sinatra. "What's this 'regret' shit?"

"Your man didn't produce the package as you warranted that he would."

"*My* man? He ain't my man. I don't do men. You got what you paid for. Sutty knows where to find the kid."

Carmine turned the valise so that he could examine the amazing electronics, which would mean nothing to him if he studied the damn thing for a year. But the data displays were interesting.

The attorney wouldn't let it go. "I repeat—the package has not been delivered."

"What's this 'package' bullshit? Talk like a real person. Sutty or someone else screws it up, that's my fault? That ain't my fault."

"Anyway, it was Mr. Sutherland's technology that located the package, not your associate."

"His tech ain't worth shit without the geek calls me. And he called twice."

"The terms of our contract have not been fulfilled."

"'Contract'? I ain't signed no contract. It's a handshake deal."

The attorney smiled thinly. "We never shook hands."

Carmine needed a hammer. Better yet, a crowbar. The lacquered metal chair in which he sat was too unwieldy for the job.

Sutty Sutherland returned to the table as Carmine rose from his chair. "The senator is on the phone with the director. They'll have agents at that house in minutes."

"This shyster," Carmine said, "he's tryin' to hose me. I got a five-million fee owed here."

Sutty shook his head. "You reached too far, Carmine. Twenty freaking million. If this Max Schreck had come through, then okay. But he failed you, he failed us. No finder's fee."

Livid, his jaw clenched with such rage that he could barely open his mouth to speak, Carmine said, "I thought I was dealin' with *honorable* sonsofbitches. This ain't done. If Joe wants to keep his Saint of the Senate image, then this ain't done."

Smiling, nodding, Sutty seemed to be acknowledging Carmine's leverage, but then he said, "I admire how you take good care of your mother, Carmine, put her in a fine house, pay for her housekeeper and car and everything."

Carmine wanted to stick a shiv in the bastard. "Ain't nothin' I won't do for her, so don't you go there, don't you ever."

In spite of the warning, Sutty went there. "Your mother's in good health at sixty, so it's easy to take care of her. It would be harder if she was blind and crippled and couldn't speak because some heartless creep cut her tongue out. There's some really bad people out there these days, my friend, all these MS-13 gangster types from Central America, all kinds of bad people."

Sutty Sutherland and John Jones let themselves out of the apartment. They took the two suitcases of money with them.

41

A dust devil swooned lazily through a vacant lot. Transparent snakes of heat swayed off the street, like cobras charmed to the music of a flute.

Standing at the window in the room at the Holiday Inn, Jane Hawk said, "There's a motor home turning off North French."

Vikram returned to stand beside her. "That's it. Isn't the paint job cool? It's called 'pewter mist.'"

As the vehicle pulled into the hotel parking lot, Jane said, "It's a big sucker."

"Just thirty-six feet. The custom recess in the roof is where the satellite dish links to the motorized controls he installed."

"Here's a thought. If I'm right about Enrique's intentions, how do you know he did all the modifications you required? Maybe this vehicle is useless to you and we should just walk away now."

"It's good. After I made the deal, Cousin Harshad stayed in Nogales two days to ensure work was done to my specifications."

"You need something so big?"

"No. But Enrique said it's all he had in stock that he could modify and get to me so quickly."

"You can drive that?"

"Yeah, sure." He frowned. "Can you?"

"Yeah."

A Porsche 911 Turbo S followed the motor home. The deliveryman behind the wheel of the Southwind was probably Tio, Ricky's right hand, with whom Jane had dealt previously. The man in the Porsche would take Tio back to Ricky's operation outside of Nogales.

Her and Vikram's luggage was in the Explorer Sport, back at the motel where they had spent the previous night. Now Vikram carried his laptop and a small tote bag that contained the second half of the payment for the Fleetwood, due on delivery.

Jane kept both hands free. She said, "Showtime."

42

The punk kid came fully awake, his eyes fixed on the point of the immense knife.

Bobby Deacon was about to reshape the pretty boy's nose when the disposable phone rang. He had never given anyone the number. He hesitated to answer it, but intuition spoke to him, and he picked it up from the table.

The first thing Carmine Vestiglia said was, "I seen your number on the damn machine."

"What machine?"

"Never mind what machine. They got an address. They're comin' for you. Get outta there with the kid *right now,* so maybe this deal can be saved."

"Who?" Bobby asked. "Who's coming?"

"Feds. They're gonna pop you, maybe do worse to my mother. The kid ain't just our payday, he's our life insurance. *Get him outta there now, now, now!*"

Carmine terminated the call, and Bobby dropped the phone.

This was exactly what he'd been afraid would happen if he took the twenty million, so he'd turned it down, but now it was *still* happening. Wasn't that the way it always went? The powers that be were the powers who had always been, and they were the powers who would always be into the far future, masters of injustice. A little guy like Bobby Deacon, born unpretty, could work hard all his life to get ahead, and it mattered for nothing. Oh, he was allowed to have small wins—a hundred thousand dollars here, fifty thousand there. But when his one big chance came along, his self-appointed betters said, *No, this is too much for you. You have forgotten your place. You must be dealt with.* He had backed away from the twenty million, had realized the shitstorm it would bring down on him, but now they were going to kill him for even thinking about going for the brass ring. And Carmine Vestiglia was no ally, hell no, telling him to take the kid and run. Bobby hated kids. He hated dealing with them. Kids didn't have fully developed brains. They were packages of craziness, totally unpredictable. He'd had hard experience of kids. The feds were coming to kill him and grab the kid, so if he took Little Mr. Pretty with him, they would chase him forever. Anyway, he didn't have *time* to take the kid. He needed to get out of here *now, now, now.* His sweet life was falling apart, was shattering for one reason: Little Mr. Pretty before whom the whole damn world bowed and scraped. If Bobby might never put his life back together, at least he'd have the satisfaction of taking this snot-nosed brat apart—a bit of justice, balancing the scales. Getting out with the little shit would take ten times longer than just killing him and running.

As he raised high the enormous knife to plunge into the little bastard's face, Bobby glimpsed sudden movement at the periphery of his vision. He turned his head and discovered the shambling mis-jointed giant coming at him with no good intention. This was yet another injustice, considering that, as one unpretty person showing respect for another unpretty person, he'd restrained this man only to the extent necessary, leaving him more comfortable than he left old Riggowitz. Consideration is repaid with treachery.

Instead of stabbing the kid, Bobby slashed at the giant. The ungrateful sonofabitch swung a fist encased in a weird metal glove, and the knife rapped off it, a bronze-bell echo clanging through the kitchen. Numbing reverberations traveled the steel blade, through the hilt, into Bobby's hand, and he almost dropped the Rambo.

Like some freaky knight with an armored hand, the giant struck Bobby upside the head. The *klonk* passing through his skull shook a dust of darkness off the rafters of his mind, dimming his vision.

The giant was strong and quick, with long arms. He was going to win this fight, maybe with the next blow. If this was to be the end of Bobby Deacon, he would go out as an agent of justice, balance the scales with his final act. Instead of trying to cut the giant, he dodged a blow, turned to Little Mr. Pretty, grabbed the punk by the hair, jerked his head back to slash a carotid artery—

43

Jane and Vikram exited the emergency staircase at the ground floor and stepped onto the hotel parking lot.

The Fleetwood Southwind stood across five or six spaces in the last row, alongside North French Street, and the Porsche 911 Turbo S waited behind it.

After the warm night, the morning had grown warmer. Traffic noise was curiously muted in the still air. The palm trees looked weary in the pebbled planting beds. As if they had forgotten how to fly, half a dozen silent crows seemed to fall through the sun-shot sky onto the roof of a building across the street.

Tio opened the front door of the motor home and stepped down to the blacktop. Perhaps thirty, he was the size of those jockeys who rode the big-money horses. Leaving the door open behind him, he watched Jane and Vikram approach.

The driver of the Porsche remained behind the wheel and didn't switch off the engine. He'd accompanied Tio when a similar delivery had recently been made to Jane in Indio, California, south of Palm Springs. On that occasion, he never got out of the car. But she didn't trust that his purpose was again limited to driving Tio back to Nogales; he would be armed.

Of the other vehicles parked on this side of the hotel complex, none appeared to be occupied. No one else was on foot at the moment.

"*Bonita chica*," Tio said as Jane came to a halt a few feet from him, "seein' you twice in a week is like the sun shines just for me, and that's no shit."

"You're a real charmer, Tio."

A thick white welt of scar tissue bisected his Adam's apple, evidence of a throat slashing that he'd survived. The experience had failed to affect his voice.

"I hope someday I see you again with your gold hair, no wig, your own blue eyes, no funny makeup, so my breath is taken away."

"Sorry I look like a *shlump* this morning." Indicating Vikram, she said, "You know Mr. Rangnekar."

"We never met," said Tio. "But Enrique, he explained him to me. You have the delivery payment?"

Vikram held up the tote.

Tio smiled and nodded. "So let's do the deal inside."

"No," Jane said. "Let's do it right here."

Still smiling, Tio surveyed the parking lot, the windows of the hotel rooms. "It's too public for countin' money."

"Counting? Does Ricky no longer trust me?" she asked.

His smile became pained. "Enrique, he don't know this man well, but *you* he forever trusts and admires. Enrique hopes you get tired bein' a widow. You know how strong he feels about you. When you're ready so Enrique can adore you, he'll adore you like no woman's ever been adored by a man. I once told you, he's hung like a horse."

" '*Un enorme garañón*,' " she said.

Tio's smile warmed again. "You remember."

"Your description made it unforgettable. If you absolutely must count Mr. Rangnekar's money, go inside and do so. We'll wait here."

To Vikram, Tio said, "But you. You need to see the changes, your satellite-dish motor."

Jane had prepared Vikram for this. He said, "I trust Mr. de Soto. And my cousin Harshad, who oversaw the work. I saw the new recess in the roof, where I'll install the dish."

Tio's smile had frozen. He looked as if he were showing off his teeth in a Pepsodent commercial—or contemplating a prostate exam. He glanced toward the Porsche. As though realizing that a protracted silence might suggest nefarious intent, he allowed his smile to thaw a little. "It don't matter we count or don't count. Key's in the ignition. Registration, proof of insurance by the kitchen sink. You look out for your sweet ass, *bonita chica*."

"You, too." She watched him go to the Porsche and get in the passenger seat and pull the door shut.

While Tio and the driver engaged in a discussion, and while perhaps Tio made a phone call, Jane walked to the corner of the lot at the intersection of North French Street and Gila Bend Highway.

The Porsche hung a 180 and drove toward an exit from the lot. It turned left on North French and came toward Jane.

She waved. The sunlight on the windshield didn't allow her to see whether Tio waved back or displayed his middle finger.

The Porsche swung right on Gila Bend.

She watched it until it was out of sight, and she returned to Vikram. "You know what to do."

"I don't like leaving you here alone."

"It would have happened here only if we'd gone inside with Tio and let the Porsche driver come behind us. Now it'll happen on the highway. Do what we discussed."

After a hesitation, Vikram set out on foot for the motel where they had left the Explorer and their luggage.

The Southwind's door remained open.

Jane moved aft of it and stood with her back to the wall of the motor home, alert and listening.

44

Wearing the metal vase on his right hand, Cornell deflected the humongous knife and then struck the bad man—a rat-faced fiend in a red-skull T-shirt!—conked him hard on the head without touching him. Cornell didn't go totally nutbar, the way he usually did when he came into contact with someone, because this time there was no skin to skin.

Cornell expected the fiend to drop as if poleaxed, but he stayed on his feet and dodged another blow. He turned to Travis, grabbed the boy by the hair, yanked his head up. The vicious rat thrust the knife forward, intending to draw it back across the tender throat in a killing cut.

The moving blade sliced air on the thrust, light drizzling along the steel. Cornell cried out in shock and despair even as Mr. Riggowitz twice fired the gun that he'd picked up from the kitchen table. For an awful instant, Cornell thought the spray of blood must be from the boy. It wasn't. Travis hadn't been harmed. The man with the knife dropped like a game of pick-up sticks spilling from a can.

Cornell never saw anyone killed before, and he never wanted to see anyone killed again, but he was glad—thrilled!—that this fiend was dead. He wanted to grab Travis and hug him and lift him high in celebration. However, though he loved Travis, he dared not touch him and thereby fall into a seizure of revulsion, incapacitating himself perhaps for hours.

Delighted as he was by the death of the fiend, Cornell was no less horrified that the child had witnessed such violence and might be forever scarred by it. Because his late mother had been a drug-addicted prostitute, Cornell had lived in a tense environment and, from an early age, had seen much violence. The doctors claimed that his personality disorder had nothing to do with those experiences, that the problem was neurological. But Cornell didn't know what to believe about that. He never had understood himself, and he never thought the doctors who diagnosed him fully understood him; in fact, he suspected that the doctors didn't understand themselves, either, that maybe they even understood themselves less than they understood him. Now he said to Travis, "It's all right, the terrible things pass, they always pass. You'll be okay, you'll be okay, okay."

The boy certainly *seemed* all right. He hadn't screamed, as Cornell had screamed. He wasn't crying. He appeared to be scared, but as Mr. Riggowitz stripped away the duct tape that bound him to the arms of the chair, the boy's voice wasn't shaky when he said, "We gotta get outta here fast. They're coming."

"Who's coming?" Mr. Riggowitz asked.

"The feds. He was real close with the phone. I could hear the other guy, too. Telling him to get out fast 'cause the feds got this address. They're gonna come pop us."

"'Pop'?" Cornell wondered.

"Kill," Mr. Riggowitz translated.

As the liberated boy overturned the dinette chair in his haste to get to his feet, Mr. Riggowitz quickly crouched beside the dead man, turned his pockets inside out. He found a wallet and then an electronic key bearing the Mercedes emblem. "If the feds have an address, they know our vehicles. Maybe they don't know his."

"Wait, wait, wait," said Cornell. "I have something in my room that I need, we need."

"*We gotta go,*" the boy insisted.

"Get your tush in gear, Cornell," said Mr. Riggowitz. "We don't have time to change. Let's go already."

We don't have time to change. Those words mystified Cornell. Most of his life, he had strived without much success to change who he was. He knew that it wasn't a matter of having *time* to change, that *time* wasn't the problem. You were who you were, and changing who you were, especially in his case, was hugely difficult, no matter whether you had minutes or decades.

"Wait, wait, wait, please and thank you," Cornell pleaded as he hurried from the kitchen.

In the few days he'd known Travis, the boy had surprised him again and again with his resilience, but Mr. Riggowitz was no less of a surprise. He was a smallish man, but he didn't act small. He had a big heart and he stepped up to every challenge. He was old, but he didn't act old. He used strange words like *plotz,* which meant burst or explode, and *bubeleh,* which was a term of endearment, and *shmegegge,* which meant a jerk, but he was one of the easiest people to understand that Cornell had ever met, maybe because he always said what he meant, without hidden intentions.

In his room, Cornell dropped to his knees, peered under the bed, withdrew a pillowcase. He had brought it from his bunker in Borrego Valley in one of his two suitcases, when they'd had to flee these same bad people on Tuesday. He'd thought they were safe here in the Cantors' house, safe forever, and now three days later they were on the run again. It was like Mr. Paul Simon had sung: *You know the nearer your destination, the more you're slip slidin' away.*

When he hurried back to the kitchen, carrying the pillowcase by its knotted neck, he expected to hear wailing sirens, helicopters, maybe even gunshots, but there was none of that. He also thought maybe the boy and the old man would be gone, but they were waiting for him; of course they were; they weren't the kind of people who ran out on you. Until he had become rich by designing popular apps, Cornell's life was in part defined by people running out on him, so he still expected to be abandoned.

They had also found the dogs, Duke and Queenie.

"For a pillow you went back?" Mr. Riggowitz said. "That's *meshugge*! Let's make like we're running for our lives, why don't we?"

The dead man's vehicle was not in the driveway. The three of them, with dogs, raced out to the street, which was when Cornell realized what Mr. Riggowitz had meant when he said *We don't have time to change*. They were all in pajamas. Bernie's slippers slapped on the pavement. Cornell and Travis were barefoot; the dogs were barefoot, too, but that was their natural condition.

The only Mercedes in sight was a white vanlike vehicle parked at the curb half a block to the south. When they got to the van, the electronic key worked.

45

In the parking lot, the Fleetwood Southwind hulked less like a vehicle than like a grand vessel, as if it were meant for seafaring or launching into space.

The thing didn't need to be as large as it was, not for their purpose. It was a bold move by Enrique de Soto to push the motor home on Vikram, considering that only days earlier he had provided one of equal size to Jane, a Tiffin Allegro, which overnight he had customized to her order. He was taking the chance that she'd wonder if he had done similar work on this Southwind and might expect a trap. Of course Ricky was nothing if not bold. And if this was a setup, the lives he would be putting on the line were those of his men, not his own. Considering his macho conviction that his sexual magnetism was irresistible and that they would hook up when Jane "got over this widow thing," he might assume she wouldn't believe that he was capable of betraying her, that she would think he had promoted the thirty-six footer only to drain as much cash from Vikram as possible. After all, Ricky's habit was to wring every dollar he could from a deal.

But she knew it was a trap.

When Vikram had blundered into that black-market operation outside Nogales, his relatives in tow, Ricky had decided that doing further business with Jane, the most-wanted fugitive in the nation, or anyone associated with her was now too dangerous. He figured to take half of Vikram's money, provide the motor home, take the rest of the money, kill Vikram, reclaim the Southwind, and have Jane brought back to Nogales in chains to spend some quality time with him.

Shortly Vikram returned in the Explorer Sport and parked behind the Southwind. Because Enrique de Soto had told him what Jane was driving, he'd known the Explorer had a rear tow hitch. He'd ordered the motor home equipped with compatible gear and a built-in electric winch. He and Jane would need about ten minutes to winch the SUV just high enough to hitch the back of it to the back of the motor home, so that only its front tires met the pavement, then install the wiring package and the auxiliary brake lights.

46

Looking for new wheels, Tio and Diablo cruised. They couldn't follow the Fleetwood in the Porsche. The bitch would make them before they'd gone a mile.

In fifteen minutes, Hawk and Rangnekar would have yoked the Explorer to the motor home and be gone. There were three main routes out of Casa Grande. West on I-8 to Gila Bend. North on I-10 to Phoenix. South on I-10 to Tucson. Also at least two state routes. They had to get back to the Holiday Inn before the motor home split. Otherwise, they were screwed.

Tio didn't want to face Enrique without the bitch on a leash. He might as well slit his own throat this time.

Street by street, they made their way into a neighborhood. Nice little stucco houses, as boring as church.

Cars parked at the curb. None of them cool. He would have to check twenty or thirty to find one with keys in it. Anyone watching would call 911.

A chicken-necked stick-thin white-haired woman. Big straw hat, long-sleeved T-shirt, khakis. Washing her Buick in the driveway. The garage door was open beyond her.

Did old ladies wash their own cars? Not often. It probably meant there wasn't a man in the house, at least not right now.

Diablo drove past the place. Pulled the Porsche to the curb.

Because he was small, could pass for ten years younger than he was, and had an innocent face, Tio took the job. Dreaming up a story to snow the old bitch, he got out of the Porsche. He walked back to the target house.

Shit happens, it happens all the time, that's life, but good luck happens, too. Just then some really good shit happened to Tio. Before she saw him approaching, the woman dropped the hose. She went into the garage for something. No neighbors in sight. He followed her in there. He drew the pistol from the belt holster under his untucked shirt.

She took a big plastic bottle of something off a shelf. When she turned, he got in her face, pressed the muzzle of the gun into her gut. "I don't wanna hurt you, Granny. I just want your car. You do right, don't lie to me, you'll be okay."

She said the key was on the front seat. Said her husband was long gone. She lived alone. She told him he was hardly more than a child, he should think about his future, take a different path. He said he *wanted* to go straight but was dirt-poor and scared. She told him about Jesus while he moved her inside the house. In the kitchen, he pistol-whipped her to the floor. When she lay unconscious, he dragged her into a walk-in pantry. He closed the door. He tilted a dinette chair under the knob to keep her from getting out until someone found her.

Outside, he rolled up the hose on its reel. Took a bucket and sponge from the driveway, set them in the garage.

The key lay on the seat. He started the engine. A remote control was clipped to the sun visor. He put down the garage door.

Diablo followed him to a supermarket parking lot, where they left the Porsche. In the Buick, Diablo driving, they headed back to the Holiday Inn.

47

Jane retrieved her tote bag from the Explorer and took from it a six-ounce bottle with a pump spray, which she slipped into an inner sport-coat pocket. She extracted a basic Taser from the tote and clipped it to her belt.

The only door to the Southwind was aft of the cockpit. Jane entered first, Vikram behind her. Immediately to her right was a free-standing Euro recliner, beyond that the cockpit with its two big comfortable seats. Directly across from the door stood a sofa.

After pulling the door shut, Vikram went directly to the driver's seat. Tio had left the electronic key in the cup holder.

After drawing the Heckler & Koch Compact .45 from her shoulder holster, Jane sat on the edge of the recliner, facing the back of the motor home, which was revealed only by smoky-bronze light that penetrated the tinted windows: the kitchen immediately to her left; the dinette opposite the kitchen; beyond the dinette, a lavatory; and at the end of the vehicle, a bedroom.

She figured two of Ricky's people must be aboard. In addition to Tio and the driver of the Porsche, one additional man might have been enough to successfully spring their trap, depending on their plan of action. But Ricky liked to have insurance. Four against her and Vikram would feel right to him. Five would be too many in the tight space of the motor home.

Vikram started the engine.

The hinged door to the bathroom was closed. Likewise the sliding door to the bedroom. The two men could be in either space. Or one in each. Or neither in either.

Maybe the sofa, a foldout sleeper, wasn't what it appeared to be. The spring-loaded mattress could have been removed from it and the sofa-cushion platform could have been raised to provide a space in which a man could lie secreted. Maybe the refrigerator-freezer was only a faux front behind which a gunman could stand full height.

The Southwind began to move.

Okay, bedroom and bath. Ricky would not have felt the need to be more clever than that. They had done a lot of business together. He expected her to trust him and enter the Southwind with Tio for the count. It was supposed to be over by now.

They would have a backup plan. From the Porsche, Tio would have called one of the men in the motor home. They weren't likely to act while the Southwind was on the streets of Casa Grande. They would figure to let her and Vikram settle in, relax. Outside of town, on whatever open highway, maybe she would be in the copilot seat, unsuspecting and easy to take from behind.

They didn't want to kill her if they could avoid it. Their assignment was surely to take her back to Nogales, to be Ricky's pump for however long he remained interested in her. They probably intended to subdue her with a Taser or maybe a compressed-air pistol that fired a sedating dart. They were also ready for her to visit the bathroom, where she could be taken by surprise.

When Vikram braked for traffic at the exit from the parking lot, he glanced back at her. She nodded and rose from the Euro recliner.

As Vikram eased the Southwind and attendant Explorer Sport into the street, Jane aimed the Heckler at the ceiling and moved toward the rear of the big vehicle.

48

Verna Amboy is interested in observing how Charlie Weatherwax will extract the urgently needed information from Ganesh Rangnekar. Together, they escort the hapless young man to one of the four offices at the back of the enormous main room of the warehouse, where the sounds produced are less likely to be heard beyond the walls of the building. Charlie carries his large black satchel of instruments.

Having participated in other such sessions with the one and only Charlie, Mustafa al-Yamani has nothing more to learn about the subject of extreme interrogation. He is pleased to let the fetching Ms. Amboy assist the master interrogator. Meanwhile, he sits at the folding table, near the computer that once again displays the words YOU HAVE BEEN VIKRAMIZED.

He does regret forgoing the opportunity to watch the lovely Verna's face as Charlie progresses from needles and pliers to the application of electric current to the subject's testicles. Mustafa wonders if her nostrils will occasionally flare like those of a cat, if she will at any time lick her lips, whether her face will flush, and what might be seen in her dark, unfathomed eyes.

But there is much more to life than work and the mysteries of one's colleagues. Mustafa takes this opportunity to peruse an issue of *GQ* in an earnest attempt to resolve his deep perplexity regarding which fragrance for men is the most suitable for the highest social circles of the better communities of Long Island, specifically for East Egg village.

Having smelled all the fragrances that are possibilities, he remains confused. Therefore, he now decides that the answer to which is the most appropriate might lie in the name of the fragrance or in the design of its bottle. A full-page advertisement for Premium Blend by Original Penguin features not a real bottle but an artist's sketchy interpretation of the bottle, which seems to be a forced attempt to associate the product with fine art. Also, the cute image of a penguin in a tuxedo strikes Mustafa as too precious. Polo Blue by Ralph Lauren is sapphire blue with a silver cap. But Bleu de Chanel comes in a stylish black container and has the edge because the spelling, *b-l-e-u*, is classier than *b-l-u-e*. Luna Rossa Sport by Prada is red and silver and appealing—but the male model in the ad looks too psychotic for East Egg. Artisan by John Varvatos comes in bottles sheathed in macramé and appears, to Mustafa anyway, to be a fragrance more suitable for Woodstock or Portland than for anywhere on Long Island.

As he broods over this complex issue, an hour passes as if it were but a minute or two. Now it seems that the sounds of distress emanating from the interrogee have escalated quicker than usual, but perhaps a greater length of time has passed than just one hour. He is surprised that such a soft specimen as Ganesh Rangnekar is proving hard to crack.

Unable to puzzle out an answer in regard to a fragrance for men, Mustafa is drawn to the consideration of another difficult matter when he arrives at three full-page ads for hair products by Axe. He does not use anything other than shampoo, conditioner, and a fixative spray, but maybe he needs a more sophisticated approach to hair care. Axe makes something called Clean Cut Look, a pomade, but the result seems reminiscent of Vitalis oil. They also offer their Spiked-Up Look, a styling putty that produces a contemporary punky appearance. Finally there is Messy Look, a flexible paste. Axe has a compelling slogan—FIND YOUR MAGIC. Mustafa is acutely aware that good hair has an almost magical power, opening doors to social strata—and the knockout women therein—that are closed to men with inferior hair. He must give this issue more and careful consideration.

The interrogation subject's screaming has grown loud enough to concern Mustafa. Perhaps Charlie mistakenly believes the enclosed office muffles more of Ganesh's cries than is the case. Mustafa is about to get up and advise his partner that the louder sounds might carry beyond the warehouse, but before he can get to his feet, the screams subside to a miserable sobbing and then grow yet quieter.

When they resume again after a few minutes, they are well muffled; Charlie evidently has inserted a rubber ball in the subject's mouth and fixed it there with duct tape, indicating that he is about to proceed to the testicles.

There is also the matter of tote versus backpack. The backpacks in question—offered by such as Louis Vuitton and Goyard—are really not backpacks. They're man purses renamed, and they present a knotty problem for Mustafa, about which he's still brooding when, at 10:17, Verna Amboy throws open a door at the farther end of the warehouse and hurries toward him.

The absence of sounds from the interrogation subject suggests that a breakthrough has occurred. Mustafa drops his magazine, gets up from the table, and meets the woman partway.

The delectable Ms. Amboy has never looked more desirable. Her cheeks are flushed. Her nostrils are flared, her lips moist.

She says, "Jane Hawk and Vikram Rangnekar are in Casa Grande, Arizona. Right this very minute, they're meeting with a man named Enrique de Soto at the Holiday Inn on North French Street."

49

The rumble of the engine masked what little sound Jane made as she moved to the back of the motor home.

She hadn't turned on any lights. The interior was illuminated only by what sunshine passed through the heavily tinted windows. Beyond the refrigerator, shadows gathered in front of the sliding door to the bedroom, directly ahead, and the bathroom door to the right.

On her left, opposite the bath, another door probably served a pantry. It was narrow and the space it served shallow, therefore it was the only one of the three that *might* be safe to open. Pistol in her right hand and thrust in front of her, she dared it and found an empty closet with a metal bar from which clothes could be hung.

Crossing thresholds and clearing rooms was bad enough in a

house, far worse in a moving vehicle. Dealing with either of the remaining doors was as dangerous as disarming a bomb.

She wanted this finished soon, but there was no mortal urgency. If seconds had counted, she would have bulled forward. However, in this instance, giving the intruders time to expose themselves was better than taking the action to them. Because it was the last thing they would expect, she eased into the narrow closet, facing out, as if standing in a coffin. She quietly pulled the door mostly shut, leaving it ajar just two inches. From this dark lair she could see the sliding door to her left and a portion of the bathroom door.

50

Sworn to secrecy about what Ganesh Rangnekar has revealed, Verna Amboy and Eldon Clocker remain in Ontario to clean up the warehouse.

At Charlie Weatherwax's request, the state attorney general, being a Techno Arcadian, orders a California Highway Patrol escort for Charlie and Mustafa involving fifty-six officers and forty-eight vehicles, which is put together with such dispatch that it doesn't seem at all like a government operation, but as though Apple or Amazon is now running the state.

Sirens shrieking and lightbars blazing, two patrol cars precede the Mercedes G550 Squared—Mustafa driving—west on State Highway 60, south on Interstate 605, and west on Interstate 105. Other units of the CHP temporarily block freeway entrances along the route to limit obstructing traffic, and clear intersections in the vicinity of Los Angeles International Airport. A journey of fifty-two miles is completed in twenty-five minutes. Both Charlie and Mustafa are exhilarated by the rare experience of achieving speed on southern California's sclerotic freeways, as well as by a sense of their personal importance that is nearly orgasmic.

Standing by at LAX is a Gulfstream V belonging to Homeland

Security. Fueled and crewed and ready for a different mission, the jet is reassigned to Charlie and is now prepared to convey him and Mustafa four hundred miles to Phoenix, where a team of four Arcadian operatives with multiple law-enforcement and national security credentials are ready to assist.

For the three passengers who have now been displaced, the steward has provisioned a lunch of either branzino with orange beet puree, lemon oil, and candied cashews or a hamburger with bacon jam and black garlic aioli on a brioche bun. Charlie chooses the burger, and Mustafa prefers the fish, and the steward offers two suitable white wines and two appropriate reds for their selection.

The police escort and the aircraft are testaments to Charlie's reputation as an effective, ruthless agent of change, but as well to his singular powers of persuasion. He has told no one that he knows Jane Hawk's whereabouts. He has said only that he has an urgent lead on Vikram Rangnekar that he must follow himself, an inquiry that can't be delegated. The rootkits and back doors Vikram has built into a broad spectrum of agencies remain mostly undiscovered, and next to Jane Hawk, he is the greatest threat to the revolution.

Charlie is playing this close to the vest in part because he cannot tolerate someone else getting credit for the capture of the elusive Mrs. Hawk. Whoever nails her will rise into the highest echelons of Techno Arcadia and eventually have almost godlike power.

But there is also the fact that he has screwed up and needs to make this capture himself in order to conceal a misstep that could result in serious disciplinary measures by his superiors.

What Charlie Weatherwax did to Ganesh Rangnekar doesn't qualify as a random act of cruelty. There was nothing haphazard or casual about it. He conducted the session using the time-tested methods and techniques of Lenin, Hitler, Stalin, and other masters of extreme interrogation. Furthermore, what Charlie has done doesn't fit his own definition of *cruel*, because a successful act of random cruelty requires the recipient to live with the trauma, to be mentally and emotionally disabled by it, to some extent, for the rest of his life. That is not the case in this instance, Ganesh having died.

Whether the fat geek expired from a heart attack or a stroke, or from some other cause, there are rivals to Charlie in this utopian movement who will be quick to contend that his decision to resort to extreme interrogation was reckless and squandered the best chance yet to arrest Jane Hawk. If the central committee decides that he has grievously mishandled the situation, he won't be stood against a wall and shot. However, there is a chance that he will be injected, transformed into an adjusted person, and thereafter used like any other cog in the machinery of the revolution.

He won't risk such a fate.

If he'd waited the four hours until Ganesh's control mechanism had been established, he would have gotten all the information that he needed. As it was, an hour sooner than that, he learned that Vikram indeed made contact with Hawk, that they are now together, and that Vikram intends to backdoor his way to whatever information will exonerate her and bring down her enemies. He has also squeezed from Ganesh the name Enrique de Soto and the fact that, this very morning, Vikram and Hawk are rendezvousing with de Soto in Casa Grande, Arizona, to take possession of a black-market vehicle that has been stripped of its GPS and modified in unspecified ways.

All this is highly valuable intel, but there are crucial details that he failed to extract from the subject before the fatty died. Charlie doesn't know who this de Soto might be or what kind of vehicle the man is delivering to them. He hasn't acquired a list of all the agencies to which Vikram, while at the FBI, established back doors that are still undiscovered, so he can't wrap his mind around how the sonofabitch expects to obtain enough data to blow up the Arcadian movement. The biggest question also remains unanswered: Considering how Techno Arcadians within government and private industry are increasingly able to control the content of most media and police the Internet to scrub from it inconvenient truths, how do Vikram and Hawk imagine that they are going to get the full story out to any significant percentage of the population?

During their high-altitude lunch, while Charlie broods on these matters, Mustafa al-Yamani works on his laptop, hoping to identify Enrique de Soto. The man apparently runs an illegal operation, but Mustafa can discover no history of an arrest. He is able to find several Enrique de Sotos. In Arizona, however, there is only a Richard de Soto, who owns an antiques store in Nogales.

"That fat little bastard should've broken in a half hour," Charlie laments. "An hour at most."

"There is no excuse for his behavior," Mustafa agrees.

"Who could know he had a heart condition or whatever was wrong with the feeb?"

"If he knew, he should have had the decency to inform you of his condition," Mustafa says.

After a silence, during which Charlie finishes his burger, he asks, "Mustafa, what would you say is the most valuable thing you learned from your mother and father?"

"I am an orphan by choice, Charles. I long ago disowned them and have worked diligently to forget they ever existed. Please do not ask me to remember them."

"The most valuable lesson my parents taught me," Charlie says, "is that deceit and duplicity pay. They became wealthy and happy and took early retirement by pretending to be something they weren't and by gaming the system in the name of various righteous causes."

Mustafa looks up from his last bite of branzino, on which is balanced a final candied cashew. "And for some reason you hold this against them?"

"No, no. Not at all. What ticks me off is that during all the years they denied me things that would have made my childhood and adolescence more pleasurable, always citing financial troubles, they were in fact salting away huge sums they skimmed from federal grants made to the operations they ran. And I'm certain that by the time they die, they'll have used every morsel of their hoard, leaving no inheritance."

Mustafa has finished his meal during Charlie's complaint. "You are displeased by their selfishness, and rightly so. Your resentment is entirely understandable."

"I do believe it is," Charlie says.

Miles below, the Mojave lay pale and sere and as inhospitable as the hearts of parents who will not sacrifice for their children.

"During the interrogation," Charlie reveals, "the fat little creep repeatedly insisted he couldn't betray his cousin."

"Whyever not?"

"He said 'Family is sacred.' He said it over and over, like a mantra to ward off the pain."

"How strange. Deranged, really."

"I thought so, too. Anyway, he eventually broke."

Mustafa says, "May I ask you something off subject?"

"What is it?"

"As a fragrance for men—Code by Armani or Red by Perry Ellis?"

"Neither."

"I suspected as much."

"Bleu de Chanel. But only a light touch of it."

51

For five minutes, the motor home had been on the open highway, heading north on Interstate 10 toward Phoenix. By now the stowaways must be convinced that Jane and Vikram were oblivious to their presence.

Indeed, as she watched through the crack between the closet door and the jamb, she saw the bathroom door slowly swing open. A shadowy figure appeared, like some golem shaped from mud. He stepped out of the lavatory, no more than a foot from her, and looked toward the front of the Southwind. He would have seen Vikram behind the wheel. Perhaps he thought Jane was slumped down in the hulking copilot seat or sitting in the dinette booth beyond his line of sight.

He rapped once, softly, on the bedroom door to his right, and it slid open. Jane couldn't see beyond the threshold of that room, but she heard one of the men whisper something.

They wanted to capture rather than kill her, and she preferred not to kill them if she could avoid it. From her belt she unclipped the Taser that earlier she'd taken from her tote.

The other man exited the bedroom, a pistol in hand, and the two edged cautiously toward the front of the Southwind, on hair-trigger alert but focused on the wrong thing.

Jane stepped out of the closet immediately behind the pair, her presence known to them only when she Tasered the first and he cried out as he fell, the pistol springing from his hand as though of its own volition.

Startled, the other man squeezed off a shot as he turned to confront Jane, the noise like a boxing of the ears in that confined space. The round was wild, over her head. She went in under his gun arm, jammed the poles of the Taser into his throat, triggered it as the muzzle flash of a second ineffective shot for an instant bloomed in his eyes, which had rolled back in his head until they were as white as eggs. He dropped like a construct of straw and staves. She turned to the first thug, who was in the grip of a semiparalyzing seizure, and she Tasered him again. She gave the second man another shock, too, before clipping the Taser to her belt.

From an inner pocket of her sport coat, she withdrew the six-ounce spray bottle she'd earlier taken from her tote. It contained chloroform that she had derived from ordinary art-store acetone by the reaction of chloride of lime, which was bleaching powder that she had bought at a janitorial-supply store. She spritzed each man across the lower half of his face, wetting his nose and mouth, and both passed from seizure into the stillness of sleep.

In spite of the gunfire, Vikram had been steady at the wheel, but into the sudden silence he shouted, "Jane! Talk to me!"

"I'm all right," she assured him as she weaved toward the front of the motor home, ears ringing from the gunfire. "You're doing great, *chotti batasha*. Just be on the lookout for a rest area." She snatched the tote bag from beside the Euro recliner. "We'll offload these turkeys first chance we get."

She switched on the lights and returned to the unconscious men and knelt beside them. She took from the tote a cluster of cable zip-ties and stripped off the rubber band that bound them together. She zip-tied one man's left wrist to the other's right. With a chain of six looped zip-ties, she shackled the second man's right ankle to the bar handle of the refrigerator door.

Chloroform was a volatile fluid, but the effect would last well past the point that their faces dried. She didn't spray them again because they would be easier to put out of the Southwind if they were conscious.

She confiscated their guns, a Glock 17 and a Para-Ordnance P18, both 9 mm, and put them in the tote.

When she returned to the Euro recliner, just behind the copilot's seat, Vikram said, "Three miles to a rest area."

In spite of Ricky de Soto's treachery, everything was moving along rather smoothly. However, although Jane wasn't superstitious, experience had taught her that there were always rhythm changes in the course of events; the beat could switch from up to down without warning.

52

A thick paperboard image of a kitten hung from the rearview mirror of the Buick. An air freshener. It stank of pine trees.

Snapping the cat with one finger, Tio said, "Why's a kitten smell like freakin' pine trees? That make sense to you?"

Behind the wheel, Diablo Wilson said, "What you want it to smell like, bro—piss in a litter box?"

Tio grabbed the kitten, yanked hard, and broke the string by which it hung. "I hate cats. Sneaky damn animals. I hate pine trees."

"What's to hate with pine trees?"

"They make me think Christmas. I never got nothin' worth shit at Christmas."

Tio put down his window. Threw the air freshener out of the car. Put up the window.

Diablo said, "They make oxygen."

"Who does?"

"Pine trees. They make oxygen."

"What shit are you smokin'?"

"It's true, bro. Pine trees, other trees, flowers, grass, they make oxygen. We don't have no trees, then we don't have no air to breathe."

"Where'd you get this shit?"

"School."

"You went to school?"

"For a while."

"It's a waste. School messes with your head."

"You stabbed that teacher once."

"For messin' with my head."

"It's still true about the trees."

"Yeah? So just how they make oxygen?"

"I don't know exactly."

"You don't know exactly," Tio mocked.

"It's like they sort of fart it."

"Trees fart oxygen?"

"Not exactly. But they exude it."

"'Exude.' There's a fancy school word."

Diablo shrugged. "It's a word. Looks like they're gettin' off at this rest area."

Tio frowned at the motor home as its signal lights and the temporary auxiliary lights on the Explorer announced a right turn.

He said, "Johnny shoulda called by now."

Following the Southwind off the interstate, Diablo said, "Maybe him and Fidel, they didn't make a move yet."

"What the hell they waitin' for? They better not've killed the bitch. Enrique wants her untouched, wet, and ready. They screwed up, he'll cut their dicks off."

53

As the Gulfstream V descends toward the runway at Phoenix Sky Harbor International Airport, east of city center, Charlie checks his text messages. "Our team of four will be waiting for us on the tarmac with two Suburbans."

"Suburbans?" Mustafa asks.

"It is what it is," Charlie says.

"Will we need to share one?"

"Four in one, us in the other."

"How far to Casa Grande?"

"Once we're out of the airport, it looks like forty miles, give or take, straight down I-10."

In flight, Charlie has gotten through to the manager of the Holiday Inn, who has been cooperative, as he damn well better be. The hotel apparently has an adequate security system, cameras in all public places, both interior and exterior. Whatever vehicle de Soto has delivered to Jane Hawk and Vikram, there will be video of it in the hotel archives.

Once they know the vehicle, they can post it with the National Crime Information Center and otherwise bring an array of state and federal agencies into the hunt, which will be so intense that they will no doubt have Hawk and Rangnekar in custody before the day is done.

PART FOUR

No Escape

1

Willisford was more a village than a full-fledged town and evidently existed to service surrounding ranches: a market, a farm supply, a general store, an off-brand gasoline station with garage— MECHANIC ON DUTY—a bar and grill called Horseman's Haven, a clapboard church of no apparent denomination, a few other businesses, and maybe forty or fifty houses.

In the hard light and heat and dust of summer, it might have been a dreary place. But now the buildings were mantled in snow, and the boughs of the pines that softened the streets were dressed in the stoles of the storm.

A Chevy Silverado, a Toyota Tacoma, and a John Deere tractor fitted with a plow stood in front of Horseman's Haven. In that company, Porter Crockett's Ford crew-cab pickup called no attention to itself.

No doubt because of the recent storm, the bar and grill wasn't busy even late morning on a Saturday. The warm air was redolent of buttery hash browns and fried onions. Instead of heading toward a back booth, which Tom expected, Porter went to a table at the front, next to a window.

"Seems like we ought to keep an eye on the street."

As they settled into chairs, Tom said, "I just realized, I don't have any money. They took everything from me before they suited me up and sent me out to be killed."

Porter leaned forward, over the table. "Way I figure, you bein' a director with a true-life story to tell, I'll get more dollars of entertainment out of this than what little a meal's gonna cost me."

"Where I come from," Tom said, "no one would be this kind to a crazy-talking stranger."

"You're not crazy, son. Just scared shitless. In my life, I've seen enough to know the difference. I'm startin' with a beer. How about you?"

"Yes, thanks."

The well-put-together fortysomething waitress smiled broadly when she recognized Porter Crockett. She slapped menus on the table and said, "You finished that business in Kansas, Colonel?"

"All wrapped up, Louise. Darlin', the first light a cured blind man sees couldn't look better than you."

"You've got more bullshit than a herd of steers, but I love the way you sling it."

They ordered Coronas with lime, and she went away to get them.

" 'Colonel'?" Tom asked.

"Thirty years, I had somethin' of a military career. Wouldn't have served so long had I known they'd make me a damn colonel. I was born for an E-2 pay grade, nothin' higher." He picked up his menu. "It's lunch and dinner on one side, breakfast on the other. They have breakfast all day if you want it."

Tom watched a truck pass in the street. "You know a man named Wainwright Hollister?"

Looking up from his menu, Porter said, "He a friend of yours?"

"Not a friend, no."

"The bastard thinks he owns the county. Hell, maybe he does. He smiles more than a pack of hyenas, and every bit as sincere."

"He's behind this mind-control nanotech I told you about. He meant to kill me last night."

Porter stared out the window, digesting this news.

Tom couldn't read the man's expression. "Is he going to give up when the roadblock gets him nothing? Will we really be able to get back on the road in just a couple hours?"

The colonel turned his attention to his menu once more. "We'll just have to wait and see."

2

The rest area offered lavatories in a squat building surrounded by landscaping that consisted of pebbles, rocks, century plants, and reddish-brown knee-high clumps of Aureola grass. Shadows had shrunk into the objects that cast them, waiting to emerge when the day finished transitioning from morning to afternoon.

A van and a Toyota Highlander occupied the rest area when Vikram drove in from the highway. A Buick followed in his wake and parked at the farther end of the lot.

While the zip-tied men recovered from the chloroform, Jane settled in the copilot's seat. "When our sleeping beauties wake and there's no one else here, we'll put them out and get moving again."

They had a view of the other three vehicles through the driver's side window. A young woman came out of the lavatory and stood waiting near a many-bladed century plant. A minute later, her companion exited the men's side of the building, and together they left in the van.

"Looks like two in the front seat of that Buick," Jane said. They were too far away. She couldn't see more than their shadowy shapes in the car. "Why aren't they using the head?"

"Maybe they're just here to take a nap," Vikram suggested.

Groaning and muttering in the back of the motor home indicated that the thugs were regaining consciousness.

Two women and a girl of about ten returned to the Highlander and left the rest area by the exit lane.

The passenger in the Buick looked toward the Southwind and then away. At such a distance, Jane was not able to see him well, and she couldn't see the driver at all beyond him. However, the position of the man's head in relation to the window suggested he was slumped in the seat or was a boy in his early teens—or might be a man of small stature. Tio was short and built like a jockey.

When the passenger glanced their way again, Jane said, "They aren't taking a nap. Keep a watch on them. Shout if anyone gets out of the car."

Her tote stood on the Euro recliner. She carried it to the back of the motor home.

The thug shackled to the refrigerator was lying on his back. He had a sledgehammer face with yellowish-brown teeth and beard stubble that suggested a case of mange. His partner was on his hands and knees, afflicted by a series of violent sneezes.

Jane put the tote on the counter by the kitchen sink. She took from it a pair of scissors and one of the guns she had confiscated earlier, the Glock 17.

The piece of work lying on his back spewed an unimaginative stream of invective, using the F-word and the C-word as nouns, verbs, and adjectives.

She aimed the pistol at him point-blank. "Shut up, you pig." He glared but for the moment said no more. "I'm going to give you these scissors to cut yourself loose from the refrigerator. Then you're going to slide them across the floor to me. If you try to get to your feet or make any wrong move, I'll kill you. Understand?"

"Blow me, bitch."

"A real tough guy, huh?"

"Blow me," he repeated.

"You're dumber than tough. You just gave me a better idea than killing you. I'll shoot your pecker off so you won't have any reason to make that suggestion to another woman." She looked at the second thug. "That goes for you, too, Sneezy."

She dropped the scissors and held the Glock in a two-hand grip.

Yellow Teeth cut the thick zip-tie at his ankle. He slid the scissors back to her.

"Sit up," she told Yellow Teeth. "Sit down," she told the guy who was on his hands and knees.

They sat side by side on the floor, each with one wrist still zip-tied to a wrist of the other.

"Good boys," Jane said. "Now get naked and be quick about it."

Sneezy had stopped sneezing but, with his free hand, was wiping a dangling string of snot from his nose. "Say *what*?"

"I'm aware no woman has asked you to get naked before. But I've got a strong stomach. Do it."

"No freakin' way," said Sneezy.

She squeezed off a round nearly low enough to part his hair, heard it crack the sliding door to the bedroom. *"Don't screw with me, you dumb shit. Get naked or die. Two minutes!"*

All the threat had gone out of Sneezy's partner, the sad case of dental neglect. Plaintively Yellow Teeth said, "How we supposed to undress, we each got only one hand free?"

"Make the world a better place," Jane said. "Help each other."

3

Bernie Riggowitz behind the wheel of the Mercedes Sprinter, Cornell and Travis in the luxurious rear cabin with the dogs, the familiar sunny streets of Scottsdale now as strange and full of menace as any mist-shrouded moor or jungle night . . .

Since he'd come here as a child, America had been wondrously good to Bernie. He had enjoyed much success. He'd loved and been loved. His long life here was blessed and happy. Decades ago in Europe, he had known the terror of utter helplessness and the pain of grievous loss, for he'd been a child in Auschwitz, where his mother and father perished. But in America he hadn't experienced the disabling fright that came with being powerless and at the mercy of evil people who clothed themselves in the absolute power of the state. Until now. Having endured a preview of such horror during recent events in Borrego Valley, he now saw the curtain rising on the main show.

When they were well away from the neighborhood in which Nasia and Segev lived, beyond all sirens and immediate threats, he pulled to the curb long enough to look through the wallet he'd taken from the man who had attempted to kill Travis. He found $1,200 in cash. Three California driver's licenses with authentic holograms of the state seal—in the names Max Schreck, Conrad Veidt, and Charles Ogle—bore the same photograph of the man whom Bernie had shot. There were as well three Visa cards in those names, but nothing else. Whoever this man had really been, it seemed he had lived outside the law and had not been a Techno Arcadian, perhaps even in some way opposed them.

A popular aphorism held that "the enemy of my enemy is my friend," but that was a fool's wisdom. Although evil came in many shades, each was an aspect of a greater all-encompassing Evil, and an alliance of convenience with evil of any kind would in time bear toxic fruit.

Whoever and whatever this *momzer* might have been, this Schreck-Veidt-Ogle character, he had nearly achieved what Jane's enemies had failed to do, destroy her by destroying her child. His near success harried the boy and his guardians from their safe haven, with no prospect of finding another.

"What are you?" Bernie said aloud to himself, with a note of disgust. "Are you a *shmo, shmulky, shnook?*"

In the worst of times, after the most dismaying setbacks, there was nevertheless always something to be done, a right step to take, a way through the woods. Where there was life, there was hope: a truth of which the course of his own life was irrefutable proof.

He started the engine and released the emergency brake and pulled the Sprinter away from the curb.

4

Clothes were armor against the world, explaining why fashion was such a large industry. When forced to strip naked, most men felt defenseless, especially those whose self-image depended on their ability to intimidate others, who lived for power on however grand or petty a scale, whose preferred techniques of social interaction were psychological and physical violence.

When clothed, Sneezy and Yellow Teeth might have needed to be pistol-whipped before they would have revealed their names, but now they volunteered without being asked. They were Fidel and Johnny. Fidel had a little daughter named Maria whom he wanted to see grow up, and Johnny had a disabled mother to support.

More likely than not, if Maria existed, her father had never provided child support. And if Johnny had a mother, her disability was probably addiction to drugs and to the kind of men who produced miscreants like him.

"You better have no illusions," Jane said. "I'll kill you if you make me."

Fidel appeared convinced. "They say you offed your own husband, faked it like suicide."

"And maybe your little boy he's not in hidin'," Johnny said. "Maybe you whacked him, too."

Occasionally all the outrageous lies told about her proved to be beneficial.

She threw a zip-tie to Johnny and told him to reconnect his right ankle to the five ties still dangling from the refrigerator. He did as she ordered, and when she saw that he didn't pull the tie tight enough, he grudgingly pulled it tighter.

She threw another zip-tie on the floor and told them to work together to bind Fidel's right ankle to Johnny's left.

When they were incapacitated, she gathered up their clothes and carried them to the sofa. She wrapped the garments and Johnny's shoes in a ball and cinched the bundle securely with their belts. Fidel had been wearing a pair of fashionable red sneakers, and she set those aside along with his underpants, a pair of black briefs.

After retrieving the scissors and returning them to her tote with the confiscated Glock 17, she took off her sport coat and put it on the Euro recliner. She shrugged out of her shoulder holster. Untucked her shirt. Undid the first two buttons. Folded the sleeves to her elbows. When she had carefully adjusted her bra, she rolled up the bottom of the shirt and used the tails to tie it in place, converting it into a midriff-baring top, which was suitable to the hot weather, would give Tio and his friend a swath of bare skin to distract them, and assure them that she was not carrying a concealed weapon.

Settling in the copilot's seat, she handed Vikram the holster with the Heckler still in it. She looked past him, toward the Buick. "No one's gotten out of the car?"

"No one."

Following a brief but intense conversation, Vikram said, "You really think this will work?"

"You never know."

He rolled his eyes. "At least you're telling me straight."

"I always will."

He sighed. "Let's do it."

She put a hand on his shoulder. "You okay?"

"Yeah, I'm okay."

"Because I need you to be okay."

He nodded and pointed one index finger at the ceiling and said, "No one has ever been more okay than I am okay."

"Do I look plausible?" she asked.

"Better than plausible."

She fetched Felix's red sneakers from the sofa, stuffed his briefs in one of them, and went to the exit, which was on the side of the vehicle facing away from the Buick. She stepped down from the Southwind, leaving the door open behind her.

The day was warm for early spring, a dry heat that penetrated pleasantly to her bones. When Jane rounded the back of the Explorer that was yoked to the motor home, she found a three-foot snake inert on the blacktop. Not dead. Just luxuriating on the sunbaked pavement, a cold-blooded creature inspired to ecstasy rather than made somnolent by the desert sun. Because it wasn't a rattler and was not coiled to strike, she stepped over it and headed toward the Buick, listening to the drone of traffic out on the interstate, hoping this business could be concluded before another motorist decided to use the rest area facilities.

5

Tio thought maybe he'd heard gunshots over the sound made by chilled air rushing through the dashboard vents. He couldn't be sure. He made Diablo turn off the engine and put down the windows.

Nothing happened for a while. Then she appeared.

Watching Jane Hawk stride toward them like some movie goddess, Tio said, "She makes me crazy."

Diablo leaned over the wheel, looking past Tio. "The bitch has style, how she walks."

"More than style, she's got balls."

She went around the back of the car. To the driver's side. She stopped five feet from the open window, looking down and in at them as if they were some species of animal she'd never seen before.

"What's she holdin'?" Tio asked.

"Shoes," said Diablo.

Tio took a closer look. "Fidel's sneakers."

Hawk said, "We have to talk."

"Get in the back," Tio told her, and Diablo repeated it as though she hadn't heard.

She said, "If I'd gotten in the Southwind to watch you count the money, I'd be on my way to Nogales. We have to make a deal here, and I won't do it in the car."

Tio got out of the passenger door, closed it. He looked at her over the roof. "Thought I heard like a pistol."

"Fidel is a lousy shot. Missed me twice. Come around here. We don't want to be doing business on that side if someone drives in from the highway. We'll draw too much attention."

The gun in Tio's belt holster was concealed by his roomy, untucked shirt. He went around the back of the car.

She said, "You get out, too, Diablo."

"He's just the driver," Tio said.

"Maybe he's got a gun. You can see I don't. I come here in good faith. Show me, Diablo."

Diablo looked at Tio. Tio nodded. Diablo got out of the car. He wore Converse sneakers, black jeans, a five-inch metal belt buckle engraved with the head of a dragon, and a colorful T-shirt bearing an image of a stoned Jesus making the peace sign with a joint between his fingers.

Hawk said, "I guess your mama doesn't buy your clothes anymore. Shut the door."

Diablo's glare was lethal, but he closed the door.

Tio said, "You sellin' shoes or what?"

She plucked a pair of black briefs from one red shoe and threw them on the pavement. "I figured Fidel for the kind of guy who'd wear a thong from Victoria's Secret, but they're just Jockey's finest."

With a moronic, lascivious smirk, Diablo said, "You took off Fidel's underwear?"

"I made him and Johnny get naked. I was curious if they had anything in their underpants. They didn't."

The bitch really made Tio crazy. In both a good and a bad way. He started to smile, but then bit his lip.

"A bitch has tits like yours," Diablo said, "you can take off my pants anytime."

"Idiot," she said.

"There some story to the shoes?" Tio asked.

"I think they're cool," she said. "You think they're cool?"

"They're cool enough."

"They're yours then." With a flick of her wrist, she threw them in Tio's face.

6

Startled, Tio stumbled backward off the pavement, into the pebbled landscaping, and fell into an overgrown century plant with succulent, saw-toothed leaves as long as swords, which snapped under his weight but also snared him as if the plant were an enormous variegated-green spider.

Grateful for cleavage, Jane plucked the small spray bottle of chloroform from between her breasts. She bent over Tio as he rucked up his shirt and fumbled for the pistol in his belt holster, and she sprayed his nose and mouth.

Maybe Diablo was as slow-witted as he appeared, fifteen years a stoner with a permanent cannabis fog shrouding his brain, but Jane had to assume he wasn't merely standing by the Buick, waiting to be sprayed to sleep. She snatched the pistol from Tio's holster—a Smith & Wesson 9 mm with three-inch barrel—pivoted with the weapon in a two-hand grip, and saw Diablo leaning through the open window in the driver's door, reaching for a gun.

She shouted—"*Don't!*"—but he came out of the car with a pistol in hand, and she shouted again, because he still had three seconds to live if he was smart enough to grasp the opportunity. As she slow-squeezed the trigger, Vikram shouted—"*Drop it!*"—from behind the driver. If Diablo thought he had some chance against one gun, he knew he had no chance against two. He dropped the weapon just as Jane finished the trigger squeeze and, with a twitch, thwarted her aim, putting the round through the open window of the Buick, an inch or two from Diablo.

During the distraction that Jane provided to Tio and Diablo, Vikram had slipped out of the motor home and around the back of the lavatories, coming in behind them, as planned.

Now Jane dropped Tio's pistol and approached the driver with the chloroform in her left hand.

Back against the car, warily regarding the bottle, Diablo said, "Enrique, he's gonna feed you alive to his hogs, bitch."

"Ricky has hogs?"

"Five wild boars, big bastards, six hundred pounds. You cross him this bad, he'll cut you so the boars smell blood and throw you in with them. He done it more than once."

Within arm's reach of Diablo, she said, "Does Ricky think he's some Bond-film villain or what? Tell him I eat bacon for breakfast."

"They chew off your face. I seen it. You're screamin' and they're rippin' open your guts with their tusks, stickin' their snouts in. I seen it."

"Did you find it amusing?" she asked, pretty much certain that the grisly spectacle had made him laugh.

Fixated on the spray bottle, he said, "What'd you do to Tio? Is that some poison? What poison's that?"

"It's not a poison, skipper. It'll just put you to sleep for a while—and make you permanently impotent."

The short-bladed razor-edged knife was sheathed in his ornate belt buckle, as she had expected. With her right hand, she seized his wrist before he could fully extract the blade, and with her thumb she applied crippling pressure to the radial nerve.

His flushed face was a wretched mask of rage as he struggled against her grip, his green eyes bloodshot from long-term substance abuse. He had a life story: Maybe he had endured tragedies and pain, numerous injustices and insults. She didn't give a damn. Join the club; that was the human condition. What mattered wasn't what they did to you, but whether you rose above the level of the users and tormentors—or whether you became one of them and did so with dark glee.

The pinched radial nerve failed the tendons and muscles of his hand, and he suffered sudden wrist-drop, losing his grip on the half-extracted knife. His bloodshot eyes seemed afire, and his voice was hot with hatred. "You're hog food, bitch."

She sprayed his nose and mouth, and a thin but satisfying cry of despair escaped him as he raveled to the ground, as limp as an empty sausage casing.

Vikram lowered the Heckler & Koch. He said, *"Jhav!"* He looked terrified. Good. Terror was instructive. He was learning.

7

The spring heat was not yet so great in Scottsdale that certain songbirds would go silent at midday. From the nearby olive trees came the serried trills and clear notes of the southwest song sparrow and the ethereal fluting and twirling phrases of the hermit thrush.

In pajamas and slippers, Bernie Riggowitz rang the doorbell of the handsome Wrightian house. Cornell, Travis, and the dogs were in the Mercedes Sprinter at the curb, comfortable in the air-conditioned rear compartment.

Bernie felt awkward, standing here dressed for bed, but he did not feel foolish. The last time he'd felt foolish was when he'd been courting Miriam, sixty-two years earlier. He'd done the silliest things in his effort to win her heart; but she endured his lack of sophistication and his maladroit courtship, ultimately marrying him. He had never since felt foolish, for how could a man be foolish who had won such a treasure?

If he wasn't mistaken, from the trees also issued the low, whistled, liquid phrases of the American robin. Segev, his son-in-law, was a bird enthusiast. Bernie had once viewed bird-watching as an eccentric hobby and tedious. But Segev had won him over, had taught him the pleasure of learning the names of Nature's wonders. Although a casual bird-watcher, Bernie could identify twenty or thirty species by their calls and feather patterns.

Segev was an accomplished and gentle man, a perfect match for Nasia, and it hurt Bernie deeply that, by bringing Travis into their house, he'd put them in the crosshairs of the Techno Arcadians. But you couldn't abandon children in jeopardy and be allowed still to call yourself human. Nasia and Segev would understand, though he needed to get in touch with them, where they were vacationing in England, to warn them off returning home until he gave them the all-clear. He dared not dwell on the possibility that Jane Hawk might fail, that there might never again be an America, as they had always known it, to welcome them home.

He was about to ring the bell again when the door opened, and before him stood a man too young to be a mensch, too handsome to be a man of humble spiritual wisdom, but he was those things and more. "Reb Bernie! *Shalom*."

"*Shalom*. Rabbi, I'm sorry I didn't call ahead."

"Come in, come in. What is it, what can I do?"

"I apologize for the pajamas and slippers. I'm so *farmisht*, I don't know where to start."

"Are you all right?" Rabbi Colstein worried as he welcomed Bernie into the foyer. "Nothing's happened to Nasia or Segev?"

"They're okay, they're good. *Baruch ha-Shem*. But you'll think I'm *tsedreyt*, what I have to tell you."

"No, no. You're the last person I'd think is scatterbrained."

"I haven't showered this morning. I regret my condition."

"Enough with the apologies. May I get you some water? What can I get you? Come along, Bernie, come into my study and tell me what's wrong."

"What's not?" Bernie said as he was led into the book-lined room. He sat in an armchair, and Rabbi Colstein sat in one like it, facing him across a low table. "Rabbi, do you watch sci-fi movies?"

"*Star Wars*, you mean?"

"Darker than that. Like the body snatchers one."

"*Invasion of the Body Snatchers*?"

"They don't come from outer space, Rabbi. They've always been here among us, human beings, waiting for the technology that they could use to steal our souls."

8

A carrion-eating turkey vulture circled overhead, silently cleaving the sky with its six-foot wingspan, although no one had died yet.

The Buick shielded Jane and Vikram from any incoming traffic that might arrive, but they were not interrupted as they worked quickly to relieve Tio and Diablo of their clothing: shoes, socks, underwear, everything. Together they loaded the naked men into the backseat, propping them in a sitting position, leaving only their wallets and cellphones between them.

As they were bundling the clothes, a Range Rover cruised into the rest area and parked near the Southwind. A tall guy in a Stetson went into the men's lavatory.

As Vikram hurried back to the motor home with the clothing, Jane gave each of the men in the backseat a second, lighter spray, and then she got into the driver's seat and pulled the door shut. She started the engine and put up the windows and waited, her Heckler on the seat beside her.

A light sweat filmed her face, and her scalp was hot under the wig. The chilled air felt glorious. She took her pulse, and it was higher than she would have liked. Sixty-six. Her resting pulse was usually fifty-eight or sixty.

The cowboy came out of the lavatory and drove away in the Range Rover.

The Southwind began to move even as the Rover was heading toward the exit lane. Vikram brought it to the end of the parking lot and reversed into a space beside the Buick, so the starboard flank, with the only door, was toward the car.

Jane got out of the Buick, leaving the engine running. Pistol in hand, she climbed into the motor home. She took the scissors from her tote and went to the back of the vehicle, where Fidel and Johnny sat on the floor, as she'd left them.

While Vikram stood watch over the naked men, with Tio's Smith & Wesson at the ready, Jane cut the zip-tie that secured Johnny to the refrigerator. She severed the tie that bound an ankle of one man to an ankle of the other, and then she freed Fidel's right wrist from Johnny's left.

She backed away and put the scissors on the dinette table. Motioning with the Heckler, she said, "Okay, get up."

Fidel rose and, with maidenly modesty, covered his genitals with his hands.

Johnny grimaced as he rose to his feet, his teeth as yellow as rancid butter. "What's happenin'?"

"We're taking you outside to the Buick," Jane said.

"What Buick?"

"Tio and Diablo traded the Porsche for new wheels."

"You're makin' us go out there bare-assed?"

"It's a nudist event. They're naked, too."

Shaking his head adamantly, Johnny said, "I don't wanna go out there like this."

"There's no panel of judges. You don't have to worry about settling for Miss Congeniality."

"This is so wrong," Fidel declared.

"You're alive," Jane said. "You want to be dead, I can take care of that for you."

Vikram left the Southwind first and waited between vehicles. Fidel followed him, then Johnny, and Jane brought up the rear, literally.

Tio and Diablo were still napping in the backseat of the Buick, their heads lolling toward each other.

Fidel and Johnny complained vociferously that the sun-seared pavement was hot under their bare feet. They wasted no time getting in the Buick, Fidel behind the wheel, Johnny through the passenger door, into the shotgun position.

While Vikram passed their smartphones and wallets to Fidel and Johnny, Jane stepped to the back of the car and shot out the rear tire on the port side.

At the driver's window, as Vikram watched, Jane said to Fidel, "I better not leave it to you geniuses to figure out your options."

"What damn options?" Fidel fumed. "We're screwed. Four naked guys in a car with three tires."

"Oh, good. You understand the basic situation."

The sound of an approaching engine drew Jane's attention. A long-haul moving van rumbled into the rest area. It came to a stop across several parking spaces.

The driver and his partner got out of the big truck and glanced toward the Buick and went into the men's facility. If they noticed that the four men in the car were not wearing shirts, they didn't seem to think that was unusual.

At the moment, Jane's greatest concern was that the next arrival at the rest area might be an officer of the Arizona Highway Patrol trained to be suspicious of even the smallest deviation from normality.

To Fidel, she said, "First option—between the moving vans and other visitors, you can change the tire. You've got enough gas to get back to Nogales without having to stop anywhere."

"I'm not changin' no tire naked," Fidel declared.

"Well, tires are rubber. Maybe Johnny or one of the snoozers in back has a rubber fetish, he'll think it's kinky fun. Second option, you call Ricky and have him send someone with clothes. They should be here in two and a half hours, maybe two."

"I don't know we can ever see Enrique again."

"You're not afraid of a few wild boars, are you?"

Johnny said, "We're in shit up to our necks."

If perhaps he'd lost his soul years earlier, Fidel nevertheless had soulful eyes, and with them he beseeched Jane. "Mrs. Hawk, we're helpless as little kids here. At least leave us some iron."

"A gun? Like that's going to happen."

From the passenger seat, Johnny said, "Gimme a loaded magazine. Put the gun in the trunk. We won't get it till you're gone."

"Mrs. Hawk," Fidel pleaded again, "we're helpless."

"That's the point. A little life lesson. So you know how it feels. Maybe you'll learn some empathy."

She followed Vikram into the motor home and closed the door. He got behind the wheel again, and she settled in as copilot.

They waited until the driver and his partner returned to the moving van. They followed the big truck out of the rest area.

Through the starboard sideview mirror, Jane saw Johnny get out of the Buick and hurry to the trunk, no doubt to retrieve the lug wrench and the jack.

9

Charlie Weatherwax stands at a window in the hotel lobby, staring out at arrangements of low and tall palm trees that fail to lend a tropical softness to the harsh reality of the desert in which the town stands. *Casa Grande* means "big house." In 1684, a Jesuit missionary named the nearby fourteenth-century Hohokam Indian ruins Casa Grande. In a lot of old movies, gangsters call prison "the big house," which is fitting because Charlie feels imprisoned by this town.

The current manager of the hotel has been on the job only three months. He is charming, courteous, respectful. He is eager to assist the FBI, though he's been told nothing about the suspect in pursuit of whom they have come here. Charlie thinks the manager is a phony. But then Charlie thinks everyone is a phony.

Nevertheless, he yearns to commit a random act of cruelty, make this a day the polite fresh-faced sonofabitch will never forget as long as he lives. On the manager's desk is a photo of his wife and two kids. Charlie has asked about them. The wife, Viveca, is a stay-at-home mom. The son is twelve, the daughter eight. Charlie wants to locate the manager's house, pay the wife a visit, and force her two brats to watch while he Tasers the woman repeatedly, using battery after battery, until she loses control of her bladder, if not also her bowels.

The hotel has security cameras in the corridors and elevators and all other public spaces, though not in the men's and women's rest-rooms at the restaurant. All exterior doors are covered by cameras, as is every section of the parking lot, which pretty much surrounds the complex.

The cameras are working. But they aren't recording. The hotel's video archives were erased. This is no fault of the manager. The blame surely lies with Vikram Rangnekar, legendary hacker, once a tool of the FBI and now its nemesis. According to Cousin Ganesh, that frag-ile little fat bastard now dead in a California warehouse, Jane Hawk and Vikram were to take delivery of a black-market vehicle of some kind in the parking lot of the hotel at ten o'clock this morning. If they stayed in a room in this hotel, Vikram might have spent a few hours worming his way into the computer system at the chain's national headquarters and from there into this operation. Or perhaps he'd al-ready backdoored the system before he'd ever arranged to take deliv-ery of the mysterious vehicle here.

Although the hotel manager had nothing to do with the erasing of the video archives, Charlie still wants to make this the day that the sonofabitch will always mark as the moment when his life took a dark turn from which it never quite recovered. After all, a random act of cruelty isn't random if it is committed for a justifiable reason, if it is somehow earned by the recipient. The manager seems especially fond of his son, Colson, who plays Little League baseball and is the best pitcher on his team. Maybe today Colson and his dad should be taught the true nature of the world; the star pitcher will learn a little humility if someone takes a hammer to his right hand and breaks every one of his fingers.

Just then, carrying a bottle of Mountain Dew, Mustafa al-Yamani arrives with an update. "I regret to report that according to the local police, this jerkwater town doesn't have many traffic cams. It is not as sophisticated as any part of Long Island. And even if it did have many, many cameras, their video archives have been erased, too."

Charlie has expected this. "If we can't ID their vehicle here, there's no choice but to go to the source. I've called for an urgent SWAT team raid on the Richard de Soto property outside Nogales. It looks to be the place. The raid is being conducted by Arcadians in Immigration and Customs Enforcement. ICE has considerable assets in that area." He checked his watch. "It goes down in forty minutes."

"Are we to visit Nogales?"

"An Arizona Highway Patrol escort will be here in a minute or two. Even with that, we won't make Nogales till after the raid has gone down. It's a hundred twenty-seven miles, at least an hour and fifteen minutes. Requisitioning a helicopter and getting it here won't be any faster. Just you and I will go."

The four who had come with them from Phoenix would continue questioning hotel employees to learn if anyone might have noticed some kind of deal going down in the parking lot along North French Street around ten o'clock. They could also check registrations to see who paid cash for a room and what ID they used.

"I am exhausted," Mustafa says. "We have not slept all night."

"We slept most of the day yesterday."

"Yes, and now it is afternoon and time for bed again. We are like bats, sleeping in daylight."

"We're closing in on the elusive bitch," Charlie says. "I smell her."

Mustafa inhales deeply, exhales. "I do not smell her."

Charlie takes a fine cotton handkerchief from an inside jacket pocket and wipes the back of his neck, as though just looking at the arid world of Casa Grande through the window has squeezed from him a light sweat. "We didn't wait for Ganesh's control mechanism to make him compliant, and we let him die on us before we got everything we needed. If we allow Hawk to slip through our fingers, we're both going to be injected and adjusted."

Charlie waits for his partner to question the use of the word *we*, but Mustafa possesses enough good sense to defer to a superior's characterization of events.

"Pump yourself with a little speed," Charlie advises.

"I'm already flying on bennies."

"Take another one."

"What are you on?"

"A little dex-meth cocktail."

"Would you say that is preferable to Benzedrine?" Mustafa inquires, as though seeking his mentor's advice on neckties or the proper fragrance for men.

"One's no cooler than the other. Whatever pins your eyes open."

Two Arizona Highway Patrol cars appear in front of the hotel entrance, one behind the other.

"Our escort has arrived," Charlie says.

Mustafa finishes washing down a bennie with Mountain Dew. As they head toward the front door, he says, "This is going to be a memorable ride."

10

Horseman's Haven had a jukebox. Tom Buckle had never seen one other than in movies, because every restaurant in which he'd eaten during his young life had provided one kind of annoying piped-in music or another. This jukebox seemed to be stocked with nothing but country stars, past and present. Even before Tom and Porter Crockett received their meals, another patron, eating lunch and drinking alone at the bar, began feeding the machine coins, filling the establishment with songs about faithless wives and lost love and lonely nights.

The music provided cover for their conversation, and by the time they were having coffee, Tom had told the colonel everything that Hollister had revealed about the Arcadians, the nanoweb control mechanism, and the Hamlet list. He recounted the death of Mai-Mai, the twists and turns of the hunt in the snow. More than once he marveled that Porter absorbed it all with no skepticism, almost as if he already knew everything he was being told.

When Tom again remarked on the colonel's credulousness, Porter said, "Son, some years now, I been watchin' the world go crazy with technology. Twenty years, we been told the Internet and smartphones and all the new ways we get information are makin' us smarter, but lately all the studies show our attention span shrinkin' along with our IQ. There's that man builds electric cars, says we need to move to Mars to save the human race, as if a world with no air and maybe two buckets of water, a cold ways from the sun, can be some kind of paradise. Same man and some other movers and shakers say robots are gonna be a lot smarter than the folks who design and build them, but the precedent tells us think again."

" 'Precedent'?"

"Thousands of years, people been thinkin' they're smarter than God, but I've not yet seen one build a universe or a planet, or even figure how to make a brand-new bitty animal we never seen before. So when you say these Arcadians are hell-bent on changin' the world by injectin' nanomachines into people's brains . . . Well, the idea seems no less likely than schemin' to move a few million people to Mars and build cities for them when we can't even figure how to help the homeless here among us."

Beyond the window, a black-and-white Jeep Cherokee, bearing the seal of the county sheriff's department, cruised slowly along the street. An identical vehicle followed closely behind the first. A third slowed and turned into the Horseman's Haven parking lot.

Porter Crockett threw some money on the table and pushed his chair back and said, "Come with me, Tom."

"Where?"

"Somewhere not here."

Tom followed Colonel Crockett through a swinging door into the kitchen, where their waitress, Louise, was waiting to pick up a customer's order from the cook's ready counter.

"Darlin'," Porter said to her, "this here friend of mine is a good man with a bad man after him."

"What bad man?" she asked.

"Wainwright Hollister, usin' the sheriff for the search, though my friend never did break no law."

"*That* sonofabitch," said Louise, and the cook looked up from the griddle to say, "Hollister is a spooky piece of shit."

"He runs this territory like it's his own ranch," Louise said.

Porter put a hand on her shoulder. "I just need to tuck Tom here away for a little while. You still hide the spare key to your place where you always have?"

"Same place."

"Okay if we settle in for a few hours?"

"Sure, sweetheart. What about your pickup out front?"

"You walk to work today?" Porter asked.

"Like always."

"Then just say you're usin' the Ford while I stay with you a few days."

Louise kissed him on the cheek. It was the kind of casual and yet meaningful kiss that Tom would have given anything to encourage from the actors in one of his films.

"I think they'll be comin' in the front door soon," said the colonel.

"Then skedaddle," Louise said.

Porter led Tom through the kitchen, past the small staff, which ignored them as if taking their cue from Louise and the cook. They left Horseman's Haven by the back door, stepping into an employee parking lot.

Tom said, "You and Louise—you're an item?"

"I'd marry her in a minute," the colonel said, "but she's not as sure as I am."

"How long you been a widower?"

"Too damn long. It's a lonely life in the best of times, and a lot lonelier these past seven years."

11

The rest area where Jane and Vikram left the four naked men in the Buick was about fourteen miles north of Casa Grande. Twenty-six miles farther north, in Tempe, on the perimeter of the Phoenix metroplex, they stopped at a supermarket and filled the Southwind refrigerator with food and drink that would carry them through the next forty-eight hours, though Vikram thought he would need no more than half that long to fillet out the remaining truth of the Techno Arcadians: who they were, down to the last one; and every individual whom they had corrupted with brain implants.

A mutual silence had endured since the rest area, but as they headed west on Interstate 10 toward the suburbs of Tolleson and Avondale, Goodyear and Littlefield Park, Vikram suddenly broke into laughter. He laughed so hard that he almost needed to pull off the highway.

"What?" Jane asked.

He quoted what she'd said to the thug named Johnny. " 'There's no panel of judges. You don't have to worry about settling for Miss Congeniality.' "

Jane laughed. "Yeah, well, good for him there were no judges. He had a lumpy ass. Anyway, I was impressed how quick Fidel figured it out. 'Four naked guys in a car with three tires.' "

Vikram quoted her again. " 'Oh, good. You understand the basic situation.' "

She hadn't laughed this much in a long time. It felt good.

When his laughter subsided, Vikram said, "Are all the bad guys *that* stupid?"

"Not all, but most. Evil is always stupid and unimaginative. Creation is the hard thing. Destruction—evil—is easy and boring, the same short list of crimes and cruelties over and over."

Solemnity slowly settled over them. Jane sensed a revelation coming, and she was not wrong.

He said, "I guess you know what you mean to me. And I'm not talking . . . romance. I know where you are on that and always will be. Why you mean so much to me is . . . because of all you are and all you've done."

She had encountered this before, not just from him but also from others, as if an elaborate urban legend were encrusting around her. She was profoundly unnerved by it. "I'm just another girl, Vikram. Events threw me into this, events beyond my control. I didn't choose it. I never would have. It's all necessity. I'm nobody's hero."

He said, "When those corrupt bastards in the DOJ wanted me to build back doors to all those systems, I did it."

"You were doing what the deputy attorney general ordered you to do. As far as you knew, they had the legal authority."

"No. I knew damn well it was corrupt. That's why I also built a separate set of back doors that I kept secret from them, in case I needed my own wicked little babies for self-defense one day. I knew it was wrong, but it was so damn exciting . . . a challenge. I can be a show-off, a sucker for challenges."

Borrowing a gesture from him, she pointed at the ceiling with her index finger as though to say, *One important point to consider.* "Enough, Vikram. Don't beat yourself up. You don't deserve it."

"But you," he continued, determined to have his say. "You always walked a straight line at the Bureau."

"Not always."

"Yes, always. And when you realized they were corrupted by these people, these Arcadians, you bailed. You not only bailed, you also cut their legs out from under them, and you keep cutting their legs out from under them every day."

To have the respect of another was a welcome burden, but to be *revered* was to be crushed by expectations that no mere human being could fulfill. "Listen, the true me is no big deal. I'm only trying to stay alive. And keep my little boy alive."

In a remarkably short distance, the thriving suburbs of Phoenix feathered away into thinly populated desert. Pale land, pale sky. Black highway ribboning toward a horizon beyond which lay a future that simultaneously inspired hope and dread.

"I want to help you," Vikram said, "also because I must pay penance for the death of two cousins. Their names were Sanjay and Tanuja Shukla, brother and sister. Twins. Talented writers—brilliant— only twenty-five years old. A week ago, they . . . they murdered six people and then killed themselves. But they weren't killers. They could not have been. No way."

"Oh, Vikram. I am so sorry."

He had been making an effort to report this tragedy with at least minimum detachment, but a thin tremor of grief now threaded his voice. "They were both so sweet. So very kind. They were not depressed, Jane. They were successful and happy. I thought of your Nick, and at once I *knew*. Now I know for sure, because . . . because of the Hamlet list. And I must pay penance."

She said, "If they were injected with control mechanisms, they have no responsibility for what they did. But, honey, you didn't inject them. You have nothing to pay penance for."

"I've discovered the assistant attorney general is an Arcadian. He's among the thirty-eight hundred I told you about. He ordered me to build those back doors and plant rootkits in all those computer systems. He gave me the challenge, knowing I'm a show-off, a sucker for challenges."

"He's a user, and he used you. But you aren't a user. You aren't like him."

He nodded, but for a couple miles, he seemed unable to speak. Then he said, "Sanjay and Tanuja aren't the end of it. I'm afraid for my cousin Ganesh. Something is wrong."

"You spoke to him last night."

"I've called him twice since. Both times I got voicemail. We agreed—Uncle Ashok and Aunt Doris and Ganesh, all my relatives who've gone into hiding—we will keep our disposable phones charged and on for the duration, to warn one another of . . . of events."

"There could be explanations other than the worst. Did you leave messages?"

"No. I hung up before the call could be traced to source."

"Let's make a pact," she said. "Let's not kill Ganesh by *thinking* him dead. Let's think he's alive, and maybe he will be."

Vikram nodded again, unable to speak.

"You are a dear soul," she said.

The highway before them was smooth and open. Historically, however, the road to every utopia was paved with blood and bones, leading not to the dreamed-of perfection of humanity and society, but to mass murder, madness, and for a while the death of hope.

12

The cookies were homemade and crisp and tasty. The coffee was good, too, and Travis's chocolate milk looked rich.

Cornell liked the ceramic mug. It was big and pale brown and held a lot of coffee. He liked the kitchen table, too, made all of dark wood and highly polished. Everything felt very substantial, as if it might still be here long after the collapse of civilization.

The kitchen was cozy, with lots of copper pots and pans hanging overhead and golden-granite countertops and dark cabinets to match the table. It was a strange place, yet it felt familiar to Cornell, as though he had been here before, like in another life. He did not enjoy strange places, because you never knew what might happen in them, but this place felt as if nothing bad could happen here.

A puddle of fur in one corner of the room was Duke and Queenie and a golden retriever named Yankel, who had exhausted themselves in play and were now drowsing together.

He and Travis and Mr. Riggowitz sat around the table in their pajamas, eating cookies, as if they belonged here, and it was really amazing that none of them was dead.

The rabbi seemed to be very nice but crazy busy, coming and going from the kitchen, always in a hurry, reporting one thing or another to Mr. Riggowitz. Cornell never met a rabbi before. When he heard there was one in the house, he was frightened, but it turned out that he had no reason to be afraid.

The best thing about the place was Mrs. Rabbi, who had given them the cookies and brewed the coffee. She was sitting with them, making a list of what clothes they needed and what sizes they wore. She intended to go shopping shortly. Mrs. Rabbi was a pretty lady with a musical voice, but she was more than just pretty and sweet sounding. When she got up to pour more coffee and to get Travis more milk, it was like Mr. Paul Simon sang: *She moved so easily, all I could think of was sunlight.*

The Mercedes Sprinter, owned by the skinny kidnapper and would-be killer, had been tucked away in the rabbi's garage. The rabbi said a reliable man named Leshem would be coming to take it all the way to Tucson and abandon it there.

At the rabbi's request, a member of the synagogue drove by the Cantor house. He said the street "looked like an FBI parking lot."

Mr. Riggowitz and the rabbi were in agreement that the rabbi's house might be a place where the FBI would come searching for them in due time, so plans were afoot to move them later in the day.

Cornell made it as clear as possible to Mrs. Rabbi that he could wear only white socks and white underwear, never the color red in anything—never, never—please and thank you, and only sneakers, but not those made by any company with a *K* in its name. When she noted all of this on her shopping list, he untied the knot in the neck of the pillowcase, which he'd brought in his luggage all the way from Borrego Valley and which was the only thing he salvaged from his possessions at the Cantor house, and he put two packets of hundred-dollar bills on the table. "I believe this will be enough to clothe all three of us, please and thank you."

"Mr. Jasperson," she said, "this is twenty thousand dollars. It's far too much for what's on this list."

"Umm. Umm. Umm. Maybe you could buy the dogs some toys, too. The dogs like toys. They are good dogs."

13

For fifteen highly profitable years, Enrique de Soto operated out of a series of weathered barns on a former horse ranch near Nogales, Arizona, which happened to be right across the border from Nogales, Mexico. He dealt in a variety of black-market merchandise, though his biggest profit center was pre-owned vehicles stolen in the States, taken into Mexico, remade to be untraceable, stripped of GPS, and reworked to outrun anything law-enforcement agencies could afford to provide to their officers. Enrique did not personally deal in narcotics, because the potential penalties upon capture disturbed him, though he took pride in the fact that wheels of his creation had imported uncountable thousands of pounds—tons and tons—of cocaine, heroin, methamphetamine, and other substances desired by American consumers but denied to them by their puritanical government. He had created highly clever voids in those vehicles and lined them with a material of his own devising that foiled even the best-trained drug-sniffing dogs, and his only regret was that he could not file for a patent on his method of ensuring safe delivery of contra- band.

Enrique *did* engage in the importation and sale of all manner of weapons, from handguns to fully automatic rifles to bricks of C-4 plastic explosives. He also maintained a thriving business in human trafficking, conveying into the United States illegal aliens, MS-13 gang members eager to establish operations in U.S. cities large and small, terrorists from the Middle East and elsewhere, and attractive young girls drugged and sold into sex slavery.

With eleven employees on the Mexican side of the enterprise and seven on the U.S. side, Enrique had a big payroll to meet. However, his costs were low compared to other private-sector businesses, for he paid no taxes of any kind on his earnings or those of his crew. Fur- thermore, he was spared hundreds of hours of tedious paperwork every year because he filed no government forms, which allowed him plenty of time for playing video games, reading graphic novels, banging his current lady, and inventing TV shows.

If he gave up his current career and went into television-program development, he would be a great success. The greatest ever. He had no doubt about that. In fact, he had no doubt about anything. He was as self-confident as an immortal.

The latest TV idea that intrigued Enrique was inspired by the real- ization that he and his stateside employees were outnumbered by the dead people buried in unmarked graves on this acreage, most of them idiots who had double-crossed him or become inconvenient for one reason or another. They numbered fourteen, not counting the four who had been fed to the boars, of which there had been nothing much left to bury, because the pigs liked bones as much as meat. He first saw the show as a *Walking Dead* kind of thing, but he couldn't figure how to extend it past six hours. Now he thought it could be like a cross between *Walking Dead* and an Elmore Leonard crime story, about this dealer in black-market vehicles and human trafficking—call him Ricky D—who employed voodoo to control the dead people he'd killed, using them to whack his enemies and provide a kick-ass security force for the former horse ranch that was the center of Ricky D's criminal empire.

Whether for a TV crime boss or in his own life, Enrique de Soto believed in multilayered security. One of those layers was a network of paid informants in local and state law enforcement. Although too many cops believed in truth, justice, and the American way, as if that Clark Kent world wasn't decades dead, there were others who knew which way the wind was blowing and were ready to be carried along with it.

That Saturday afternoon, Enrique was at his desk, in his office, in the barn nearest the highway, which was stocked with a bedlamic variety of junk and dressed up to pass as an antiques shop to front the true business. Enrique was eating lunch and doing research by watching a DVD of a movie titled *Voodoo Dawn*. The film, a 1990 release, was rated R for violence and nudity, though for Enrique's taste, there wasn't enough of either.

The first time his phone rang, the caller was a contact inside the Arizona Highway Patrol. He reported that two units had been assigned and dispatched to provide a police escort for a pair of high-ranking officials of the FBI, to get them from Casa Grande to Nogales in record time. The destination was Enrique's address.

Enrique withdrew a Brugger & Thomet TP9 with a thirty-round magazine from a desk drawer. He bolted to his feet and went to the wall to the left of the door. He popped the plastic cover off a thermostat.

His phone rang again. A fly on the wall in the county sheriff's department urgently informed him that ICE agents were mounting an imminent raid on his property and had asked the sheriff to assist by closing the intersections of certain county roads for the duration of the operation.

"You've got probably like ten minutes," the caller said. "Or maybe just eight."

Enrique manually forced the red temperature indicator from 70 to 78 and replaced the cover on the thermostat. Eight minutes.

As he hurried through the fake antiques barn, he knew what had gone wrong for him. Jane Hawk had gone wrong for him. Jane Hawk and her geek friend Rangnekar. What kind of name was Rangnekar, anyway? It damn sure wasn't an *American* name. Foreign, un-American, *weird*. De Soto, now, that was an all-American name. DeSoto had even been an American car, built from 1928 through 1960. There never had been and never would be a car named the Rangnekar. Enrique had nothing to do with the people the car had been named for, whoever the assholes might have been, but he was proud to have a truly American name.

He departed the barn by the exit least visible from the county road, assuming surveillance might already have been established. In case he was under observation from a distance, he didn't run along the oiled-dirt driveway that served the series of five barns, but ambled as though he hadn't a care, while grasshoppers sang in the tall golden grass and the fireweed that bristled on both sides of the lane.

The first time Hawk came to him to buy a set of wheels, he should have set her up so that his guys could Taser her and tie her and take her to his apartment on the second floor of the third barn. He should have stripped her and spent the last few months teaching her just what she was good for. But she was on the run, wanted, and Enrique was just too nice a guy not to give her a chance against the feds. His biggest problem always had been that he was too nice to people, and they mistook niceness for weakness, and then he had to kill them.

Barns two and three were used for storage of parts and ready-to-roll inventory. Barn four was where authentic-looking license plates were stamped and various other tasks were performed. Barn five was reserved for vehicles that had been returned from Mexico rebuilt and marketable but that required modifications to meet the needs of a specific buyer. At the moment, all seven of Enrique's employees were busy there.

Vikram Rangnekar's Fleetwood Southwind had been modified in barn five, while his cousin Harshad had overseen the work to ensure that Enrique would do it exactly as specified. What kind of name was Harshad, anyway? Enrique should have killed Harshad and canceled the deal for the Southwind, should have killed all five Rangnekars when they first showed up, but he had this thing for Jane Hawk. He had this thing, and Vikram Rangnekar claimed to want to help her, and now it had come to this. Niceness and horniness were a dangerous combination.

Several power tools were in use when Enrique entered barn five. He shouted to be heard over them, and he cringed when he realized that he sounded just like that terrified bug in those insecticide commercials: "*RAID!*"

14

Where there had once been a forlorn and untraveled sea, tens of thousands of years before the advent of humankind, now lay a lonely vastness of sand and stone and scattered brush under a pale-blue sky empty of all but color.

At Tonopah, about fifty miles west of Phoenix, they left the interstate, passed through town on blacktop, and then headed north on a gravel-over-hardpan road that Vikram had identified during his planning. The track was crude but navigable even for a motor home towing an SUV, and they followed it into a wasteland that appeared without prospect but that might be the place where the destruction of the Arcadians began.

Maricopa County was stippled with unimpressive, largely barren mountains—the Big Horn Mountains, the White Tank Mountains, the Vulture Mountains—all stark and forbidding. But there were more flatlands than slopes, and Vikram followed a route that brought them to a place as lonely as any Jane had ever seen, where he came to a stop off the gravel.

"Nothing in the way," he said as he shut off the engine.

Getting up from her seat, Jane said, "In the way of what?"

"The dish has to have a clear line of sight toward the equator. The satellites that transmit the Internet are positioned directly over Earth's equator."

Enrique's people had created a well about nine inches deep in the roof of the Southwind, above the bedroom, reducing the interior ceiling height of seven feet to a little over six. This ensured that once Vikram installed the satellite dish in the well, there would be no danger that it would be ripped off if they passed through a low-clearance underpass or other overhang during the desperate evasive maneuvers that might be necessary in the hours ahead.

Vikram said, "Help me raise the dish package to the roof?"

"Let's get it done."

As Jane strapped on the shoulder rig with the Heckler in the holster, Vikram said, "No one can track us yet, and we're miles from nowhere."

She picked up the confiscated Glock 17 as a backup gun. "Miles from nowhere isn't the same as being miles from trouble."

15

Bracketed by highway patrol cruisers, their sirens shrilling and lightbars flashing but paled by the Arizona brightness, Mustafa al-Yamani drives the simple black Suburban with dignity, even if he and Charlie have earned—and are accustomed to—far more exalted vehicles. They are traveling Interstate 19 at such extreme speed that the road seems to have fallen away under them, as if they are flying an inch or two above the pavement, bulleting along. This is most exhilarating.

Mustafa is excited about the upcoming raid and the prospect of learning what vehicle Enrique de Soto provided to Vikram Rangnekar, but he is not focused solely on matters of the revolution. His mind is a Benzedrine wonderland of bright thoughts about the beaches of Long Island and the glittering mansions of East Egg, about Ring Jacket suits and Edward Green loafers, glamorous women in stunning dresses by Erdem and Alexander McQueen and Dior and Yolan Cris, the same glamorous women reclining naked on a blue mohair sofa by Fendi, and of course the woman of all women, his own Daisy Buchanan—or whatever her name will eventually prove to be—an incomparable beauty of the classiest kind, from a family of status, wearing nothing but Louis Vuitton ankle boots, those sexy ones in red leather and gray snakeskin.

They are deep into Santa Cruz County, Tumacácori far in the rearview mirror, maybe still twelve miles from the site of the raid, which is already under way. At their current speed, they'll be there in eight minutes. De Soto will reveal what vehicle Rangnekar bought, what modifications might have been made that will suggest something of his purpose, clues to where he might have gone after taking delivery in Casa Grande. Charlie says he smells Jane Hawk, but Mustafa smells triumph, smells the gunfire that will bring down the bitch, smells her reeking corpse, which for him is the sweet smell of glory, because her destruction will elevate Charlie and him to the very pinnacle of the Arcadian pyramid: *This* is the ideal fragrance for men.

16

The escape vehicles were stored in the fifth of the five barns, one for Enrique and for each of his seven employees. In anticipation of an eventual raid, they had planned to flee overland by multiple preplanned routes and would cross the border not at checkpoints, but through the wilds.

Enrique kept no business records or client lists in Nogales, Arizona. Everything incriminating remained in Mexico, in the files of Purify the Planet Now, a nonprofit that ostensibly supported environmental causes, but in fact was the repository of Enrique's fortune and manager of his many legitimate investments. The organization also performed work beneficial to the earth by planting as many as thirty trees each year, as well as by banning the use of plastic cups and straws in its offices.

Although Enrique would lose significant inventory and some expensive equipment in the forthcoming raid, it was a pittance when compared to his net worth. Finding a new U.S. property from which to operate in the future and acquiring a new identity supported by deep documentation would be a bother, but he had been through all that previously when he had become Enrique de Soto.

Riding eight Honda 250cc motocross bikes with Bridgestone M78 rear tires that could devour hard terrain, Enrique and his crew racketed out of barn five like a swarm of hornets fleeing a burning nest and split into ones and twos, following five different overland routes to the border. Simultaneously, a screaming chorus of sirens announced the explosive entrance of maybe ten ICE and Homeland Security Suburbans, Jeeps, and Dodge Chargers that burst off the county road onto the property so abruptly they seemed to have erupted through a veil between this world and one parallel to it.

Glancing over his shoulder, Enrique saw three all-wheel-drive vehicles trying to chase down the motorcycles, a fruitless pursuit considering the superior maneuverability of the bikes. The other units were fanning out to secure the five buildings—which was when the barns blew up, one after the other.

17

In the barren wastelands of Maricopa County, along a crude gravel road, far from the nearest highway . . .

Together, Jane and Vikram created a snug rope sling around the satellite-dish package. He climbed onto the roof of the Southwind by way of a ladder on the port side, taking the end of the sling rope with him, and then pulled the dish up. She ascended to the top of the vehicle and assisted with the installation, fitting the dish to a motorized adjustment arm that would keep it angled south toward the equator even when the motor home was in motion.

The coaxial cables of the dish passed through gasketed holes in the roof well and into the bedroom below, where Vikram would shortly connect them to modems at the computer setup that had been installed by Enrique under the watchful eye of Cousin Harshad. The bedroom had no bed, only a built-in workstation with two computers, attendant equipment, and a wheeled office chair.

In the Southwind, Vikram gave Jane an earpiece with a pendant microphone. "Walkie-talkie. To send, just touch the mic casing with your finger, like this, before speaking."

She touched the mic, spoke, heard the ghost of her voice issue from his earpiece. Another touch cleared the line for his response.

"When you're behind the wheel or anywhere else, we'll remain connected while I'm buccaneering through various computer systems. Periodically I'll switch from one to another of those thirty-six Internet service provider accounts I mentioned, so that I'll appear to be different users. Some security programs have a suspicious-user alarm triggered by activities that don't conform to one or another average pattern of engagement—like maybe an unusual length of time spent in their system. Switching from one ISP to another ought to conceal that it's the same user."

"'Ought to'?" she asked.

"If I'm hit with a locked-on alert, I'll disconnect before they can get a fix on our location, then I'll reenter through another ISP account."

"Suppose they locate us anyway?"

"It's not going to be easy for them, considering we're tapping into the Internet by satellite. But if they get a fix on us anyway, then you've got to haul ass while I try to finish getting what we need."

The bespoke Southwind was fitted with two auxiliary fuel tanks. All three tanks had been filled in Tempe. They contained sufficient gasoline to power the idling engine through the rest of Saturday, well into Sunday, with enough remaining to go on the run—for a while.

"How long till you're online?"

"Maybe twenty minutes."

"I'll start the engine. Then what can I do?"

"Be ready," he said. "Just be ready. I guess you should have brought a book to pass the time."

"Got one in my head. *The Book of What If.* Infinite number of pages and scary as shit."

18

Charlie Weatherwax is accustomed to entering the scene of a raid in the wake of the team that subdues the miscreants. Homeland Security is a bureaucratic nightmare, like a bizarre Hieronymus Bosch painting come to life, but the armed grunts on the ground are competent, especially those in ICE, which is under the jurisdiction of Homeland and reliably conducts efficient raids like the one targeting Enrique de Soto.

But when Mustafa pulls their Suburban off the county road onto the de Soto property and brakes to a stop, Charlie finds a vista of chaos unlike anything he could have anticipated. Five big fires are raging, flinging into the sky dazzling sheets of blue-orange flames like flocks of mythical phoenixes reborn from their death pyres. Continuing detonations shudder the burning walls of the barns as containers of combustible materials and the fuel tanks of vehicles succumb to the heat, swelling and bursting. Smaller fires flicker across the fields of dry grass, where burning embers have fallen, and half a dozen blackened cottonwoods stand ablaze like many-armed demons in some crazed vision of Hell. Two ICE vehicles, having been near the buildings when the explosions occurred, are already shells filled with fire, canted on melted tires, and the dust-control oil that has been sprayed on the dirt lane is acrawl with iridescent beetles of blue flame.

ICE agents are running for their vehicles. Some are shooting while on the run, in violation of their training. Charlie cannot at first understand what has panicked them or at whom their gunfire is directed. Then the first massive creature appears, at least six hundred pounds of low-slung, fast-moving muscle, a horrific vision of Death on cloven hooves.

"What is that?" asks Mustafa in alarmed bafflement. "Is that a pig, a hog?"

"A wild boar," Charlie says.

"It has horns like a steer."

"They're not horns. They're tusks. It's a boar."

"Are there wild boars in this territory?" Mustafa asks.

"No. And these look like they don't belong in North America. Too big. They're maybe European forest hogs, maybe from Germany."

"How'd they get here?"

"This Enrique lunatic must have imported them through South America and then smuggled them across the border. And fed them well."

The smoke from the barns rises straight into the sky, but the lesser smoke from the spotty grass fires now feathers out across the property like a thin fog, bringing an eerie dreamlike quality to the scene.

Two additional boars appear. One catches up with a fleeing ICE agent, and the consequence gives credence to the belief that nature is not reliably a friend of humanity.

"Ouch," says Mustafa. "I gather these animals are carnivores, or at least omnivores. But are they always this frenzied, is that why they're called 'wild' boars?"

"By nature, they're ferocious and easily incensed. But these are especially pissed by the fires, the explosions, the gunshots."

Now there are five gigantic boars plunging this way and that among the small fires in the field, squealing with such outrage that their chilling voices carry above all else.

The largest of the creatures, finding itself facing the port flank of the Suburban from a distance of twenty yards, freezes and raises its massive head and seems to fixate on the vehicle. It paws the ground with one hoof.

Mustafa locks the doors. "Should we retreat to safer ground?"

"Just wait," Charlie advises. "Someone will take them out."

"Who? Who will take them out?"

Head lowered, the boar charges. Its skull is thick, a slab of bone that makes an effective battering ram. When it slams into the Suburban, the metal of the driver's door shrieks and buckles, the window glass cracks, and the vehicle rocks on its tires.

The beast stands about three and a half feet tall. However, it can rear somewhat on its hind legs, and when it does, it comes face-to-face with Mustafa, its tusks rattling against the cracked window, chisel-edged teeth revealed in a snarl, its beady eyes two pools of dark glistening hatred. As the window shatters, the animal drops to the ground, and glass wet with thick porcine saliva tumbles into Mustafa's lap.

Snorting, grunting, the boar turns from the Suburban and trots back through the haze of smoke to the point from which it launched its assault, evidently not injured. It circles and circles, glancing repeatedly at them, as though trying to make up its mind whether to attack again.

"I don't eat pork," says Mustafa. "I never have."

19

The town of Willisford flanked the east-west county road and boasted one additional long, parallel street—Gower's Lane—on the south side of which stood the simple two-story house belonging to the waitress at Horseman's Haven, Louise Walters.

The rooms were spotless. Pale-gray walls with white ceilings and white woodwork. An open floor plan more elegantly conceived than the exterior of the house. Contemporary furnishings, soft-edged and welcoming, had been brought together with such style as to suggest that Louise watched a lot of home-makeover shows on television.

Neither draperies nor shades covered the windows. Each was flanked by glossy white shutters that could be closed when privacy or sun control was wanted. The shutters featured wide, adjustable louvers.

On the second floor, in the master bedroom, Tom Buckle and Porter Crockett stood side by side at a large window. They peered between the louvers, past a decades-old bare-limbed sycamore that dominated the front yard.

How prudent Porter had been to hustle Tom out of Horseman's Haven immediately on seeing the Jeep Cherokees bearing the sheriff's department shields. The two had crossed an alley, passed through the property on which stood a clapboard church with a shingled steeple, and hurried east on Gower's Lane for a block and a half before coming to Louise Walters's residence. At the colonel's suggestion, rather than tramping through the fresh snow on the front walkway and around to the back of the house, thus leaving two distinct sets of footprints, they kicked through it, disturbing it to such an extent that several people might have come and gone from the house. By the time they left their boots in the mudroom and went upstairs in their stocking feet to the master-bedroom window, a Dodge Charger, also from the sheriff's department, was cruising by slowly, quietly along Gower, traveling east to west, its tire chains leaving crosshatch patterns in the snow.

Three shorter streets connected Gower and the county road, including Fortnam Way to the west of the Walters house. The Dodge stopped there, in the intersection, its lightbar flashing.

When Porter leaned close to a gap between louvers and squinted east toward Barkley Way, he said, "Another patrol is blockin' that intersection."

"They know I'm here," Tom said. "How can they know I'm here? The tracking device was in my jacket. I'm sure of that."

"Maybe they don't know any damn thing, son. Maybe they only

suspect. If they knew your certain whereabouts, they'd already be surroundin' the house. Instead, they seem suspicious of the whole town."

20

Leaving the engine running, Jane Hawk stepped out of the sweet cool air of the Fleetwood Southwind into the warm desert afternoon and closed the door behind her. She stood for a moment, staring at the gravel road dwindling south toward I-10 and northwest toward the tiny town of Aguila and State Highway 60.

She walked around the motor home and studied the arid plain to the east, as if it might be a preview of a future Earth that would become a desolation from pole to pole.

At least the land was bright, unlike the world beyond the night window in her dream. She walked a short distance into it, to a rock formation about three feet high and forty feet long, segmented like the vertebrae of a Jurassic-era skeleton that uncountable millennia of wind had gradually exposed.

She sat on the spine of that imagined reptilian terror and watched the motor home and listened to the stillness and considered what would need to be done next if Vikram indeed acquired the names of every Arcadian, those of all the people they had adjusted with nanoweb brain implants, and the location of laboratories in addition to the Menlo Park labs of the late Bertold Shenneck. No matter how she approached the problem, one particular action rose to the top of a list of options. In fact, it wasn't just an option, but instead a necessary subsequent step, essential if the Arcadians were to be defeated. As she contemplated it, she grew cold in the desert sun.

Smoothing one hand over the stone beside her, studying the patterns of the minute particulates that composed it, she marveled, not for the first time, at the baroque intricacy of matter and the innumerable forces, known and unknown, that forged and shaped even the most seemingly simple things.

A section of the stone proved to be fractured, and it wobbled under her fingers. She lifted an inch-thick piece twice the size of her hand, revealing a cuniculus, a winding burrow, about half an inch in diameter. Some tiny creature—possibly worm or beetle—had excavated this during Earth's long preparation for the advent of humanity, perhaps millions of years before the earliest women and men, when this stone might have been just superthick mud hardening under great pressure.

Before her lay exposed a mere portion of the tunneler's work, neither its beginning nor its end, and she could only guess at the intent behind this industrious labor. Whatever the motivation and the goal, the purpose of the ancient excavator had been important, as all things were important, even essential, on the foundational level of the world, from which all else that came had been shapen.

She was but one woman, one small being in an infinite universe, another tunneler making her way through a medium different from mud, through a stratum of human society that was corrupted by a lust for power and utopian ideology, that mocked the concept of free will and therefore despised freedom. She was excavating a long and twisting cuniculus through the foundation of the Arcadian revolution with the purpose of weakening it, that it might collapse in ruins.

She mattered no less than any person of goodwill—though she mattered no more, either. There was the work you sought in life and the harder work you were given that you wouldn't have chosen. The truth, if you dared face it, was that you could never know with certainty which work mattered more, which would shape a better future; therefore, you couldn't focus only on what you wanted and ignore what was needed of you. However, Jane was no blind worm or squirming beetle; the twists and turns that she took daily in the excavation of her cuniculus were decisions made with free will, which must be used in service to truth, because free will in service to falsehood was the source of much death and all earthly horror.

Chilled in the Arizona heat, considering what would be required of her if Vikram succeeded, she heard a motor purring. She looked up and saw the satellite dish assuming a new position, the high-gain antenna at its center pointing due south toward the sky above the equator.

She rose from the spine of stone and returned to the motor home and went to the bedroom at the back.

Grinning, Vikram swiveled in his office chair to face Jane. "I'm on-line. My wicked little babies await."

"Before you start," she said, "I need you to send an email for me." She gave him the address and the message.

21

Standing at the window in Louise Walters's bedroom, shifting his attention between the patrol cars blocking the intersections half a block to the east and half a block to the west, Tom Buckle said, "If they do a house-to-house, we're screwed."

Coming out of the adjoining bathroom after considering the possibilities of the supply closet in there, Porter Crockett said, "They'd need a bushel of search warrants."

"These aren't people who give a damn about warrants. Anyway, all they need is a judge who's like them—or who's been adjusted."

"I suspect the sheriff himself has one of them webs on his brain," Porter said.

"And maybe all his deputies."

Past the sycamore tree, beyond the single-story house across the street, beyond the alleyway behind the house, at the farm supply facing onto the county road, one of Wainwright Hollister's Sno-Cats hoved into view and came to a stop in the parking lot.

Before Tom could call Porter's attention to this development, engine noise from a significant vehicle growled along Gower's Lane.

The second Sno-Cat appeared in the intersection at Fortnam, tracked past the patrol car there, entered this block, and stopped. Four men in identical storm suits disembarked from it.

With a shudder, Tom said, "Rayshaws."

22

The fires are subsiding, the barns collapsing. Using a sniper rifle, from the roof of a Suburban, an ICE agent, a former Navy SEAL, has killed three of the wild boars. The other two have galloped away to the east, heading toward the luckless outlying neighborhoods of Nogales to wreak whatever havoc they can.

This guy who works for Enrique de Soto went for a tumble when his bike hit a boar and flipped airborne over the animal. He claims his name is Hugo Chávez, which is unlikely. For one thing, he doesn't resemble the dead dictator. He's a blond, blue-eyed, Germanic slab. He has no ID to support his claim to have governed Venezuela into ruin. He wishes his captors to believe that he lost his wallet in the collision with the boar.

Hugo Chávez is a problem for Charlie Weatherwax. The man has broken his wrist, which is swollen and surely painful, but that isn't why he is a problem. Hugo seems to have a high pain threshold, and he's one of those macho men who would strive to hide his discomfort if you pinned his hand to his thigh with a nail gun. Anyway, Charlie doesn't care about Hugo's pain or his need for medical attention.

The man is demanding an attorney, but that isn't a problem, either. Charlie doesn't believe in attorneys for the defense, only for the prosecution. Besides, the odds that Hugo will live long enough to find himself in a courtroom are worse than a sloth's chances of making it across a NASCAR raceway during the main event.

The problem with Hugo is that Charlie and Mustafa do not have a Medexpress carrier containing a nanotech control mechanism, and even if they could arrange for one to be brought to them in short order, they don't have the time to sit around waiting for the nanoweb to form in this wise guy's brain. They need to get a lead on Jane Hawk sooner than now, by any means necessary.

The destruction of the barns is a double blow to Charlie. Any records Enrique de Soto might have kept, regarding vehicles sold to Rangnekar and Hawk, are ashes. Hugo is the only potential source of information. But no place remains on the property where the man can be adequately interrogated. Anyway, not all of the agents who were impressed into this raid are Arcadians; several are common plebs who wouldn't find Charlie's techniques acceptable.

They load Hugo into the back of their Suburban, supposedly to convey him to the nearest federal detention facility. Charlie sits next to him with the muzzle of a pistol jammed in the fool's side in case that, in spite of his shattered wrist, he decides he has a chance to escape.

Mustafa drives not north on I-19, but northeast on State Highway 82 toward Patagonia. Along the way are some isolated properties set back from the two-lane blacktop, and Mustafa pulls off the road to look over a few of them.

Hugo Chávez senses something amiss in the way that he is being conveyed to an arraignment. Even though he isn't familiar with FBI protocols, he expresses his concern. "This is shit, man, what you're doing here. What is this shit?"

Charlie says, "Shut up."

"Nobody can tell nobody to shut up, man. That's just cop shit. I got free speech rights just like you do."

"Shut up."

"I need a hospital. You see this wrist? You *see* this? I could say you done this to me. Police brutality."

Charlie says nothing. He can say nothing in such a way that it alarms people into a silence of their own, which is what happens to Hugo Chávez.

23

The limestone-clad building had once been a fraternal club, but the sign above the entrance now said RED, WHITE, BLUE, AND DINNER. A line in smaller lettering promised three square meals a day.

This privately funded facility, serving San Diego's poorest citizens, was quiet between lunch and dinner. In the main dining room, the tables were empty, the cafeteria line not staffed at the moment.

Cooks toiled busily in the kitchen, and the air was fragrant with sautéed onions, chicken soup in process, and chili bubbling in a five-gallon pot.

The kitchen manager's office had a desk, computer, shelves of cookbooks, and two windows that were painted black. The bearish man at the desk, working on accounts payable, was Dougal Trahern, whose charitable foundation, funded by his years as a wise investor, financed this operation.

Three weeks earlier, on a seventy-acre Napa Valley ranch, he had taken three bullets—one in the thigh, one in the gut, and one in the chest. Miraculously, he had suffered no organ damage, but he had almost died from a loss of blood.

The ranch had belonged to Bertold Shenneck, now deceased, creator of the nanoweb brain implant. Dougal invaded the place in the company of Jane Hawk. He had come unscathed through a previous career in the U.S. Army, during which he'd been awarded the Distinguished Service Cross—one step below the Medal of Honor—so his wounds at Gee Zee Ranch seemed like the war at last catching up with him.

Charlene Dumont, who doubled as a cook and a cafeteria-line manager, stepped through the open office door and closed it behind her and said, "You wanted to see me?"

"Please have a seat, Charlene."

She settled in the chair in front of his desk. She was a black woman shaped like a plump hen, with a face that could be as sweet as that of a gospel singer enraptured by songs of Jesus or as stern as that of a drill sergeant. She was one of the finest people Dougal had ever known, and he'd known more than a few.

"I have lasagna in the oven, chili on the stove, and my veggie-prep boy cryin' in a corner 'cause the Roma tomatoes remind him of this girl he just lost. He's too soft in the head to realize she's the worst thing ever happened to him and it's better she's gone to torment some other poor fool. So don't you go givin' me the whatever about the price of fresh cilantro. I'm not in the mood."

"Cilantro isn't on my mind," Dougal assured her.

"Whatever it is," Charlene said, "you have that thundercloud forehead I know too well."

"You remember three weeks ago, I had my appendix removed—"

She interrupted. "It wasn't appendix, no matter what you say. I know a man recoverin' from a gunshot when I see one."

If Dougal had gone to a hospital, attending physicians would have reported the wounds to the authorities. Therefore, prior to the assault on Shenneck's ranch, they had arranged to receive treatment, if needed, from a former army doctor currently in private practice who was willing to keep secrets. Dr. Walkins had been given their blood types; he had a source for as many units as they might require. For two weeks, under Walkins's care, Dougal recuperated in the home of an old army friend in Napa Valley before returning to San Diego.

"A man doesn't lose thirty pounds of himself recoverin' from appendicitis," Charlene said, "or spend two weeks in bed doin' it."

Dougal sighed. "Tell me again—what medical school did you graduate from?"

Charlene said, "The street."

"Whether it was appendicitis or something else, I'm not going to argue with you about it."

"Good. Because I can't be argued into stupid."

"I hate to admit it, but I'm still not able to get up a full head of steam."

Her expression softened. "You're more than halfway there. It's only a matter of time. You'll be your old self soon enough."

The expedition that he had taken with Jane Hawk had begun to heal a lot of old traumas that were deeper than mere bullet wounds. On balance, blood loss and nearly dying and a tedious recovery were worth enduring for the changes the experience had wrought in his mind and heart.

"You remember the woman I went north with three weeks ago—Alice Liddell."

"So she called herself both when she first came here and when she came back the Monday after your . . . appendicitis."

At Gee Zee Ranch, in spite of a pitched battle with rayshaws, Jane had acquired flash drives packed full of Bertold Shenneck's research as well as ampules containing nanoweb control mechanisms stored in a cooler with ice. The following day, a Monday, she had arrived here, having acquired a Medexpress carrier from a medical supply outlet. She had left the carrier, and the ampules therein, with Charlene Dumont. Ever since, the carrier had been in the refrigerator in Dougal's apartment on the top floor of this building.

"I've had an email from her," Dougal said. "She badly needs that Medexpress carrier she left with you. I want to take it to her. More than anything, I want to do that. But I'm still shaky from time to time, and this is too important for me to risk failing her."

"Where's she want to take delivery?"

"I don't know if she's there yet. What she needs is someone to be waiting at the Best Western Rancho Grande Motel in Wickenburg, Arizona, for the next two days. She'll make contact. As I recall, you took quite a liking to her when she first came here."

Charlene nodded. "She shines."

"She's very beautiful," Dougal agreed.

"Like I care about beautiful. When I say that girl shines, I'm talkin' her heart and soul." She leaned forward in her chair and scowled with disapproval. "You don't imagine you and her . . ."

"Good grief, no. I'm an old burnt-out case, Charlene. If life could have played out different for me, I'd have wanted nothing better than to say she was my daughter."

Sitting up straight, she said, "So where's this Wickenburg?"

"I looked it up." He pushed a Google map across the desk. "Fifty miles northwest of Phoenix. You'd need to fly into the city, rent a car there. But you don't have medical credentials from Street University, so any airline will be suspicious of that Medexpress carrier. What's the fluid in those ampules? Could it be explosive? That's the way they'll think. You can't risk having it loaded as regular luggage. If it's lost . . . Well, I don't know, but I'm pretty sure it would be a disaster for Alice if it were lost. So I've booked a private jet to Phoenix."

Charlene said, "The unfortunate clothes you wear, the way you live in that monk's cell you call an apartment, I forget you're a man with money, even though you're always givin' it away. How do I dress for a private jet?"

"Any way you like. But, Charlene . . . this could be dangerous. I don't think it will be, considering what little you've got to do with it. But it could be."

Crossing her arms on her ample bosom, face radiating righteous indignation, she said, "Don't you go insultin' me, Dougal Trahern."

"I'm only warning you."

"If you think I'd turn tail from a little bit of trouble on your behalf, then you must believe I have no gratitude. Didn't you once lift me up when I was in the gutter?"

"You were never in the gutter."

"I was down where down don't get lower. You made me believe in myself and gave me hope."

"I gave you a chance. You lifted yourself. Watching you lift yourself lifted me. We're even. So now if I'm sending you off to Wickenburg, I want you to understand the danger. You need to know Alice Liddell's real name."

Charlene rolled her eyes. "Lordy, the man can be dense. She's all over the news since you had your 'appendicitis' and you think I don't know she's Jane Hawk?"

He raised his formidable eyebrows, which he sometimes did when words failed him.

Charlene continued, "Whatever she is, that girl's no monster, which means the real monsters are those who're callin' her that. I've known their type all my life, the kind who make themselves big by makin' other people small."

From a desk drawer, he removed a disposable phone. "She left this with me in Napa. It's how she'll contact you in Wickenburg."

Charlene took the phone. "Life's been so smooth for so long, a little danger will add spice. Tell her I'll be there in Arizona."

"I don't know how to reach her. The email came with no address for her. Never saw anything like it. But I never saw anything like her, either. Maybe she suspected I wouldn't be my full self yet, because she suggested she'd trust you if I couldn't be there."

Charlene rose from the chair. "When I get back, you can tell me her true story. Meanwhile, will there be a fine dinner on that jet?"

"I know what you like. I've already arranged it, though it won't be as good as your cooking."

"Nothin' is." She gestured toward the two blacked-out windows. "You're not a man who wants to hide from the world anymore. When you goin' to unpaint that glass?"

"I thought maybe in a week or two."

She shook her head. "Why not do it tomorrow? When I get back from Wickenburg, I'd like to see you sittin' here in the light."

24

Wainwright Hollister sits alone in the Sno-Cat that is parked at the farm supply, keeping warm while the search is organized. He will join the others later.

The town is blanketed and draped in snow, the roofs capped in white, huddled and humble and small like some modern-age farmland Bethlehem. Wainwright Hollister hates the place.

Of several homes that he owns, Crystal Creek Ranch is farthest from a city, making it ideal for his center of operations during the last stages of the revolution. If at some point certain potentially hostile elements in the existing power structure—or even the TV-besotted

Internet-mesmerized cud-chewing public—should become wise to the Techno Arcadian ascendancy, the crisis will then necessitate greater violence. Thousands of assassinations will be carried out in a few days, not merely by those hollow, murderous creatures Bertold Shenneck named rayshaws, but also by platoons of adjusted people living unrecognized in numerous places of great importance. In the Department of Justice, the associate attorney general is adjusted, as are the heads of the antitrust, civil rights, and criminal divisions, and as are the executive secretariat, the head of the office of public affairs, and the director of the FBI, as well as a hundred agents working under him. Together, in a coordinated assault launched from within, they could liquidate most people in the higher echelons of the DOJ. In the Department of State, an adjusted person serves as the chief of staff and assistant secretary for public affairs; ten others, plus half the officers on the department's security staff, are adjusted and ready to be controlled for whatever purpose. Enough White House aides and Secret Service agents have been injected with control mechanisms that the executive branch could be decimated in an hour. Hollister would rather take two more years to raise the number of the adjusted from the current sixteen thousand to maybe forty or fifty thousand, particularly saturating the military command with them. But if a crisis comes sooner, the streets will run with blood, and portions of some cities will burn. Better, then, to site the chair of ultimate power in a place as remote as Crystal Creek Ranch, where he can pull the strings of revolution without being in the thick of it.

The drawback is that, during the ramping-up toward the seizure of ultimate power, he must for the most part live in this tedious, bucolic county with its dismal litter of little towns, among the rustic residents, none of whom, if invited to dinner, would know the salad fork from the fish fork. Lonely is he who wears the crown, at least until everyone knows the name of the king and understands what he can do to them if they do not become precisely the kind of people he wants them to be.

He is in Willisford now to put an end to Thomas Buckle. The next to last driver screened at the barricade on I-70 reported seeing a vehicle ahead of him depart the highway and go overland. He had been at some distance from it; because of the chaos of snow and the confusion of the roadblock, he could say only that he thought it had been a truck of some kind or van or SUV, and that it had been dark in color, blue or gray or black. Given the point at which the vehicle had gone overland, it could have found only one paved route nearby, the county road that led either north past Crystal Creek Ranch or here to Willisford, south of the interstate.

With the forces at his command and considering the ruthlessness with which he can pursue this hunt, Hollister is confident that Tom Buckle is already as good as dead. There is no escape for him.

25

In spite of its weirdly ornate skeleton of timbers festooned with beards of dead grass and brush borne by the tempests of other days, the weather-beaten structure, perhaps meant to pump water from a well, sufficiently resembles a windmill that it can't be mistaken for anything else. However, as the thing looms over the small house, stark and eerie against the sky, its vanes unmoving in the languid air, it also seems, at least to Mustafa al-Yamani, like a monolith erected by some cult of shamans, placed here as a warning of doom impending. No doubt the bizarre consequence of the raid on the de Soto operation has rattled him and left him vulnerable to paranoid imaginings.

Under a corrugated rusted-metal roof sits a small stucco house with a sagging wooden porch that hasn't been painted in years. It waits at the end of a weedy dirt lane, about forty yards from the highway, without landscaping other than cactuses that appear to have been half devoured and their forms made grotesque by whatever rot or diseases afflict such plants.

No place could appear more deserted than this. Nevertheless, as

Mustafa puts the car in park, he says, "I'll go knock." He leaves the engine running, the air conditioner blowing, and Charlie in the backseat of the Suburban with Hugo Chávez.

Although it seems as if the mere rap of his knuckles might separate the front door from its hinges and collapse it into a long-abandoned realm populated only by spiders and their prey, his knock is answered by a mass of wrinkles with a lush white beard and bushy eyebrows under which gleam eyes as green and clear as Midori liqueur. The old man wears a straw hat, no shirt, bib overalls, and tennis shoes without socks.

"FBI," says Mustafa, flashing his ID. "I'm looking for a Mr. James Farkus."

"Farkus? Never heard of him," says the codger.

"May I ask to whom I'm speaking?"

"Name's Roger Hornwalt."

"Is this your residence, Mr. Hornwalt?"

"Been my own place fifty-four years. Never owed a penny to a bank or anyone else."

"Sir, do you think that Mrs. Hornwalt might have heard of James Farkus?"

"There isn't any Mrs. Hornwalt and never was. Not even a damn dog. Just me and my books, the way I like it."

In fact, the old man is holding a leather-bound volume in his right hand, and for a moment Mustafa thinks it is the very same edition of the novel he most cherishes. "Is that *The Great Gatsby*?"

Hornwalt frowns. "What, this? No, no." He holds the book so that Mustafa can see the spine.

The old man is reading something called *Faust*, of which Mustafa has never heard, written by an author with the absurd name Johann Wolfgang von Goethe.

"I regret this, Mr. Hornwalt. But time is of the essence."

"Regret what?" Hornwalt asks.

Mustafa draws his pistol and shoots the old man dead. Hornwalt falls backward into the house, making it easy to drag him off the threshold and farther inside.

Curious, Mustafa pauses to examine the book. It's over four hundred pages of verse. *Verse!* Hornwalt is obviously one of those lifelong desert dwellers Mustafa has heard about, eccentric in youth and full-on crazy by midlife.

Mustafa returns to the Suburban and opens the driver's door. He switches off the engine and says to Charlie, "This place is plenty private enough for what you need to do."

Charlie carries the satchel of interrogation instruments into the house, and Mustafa escorts Hugo Chávez, who protests every step of the way, cupping his broken wrist in the palm of his good hand.

Much of the residence is lined with leather-bound books. The small but cozy living room features an armchair with footstool, a sofa, and reading lamps. It is open to the kitchen. Between the two spaces stands a chrome-legged table with a red Formica top and two chrome chairs with red-vinyl upholstery.

This is a far cry from an elegant mansion in East Egg village, but it is undeniably cozy. Except for the corpse and the mess on the floor around it.

As Hugo is led to the table, he says, "Shit, you killed him, man. Why'd you kill the old dude? Just to grill me here?"

"We're in a hurry," Mustafa explains as he forces Hugo into a chair. "We couldn't keep looking for a place all afternoon."

Charlie sets his satchel on the table. "I'm not going to grill you, Chávez. I'm going to torture the truth out of you."

"You popped him *in the face*," Hugo Chávez declares with withering reproach. "You didn't have to pop the dude *in the face*. You can at least leave a man his face."

Baffled by this curious assertion of homicide etiquette, Mustafa reminds their prisoner: "We're in a hurry. Time is of the essence. A point-blank face shot, and it's over."

From the satchel, Charlie extracts a length of leather with a buckle on each end. He instructs Mustafa to cinch it tightly to the prisoner's neck and to the stretcher bar between the legs of the chair, taut enough so that Hugo can't get to his feet.

"What kind of people are you, poppin' some old dude for answerin' his door? Stall it out, man. Stall it out. You're goin' downhill toward a cliff."

Charlie smiles and shakes his head. "Such moral outrage. As though you haven't killed people."

"Shit, I only offed slobs I was told to off, not anyone just 'cause I wanted to, not just 'cause *they answered their damn door!*"

Removing an array of stainless-steel instruments from the satchel and placing them on the table, like a surgeon setting out the tools of his healing art, Charlie says, "The gentleman on the floor wouldn't trade places with you if he knew what is about to happen here. A quick death is merciful."

Perhaps the glaze of sweat on Hugo Chávez's face is caused by the pain of the broken wrist rather than by fear of what will be done to him, but he can't take his eyes from the tools and devices that Charlie withdraws from the seemingly bottomless bag.

"I been hangin' with some hard sonsofbitches," the prisoner says, "red-eye guys who'd slit the throats of their own sisters if they had a half-good reason, but it's not like they don't have their own ethics. In their way, they have ethics, man. You assholes in your suits, you don't have ethics, you're the worst of the worst."

He is talking himself into a state of blind terror.

Mustafa is convinced that Hugo will soon drop his macho pose and tell them what they want to know. Soon they will have what they need to find Jane Hawk. Her run is over. There will be no escape for her.

PART FIVE

Jane in Chains

1

Via satellite, swimming in the electronic bloodstream of the Internet, Vikram backdoored the computer system at the Food and Drug Administration offices in Rockville, Maryland. He used his password to activate the shadow-booked ISP account he had established, and from there he continued the research he'd been conducting for weeks.

Among the 3,800 names he had identified as Arcadians, there were many connections: mutual acquaintances, business relationships, conferences attended, club memberships, the colleges from which they graduated, the private schools where they sent their kids—a couple hundred potential identifiers altogether. Not every Arcadian went to the same university or attended the same conferences, of course, but he'd learned that if a suspect shared as many as twenty connections with a known Arcadian, the chances were high that they, too, were of that cabal.

Then it was time to hack into the computer system where the person worked—if Vikram didn't already have access through one of his wicked little babies. Time to search their email archives using an algorithm he had devised to sift from the haystack those little incriminating needles that were Arcadian identifiers: names like *Aspasia* and *Hamlet* and *Shenneck*, terms like *adjusted person* and *central committee*. Those words were always used in a context that didn't appear sinister unless you knew, as Vikram knew, to what nightmarish future these people had committed their fates and fortunes.

Recently, he had discovered a golden nexus, a link shared by *all* the Techno Arcadians he had thus far identified: regardless of their apparent position in the organization that employed them, whether high or low on the ladder, each had been granted official security clearance in an extraordinary, expedited fashion, often in as little as one week. If they didn't already possess it, Arcadians in the military and all government agencies were granted access to the most top-secret files regardless of their rank and in spite of questionable associations in their past that ought to have been cited to deny them. In private industry, which jealously guarded secrets that gave it competitive advantages, Arcadians were quickly brought into the innermost circles of those with easy access to privileged information. This happened to the consternation of many non-Arcadians who witnessed it, couldn't explain it, and complained about it to one another in their own emails.

Now, ostensibly from the Food and Drug Administration offices in Rockville, Maryland, Vikram backdoored the NSA Data Center in Utah. He began searching their archives of government and military security clearances for the names of those individuals who had received radically expedited approval as well as for the names of those who had vouched for them.

Although he had installed a rootkit in the NSA system and was operating at such a low level that he left no tracks, although even the most skilled IT security specialists would have great difficulty detecting his activity, after half an hour he skipped out of the Food and Drug Administration system. He slipped into the Department of the Interior system, activated a shadow-booked ISP account in the Fish and Wildlife Service, and returned to the NSA to continue his work. Half an hour later, he spoofed into the NSA again through the National Highway Traffic Safety Administration at the Department of Transportation.

In an hour and a half, his list had grown from over 3,800 names to more than 4,100.

2

Although the storm had passed and the wind had sailed away with it, the spent clouds dropped anchor over Willisford. The sky hung low and gray and motionless. Light fell bleak on the mantled town, and what had appeared Christmas-card perfect now seemed to betoken death.

Watching through the louvers of the shuttered window, Tom Buckle saw teams of four men, two in uniform and two rayshaws in their identical storm suits, moving house to house on the farther side of Gower's Lane. They knocked on doors and were either invited inside or forced their way in against objections.

At one residence, no one answered the door. After a conference among themselves, one of the men produced an object Tom couldn't identify, stooped to the lock, and apparently picked it. The four went inside.

"They'll be over here soon," Tom worried.

"I know this house well," Porter Crockett said. "Can't figure anywhere smart to stick you away. They'll for sure check the cellar, attic, closets."

"Maybe we can slip out the back, go somewhere else, go overland to somewhere else."

"There's nothin' but open range back of here, maybe two miles before you get to any ranch house, and damn few trees or anythin' else for cover."

A distant clatter, familiar but not at once identifiable, grew swiftly louder.

"Helicopter," said Porter.

They stood staring at the bedroom ceiling as the roar of the engine and the rhythmic chop of the rotary wing swelled in volume. The helo passed overhead at low altitude, cruised out beyond the county road to the north, and then seemed to circle back in a wide loop.

"They got themselves some aerial surveillance," said the colonel.

"We're goin' nowhere from here. And two measly pistols don't give us a sportin' chance of shootin' our way clear."

3

Mustafa browses the bookshelves, wondering how a man as well read as Roger Hornwalt could have been such a bad dresser with no sense of style in his household furnishings. Meanwhile, Charlie Weatherwax does what he does so expertly.

Sometimes a guy in Hugo Chávez's circumstances cracks quickly, because his macho is merely an attitude intended to display to his friends and associates the toughness that they likewise project for the purpose of impressing and intimidating him and others. When he swims with sharks, the only way to avoid being eaten is to convince them that he, too, is a shark, a great white. But when there's none of the old gang to see, no likelihood that his weakness of heart and mind will be reported to anyone who knows him, he can soon crumble, especially at the threat of pain and disfigurement.

This is what Mustafa expects to happen with Hugo. However, for an hour the Germanic hulk endures the pain of the broken wrist and numerous cruelties that Charlie inflicts upon him, and he refuses to answer questions.

Mustafa has witnessed this before, as well. The problem is that Hugo saw the old man shot in the face, and he assumes that his fate will be the same once he has told them everything they want to know. Terror can make any man irrational. The rational course of action in these circumstances is to avoid more torture by answering questions truthfully as they are asked. If death is unavoidable—well, then, a reasonable man will want to die with the least possible amount of suffering. A man with a poorly ordered mind, however, as Hugo's is poorly ordered, will sometimes arrive at the absurd conclusion that the longer he stays alive, even at the cost of terrible pain, the better his chances of survival. This foolish conviction is based on the hope that a miracle will occur. Perhaps a cop cruising past on the highway will see the Suburban, will for whatever reason surmise that something must be amiss at the Hornwalt residence, and will ride to the rescue. Or maybe the dilapidated windmill will at last collapse onto the house at the most opportune moment, killing Hugo's tormentors but sparing him. This is magical thinking, but the plebs of the world are frequently guilty of it.

Perusing the books in Roger Hornwalt's collection, Mustafa comes across *The Great Gatsby.* It is a slim volume because, for all its richness, the story is not a long one. The novel is bound in midnight-blue leather and, both front and back, features an inlaid Art Deco pattern in lighter blue and gold.

Mustafa turns the treasure over and over in his hands, strokes the ribbed spine with one finger, riffles the pages, marvels at a half-dozen elegant full-page illustrations rendered in pencil.

If Charlie should take another hour or even longer to break the foolish Hugo, reading a few chapters of this precious book might be an agreeable way to pass the time. Mustafa has never read F. Scott Fitzgerald's immortal work, though he has seen the Robert Redford movie forty-six times, the version starring Leonardo DiCaprio four times, and the TV version with Toby Stephens once.

But, no. He returns the volume to the shelf. However much time Charlie takes to wring the truth out of Hugo, it will not be long enough for Mustafa to finish the entire novel. He does not want his first reading of this book, which has so inspired him, to be in fits and starts. He will one day read the tale in a single sitting. In truth, he is also somewhat afraid that after the glamorous film with its sumptuous sets and spectacular costumes—not to mention the incomparable Robert Redford—the book might be a disappointment. Anyway, Mustafa is not much of a reader.

As Mustafa turns away from the bookshelves, the clench-jawed, stoic, stubborn Hugo at last screams like a little girl, which is a promising development.

4

For dinner, Jane brought Vikram one deli-made Reuben sandwich purchased during the stop in Tempe, a bag of green-onion-flavored potato chips, and another twenty-ounce bottle of Coca-Cola. Earlier, at his request, she'd provided him with pretzels, cashews, peanuts, chocolate chip cookies, Oreo cookies, a bar of dark chocolate, and a bag of M&M's. The slim, would-be Bollywood star with great dance moves evidently had the metabolism of a hummingbird, at least when his brain was overheating during a data chase, because he nibbled continually when buccaneering through the systems he targeted. He went at the sandwich as if he'd had nothing but water for the past week.

"That guy you touted me on to, Wainwright Warwick Hollister, a billionaire's billionaire, big-time adviser to presidents, big-time philanthropist," Vikram said, as if speaking to his sandwich or the computer.

"A total phony," Jane declared.

"Why do you say that?"

"You see him on TV, in the papers, wherever, he's always got a smile as wide as his head. He's never without a huge smile. Anyone who smiles all the time doesn't mean it. The needle on my creep detector always hits the red peg when I see him."

"Impressive scientific analysis."

"Sometimes a gut feeling is as scientific as a Geiger counter. Was I right when I put you on to him?"

"Those political appointees high in government bureaucracies who're also on my list of Arcadians—many at one time or another worked for one of Hollister's companies. Plus most of the Arcadians who received expedited security clearances cited Hollister as a character witness. And the politicians on my list . . . every one of them was backed extravagantly by a political action committee that Hollister funds out of his pocket."

"Look at his charitable foundation," Jane advised.

"I'll stay on him hard," Vikram said. "And dive in and out of the NSA more frequently. Short forays. In case some security geek, like a remora fish, tries to sucker himself to me." He took a bite of his sandwich, put it aside, wiped his hands on his shirt, and began finessing the keyboard at one of the two computers, leaning toward the screen with the intensity of a shark stalking prey.

Jane returned to the kitchen. She retrieved her sandwich and a bottle of Diet Pepsi from the refrigerator.

The Southwind's engine idled, powering Vikram's computer and the satellite dish, but Jane turned on no lamps.

No other vehicle had used the gravel road during the afternoon. Nothing moved in the grim vista beyond the wide-screen window.

She ate dinner in the copilot's chair, watching the last light fade from the day. She hoped that she was wrong about what would be required once Vikram finished his work, but she suspected that hope would not be fulfilled.

Night settled on the land as softly as a dream upon a sleeper. The stars were numberless, arrayed in the constellations named by astronomers now dead for centuries, and the glow of distant galaxies lay faint upon the desert floor.

5

When Porter Crockett opened the front door, standing before him in the porch light was the four-man search party led by someone whom he knew. A few years earlier, Andy Goddard had been the star of the football team at the county's only high school. His father, a friend of Porter's, had been the sheriff a decade previously; and it was assumed that Andy would one day be elected to that position. He was a personable down-to-earth young man with a long list of friends.

On this occasion, however, Andy Goddard wasn't as he had always been before. As if it had never shaped a smile, his face remained
as solemn as that of a mortician at graveside. "Colonel Crockett."

"Good evenin', Andy. What's all the commotion about? Escaped
prisoners from the penitentiary?"

Goddard spoke without emotion, as if he might be walking in his
sleep. "We've got to search the house. We're authorized by a FISA
court order, in urgent pursuit of a suspect in a national security matter. A post hoc copy of the warrant might later be provided. I advise
you not to obstruct us."

"You might remember I been in uniform myself. Wouldn't want to
make your hard job harder."

Porter stepped aside to admit them, and they entered in their
snow-caked boots, without concern for the flooring.

The two men whom Tom had called rayshaws regarded Porter
with eyes like holes burned by cigarettes in the cloth of their faces.
They drew pistols from belt holsters and split up. One went upstairs
with a deputy, and the other moved off into the ground floor, while
Andy remained in the foyer.

"Anyway," Porter said, "do whatever you need to do. It's not my
house."

"I'm aware of that." Goddard surely knew that Porter and Louise
had been flirting with the idea of marriage for a while. He ushered
the colonel through an archway into the living room, pointed to a
chair, and told him to sit, as though they had never eaten a meal together or gone dove hunting, or shared a few beers and laughs.

"National security matter here in sleepy little old Willisford," Porter said. "What's this sorry world comin' to?"

Goddard remained all business, standing to one side of the archway, alert to sounds from elsewhere in the house. "That's your crew-
cab Ford parked at Horseman's Haven."

"A beauty, isn't she? That truck's as tough as I like to think I used
to be. Louise drove it to work this mornin'."

"Why didn't she drive her own car?"

In fact, she had walked. But Porter said, "Her car was in the garage. We got up late, and with all this snow, we didn't have time to shovel the driveway."

"So your crew-cab was in the street all night?"

"Left it there when I got back from visitin' my daughter over to Kansas."

"When was that?"

"When I got back from Kansas? Wednesday afternoon 'round about three o'clock."

"This is Saturday."

Porter smiled, nodded. "Me and Louise have had ourselves a nice little visit."

"You weren't driving on Interstate 70 this morning?"

"In that storm? Son, the older I get, the less willin' I am to risk breakin' my stuff. You'll tame yourself some, too, when you get to be my age."

From an inner jacket pocket, Goddard produced a printout of a photograph, unfolded it, and held it toward the colonel. "You ever see this man?"

Porter leaned forward on his chair, squinting at an obvious publicity photo, a head shot of Tom Buckle. "Why, don't he look about as innocent as a Mormon missionary."

"Does he?"

"I mean for a dangerous national security fugitive, he looks just like the boy next door."

"You haven't seen him?"

"No, sir, not in this life."

They passed a few more awkward minutes before the other three men returned. The colonel showed them out, wished them success in their search, and said, "God bless America." He closed the door and watched them through a window in it as they headed down the front walkway to the street. He felt as if four highly advanced robots had visited, pretending to be men, remarkably lifelike constructions, but not quite convincing as human beings.

He hurried upstairs to the master bedroom. At the foot of the bed, he removed the colorful folded afghan from the hope chest and opened the lid. It was basically a big cedar-lined box—five feet long, three feet wide, two and a half feet deep—and Tom lay curled within it like a walnut in its shell.

6

Saturday evening. The IT security room is cool, most of the workstations deserted, the lighting subdued, the electronics humming softly. Celery sticks in one plastic bag, carrot slices in another, chunks of jicama in a third. A can of Red Bull close at hand.

Because Felicity Spurling hasn't taken time to wash her hair in four days, she has it tied in a ponytail and is wearing a cap that declares FUCK OFF, I'M WORKING. Those four words are not meant to amuse or have shock value; they are to be taken seriously, because when Felicity is working, she has no patience for small talk. For four days, she has been *in the zone*, working most of the time, going back to her apartment only for some sack time, deeply resenting the need to sleep. She is only vaguely aware that the weekend has come and that this is one of her days off.

Felicity grew up as the middle child in combat with four high-energy brothers, raised by their widower father—a gym teacher and football coach—after their mother died in childbirth. She knows how to throw a football, steal a base, make a jump shot, block a goal in soccer, and in general how to win, win, win. She can spit watermelon seeds as far as anyone else can. She can escape a determined noogie-giver's grip and give as good as she gets. She can hold her liquor, beat the shit out of anyone her size or even a little bigger, and cuss as fluently as anyone who stands up to pee instead of having to sit. There are many things Felicity has never learned about being a woman, which is all right with her. She's a woman in a man's world, in a man's profession, and what she cares about above all else is proving that she's better than all the snarky dicks who might want to take her job.

As the second assistant manager of IT security at the National Security Agency's million-square-foot data center in Utah, she is willing to work longer and harder than anyone, and it goes without saying that she works smarter. She is so tech savvy that some claim she must be a silicon-based life-form. Felicity is a past master, a wizard—a *mahatma!*—at every video game she ever played. At twenty-six, however, she is beyond the games of her extended adolescence. The future has been revealed to her; it is magnificent. Recruited by the revolution, she is now an Arcadian. The day draws near when she will not manipulate mere avatars in an intricately detailed fantasy world, but instead will manipulate real people in the real world and have *power,* power that is actual, not merely power that is measured in points scored and advancement to the next level of game. After the revolution, as an Arcadian, she *will be always at the highest level.*

She is excited to be leading three lives. Friends and family think she is merely a data analyst for an obscure government agency. In fact, she is an agent—office-bound but still an agent—of the NSA. And now she is also a techno guerilla secretly serving the revolution from within the nation's primary intelligence-gathering apparatus. Too cool.

Her first big job as an Arcadian is to stop Vikram Rangnekar, who is assumed to have created back doors of his own, including one into the NSA, while at the FBI. If he is now working with Jane Hawk, as suspected but not proven, the ocean of data archived by the NSA is invaluable to him. Felicity needs either to find the rootkit that he seeded in the system and rip it out—or catch him in real time swimming through the data, tag him, and track him to source.

If she should be so fortunate as to get a fix on Rangnekar, she has been instructed by her boss here in Utah, also an Arcadian, to inform him second, after first contacting the agent leading the hunt for the hacker. The phone number for the agent, Charles Weatherwax, is programmed into the directory of her smartphone.

However, Rangnekar's design skills are so refined, so elegant, that his handiwork is invisible, leaving her only the hope of being alerted to his presence when he's inside the system. As a result, Felicity has crafted a series of security fixes, including a program to trigger alarms when someone is diving deep into data chasms and seeking information that might be related to the revolution.

These triggers are words, phrases, and names supplied by her cell leader, who received them through a regional commander, who was given them by the central committee. Felicity doesn't know why these words are associated with the Arcadians; she has been told to avoid researching them and speculating, lest she develop a breadth of knowledge that makes her a liability to the revolution.

At 9:11 P.M. mountain time, as Felicity is leaning back in her chair, taking a brief jicama break, her computer issues a tone that signifies suspicious activity. A name appears in red on the screen: DIEDERICK DEODATUS FOUNDATION. It is one of the trigger words and phrases provided by the central committee.

7

High on sugar, deep in the murky world of Wainwright Hollister, Vikram discovered that the NSA, in addition to its hundreds of other interests, gathered and stored information on scores of charitable foundations about which it had suspicions of one kind or another. Some were fronts for extremist groups, by which funds were channeled to anti-American causes and to support terrorism. Others seemed to be banal organizations that, innocent of wrongdoing, became entities of interest for bogus reasons; but once brought to the attention of the intelligence bureaucracy, they would be suspect until the universe stopped expanding and collapsed back on itself.

According to the mission statement for the Diederick Deodatus Foundation, it was established by Wainwright Hollister and funded with $3 billion of his tax-deductible contributions, in honor of his only sibling, Diederick Deodatus Hollister, whose life tragically ended in the crib when he succumbed to sudden infant death syndrome. Although Diederick hadn't died of any malignancy, the foundation was formed to research cures for childhood cancers.

Vikram noticed that everyone on the board of directors was also among those he'd identified as Techno Arcadians, including the late billionaire D. J. Michael, with whom Jane had survived a showdown in San Francisco.

Poring through the foundation's grant recipients over the past six years, he saw a few institutions known for cancer research. But the larger grants had been to nonprofits of which he'd never heard. After making a list of the latter, he retreated from the NSA system to research them through conventional Internet sites.

8

Felicity Spurling has at her command state-of-the-art track-to-source software, which she employs to get a fix on the intruder in the Diederick Deodatus Foundation archives. He has not come through an official portal, but instead through a back door. The hacker opens a file on the employees of the organization, occupies himself with that for a few minutes, drops out of it, and opens another file filled with information about the board of directors. Felicity has his electronic thread, his tail, the software does the tracking, and a point-of-origin citation appears boxed on the screen:

FEDERAL AVIATION ADMINISTRATION
DEPARTMENT OF TRANSPORTATION
800 INDEPENDENCE AVENUE SW
WASHINGTON, D.C.

Admission to the NSA system is strictly limited to approved individuals in various intelligence services and to certain high aides to the president. No flyboy or desk pilot at the FAA is authorized to access the Utah center, nor is anyone at the Department of Transportation, for that matter.

Which indicates that someone with knowledge of a back door—surely Vikram Rangnekar, he who built it—is spoofing into the NSA through the FAA to hide his true location.

Spoofing won't save him. Felicity can track him through any labyrinth he has built to conceal his whereabouts. The keyboard and touch pad give her the power of a bloodhound, and his trail cannot be lost in a swift-running stream.

She has hardly set to work, however, when he closes the file on the foundation's board of directors and drops out of the system. Gone.

"Shit, shit, shit, shit, shit!" Felicity chants, as yet making little use of the colorful cussing she learned in a family of ornery brothers.

Eighteen minutes later, her computer issues the familiar tone signifying suspicious activity, and the words DIEDERICK DEODATUS FOUNDATION once more appear in red on the screen.

9

Searching five websites of the nonprofits conducting scientific research, supposedly regarding childhood cancer, Vikram discovered that Shenneck or his wife, Inga, or both, served on the boards of every one.

Vikram had found the primary source of the funding for the nanoweb control mechanisms. Perhaps he had also found the chairman of the Arcadians' central committee: Wainwright Hollister. And now he knew as well the location of their several laboratories.

Rather than devote time to penetrating the Diederick Deodatus Foundation by establishing a back door, he returned to the National Security Agency's computer system. The NSA already had an exhaustive file on the foundation, though apparently they had not effectively investigated it. Within their archives, he might find more of what he needed.

He ate another Oreo.

10

When after eighteen minutes he returns to the NSA system and dives straight into the agency's archives on Diederick Deodatus, the intruder knows what file he wants. It is labeled DONORS.

Another point-of-origin citation appears on the screen within seconds:

GENERAL ACCOUNTING OFFICE

441 G STREET NW

WASHINGTON, D.C.

Felicity doesn't know what the General Accounting Office is. Washington is home to a gajillion agencies and bureaus, and probably half the people working in them don't know what their organization really does or why it exists. But she knows for sure that nothing called the General Accounting Office has authorization to enter the NSA Data Center.

Rangnekar—it has to be him—has ricocheted through the GAO from elsewhere, and track-to-source software seeks to backtrack him from there through whatever telecom exchanges he has bounced.

Before track-to-source can give her the first twist in his trail, a boxed alert appears in the upper right quadrant of her screen: "DONORS" > 5,260 ENTRIES IN 24 TRANCHES > DOWNLOADING TRANCHE 1.

The foundation had 5,260 active donors in twenty-four files, corresponding to the first letter of each donor's last name. As Felicity watches, the number of the tranche changes from 1 to 2 to 3 to 4 at an alarming pace. The sonofabitch is a data vampire, sucking with incredible speed.

The number reaches 14 before track-to-source turns its point-of-origin citation from regular font to bold, and announces it has CONFIRMED ORIGIN, thereby claiming the hacker is actually in the General Accounting Office on G Street and hasn't spoofed into the NSA system through a chain of exchanges.

"Bullshit," Felicity declares. "Bullshit, horseshit, your mama eats shit."

She instructs track-to-source to run the tail again. Then she goes to the icon field at the top of her screen and keys one that looks like a bullhorn. This activates a soft alarm tone throughout IT security and summons other on-duty personnel to her workstation.

The intruder downloads the twenty-fourth tranche of donor names and drops out of the system.

11

Using a dex-meth cocktail as a substitute for sleep requires a precise calculation of the size and frequency of dosage in order to avoid unfortunate symptoms. This is especially tricky for Charlie, because he isn't a regular user with known tolerances. If he takes too little, at some point he'll amp-out too soon, drop into total exhaustion at a critical moment, and require a day to recover. If he takes too much, he might become hyperalert, fidgety, irritable, and aggressive, while unaware that his judgment has been impaired. Even without drugs, Charlie has a tendency to irritability and aggression, and he realizes what a wire he walks when using chemical stimulants.

After leaving Hugo Chávez dead in the book-lined house of Roger Hornwalt, the amphetamine-powered team of Weatherwax and al-Yamani heads back toward Nogales with Mustafa at the wheel, their headlights like the bright swords of knights setting forth into battle. Charlie feels good. He feels *great*. As alert as a cat. As quick as a skink.

High on a wire but perfectly balanced. Thanks to the interrogation, they know their quarry is in a thirty-six-foot Fleetwood Southwind, towing an Explorer Sport, although Hugo was unable to remember the license-plate numbers that Enrique de Soto had provided for either vehicle.

When they acquire cellphone service at the perimeter of Nogales, Charlie places an encrypted call to Gary Greenway, the senior of the four agents attending to matters at the Casa Grande Holiday Inn. He doesn't mention Jane Hawk. He is determined to have her in his sights before breaking the news to anyone that she is definitely with Vikram.

Following the sudden death of Ganesh Rangnekar from a heart attack or aneurysm, they had lost the chance to find the infuriating bitch earlier in the day. Now he has no choice but to compensate for that screwup by nailing her—or forever conceal his error. For the record, they are on the trail of Vikram Rangnekar and no one else.

He tells Gary Greenway that they are seeking a Fleetwood Southwind towing an Explorer Sport. From Casa Grande, the vehicle could have gone south on I-10 to Tucson, north on I-10 to Phoenix, or west on I-8 to Yuma.

Currently, in all cities with a population greater than one hundred thousand, key-intersection cameras—including interstate ramps and connector loops—record 24/7 and transmit their traffic video to archives, including those at the NSA. If Rangnekar took delivery of the motor home at 10:00 A.M., hooked the Explorer to it, and was on the road half an hour later, there are different windows of time, in each of the three metropolitan areas, when he might have been captured by a camera. The two yoked vehicles provide a unique image and should be easily identified.

"It's tedious," Charlie tells Gary Greenway, "a lot of video, but you four get your eyes on it, find where the sonofabitch went."

When Charlie terminates the call, Mustafa says, "You didn't mention the Southwind was converted for a motorized satellite dish."

They are racing through the Arizona night toward Casa Grande without a highway patrol escort. The Suburban has a siren, which

Mustafa uses as needed, and though the vehicle isn't fitted with a lightbar, it has flashers that he leaves on for the entire trip.

"Why do you think he wants a motor home with a satellite?" Charlie asks. "Hmmm? What do you surmise from that information?"

"He wants to penetrate sensitive computer systems in search of whatever. He wants to make it as difficult as possible to be tracked while he's doing it."

"And?" Charlie presses.

"He wants a secure connection, so he can't be cut off just by someone identifying his phone or cable service and shutting it down."

"And?"

"He wants mobility, so no one can easily track his signal to its source and show up at his doorstep."

Charlie says, "These extraordinary measures that he's taken, *that he and Jane Hawk have taken*, suggest they're after what information?"

For half a mile, Mustafa considers his answer before he says, "A complete roster of Arcadian membership, all our names."

"Names, lab locations, research records," Charlie suggests. "Maybe the names of everyone who's been brain-shagged."

"This is most worrisome," Mustafa declares as he uses the siren to clear their way through a patch of congestion. "Why aren't we at once reporting this to our cell leader?"

Charlie lays it out for him. "We got the satellite information from Hugo Chávez, and we got Chávez in the raid on Enrique de Soto's operation. How did that raid go? If you had to write a report, how would you characterize that raid?"

"It did not go as well as hoped. Two agents dead in a barn explosion, three killed by giant pigs, one shot by friendly fire."

"And why did we have to pull the raid in the first place?"

Mustafa considers the question for only a quarter of a mile this time, at ninety miles per hour. "Because we kept to ourselves the information we received from Ganesh, and we arrived in Casa Grande only after Rangnekar and Hawk left in the motor home."

Charlie conducts a further analysis of their predicament. "And Rangnekar had taken out the hotel and municipal cameras, so there was no record of what vehicle was delivered to him. We were Vi-kramized."

"Not for the first time," Mustafa adds.

"Not that I have any problem with people from India, I want that understood, but *I hate this bastard.* We were in Casa Grande because we were previously Vikramized at the warehouse in Ontario." Charlie emphasizes each word by pounding the side of his fist against the dashboard: "I hate this asshole Rangnekar."

Mustafa accelerates past a hundred miles an hour. His demeanor is usually placid, but now in the light of the instrument panel, his face is wrenched with hatred. "And before *that* we were Vikramized at the Stein house in La Cañada Flintridge."

"If we pass along the information about the satellite dish, this will be taken out of our hands and—"

"—given to the butt-kissers who rank above us."

"Exactly. Even if they catch Rangnekar and Hawk, we'll get no credit, but they'll damn sure make an issue out of—"

"—out of all the times this terrible man pulled the rug out from under us," Mustafa finishes.

"And you know what that means."

"We are screwed."

"Brain-screwed."

At a hundred ten miles an hour, the tires stutter across every ir-regularity in the pavement and the chassis rattles on the frame.

With bitterness that has a Benzedrine edge, Mustafa says, "We started this in a luxurious, bespoke Mercedes-Benz G550 Squared with a biturbo V8, and now we are reduced to a common Suburban. My suit is wrinkled, and my shoes badly need a shine."

"We'll find them and kill them," Charlie insists. "What these shit-heads don't want to understand is, even if they obtain all this infor-mation, they won't be able to get it out to the public. We have people—Arcadians and adjusted plebs—in control of the media, the Internet, law enforcement, the intelligence community, both major political parties. This country is ours. America is over. Arcadia is ris-ing in its place." His voice has become harder as he speaks, and cold with passion, sending an icy thrill through him, as if he is listening not to himself, but to an orator of considerable power. "And if these two pieces of shit find a sympathetic ear, whoever the hell it is, we'll inject the sonofabitch or order some brain-screwed pleb to whack him and then kill himself. Jane Hawk is too late. Beautiful monster? Contemporary Joan of Arc? No. No, no! She's nothing. She's just a gash, a pump, a piece of ass who doesn't know her place. But she's going to learn soon enough, damn soon. We've infiltrated too deeply. The revolution isn't just beginning. It's nearly over." He looks out the side window at the deep darkness of the desert lying under a moon that illuminates little and stars that are configured without meaning. "It's over, and so is she."

12

At 9:31, Jane Hawk was walking the land around the Southwind, listening to the sounds of silence. At first the desert seemed as eerily hushed as an airless moon. But when she stood very still and quieted her mind, the night offered a subtle chorus of clicks and rustlings, wordless whisperings, the thrum of bat wings overhead, the faraway, forlorn voice of a coyote like a faint cry in a dream, and the soft susurration of a barely felt breeze licking the stems and leaves of sage, of mesquite.

She was startled when Vikram's voice bloomed in the earpiece of her walkie-talkie: "Come see this."

She tapped the mic—"On my way"—tapped it again to disconnect, and returned to the Southwind. She locked the vehicle behind her and made her way back through the dark interior. Slid open the door to what had been the bedroom. The place was illuminated only by a lava lamp—his preferred work light—and computer-screen glow.

Sitting at his workstation, in the amber light of the lamp and the ameboid shadows cast by the ceaselessly changing red-wax forms within it, Vikram looked like a magical figure, as if he were some wizard who should be dressed in a long blue robe patterned with stars and crescent moons.

He held up a pair of flash drives. "Two copies of the complete roster of Arcadians."

"You're sure?"

"Five thousand two hundred sixty names and addresses, including Hollister. They're listed in the Diederick Deodatus Foundation files as 'donors.' Some have given as little as a hundred bucks, others millions. But they're not just donors, they're Techno Arcadians. That list I compiled on my own? Every one of them is one of these donors."

She accepted one of the flash drives. "Amazing."

"Beside some donor names in their records are the letters *CL*. Which I suspect means 'cell leader.' Beside a fewer number is *RC*, which probably means 'regional commander.' Given the high-power names on the foundation's board of directors, I'll bet my *golis* they're also the revolution's central committee."

The flash drive seemed too small and light to hold within it the fate of the world, the hope of the future. "The research labs? Where they produce the control mechanisms?"

"A small number of nonprofits received enormous grants from Deodatus. Shenneck and his wife were on the boards of all of them. I've made a separate file on the flash drive."

"This is brilliant, Vikram."

He shrugged. "The irony is, I couldn't have done any of it if the black hats at the DOJ hadn't assigned me to build all those back doors, unwittingly giving me the chance to create others of my own. One of the regional commanders and two central committee members—they're the ones who asked for my wicked little babies in the first place."

Fingering the flash drive, Jane said, "I wonder . . ."

"What?"

"Why they didn't inject you and control you before assigning you to do so much that was illegal."

"Maybe I started that work before they perfected their control mechanism. They had nothing to inject. My wicked babies go back some years."

"But wouldn't they inject you after the fact, to be sure you never turned against them?"

After a silence, he got to his feet. He didn't know what to do once he was standing. If he was one of *them*, there was nowhere to run from himself. As if afraid to face her, Vikram stared at the computer, at the lava lamp with its ever-changing shapes. "You're spooking me."

"I'm spooking myself."

When at last he looked at her, a glint of fear sharpened his gaze. "How would I know if I was . . ."

"You wouldn't." She hesitated before saying, "Uncle Ira is not Uncle Ira."

That was the current access sentence that opened an adjusted person to total control. It came from a 1955 novel, *Invasion of the Body Snatchers* by Jack Finney. If Vikram were one of the adjusted, he'd have responded with "Yes, all right," and would thereafter have obeyed her every command; but he did not.

The original access sentence had been "Play Manchurian with me," a reference to Richard Condon's famous novel about brainwashing, *The Manchurian Candidate*. When she'd learned that one, the Arcadians had reprogrammed the adjusted people—probably with phone calls—and installed the Finney quote.

"They know you're aware of the Uncle Ira command?" he asked.

"Yes."

She realized what he meant. Maybe he *was* adjusted, but had been reprogrammed with a sentence she didn't know. Which might be why he didn't respond to the command she'd just given him.

"When did you learn about Uncle Ira?" he asked.

"A week ago."

He shuddered and let out his breath in a sigh of relief. "I fell off their radar ten days ago, before they would've changed the command. If I was adjusted, I'd still be responding to Uncle Ira."

She put her arms around him, and he held her tightly as well.

They stood that way for a long moment before he let go of her. "I still have to find the names of the people they injected. The adjusted people."

"In the files of the same charitable foundation?"

"There's no reason for them to store the data somewhere else. They obviously think the foundation is perfect cover."

"Get it done, Vikram. I feel as if we're running out of time."

He dropped into his chair and swiveled to the screen.

Leaving the room, Jane slid the door shut. She went forward to the copilot's seat. She wanted a double vodka to steady her nerves. She didn't allow herself to have it.

The wide-screen windshield presented far more night sky than desert, for the land was flat, while the heavens were concave and all-commanding. The sight of countless suns in that vast void had often inspired her to cope when coping seemed too difficult. Stars reminded her that the universe—and life—had infinite possibilities but also that her powers of mind and body were modest in the scheme of things, that when a terrible task lay before her, it couldn't be accomplished with fierce will alone, but required also humility in the presence of grace.

On this occasion, however, the wealth of stars conjured in her imagination an evil, glimmering constellation of junction points in a nanoweb secreted in the darkness of a skull, and thinking of the mission ahead sent cold tremors through her.

13

Wainwright Hollister, who hunts people for sport and can control more than sixteen thousand men and women as if they were puppets and he the puppeteer, prides himself on his physical and mental stamina. But he sleeps in the Sno-Cat at the Willisford Farm

Supply, while others, all marionettes under his command, continue to quarantine the town and conduct an exhaustive search.

He dreams, and the dreams are of the kind that might chase another man awake, screaming, but Hollister has a high tolerance for horror. He is nine years old again, creeping stealthily through the great house to the nursery where his infant brother sleeps. The night nanny has gone to the kitchen for a piece of cake. A mobile hangs above the crib, colorful plastic birds that will circle to a soft, cheerful tune if they are activated with a remote control. On a nightstand, the lamp base is a ceramic teddy bear, the shade of pale-blue silk, the three-way bulb at a low setting. Pillow in hand, young Hollister approaches the crib, which is much larger than he remembers it. As he quietly lowers the railing to facilitate his assault on this would-be thief of his inheritance, he is surprised that Diederick is not, as usual, snug in knitted pajamas, in plain sight. There is a blanket, though there has never been a blanket before. Mother worries that a blanket might dangerously entangle her precious angel. He grips a corner of the blanket, and as he throws it aside, he realizes that the shape beneath it is too large to be Diederick. Before him lies naked Mai-Mai. Although part of her head is missing, she opens her eyes, which are sunken in her skull, and reaches for him with both arms and spreads her thighs and smiles and says, *Come die in me.*

The dreams flow one into another until someone speaks his name—"Mr. Hollister, sir, Mr. Hollister"—and gently shakes him by the shoulder until he wakes.

Deputy Andy Goddard is in the driver's seat.

Hollister yawns, stretches, sits up straight. "Have you found him? Have you found Thomas Buckle?"

"No, sir. He's not here. We've searched everywhere. I don't think he was ever here."

Hollister has little patience for such defeatism, and he at once wonders if it might be more than mere pessimism and laziness. Bertold Shenneck always insisted that adjusted people were not only incapable of disobeying a master's order, but were also incapable of deceit. But Hollister isn't convinced of their absolute reliability. Husbands deceive wives, and wives deceive husbands. Mothers deceive sons, and sons deceive their mothers. Deceit might be the defining quality of human beings. In a world where duplicity, fraud, and subterfuge are rampant, perhaps even a brain trapped in a neural lace can be full of cunning and trickery.

"Search it again," he commands Deputy Goddard.

"Again? Sir, you mean the entire town?"

"That motorist saw a truck or SUV leave the interstate and go overland. If Buckle was aboard the damn thing, it definitely didn't go to my ranch. It could have come only here."

Goddard's tone is apologetic, submissive. "Or, sir, maybe whoever picked him up . . . maybe they just drove straight through Willisford."

"And went where? To some isolated ranch where no one is likely to take him in? No. If Buckle's not here, then he's gone for good, and he's damn well *not* gone for good. He's mine, and I'll get him."

"The men are exhausted, sir."

Although Deputy Goddard seems by all measures subservient, his complaint strikes Hollister as half a step away from disobedience. "Gallons of coffee. Caffeine pills. Amphetamines if you have them. Stay on your feet and stay on the job. I have never failed, and I won't fail at this. The ones before Buckle were easy. They were nothing. And he's nothing. *Nothing.* Find him."

"All right. Yes. We'll find him."

A weariness still infects Goddard's voice, and it infuriates Hollister. If adjusted people cannot be used until they collapse, if they have to be *coaxed* to perform to their furthest limits, they are hardly better than the lazy and shiftless plebeian hordes who have made this world so much less than it should be.

"He's here," Hollister insists. "I've seen signs and portents. Scarlet silk and a dead woman walking. He saw her die, and as long as he's alive to bear witness, she'll stalk me. Only when he's dead will she stay dead. Do you understand, damn it?"

Goddard stares at him, unsure what to say.

"You pathetic excuse for a deputy. Say, 'Yes, sir. Yes, sir, I understand.'"

Goddard nods. "Yes, sir. Yes, sir, I understand."

After Goddard departs, Hollister tries to sleep, but he can't. When he opens his eyes, he sees a familiar figure in the farm-supply parking lot, standing in the snow under a lamp. Naked, she holds a dead infant in her arms.

14

Five IT security staffers gather around Felicity Spurling's workstation, all men of course, and she the lone woman in the room.

They are waiting for Vikram Rangnekar—and it *is* Rangnekar, it can be no one else, she is *this close* to being the one who nails the dipshit—to return to the NSA system.

One of the guys, Gregor, picks up her Ziploc bag of jicama chunks and appropriates a few for himself. She might tolerate such poaching if he was one of the other four, but Gregor is a freak and a wuss with no chin and with hair sprouting from his ears, though he's only thirty. She would rather die than let him in her pants, where two of the other four have previously found their way. She takes the bag from him, seals it, and puts it down without comment.

After eleven minutes, one of the alarms that she designed is triggered, and again the words DIEDERICK DEODATUS FOUNDATION appear in red. "Here we go," she says.

The hacker's point of origin appears:

MINE SAFETY AND HEALTH OFFICE
DEPARTMENT OF LABOR
200 CONSTITUTION AVENUE NW
WASHINGTON, D.C.

Blue-eyed, red-haired Derek says, "He's working through a shadow-booked ISP account. No one from Mine Safety has legitimate entrée to *us*, and anyway no one's there at this hour on a weekend." Derek is one of those with whom Felicity has slept. His technique in bed is as obvious as the observation he has just made.

As track-to-source seeks to follow Rangnekar's electronic tail to its true end point, a boxed alert appears on screen: "POTENTIAL DONORS" > 16,912 ENTRIES IN 26 TRANCHES > DOWNLOADING TRANCHE 1.

At the bottom of the boxed alert is a bar meter showing the percentage of the tranche that has been downloaded.

Mike, with whom Felicity hasn't slept but would in a minute, says, "That's crazy speed. Data's draining down this guy's pipe as if a hundred porn stars are sucking on the other end."

The intruder is taking the third tranche when track-to-source bolds the regular font of the Mine Safety address and announces CONFIRMED ORIGIN.

Felicity lets loose with a string of expletives.

Warren Farley giggles too girlishly. He is a former Seventh-day Adventist who now believes that God hasn't yet been born and will eventually be an artificial intelligence created by scientists. He is easily titillated. "Spurling, you're such a bad girl."

Gregor says, "We should get someone in Washington over to Mine Safety just in case that *is* where he's operating from," and he picks up the phone from Spurling's workstation.

The other four guys begin talking at once as the intruder pulls the cork on the fourth tranche, their excited voices reminiscent of turkeys gobbling. As far as she knows, Felicity is the sole Arcadian among them, and as their commentary washes over her, it's obvious why that should be the case.

She directs track-to-source to try again, but less than a minute later, the hacker drops out of the system.

Not two minutes pass before he's again in Diederick Deodatus, in the potential-donors file, downloading once more, beginning with the fifth tranche.

Lenny Morton, who talks less than the others and seems slow, who is *wonderfully* slow in bed, says, "He's got a VSAT setup."

Felicity shakes her head. "If he did, track-to-source would tail him to a telecom satellite—it's just another exchange."

"Then this isn't public telecom," Lenny concludes. "Milcom. A Department of Defense military-communications satellite."

"How the hell would he crack a milcom satellite?"

"He cracked *us*, didn't he? The guy's a wicked genius."

Track-to-source provides a point of origin:

INDIAN AFFAIRS

DEPARTMENT OF THE INTERIOR

1849 C STREET

WASHINGTON, D.C.

As the intruder drains the sixth tranche, another alert appears on Felicity's screen in red letters: DIEDERICK DEODATUS FOUNDATION.

"What the hell? We now have *two* of them."

The new arrival enters the potential-donors file and begins downloading the tenth tranche, as the first hacker moves on from the sixth to the seventh.

"Same guy," Felicity says. "Opening two pipes, trying to drain what he needs before we can get a fix on him."

Track-to-source gives the newcomer's point of origin as the Office of Food Safety at the Department of Agriculture.

Lenny hurries to his workstation, two away from Felicity's. "We've got a legit relationship with the milcom-sat system. Their NOC should be able to pinpoint the sonofabitch."

15

When Mustafa follows Charlie into the Holiday Inn suite where the four agents from Phoenix are supposed to be reviewing archived traffic-camera video from three metropolitan areas in search of a Fleetwood Southwind towing a Ford Explorer Sport, he finds not one of them busy at a laptop. They are sitting around a table, chowing down on room-service food, drinking beer, engaged in conversation they find highly amusing.

Mustafa is angry, partly because it seems to him that they do not understand the gravity of the situation, do not grasp what is at stake. His future on Long Island is at stake, damn it, his mansion in East Egg village, his chance to marry his own Daisy Buchanan, to have his name changed to Tom Buchanan or Nick Carraway, to get what Gatsby failed to achieve, to be accepted by the old-money crowd, to live forever in the green light of the orgastic future. He is also angry because, well, he is buzzing so intensely on Mountain Dew and bennies, those little cross-tops, that he's seeing golden auras around some people, as if they're haloed angels, which of course they aren't. And he is plagued by a persistent ocular migraine—no headache, merely a chain of twinkling lights floating through his field of vision, which would make it difficult for him to read if he had any interest in reading anything.

But it turns out that the four agents are celebrating the recent discovery of four traffic-cam video catches that show the Southwind with Explorer in tow. First, as it passes through Tempe. Second, as it pulls off the street into a supermarket parking lot, apparently so Rangnekar can fill the larder. Third, as it enters westbound Interstate 10 at Fifty-Ninth Avenue in southwest Phoenix.

The fourth catch was made by an Arizona Highway Patrol unit equipped with 360-degree scan capability, which was stopped on I-10, short of the exit to Tonopah, while the officer issued a speeding ticket to a motorist. The Southwind exited I-10 at Tonopah.

Charlie gives Mustafa a meaningful look, because they both know what this means. Rangnekar and Hawk want a private place, far from any likelihood of an encounter, where they can attach the satellite dish and get down to business.

Gary Greenway, the agent in charge here, has taken the liberty of negotiating an emergency loan of a helicopter from the Bureau of Indian Affairs, which manages the vast Papago Indian Reservation immediately southwest of Casa Grande. The aircraft, with pilot, is standing by in the hotel parking lot along North French Street. The flight to Tonopah should take less than thirty minutes. When Charlie and Mustafa arrive there, an all-wheel-drive vehicle belonging to the Arizona Highway Patrol will be waiting for them in a vacant lot along Indian School Road, across the street from the Shell station.

In the elevator, Mustafa says, "They totally piss me off."

"Who does?"

"Greenway and the other three."

"They did their job," Charlie says.

"Sitting up there stuffing their faces and guzzling beer while we're running from one damn place to another."

"Because we've got to cover our ass, remember, and no one will work as hard to cover it as we will."

"They piss me off anyway, with their halos. You don't have a halo, Charles."

"Neither do you, my friend." As they reach the ground floor, Charlie says, "Maybe no more bennies for you."

"In a little while, just one more," Mustafa says. "I feel that if I do not take one more, my teeth will melt right out of my head."

The helicopter is a four-seat Robinson R44 Raven. The pilot's name is Cynthia Red Coyote, who looks nothing like Daisy Buchanan ought to look, but who stirs Mustafa's interest, anyway.

As they lift off for Tonopah, Charlie's smartphone rings.

16

Using two computers, the intruder downloads all twenty-six tranches in the potential-donors file. Instead of dropping out of the NSA system, he moves on to a Diederick Deodatus Foundation file labeled LEGACY DONORS, which contains 9,410 names in twenty-three tranches, and he starts sucking out that data as well.

He is now downloading tranche 15 with one computer and tranche 20 with the other, when Lenny Morton, two workstations away from Felicity Spurling, quietly announces, "Milcom NOC has a fix on him," which electrifies Felicity and the geek squad around her. Lenny reads the longitude and latitude from his screen and then says, "Maricopa County, Arizona. Twelve point four miles north of a tiny town named Tonopah, apparently on a dirt track or gravel road in what seems to be a really desolate area."

Feeling as if she's hit a long one with all the bases loaded, Felicity snatches up her phone, calls Agent Charles Weatherwax, and repeats the information to him.

Rangnekar is still draining data out of the legacy-donors file, but the peak moment has come and gone. Everyone drifts away from her workstation, except for Gregor, who picks up her bag of carrot sticks and poaches a few.

"That totally rocked," he says, crunching the carrot, his weak chin sort of wiggling at her.

Without replying, Felicity takes the Ziploc bag away from him and seals it.

Gregor remains clueless. "You're always working. Take a day off tomorrow, and let's do something together."

Felicity reaches back into her recent adolescence for a bit of snark. "You don't want to do anything with me, Gregor. I have a case of crabs."

His face brightens. "I love crab. You cook, I'll bring a good white wine."

17

Vikram's voice crackled in Jane's earpiece: "Come here quick."

She went to the back of the motor home and slid open the door. "What is it?"

"We've been followed home. They'll be on their way."

"Drop off the satellite, and I'll get us rolling."

"No. Change of plans. I've got nearly everything."

"So soon?"

"I'll have it all in another few minutes. We'll stay uplinked, get the last of it, and leave the motor home here. Start unhitching the Explorer."

No less hopeful than fearful, grateful for the promise of victory even as she dreaded what the cost of it might be, she went forward again, grabbed the flashlight and toolbox from behind the copilot's seat, and stepped out into the warm starlit night.

She had been working only two or three minutes when all the lights came on inside the Southwind. A moment later Vikram appeared and began to assist her.

"If they can use the highway patrol," he said, "troopers will be coming fast for us straight up from the interstate."

"Count on it. They've got tentacles everywhere. They can use everyone."

The Explorer had all four wheels on the ground.

Disconnecting the auxiliary brake-light cables, Jane said, "I can finish this. Get my tote bag and whatever you don't want to leave behind."

"Just one laptop," he said and hurried back inside.

18

The deputies finally allowed Louise Walters to go home from Horseman's Haven, although they insisted that she walk rather than drive the Ford crew-cab.

When Porter Crockett opened the back door to her house in answer to her knock, she came into the mudroom in a state of high agitation. "They've all gone stark raving crazy, quarantining the town and won't say a word about why except for flashing a picture of your friend. They're like gestapo in some old movie. This *is* still America, isn't it?"

"Maybe not so much anymore," Porter said, helping her off with her coat. "Tom knows. He can explain."

She sat on a bench to slip out of her boots. "They're still holding this morning's customers in the restaurant. Won't let them get in their cars and go home. When Carl Volk tried to leave, it got real ugly. Porter, they clubbed him to the floor and dragged him to a table and cuffed him to it so he couldn't get up. These people acting so crazy—I've known some of them most all my life, but now they're like strangers." Her hands shook as she put on a pair of penny loafers that she'd left there earlier. "Where is he?"

"In the kitchen. Just had us a bite. The blinds are closed. No one can see him. They searched here earlier, but we outfoxed them."

Louise went into the kitchen, Porter trailing after her, and Tom Buckle got up from the table, where he was having a mug of coffee. "Ms. Walters, I'm so sorry about the trouble I've caused."

"You're not the trouble, young man. It's these deputies gone wild that scare the bejesus out of me. And however you and Porter outfoxed them, we better hope you can do it again. Out on the main street, they're starting to search again every place they already searched before."

19

Jane behind the wheel of the Explorer. Vikram holding fast to the grab bar above the passenger-door window. Barrages of gravel rattling against the undercarriage. They rollicked across the rutted terrain of the Sonoran Desert.

She dared the headlights because it wasn't likely the Arcadians would be able to find a helo near enough to launch an aerial search this fast. Soon but not yet.

"You're sure the potential-donors file is actually the list of people they've injected?"

"You said Booth Hendrickson, when you broke him, he told you over sixteen thousand."

"Yeah."

"The list of potential donors is sixteen thousand nine hundred twelve. And then there's the legacy donors. Legacy donors usually means people who bequeathed money in their wills. But that's not what these bastards mean by it. I suspected it might be a list of those chosen for self-destruction. Nine thousand four hundred ten people. Jane . . . I checked for Nick. His name was there."

Emotion trapped the words in her for a moment. "Hamlet list."

Three miles north of where they had left the motor home, Vikram said, "There it is," pointing to a cairn of loose stones that marked the intersection.

The gravel road continued northwest for twenty-two miles to the town of Aguila and U.S. 60, an undivided old federal highway that, if they followed it westward, would lead them between the Harquahala and Harcuvar Mountains, into La Paz County.

The dirt road to the right led directly north-northeast for about eighteen miles, past the Vulture Mountains. It also came to U.S. 60, just west of the larger town of Wickenburg, which had a population of just over seven thousand.

"You'll need the headlights all the way," Vikram warned as she turned onto the dirt. "My research says there ought to be some tire tracks to follow if the wind hasn't blown them away. And there's also supposed to be a small cairn every mile to mark the route, but who knows if the people using this track actually maintain them."

Accelerating, Jane said, "Who the hell *does* use it?"

"Damn if I know. Probably nobody at this hour. It could be easy to lose the track at night, even with headlights, and maybe never find your way back to it."

"I'll call out every mile," she said, "and you spot the cairns for me."

Despite a fissured, cratered landscape roughened through millennia, Jane was able to press the Explorer to sixty miles per hour and still hold the twitching wheel. They ought to see a new cairn every minute.

In the sidewash of headlights, tall saguaro cactuses stood here and there like mournful penitents or angry transgressors, their arms raised as though either begging for divine compassion or cursing the heavens.

"That email I sent for you by satellite," Vikram said. "This Dougal Trahern. Is he the guy who went into Shenneck's Napa ranch with you?"

"Yeah, but I don't expect it to be him in Wickenburg. A rayshaw shot him up bad a few weeks ago. One mile."

After a hesitation, he said, "There's the cairn."

A county sheriff's unit—perhaps even two, but not likely—might be assigned to the seventy-nine-mile length of U.S. 60 that ran from the minuscule town of Brenda east to Wickenburg. However, it was such a long, lonely stretch of highway that the chances of a patrol being close enough to cut them off at the end of this dirt track weren't good enough to inspire a betting man to place a wager.

"Mile," she said.

"Cairn," he replied almost at once.

They were less than fifteen minutes from U.S. 60.

Although Jane's heart labored, she didn't fear encountering a cop ahead or being overtaken by pursuers from behind. Her rapid pulse rapped the rhythm of a dread far greater than anything the Arcadians or the unwitting authorities who assisted them could inspire.

20

By the time the helicopter touches down in Tonopah, near the Shell station, which looks like the social hub of the town, Charlie Weatherwax has figured it out, thanks to a map the pilot, Cynthia Red Coyote, has displayed on her GPS for his study.

Rangnekar and Hawk have chosen northern Maricopa County as the location for their assault by satellite, because it's a short haul from Casa Grande, where they took delivery of the Southwind, and because it is so remote that, if necessary, they could have tucked in for a day or two without attracting attention, perhaps without being seen by anyone whatsoever.

But they've come here also because a network of gravel roads and even some serviceable dirt tracks provide numerous escape routes into the vastness of La Paz, Mohave, and Yavapai Counties, which are thinly populated and therefore thinly policed. Under cover of night, they plan to ditch the motor home and, in the Explorer, vanish into that wasteland before authorities can organize the large number of officers necessary to cordon off the area.

Or that's what they *want* Charlie to think. But he has much experience of deceit, beginning in childhood, and he is convinced that they will instead switch to a dirt track that will bring them to U.S. Highway 60, west of Wickenburg. Intuition would suggest they would avoid even passing through a town that has a small sheriff's department substation, as Wickenburg does, but Charlie is a master of counterintuitive moves that have in the past paid off.

Deputy Vaughn Cooley, in a sheriff's department Jeep Cherokee, is waiting when the helo touches down in Tonopah.

Ms. Red Coyote regards the Bureau of Indian Affairs as being above further assistance to law enforcement. She claims that she can't join in a night search because her chopper isn't equipped with either infrared or night-vision gear. She is impervious to both Charlie's charms and threats, and she takes off with such a smug smile that he would like to cut off her lips.

As Charlie orders Cooley to alert the substation in Wickenburg to be on the lookout for a metallic-gray Explorer Sport, Mustafa al-Yamani washes down another cross-top with the last warm soda in his bottle of Mountain Dew.

21

Having spent her busy life in the lushness of San Diego and environs, on the shores of a vast sea, Charlene Dumont didn't know quite what to make of Wickenburg. The tall palms with short shaggy fronds. Scrawny-limbed trees with small drab leaves. Pea gravel where she expected grass. Everywhere low beige and sand-colored buildings, as if months of hundred-degree temperatures, decade after decade, had withered them down from greater height. Blacktop streets fried to gray and crawling with wiggly lines where tar had been used to fill cracks made by the sun. And everywhere, so much open space—wide streets, wide lots, vacant land—gave her an exhilarating sense of freedom but one that alternated with an equally disturbing sense of emptiness, loneliness.

She arrived in daylight from Phoenix, driving a rented SUV—a GMC Terrain Denali—per Jane's instructions in her email to Dougal. Charlene walked the town both in daylight and after dark, always with the disposable cellphone in her handbag.

By the time it rang at 10:22, she was in her room at the Best Western, watching cable news. They were running a segment about Jane Hawk, portraying her as a demonic kill-crazy witch, claiming she murdered her husband and most likely her missing little boy. It was such a strident, feverish piece that only a total fool would think it was anything but propaganda. Charlene Dumont was no fool, but she knew there were plenty of dunderheads out there who would believe every word of this drivel, so that by the time the phone rang, she had no capacity for exhilaration and instead felt as though the emptiness of the Sonoran Desert had leached into her.

She took the call. "Hello?"

"Charlene?"

"The one and only."

"I'm more grateful for this than you can ever know."

"No gratitude needed, child. Our mutual friend says he wishes you were his daughter, and I sure wish my daddy had been like him, so that makes us sisters."

After a silence, Jane said, "I'm going to do my best to get you in and out of this with as little risk as possible."

"When I'm in, I'm in," Charlene said, "just like your would-be daddy is with people, so no more of that. What is it you need?"

"The town library is only a few blocks from you."

"I know it. Spent some time tourin' the burg."

"Behind it, there's a parking lot, across the street from a shopping center. How soon can you meet me there?"

"Five minutes."

"You won't be going back to the motel."

"The bed's firm, the room's clean, but I'm too much a city girl for Wickenburg. Already I feel I'm fillin' up with desert sand."

"There's a man with me, so don't spook when you see him. I wish he were my brother, so maybe that makes him yours, too."

"We got us a growin' family," Charlene said. "See you in five."

22

To Mustafa al-Yamani, the Fleetwood Southwind seems to be perspiring like a great beast as it stands here in the desert night. It is sweating light. The brightness inside the vehicle streams out like a liquid into the arid land and forms pale pools on the earth.

Charlie and Deputy Cooley are conducting a quick search of the motor home while Mustafa stands at a pool of light, expecting to see his reflection, as he would in bright water, but there is no second Mustafa peering up at him. There is only one Mustafa, glistening with his own lather as his heart maintains a resting rate of maybe a hundred beats a minute. Mouth dry. Eyes itching. His clothes are rumpled, dust-streaked, unsuitable in polite Long Island company or wherever else the elites gather, and sour sweat isn't an acceptable male fragrance in any circles to which he aspires.

He is not angry by nature, certainly not nearly to the extent that Charlie Weatherwax is always raging on some cellular level, but now he's as furious as he is afraid. Restless, agitated, he feels as though he's running in place while the world crumbles in his wake, a void opening behind him, from which he can't escape. The right shoes and socks, the right necktie, the right male fragrance—none of it gives him an advantage in this situation. He knows his anger, fear, and agitation have more to do with the fact that he's flying on Benzedrine than with the setbacks they've endured, but that doesn't make his feelings any less important, any less real.

He wants to kill someone. He understands as never before the *relief* that Charlie must experience when he wastes someone like Hugo Chávez or Jesus Mendoza. Life frequently drops boulders in a man's path, infuriating twists of fate, and there's nothing he can do but struggle around or over them; but no relief is to be had in merely persevering. When the hateful obstruction is another human being, however, a man's stress level can plummet and profound relief ensue with the expenditure of a few bullets.

Charlie and the deputy exit the motor home, switching off the lights behind them. Now it is the darkness that seems like a liquid, washing around Mustafa, a threatening tide.

Charlie is in a hurry, and Deputy Cooley will drive the Jeep Cherokee, so Mustafa gets into the backseat alone. He wishes he were driving. Because he has nothing to do in the back of the vehicle, his agitation grows, his fear, his desperate need for relief. The darkness in the footwell seems to be crawling up his legs.

As they race north, leave the gravel road, and angle northeast on the dirt track, toward Wickenburg, he considers shooting Cooley in the back of the head and taking the wheel. He knows this isn't a good idea. The Cherokee might go out of control and crash. And if that didn't happen, there would be a lot of biological debris in which Mustafa would have to sit, further soiling his expensive suit. Besides, Cooley isn't a serious obstacle, only an annoyance because of his insistence on driving, and killing him might not bring the desired relief.

Mustafa will have to wait. He will find someone to kill in Wickenburg. Until then he will have to wait. He fidgets in the backseat. He keeps wanting to ask, *Are we there yet? Are we? How long until we'll be there?* But he controls himself. He is very good at controlling his impulses. He wants to take another bennie, but he does not. He might not even take one if he had some Mountain Dew left with which to wash it down.

23

The antique-looking lampposts in the parking lot behind the library were widely spaced. Jane had parked the Explorer as far from one of them as she could, though she found no place where shadows were as deep as she would have liked.

If the library had security cameras, they were focused on its doors. There were none in the parking lot.

The shopping area on the other side of East Yavapai Street was closed. Wickenburg appeared to be an early-to-bed town, and little traffic plied its streets at this hour.

As she and Vikram waited for Charlene Dumont, Jane couldn't stop thinking about Cornell Jasperson, one of the guardians of her boy. Cornell was a stone fan of Paul Simon, in whose music he found a guide for his troubled life. In moments when he was fearful and a bit pessimistic, he sometimes repeated a line from a song that now flowed repeatedly through Jane's mind: *The nearer your destination, the more you're slip slidin' away. . . .*

When the Terrain Denali entered the lot from the street, Vikram put up the tailgate of the Explorer, and Jane directed Charlene to back her SUV up to theirs, to facilitate the rapid transfer of their luggage.

Two minutes later, they were leaving the library lot, heading south on U.S. Highway 60. In forty miles or so, they would arrive in the western suburbs of Phoenix.

Of course, *the nearer your destination, the more you're slip slidin' away. . . .*

24

Charlie Weatherwax has come a long way from a suite in the Peninsula Hotel in Beverly Hills to this desert backwater, leaving three dead bodies in his wake. This does not count the deaths that occurred during the raid in Nogales, which accrue not to his credit or blame, but rather to Enrique de Soto's. All of this has gone down in not quite thirty hours, though he feels as if a month has passed since the Peninsula. Partly this distortion of time is a result of the dex-meth cocktail with which he has been staving off sleep, but it is also a consequence of the quiet desperation that arises from the inescapable feeling that he is in a long death spiral.

A sheriff's patrol car waits in the parking lot behind the Wickenburg Public Library when Deputy Cooley arrives with Charlie and Mustafa. The department dispatcher alerted Cooley en route that the Explorer Sport has been found abandoned.

The deputies stand at a distance, conceding jurisdiction to the FBI, while Charlie and Mustafa pretend to search the Explorer for clues. In fact, as they check under seats and look in the glove box and lift the floor mat in the cargo area to inspect the spare-tire well, they expect to find nothing of interest, and they are going through this charade primarily to be able to confer in private, keeping their voices low.

"Our assignment was to find Vikram Rangnekar," Charlie says. "Isn't that right, just Rangnekar?"

"That is right," Mustafa agrees, nodding vigorously. "That is exactly right, exactly. You have put your finger on it exactly."

"So who besides you and me knows for sure that Rangnekar found Jane Hawk and is working with her?"

"Verna. Verna Amboy. She was with you when you interrogated Ganesh. She is not my type, but I would like to see her naked."

"Don't take another bennie," Charlie warns.

"No. I will not. If I take another, I will implode."

"Amboy will most likely tell her partner, Eldon Clocker."

"But they are sworn to silence about what happened in that warehouse," Mustafa reminds him.

"Did either of us say anything about Jane Hawk to Gary Greenway or the other three in Casa Grande?"

"We did not, no, not a word, no, never," Mustafa insists.

"Hugo Chávez knew, but we're the only ones who spoke with him."

"Yes, only us, and he's dead, very dead," Mustafa said. "We will have to kill Amboy and Clocker."

"Of course," Charlie agrees, "but that can wait until tomorrow or the day after. Right now we need a story for our cell leader."

"What is our story?" Mustafa wonders.

"We're still hot on the trail of Vikram Rangnekar, and because of something Chávez told us, we have reason to believe that, after using his satellite dish and abandoning the motor home, he intended to make his way to a safe house."

"Safe house? What safe house? Where? Where is the safe house?"

"We don't know. But we have a lead, a slim lead, and we're going to follow up on it tomorrow, as soon as we get some sleep."

"But we have no lead, none, none at all, and Rangnekar might have gone anywhere," Mustafa worries, "so what do we do tomorrow?"

"Fake it. What else? Phoenix is a big city. No one can blame us if Rangnekar loses himself in it."

"Why would he go to Phoenix?"

Charlie sighs. "Because that's the nearest place to here where we can get rooms in a four-star hotel."

"Yes, I see. I see. You are brilliant, Charles."

"I know."

They conclude their pretense of searching the Explorer and motion for the deputies to join them. Charlie asks that the vehicle be impounded by the sheriff's department and held until the FBI can arrange to take possession of it. He asks Deputy Cooley to drive them to the Arizona Biltmore in Phoenix, approximately an hour away, and Cooley shortly receives permission from his superiors to do so.

On the way out of Wickenburg, Charlie places a call to Gary Greenway at the Casa Grande Holiday Inn. He directs Gary and the three other Arcadian agents to bring the Suburbans to Phoenix, a one-hour drive, take rooms for themselves elsewhere than at the Biltmore, and be ready to meet at nine in the morning.

With a second call to an Arcadian facilitator within the DOJ, he arranges to have his and Mustafa's luggage, which is still in their rooms at the Peninsula Hotel in Beverly Hills, flown overnight to Phoenix and delivered to the Biltmore sharply at seven o'clock in the morning.

Whatever fearsome shitstorm might be coming, it's nonetheless exhilarating to be a revolutionary when the government you're bent on overthrowing is generously providing you with every imaginable luxury at its expense.

25

Efrata Sonenberg was ninety years old but still spry enough to hurry up and down the hidden staircase, seeing to the needs and comfort of her guests: handsome Mr. Riggowitz, the strange but sweet Cornell Jasperson, the darling boy, and the two well-behaved dogs.

The secret basement had been equipped with four beds, one more than currently needed. Earlier, Efrata had stripped off the plastic dust covers that had long covered the mattresses. Before the guests had arrived, she and her daughters, Orlee and Nophia, had dressed the beds in fresh sheets and pillowcases. They supplied the bathroom with plenty of towels and toiletries, and stocked the refrigerator. For the duration, the dogs would remain upstairs, where Efrata and Nophia—who had lived here four years, since the death of Victor, her husband—could take care of them.

Orlee and Nophia and Cornell and the handsome Mr. Riggowitz

were sitting at the table, having a late nosh and playing cards, which Efrata had found was a reliable way to settle one's nerves.

The boy was in pajamas, in bed, unable to sleep in spite of the late hour, sitting with his back against the headboard, holding a large glass containing a root-beer float that Efrata had made for him. She sat in a chair beside the bed, with a storybook in hand, but Travis was too full of questions to listen to a fairy tale.

"Why did you hide a whole cellar?" he asked.

"Well, because for a long time in my childhood, I lived every day in fear."

"Of the cellar? Did it have a monster in it?"

"No, not of the cellar. In fear of those who might find me hiding in the cellar. I'm sort of a crazy lady, you see."

He cocked his head and regarded her dubiously. "You don't look crazy. You make good root beer."

"Well, I'm crazy enough, I assure you. I never quite got over that fear. In fact, I never got over it at all. Not even here in beautiful America. I always wanted a place to hide—or to hide others—if the world turned darker. It's a complicated story, dear, and too scary for a child your age."

He spooned some ice cream from the glass. "How'd you make this cellar here and keep it secret?"

"When my hubby, Sam, and I built this lovely house, the basement wasn't secret at all. But my Sam indulged me. He always did. He was the kindest, gentlest man. We designed the place so the stairs could later be hidden away and everything down here lost to memory."

"But why?" he asked again. "Tell me. I don't scare easy. I'm an FBI kid, you know."

She considered him for a long moment and then put aside the book. "When I was a child about twice your age—"

"How long ago was that?"

"Oh, I suppose almost eighty years ago."

"Wow! You are *really* old."

She laughed softly. "I really am. Some days it amazes me how old. Anyway, this was in Holland. My entire family was saved when some good people hid us in a portion of their basement, which they walled off so no one knew it was there."

"Where's Holland?"

"In Europe, half a world away from here."

"Who were you hiding from?"

"Nazis. Have you heard of them?"

"Nope. I heard of vampires and werewolves. But I don't think they're real. Were the Nazis monsters?"

"Yes, honey. They were terrible monsters."

"Did they want to eat you?"

"That's pretty much what they wanted, yes. Now finish your root beer. It's late, and growing boys need their sleep."

When he finished his treat, she took the empty glass from him and set it aside and tucked him in and kissed him on the brow.

He reached out and put his hand on hers. "I'm glad the monsters didn't eat you."

"Thank you, Travis. I like to believe they would have broken their teeth on me if they tried."

"Do you think they'll eat me?"

"No chance, sweetheart. You're safe here. There are no monsters here."

"My mother's out there alone somewhere, and I know they really want to eat her."

Although Efrata's parents had survived, her grandparents, whom she'd loved so much, had perished. The enduring memory of that loss made it difficult for her to be to any degree a Pollyanna, but she believed what she said to the boy. "Honey, there's a world of people out there who love your mother, people who've never even met her but somehow know the truth of her, and when she asks for help, I'm sure there's always going to be people who stand beside her when she needs them."

26

Bound for Phoenix in the patrol car, alone in the backseat, with Mustafa up front next to Deputy Cooley, Charlie receives an urgent encrypted call from his cell leader, Raimundo Cortez, the attorney general of the state of California. He's a sarcastic prick, but Charlie has to answer to him.

Cortez reports that the Techno Arcadian central committee has minutes ago learned that among the nearly infinite oceans of data stored in the National Security Agency's facility in Utah is an exhaustive file on the charitable foundation that serves as a front for the revolution's activities. Somehow, Vikram Rangnekar made a connection between this foundation and the revolution. He now has the locations of all laboratories, the names of every Arcadian, and the names of every hapless pleb who has been brain-screwed.

"Where the hell are you?" Cortez asks.

"On our way to Phoenix, less than an hour out."

"Tell me you're not doing your Inspector Clouseau act. Tell me you have a lead."

"He's there," Charlie lies. "In Phoenix."

"Rangnekar?"

"Yes. I'm not in a position to talk freely at the moment."

"Screw that. Talk. Where is the little puke? Where in Phoenix?"

"In a safe house," Charlie lies.

"The address?"

"We just know a safe house in Phoenix."

"Who's your source?"

"This guy, Chávez, who tried to escape a raid we conducted in Nogales. His motorcycle flipped. He was fatally injured. We only had a few minutes with him before he was gone."

Cortez is furious and perhaps panicked. "That's all you got out of the scumbag, some bullshit about some safe house that could be anywhere in Phoenix? Phoenix is—what?—the sixth largest damn city in the damn country? That's the needle in a haystack you're handing me? *That's all you've got?"*

Because he can see in his mind's eye an ampule of amber fluid draining into a vein in his arm, Charlie buys time by supporting one lie with another. He doesn't know Phoenix well, so he refers to that part of it with which he's vaguely familiar. "Chávez said it's within walking distance of the state capitol building. That's all he knew."

Cortez's anger swells. "Walking distance? How's the asshole define walking distance? Six blocks? Ten? Twelve?"

"I can't ask him, sir. He's dead. But our target is somewhere within walking distance of the capitol, which is off West Jefferson Street, between Seventeenth and Eighteenth Avenue."

"We'll flood the zone," Cortez declares. "We'll throw everyone we have in there, but we can't get an operation this big mounted before morning. If he splits before we have the area sealed, we're totally screwed—all of us, including you, Weatherwax."

A third lie is necessary. "Chávez thought our target is going to be in the safe house for at least a week."

"You just remembered that? You didn't think that little detail mattered?"

"Sorry, sir. I'm tired. Exhausted. Wiped out. My partner and I haven't slept since Friday afternoon. We're on our way to a hotel."

With withering sarcasm, Raimundo Cortez says, "Heroes of the revolution. All right, get some sleep. But be ready to roll by eight in the morning." He terminates the call.

For all Charlie knows, Vikram Rangnekar and Jane Hawk are headed northwest from Wickenburg toward Kingman. Or north toward Prescott. Or northeast toward Flagstaff.

Turning in the shotgun seat to look back at Charlie, Mustafa says, "Trouble, Charles?"

"Nothing we can't handle," Charlie lies, hoping he'll come out of this smelling as sweet as his greedy, deceitful parents, who have done so well by lying their way through life.

27

The first motel on the west side of Phoenix had only two vacancies. The second had more rooms available, but they were not contiguous. The third could give Jane three rooms side by side, with connecting doors. Still being Leslie Anderson, she produced ID and paid cash in advance, casually mentioning that she was traveling with two siblings, which made the Anderson family a multicultural wonder.

She took the center room, with Vikram to the north and Charlene to the south. Together they unloaded the GMC Terrain Denali shortly before midnight.

As they pulled bags from the SUV, Jane said, "Vikram, can you set up your laptop right away, review the data you downloaded onto those flash drives?"

"Yeah, sure."

"Are you able to search those names by geographic location?"

"In like a minute."

She told him what she needed.

While Vikram was carrying bags into their rooms, Jane put a hand on Charlene's shoulder. "Don't go to sleep right away. I need to talk to you, just you and me, in half an hour or so. That okay?"

"Honey, if insomnia was a country, I'd be queen. You come see me whenever you want."

After unloading the rest of her luggage, Jane got a Coke and a bucket of ice from the vending-machine alcove. Worshipping light, two large moths repeatedly offered their soft bodies to the four recessed bulbs in the ceiling, a quartet of gods indifferent to their desire to sacrifice themselves.

In her room, she retrieved a pint of Belvedere vodka from a suitcase, fetched a glass from the bathroom, and fixed a strong drink. She needed it to grease her thought processes. And to boost her courage.

Unable to stop the ice from rattling in the glass, she set the drink on a small table beside an armchair.

She unlocked the first of the two connecting doors and rapped softly on the second. Vikram unlocked it, and they faced each other across the double threshold.

Behind him in the otherwise shadowy room, the screen of his laptop glowed like some mystical instrument through which an oracle foresaw the future.

In answer to the questions Jane had asked as they'd unloaded the SUV, Vikram spoke softly, as if events had harried him into a state of acute wariness and suspicion, until he felt as though even a motel chosen at random might be a listening post manned by their enemies. "Yeah, there are more Arcadians in a state capital, like Phoenix, than in other cities. And of the top ten cities in the country, by population, Phoenix is the only one that's also a state capital. The less important the state, the smaller the contingent. Arizona is important, Phoenix is important, so there are a hundred forty-nine Arcadians in state government, industry, and media, as opposed to sixteen in the entire state of Wyoming."

She found herself speaking as softly as he did. "And how many people with brain implants?"

"Of the almost seventeen thousand adjusted people, two hundred eighty-six are in greater Phoenix. Why do you want to know?"

"We've got proof. All these names you've found. The research files I got from Bertold Shenneck's house in Napa, the incriminating videos from Anabel Claridge's estate. But now . . . what next? How do we get the truth out there? Who can we trust?"

"I've been wrestling with the same question."

"Any ideas?"

He didn't answer at once. He'd always been a perpetual-motion machine, energized and ebullient, but now he appeared profoundly weary. His solemnity was that of an executioner with a conscience, who understood that a counterrevolution was essential to prevent the Arcadian movement from enslaving the nation and then the world, but who also knew that there would inevitably be much violence and that perhaps there would be no safe harbor for either him or Jane.

Finally he said, "I have a few ideas. I don't like any of them. I need to sleep on it."

"I hope you *can* sleep. We need you clearheaded. You've done brilliant work, *chotti batasha*. You're amazing."

"But too slow to the fight."

"Never waste energy beating yourself up. Other people are always standing in line to do it."

His smile was a curve of melancholy.

"I'll sleep," she said. "You will, too."

He nodded. "Let's leave these doors closed but unlocked. So we can be together quickly if . . . if someone shows up, if something happens."

"Good idea."

"And if I can't sleep," he said, "I'd like to just sit in the dark with you. Just sit near you in the dark. Then maybe I'll be able to sleep, after all."

28

Hollister is napping in the warmth of the Sno-Cat, getting out only to urinate, never lingering once he completes his business, for *she* is always out there, naked and brainless, with the corpse of the infant in her arms. She will be there until the moviemaker is dead, for somehow Buckle has conjured her.

The town lies in midnight stillness, with no one about except the searchers, but considering the hour, there is an abundance of light in the houses and other buildings, the residents alert to the strangeness of their situation and no doubt frightened, as they should be.

Throughout the afternoon and evening, they have been without phone and Internet service, have been confined to their homes and businesses. Sooner or later these conniving yokels, these ignorant fools, will submit to Hollister as their rightful ruler. They will cease colluding to hide the filmmaker from him.

He would like to be part of the search, to prowl through their blighted dwellings, be amused by their taste in décor, see them realize, in his presence, the insignificance of their lives. But in light of the fact that more than a few of them have guns, he elects to wait to venture among them until Buckle has been found.

He has taken Andy Goddard's advice and has replaced the weary deputies with fresh ones. It matters not who he uses to conduct the search. They are all adjusted people, his to use as he pleases. He has also brought in fresh rayshaws from the ranch security force.

They are coordinating with one another through the whispering room. There has been no catastrophic psychological meltdown as recently happened in Borrego Springs and Borrego Valley, when one unstable individual infected others with his madness by broadcasting it directly into their minds. The technology works. It is reliable. If it weren't reliable, the revolution would be fated to fail, and that is not the case. Hollister does not fail.

He has decided to purge from the central committee those who want to strip the whispering room from the programs of the adjusted people. As soon as this business in Willisford is finished, he will order their execution. He will not be resisted. Throughout his life, he has conquered all resistance. He has no memory of a time when he lacked great wealth, and therefore no memory of a time when he was without absolute power.

Mai-Mai thought she had acquired power over Hollister when she told him that she was pregnant, but she didn't understand that woven across her brain were gossamer chains of enslavement, that her free will was an illusion, and that he would not permit an heir. No one can deceive him, win against him. He has always crushed opposition, and he always will.

He needs to urinate again, but she is out there under one of the parking-lot lamps, holding dead Diederick, and each time that he exits the Sno-Cat, she slowly approaches him. She seems to have no fear of him. He doesn't understand what the woman intends. It's difficult to crush the opposition when she has no fear and when her intentions are mysterious.

29

Jane sat in darkness but for the television, on which Jurassic monsters provided something to fear that in fact need never be faced in life, fantastic shapes of shadow and light playing across her face, suggestions of reptilian ferocity glimmering within the ice in her glass.

This was not a time for tears, for brooding about what might have been or wishing for what could never be. There was a precious child for whom she would sacrifice her life if there was no other way to protect him and guarantee him a worthwhile future. This was a time for cold calculation, as free from emotion as possible.

Having slept only a few hours earlier Saturday, in an armchair in the Casa Grande Holiday Inn, Jane would have liked nothing better than to sleep in this chair, in this Phoenix motel, as Saturday at last became Sunday, but the terrible prospect before her made sleep impossible.

As quiet and safe as this place seemed when compared with the unrelenting danger and frequent violence of the past few weeks, she was in a crisis. She needed to get off the X, take action, because when she wasn't moving to deal with a threat, the threat would come to deal with her.

However, she needed to think this through, be certain that the one way she saw before her was indeed the only viable way, before she acted precipitously.

They had acquired everything they needed to destroy the Techno Arcadians, proof of unprecedented evil and horror, reams of evidence more complete than that in any case brought before a court since the Nuremberg trials in the wake of World War II.

A time had existed when the safest thing to do would have been to approach a newspaper or TV news operation that had a sterling reputation, give them the scoop of the century. But the public's trust of the media was at an all-time low, and at least in part for good reason. More important, many of the biggest names in journalism had been injected with nanoweb brain implants or in some cases were Arcadians. Reporters existed who were neither adjusted people nor among the wicked, but they weren't necessarily the media gatekeepers who decided what was news and what was not. Making common cause with reporters who could not blow open the media walls with the story would only ensure they were all murdered or brain-screwed. Jane had already tried that approach with an acclaimed journalist, Lawrence Hannafin, who had proved to be a paragon of deceit and treachery.

Perhaps there were those in Congress who could be trusted, whose names didn't appear on any of the lists Vikram had obtained. But there was no way that she could approach them, not after she'd been demonized in the media, indicted in absentia by a grand jury, charged with treason and multiple counts of murder.

Even if she could contrive to meet in a private place with a powerful, charismatic senator who could command the attention of the media, she would need to convince him or her that the conspiracy was real, which would not be easy, even with mountains of evidence. Nanoweb brain implants; adjusted people shorn of free will, memories edited; human beings turned into biomachines programmed to kill; thousands on the Hamlet list slated for extermination . . . Even in a time when noted entrepreneurs and wizards of technology like Elon Musk and Ray Kurzweil and numerous others spoke glowingly of the Singularity, the yearned-for event when human brains and computers would meld to form a superior species, the Arcadian story could sound like the fevered imaginings of the tinfoil-hat crowd.

And suppose she could convince this senator that all of it was true. Would he do the right thing, or would he try to escape both responsibility and threat by seeking to become one of the Arcadians now that he knew of their existence? Courageous politicians existed, as did albino tigers and two-headed frogs. But she was loath to put the life of her child and the future of all children in the hands of a public figure whom she didn't know personally.

A decade ago, there might have been a way to use the Internet to push a tsunami of truth about the Arcadians from shore to shore of social media. But these days the Internet was flooded with so many flavors of rage and rant, with so much fake news, with such torrents of paranoia, that the Arcadian story would probably wash through the system in a week, perhaps winning a few believers while inspiring loud, mindless mockery. Anyway, Arcadians threaded through social media companies would quietly, quickly censor everything she posted, draining from the truth enough of its substance to leave it hollow and unaffecting.

The one way forward that she had identified remained the only way that seemed to offer any hope for Travis and for the future generations of which he was, to Jane, a symbol. For her, this was a dark kind of hope, demanding a foreboding passage that mere days ago she could not have contemplated.

From a pocket she extracted the half of a broken locket that Travis had found and given her weeks earlier: a silver oval in which was embedded a soapstone cameo that he felt resembled her. He wanted to believe the locket was magical, that some fate had guided him to where he found it on water-smoothed stones beside a clear-running stream. He hoped that it would protect her from harm as long as she carried it. She worked the oval between her thumb and forefinger, not as if it were a wishing stone by which her triumph would be assured, but because she could not caress her child, only this he had given her, only this.

For millennia, people had lived and died and been forgotten, vanished from history by the billions. Even the most famous and celebrated would not be remembered forever; in mere decades or centuries, they also would be forgotten, those who had lived like angels and those who had lived like devils, all gone with their fame as if they had never existed. Time was relentless and the world was not Gaea, not a caring mother who cherished her children. The world remained indifferent to their struggle. In the end, the true end, the final accounting of the universe, fame did not matter, and mere celebrity was the pursuit of fools. Wealth and power meant nothing in the long run. What mattered was what you did in private, when no one was looking, when you either lived by the values you claimed in public or you didn't. The truest and most terrifying thing about the human condition was that if you remained faithful to your values even behind closed doors, no one in this busy world cared but you yourself. You were your only taskmaster, at liberty to deceive the world and lie even to yourself, to be a monster in the secret cellar of your soul. Neither the billions who had come and gone nor the billions yet unborn would think less of you—or think of you at all. This was the beauty and the terror of free will.

One way. One path. One hope. The whispering room. And no one to go there but her.

She finished the vodka-and-Coke.

Leaving the dinosaurs to caper on the screen and cast their flickering ghosts across the walls, she went to the dresser and picked up the Medexpress carrier.

She unlocked and opened the first of two connecting doors to Charlene Dumont's room and knocked lightly on the second.

When Charlene opened her door, Jane said softly, "I need your help to save my child."

PART SIX

Free Will

1

They sat across from each other at a small round table by the curtained window, where a motel guest might read the free morning newspaper or eat a complimentary breakfast of a sweet roll and coffee. Nothing about the scene was dramatic, not even the lamplight or the fall of shadows, with which a moviemaker might have dressed such a set; everything about it was mundane—except for the words Jane spoke as she laid out the truth of the Arcadians.

Charlene listened and did not interrupt, as if she knew from the outset that, crazy as it might sound, Jane's story was true in each new and astonishing detail. The street was a hard school, and you didn't graduate from it unless you developed a reliable bullshit detector. There was also the fact that she had such deep respect for Dougal Trahern that she would never second-guess his considered opinion of anyone; and Jane came with his strongest endorsement.

Perhaps Dougal would have denied Jane his help in performing this grim task. His life had been scarred by exceptional traumas beginning when he was ten years old, and those events were of a nature that impressed on him the essential truth and importance of free will. Furthermore, after what he and Jane had been through at Bertold Shenneck's ranch in Napa, he had said he loved her like a daughter, and no loving father, even a surrogate father, would want to assist a daughter with this injection.

Unlike Dougal, who'd never had children of his own, Charlene Dumont had known the joy of a daughter and a son—and had lost both. Larisa died of cancer at five. Jerome had been killed in gang-banger crossfire when he was nine. The deaths came one year apart. Charlene would have given her life for either child, and she understood that Jane could do no less.

"But, honey," she said, "this isn't just dyin' once for your sweet boy. This could be a livin' death. This could be like dyin' for him every day, over and over again, for all the rest of your life."

"Not if it goes like I think it will. And if it doesn't, well, once the nanoweb is established, Vikram will be my controller. If worse comes to worst, he can save me from lifelong enslavement by ordering me to kill myself."

Charlene closed her eyes and shook her head. "You say it so matter-of-fact. That is a woeful thing for the poor man to have on his conscience."

"I know it's wrong to ask it of him. But he'll understand. He's a decent man with a good heart. He wants to pay penance for things he's done, and he'll see doing this, taking on the weight of this, as penance."

Raising her eyebrows, Charlene said, "You haven't asked him yet?"

"No. If I tell him what I'm going to do, he'll try to argue me out of it. We don't have time to debate. We've just about run out of time. With all their resources, they're closing on me fast. Instinct says this is my last shot, and instinct has never done me wrong."

Charlene reached across the table. Jane took the offered hand and closed her eyes. They held tightly to each other for a long moment.

With Jane now were her mother and her husband, both gone from this world and yet no less full figures in her heart as they had been when alive. Death conquered only the body, not what was ineffable but real. She thought of a Dylan Thomas poem that Nick had given her before he'd shipped out for a black-ops mission overseas. He had not marked the two lines that were important to him, and he didn't need to cite them, for she knew them on first reading: *Though lovers be lost love shall not; / And death shall have no dominion.*

She opened her eyes. "Charlene, I'm sorry as I can be to ask you to help me. If it was a simple injection, I could manage that myself. But it's damn complicated. I don't have three hands, and I don't dare screw this up. I know it won't be easy for you."

Charlene gave Jane's hand a final squeeze before letting go. "Easy and right aren't the same thing. Nothin' new about that."

Jane looked at the Medexpress carrier, which stood on the table. The digital readout showed an interior temperature of forty-six degrees.

"It's within the range that keeps the nanoweb viable. Has it always been below fifty-five degrees since I gave it to you three weeks ago?"

"Far as I know, yes. I never opened it, and Dougal always kept it safe, with his fridge turned down to thirty-five. It was forty degrees all the way here from San Diego. So if it's climbin', maybe it's good you didn't get here a week from now."

Jane got to her feet and stood over the carrier. *Why is it six degrees warmer?* She pressed the handle aside and opened the lid.

Instead of everything she expected, everything she *needed*, under the CryoMax modular cold packs that were still largely frozen, the carrier contained only a zippered leather shaving kit in which a man might pack his electric razor, preshave, aftershave, and other toiletries. When she opened the kit, it was filled with two or three pounds of gravel, stones from the very road that she and Vikram had taken into the desert north of Tonopah.

2

With Charlene close behind her, Jane hurried through her room, pulled open the first connecting door, pushed open the second, and went into Vikram's room.

He sat at a table identical to the one on which she had left the raided Medexpress carrier. Standing over Vikram was a somewhat younger man who shared his heritage and might have had his same smile if anyone had been smiling.

On the table lay the length of rubber tubing used as a tourniquet.

A cannula had been installed in the target vein, and the first of three large ampules of cloudy amber fluid was being infused into Vikram's bloodstream. The other two ampules floated in one of the motel's plastic buckets, which was filled with ice and water.

With his free hand, Vikram indicated his companion. "This is my cousin Harshad, who waited at that abandoned school in Las Vegas for the delivery of the satellite dish. His parents are Uncle Ashok and Aunt Doris. His brother is . . . Ganesh."

Jane said, "Stop now. Don't infuse the other two ampules."

"Too risky," Vikram said. "The one I've received is on its way through the blood-brain barrier. It needs the other two if it's to form properly. What happens if it can't become what it was designed to be, all those tens of thousands of nanoparts forever bumping against one another inside my skull, trying to assemble? A stroke? Catastrophic failure of the brain's natural electrical activity? What would I be then? What strange version of myself?"

Briefly Jane stood frozen in tumult, her heart laboring through each heavy leaden convulsion, as if it had forgotten the automatic rhythm it had known through all its years of life, as though she must consciously will it to beat against the multiple gravities that weighed upon it like a mile of ocean upon the hull of an abyss-traveling vessel.

Her mind no less oppressed than her heart, she went to the plastic ice bucket and peered at the floating ampules. "There were six in the carrier. Two complete control mechanisms, labeled with the date of production. Where are the other three?"

"You can't have them," Vikram said. "I opened them and poured them down the sink drain." She started to speak, but he raised his free hand to silence her. "By morning, when I'm . . . adjusted, I won't know what's happened to me. That's how it works, right? The program wipes from my memory the truth of my condition."

"Not quite. Others who are injected don't know anything more than that something's been done to them against their will. They don't know what the injection was or why they received it. After the nanoweb is in place, a controller instructs them to forget being restrained and injected. But you already know everything about the implant, and I won't tell you to forget. You'll know what's happened and why. You'll be unique among those who've been adjusted."

"Still, doesn't someone have to unlock me with a key sentence, to activate my program, so I can access the whispering room? I need a controller."

"Maybe not. Maybe you only need me to counsel you, not control. Maybe you can do what needs to be done yourself, although you might be confused. We're in uncharted waters."

"Other than me," Vikram said, "only you know what has to be done. And though I love Harshad and my brother and all my family, there's no one but you in this world I trust to have control of me, to be in possession of my mind and soul, if it comes to that."

When she was able to speak, she could barely summon the words in a whisper. "I didn't ask this of you."

"No. You didn't. You never would."

"God, I wish you hadn't."

"Given the alternative, I'm so very glad I did."

Harshad fished the second ampule from the ice water.

3

One bedside lamp aglow, otherwise the room in shadow. Jane at the table with Vikram, much to be said and much for which there were no words.

This was a city of fewer sirens than most, as if the curative dry heat baked some of the lust for violence from its populace. But there were engine sounds in the night, the periodic clank of an ill-fitted manhole cover protesting a tire, and occasionally voices in the distance. A drunkard in his wandering passed along the street, singing that old

Cole Porter song "I've Got You Under My Skin." Although he was in fine voice, he sang in an inappropriate key, so that it sounded like a threnody accompanying a funeral procession, giving the words an eerie subtext.

With backup flash drives of the data Vikram had taken from the NSA, Harshad now set off on an urgent mission. Unknown to Charlene Dumont, alerted by Vikram, Harshad had been at the Best Western in Wickenburg, where she'd taken a room to wait for Jane's call. He'd followed her to the rendezvous with Jane, then here to Phoenix.

Charlene felt bound to Jane and Vikram by the enormity of what had happened in this room and by the terror of what was happening in the world beyond these walls. She wanted to stay through the morning mission rather than return to San Diego. If she could have slept, she didn't try. She sat in the armchair with her well-worn rosary, silently meditating upon mysteries sorrowful, joyful, and glorious.

On the crook of Vikram's right arm, a Band-Aid bore a spot of blood, the only evidence of his sacrifice.

A chill passed through Jane, different from any she had felt before, as cold as the light of a winter moon, but of such strange character that she sensed it was a quiver of warmth when compared to some great arctic sea of cold that could rise within her and drown her if anything worse happened to Vikram than the wrong to which he had already been subjected. She had done terrible things since the Arcadians had murdered Nick. Although the acts she committed had been essential, even justified, they were nonetheless terrible. Perhaps the worst for which she must account was bringing Vikram to a point where he'd done this to himself out of . . . Out of what? Love for her? Worse, out of adoration? Adoration that she had failed to work hard enough to discourage? The intuition by which she lived now told her that if Vikram, in her control, suffered worse than what he had already endured, she would have earned her hell in this world as well as in any world to come.

Each of them had an open can of Coca-Cola, and there were two more cans nestled among cubes in the ice bucket. She had gotten a bottle of caffeine tablets from her tote, and both she and Vikram had chased a pair with cola.

In light of what was happening to him, neither of them could sleep, yet when the time came to act in the morning, they needed to be as clearheaded as possible.

Jane said, "When did you know what I meant to do?"

"Soon after you had me send that email to Dougal Trahern, just after I had the satellite dish up and running."

"Even then? But how could you know?"

"You said we might need to select an Arcadian or two, inject them, control them, and direct them to confess all in some public forum. But I couldn't see how that would work, with an army of them closing in on us, or why it would be necessary if I could get all their names and the locations of their laboratories. But then I realized . . . once we had it all, how would we get the truth out through media the Arcadians infest? They have countless ways to thwart us, silence us."

She said, "It's not unlike being in the old Soviet Union, with all channels of communication clenched in the fist of the state, with every dissident branded insane, stifled at once, and sent to an asylum to get his head straight."

"Except for their one weakness. The whispering room."

If they could have gone to one of the adjusted people on Vikram's list, could have accessed him and used him to do what must be done, Jane would never have considered injecting herself. But the Arcadians had changed the access sentence, "Play Manchurian with me," immediately when they knew she'd learned it from Bertold Shenneck. And when she took down Booth Hendrickson, of the DOJ, they realized she had learned the new sentence, "Uncle Ira is not Uncle Ira." So they would have reprogrammed the adjusted people yet again. With no way to learn the newest key sentence, at least not in a timely fashion, and with time running out . . . she had seen no alternative.

"I've thought it through," Vikram said. "There's no other way."

For the rest of Jane's life, however long or short it might be, she would always wonder if *she* had thought it through well enough, if she shouldn't have dared delay another day, to work through the Gordian knot that was their situation, even at the risk of being found and enchained.

4

According to their labels, the ampules contained the most recent iteration of the control mechanism. The first nanowebs had taken eight to twelve hours to install. But this one should be in place in four hours, shortly after five o'clock in the morning.

Jane did not sit across the table from Vikram any longer, but at his side, the better to monitor his condition. Occasionally she took his pulse or held a palm to his forehead to feel for fever, as she had sat bedside with Travis when he was stricken with the flu. Often she touched Vikram not in the role of nurse, but to reassure him—and herself—that he'd be okay. This also was reminiscent of times when Travis had been ill: squeezing his shoulder, smoothing the hair back from his forehead, holding his hand.

"You didn't give the elephant a chance to miss you," she said. "You stepped right out in front of it."

"I guess I did, but I haven't been trampled. I'm okay. I don't feel anything strange." He pressed the fingertips of one hand to his forehead. "I thought I'd feel those tiny constructs moving, swarming in my head. But there's nothing."

"No fear," she said.

He smiled. "No fear."

Charlene brought a straight-backed chair from Jane's room and joined them at the table. "I'm not much of a drinkin' woman," she said. But using Jane's pint of Belvedere, she had mixed a vodka-and-Coke for herself. "I don't know how to feel. I've always held tight to hope, but I'm in a dark place now, and the longer I have to think about what you told me, the darker things seem. People who tell us they're our leaders, our betters, them that claim to know how the future should be shaped—seems the smarter they get, the less they know. The more progress they force on us, the more ignorant they are about the consequences. They don't realize there's truest evil in the world that'll make misery from their progress, so they don't guard against it. Worse, the smarter they get, the less they're able to see evil in themselves. What if in the mornin', after you do what you're gonna do, you can't bring down these Arcadian fools?"

"We'll bring them down," Jane said. "There's no alternative. They've given us a way to do it, and we'll bring them down."

She wished that she were as confident as she sounded.

5

Since their hours in the desert north of Tonopah, Jane had been mentally composing what she would broadcast through the whispering room to other adjusted people once her brain implant had installed and Vikram had become her controller/counselor. Now that their roles had reversed, she worked with him to craft the message as succinctly and powerfully as possible, and Charlene suggested certain tweaks.

They had just finished that task when Vikram's crisis came at four o'clock in the morning.

From what she'd reviewed of Bertold Shenneck's research records that she had recovered from his ranch in Napa, Jane knew some people experienced no symptoms related to the assembling of the gossamer nanoweb, while others were afflicted by strange smells or sudden foul tastes or noises that no one else heard. A few experienced intense anxiety without apparent cause, though their distress was sometimes associated with a crawling sensation inside the skull.

At the table with Jane and Charlene, Vikram suddenly broke into a sweat and clasped his hands to his head, his face drawn and gray, his eyes widening as though with the sight of horrors that only he could see. His expression was as ghastly as that of the tormented man in the famous painting *The Scream* by Edvard Munch. "Spiders, listen to them, spiders. Oh, God, I'm full of spiders laying eggs. *Spiders behind my eyes.*" He groaned, whimpered like a wounded dog, gagged with revulsion. Tremors racked him, and he rocked violently in his chair.

"Let's get him to bed," Jane said.

She and Charlene lifted Vikram from his chair and, between them, brought him to the bed as his legs failed him. Lying on his left side, he pulled a pillow to his face and muffled hoarse cries of anguish with it. He seemed to be unable to hear what was said to him, unable to answer questions. Whether his suffering was mental or physical, or both, it appeared existential, as if at any moment he would be gone. Chilled and trembling, Jane stood watching him. She felt powerless and guilty and sick with grief. If a man had been entered by a demonic butcher intent on filleting his soul from him, the torment caused by that invader wielding its psychic knives might have resulted in such distress as this. She found herself upon the bed, spooned against Vikram's back, embracing him as if he were her child, holding him as though, by some mystical transference, she could relieve him of his pain and take it into herself, and not just his pain but the hideous consequence of the injection. Her face wet with tears, Charlene settled onto the bed as well, and together she and Jane held the boy—for he seemed now so like a helpless child—as he shuddered and quaked and ultimately surrendered the dominion of his mind to the nanoweb, to a program of enslavement designed by those who considered themselves his superiors but were in fact only emotional cripples, sociopaths without the capacity to know truth.

6

Vikram's crisis lasted almost half an hour before quickly subsiding. Exhausted, he slept forty minutes in the arms of the women.

Against all expectations, Jane slept part of that time, too. She startled awake at 5:20, when Vikram sat up and, in a voice as dry as Sonoran sands, asked for something cold to drink.

She left the room and went to the vending-machine alcove and bought three cans of cola. Of the two large moths she had seen hours earlier, one lay dead upon the concrete floor in fans of wing dust it cast off in its final throes. The other lay near it, fluttering feebly in the last minutes of its life.

When Jane returned to the room, Charlene was sitting on the edge of the bed with Vikram. He was bent forward, his head hung low, his hands cupping his knees. When he heard the pull-tab pop on the first can, he looked up and reached out with one hand.

Jane opened a Coke for Charlene and one for herself.

Vikram drank greedily. He set the empty can on the nightstand.

After putting her unfinished cola on the small round table, Jane knelt before him and took his hands in hers. "*Baba*," she said, for she had learned from him that it was an affectionate form of address in Hindi. "*Baba*, how is it now?"

He met her eyes. "I believe it is done, Jane-ji."

"Then should I . . . ?"

"Yes."

She rephrased it. "*May* I, Vikram?"

"Yes, *bhenji*."

"What does that mean?"

" 'My beloved sister.' "

Still beside Vikram, Charlene resorted to her beads again.

Although this control mechanism was of the latest generation, it had been produced before the key sentence that unlocked the mind of an adjusted person had been revised.

Therefore, after a hesitation, Jane whispered, "Play Manchurian with me."

"Yes, all right."

She wanted to believe that nothing changed within his eyes, that she only imagined a sudden diminishment of their light, a new and awful meekness, subservience.

"*Baba,* am I with you?"

"Yes."

"I mean not just here in this motel but . . ."

"Within me. Yes. The mind has many chambers, and you're in all of them now. Wherever I turn, you are there. What may I do for you?"

"Do you know the whispering room?"

"Yes."

"Do you understand how to enter it and speak to others . . ."

"Others of my kind? Yes."

It was an exaggeration to say that the words *others of my kind* broke her heart, but the bruise it left would be enduring. She needed a long moment before she was able to say, "Then we're ready. Don't forget this exchange we've had. Never forget anything that happens while you're . . . controlled." She closed his program by saying, "*Auf Wiedersehen.*"

"Good-bye," he responded, as he had been programmed.

When his hands tightened on Jane's, she said, "Vikram, do you remember what just happened?"

"Yes. I am adjusted but, unlike the others, I know that I am."

"Can you use the whispering room without being told to do so?"

"No. My program can be activated by someone, like you, either in person or *through* the whispering room. But I have to be in a controlled condition before I'm able to communicate that way with the others."

"Then we will be side by side through all that's coming."

"And what is that?" Charlene asked, looking up from her beads. "I'm almost afraid to ask, and I'm for sure afraid *not* to ask. What is comin'?"

7

Morning light in Willisford, Colorado, reveals that the skin of clouds has for the most part been peeled away from the bright fruit of the sky, which is ripe and round and pendulous in its blueness. The crystallized town lies as quiet as a deeply buried strata of quartz, its residents paralyzed by an overwhelming sense of peril and by bewilderment as to the reason for their quarantine.

In the early light, two rayshaws at last escort Wainwright Hollister on foot from the Sno-Cat in the farm-supply parking lot to the home of Louise Walters. During a second and more thorough search, Thomas Buckle has been discovered hiding in a hope chest at the foot of a bed. The house is secure. Louise and her paramour, Porter Crockett, are restrained in that very bedroom, where later they will be injected with control mechanisms and brought to heel.

This moment of triumph would be exhilarating for Hollister if not for the artist who obediently destroyed her art at his command, who at his order serviced his every sexual desire with eagerness, a little maidservant whore who never was anything other than a slut with a pretense to artistic talent, a humping animal. The brainless naked bitch with the perfect body and the now grotesquely distorted face, holding the smothered infant, as though she is a Madonna of death, appears from behind a tree, leaving no footprints. Appears in the street, standing sentinel. Steps into sight on the front lawn of the Walters house. Each time she comes slightly nearer to Hollister than she has previously dared.

In the house, as he follows the hallway toward the kitchen, he thinks he sees the menacing shape of her in the shadowy living room, but isn't sure. He passes archways and open doors with caution, in spite of the rayshaws with him.

Thomas Buckle is zip-tied to a chair at the kitchen table and watched over by a rayshaw. At the sight of Hollister, the filmmaker tries to appear stoic, even defiant, but anxiety has drawn lines in his previously smooth young face. Hollister can read eyes as well as a gemologist can read the value of a diamond by its clarity, its carats, and its way with light. In Buckle's eyes, he sees fear. Before this confrontation is over, he wants to see pure terror in those eyes, followed by desperation, and finally despairing submission.

Settling into a chair across the table from Buckle, Hollister smiles with contempt. "What kind of coward hides in a hope chest, curled like a baby in the womb?"

The director says nothing.

"Instead of counterstalking me as a real man would have done, one on one, mano a mano," says Hollister, "you ran. You hid beneath a bridge, stole my snowmobile and fled on it, fled with Crockett, hid behind the skirts of a waitress, and cowered in her hope chest."

"It was mano a mano," Buckle complains, "only in the lie you told yourself. You have an army."

"And now you whine like a child." Hollister shakes his head as if to say *What a pathetic specimen.* "What is your story, Tom?"

" 'Story'?"

"What did you put in my food at lunch?"

"I don't know what you're talking about."

"You put something in my food."

"I was nowhere near your food."

"Then what did you put in my drink?"

"I was nowhere near your drink, either."

Hollister leans over the table, the better to read Buckle's devious eyes. "My father had his thousands of novels. He said all the truth of the world was contained in fiction, in the work of storytellers. I read a few of them and saw no truth, nothing but myths and superstitions, wishful thinking and sentimentality and asinine opinions. You're a storyteller, Tom, making your little films. So tell me your story."

"You aren't making sense. I don't know what you want."

Hollister sees Mai-Mai from the corner of his eye and turns his head. She stands before the refrigerator, as though it is a white coffin out of which she has stepped, the infant in her arms.

In that gunshot-distorted face, her smile is evil, her eyes sunken into a vacancy. She's but ten feet away in the small kitchen.

Hollister leans even farther over the table, no longer smiling. "I don't believe in spirits, ghosts. I will not be haunted. *I will not.* What have you done, you bullshit artist?"

Buckle is agitated now, straining in his bonds, his fear evident in the pulsing arterioles in his temples, a beadwork of sweat on his brow. "I don't know what you're talking about."

"Liar. That's what storytellers are, isn't it? Liars? Paid liars? Will you lie and say you don't see her there?"

Faking bewilderment, Buckle looks where Hollister points. "See who?"

The filmmaker's deceitfulness infuriates Hollister. "Somehow she's here because of you. How is this trick performed? My food, my drink contaminated? It's the only explanation. Mai-Mai is *here*."

Buckle regards him with feigned astonishment. "She's dead. She can't be here. You killed her."

"The dumb bitch shot herself."

"Because you told her to."

Hollister pounds the table with his fist—once, twice, a third time. "She's here, she's here, her skull blown out, baby Diederick dead in her arms."

Buckle's agitation passes, and he goes very still in his bonds. His voice is a whisper, not tremulous as it ought to be, but instead accusatory. "You're insane."

Hollister shouts, *"Bring it!"*

One of the rayshaws who accompanied him from the Sno-Cat enters with a Medexpress carrier and puts it on the table.

"Your stories are all lies," Hollister declares. "But I'll have the truth from you."

8

Charlie Weatherwax and Mustafa al-Yamani, in their suite at the Arizona Biltmore, achieve five hours of deep sleep by countering Saturday's amphetamines with one-hundred-milligram tablets of phenobarbital. Charlie responds to his wakeup call. But then he is forced to use a bucket of ice water and considerable brisk slapping of the face to get Mustafa out of bed.

Showered, dressed in fresh clothes from the luggage that has been delivered to them by jet from the Peninsula Hotel in Beverly Hills, fully caffeinated with coffee from room service and tablets from Charlie's apothecary, they arrive by Suburban at the operation-command center in Wesley Bolin Memorial Park directly east of the complex of buildings around the Arizona State Capitol.

The search for Vikram Rangnekar is based on the information—actually bald-faced lies—that Charlie provided to his cell leader, Raimundo Cortez, the previous night. However, because he and Mustafa were incapacitated while the operation was being put together, they aren't in charge of it. This is ideal, because when the Mumbai bad boy can't be found where he doesn't exist, they can credibly claim that the blame lies with the incompetence of others rather than with the intel they provided.

The head of the effort is the special agent in charge of the FBI Phoenix office, Lambert Ash. He is one of nine Arcadians overseeing another 110 non-Arcadian agents—Bureau and Homeland Security in a rare joint operation. They are saturated through an area bordered by Madison Street to the south, Twenty-First Avenue to the west, Van Buren Street to the north, and Seventh Avenue to the east.

Lambert Ash and the other Arcadians, sans Charlie and Mustafa, apparently fancy themselves strategists and clairvoyants. They have reached the conclusion that Rangnekar would go to ground in a safe house in this area only if he has designs on the state legislature, the capitol building, or some important office within the capitol complex. Otherwise, surely he would avoid such a well-policed area.

Therefore, in addition to traditional search methods, Lambert Ash has equipped thirty-six agents with sunglasses-mounted cameras equipped with facial-recognition capability, produced by LLVision Technology, a Beijing-based company. The eyeglasses are wired to handheld devices that contain an offline database of ten thousand faces of interest to authorities. Rangnekar's face is one of these, as is that of Jane Hawk, because there is reason to believe, based on their past association at the FBI, that they might be working together. Once a camera captures a face, it can make a match with those stored in its database in just six hundred milliseconds. If either Vikram or Jane ventures onto a street within the purview of this operation, they will be identified and captured.

Charlie has concealed the fact that Rangnekar and the elusive Hawk bitch are indeed now working together, so that he and Mustafa can find and capture them and receive all the credit. He might be distressed that Lambert Ash is now in the Jane hunt—if there were a chance in a million that she is within the perimeters of this search area. But she is most likely not anywhere in Phoenix, and certainly won't be found skulking through the highly policed neighborhoods around the capitol.

A tent has been set up in Wesley Bolin Memorial Plaza, in the heart of Wesley Bolin Memorial Park, to serve as a communications center for the operation. Coffee is provided, along with bottled juices, a variety of doughnuts, and trays of small sandwiches ranging from egg salad to roast beef with cheese. Charlie and Mustafa, suffering from drug-cocktail hangovers but with serious appetites, avail themselves of the buffet. They stay within the shade of the tent, amused by the urgency infecting the other agents.

From time to time, Lambert Ash or another Arcadian asks them a question about Rangnekar. They are pleased to answer if they have the wanted information, as long as it is not particularly helpful and as long as they are not expected to offer an opinion of any aspect of the search plan that might result in their sharing responsibility for its inevitable failure.

Because Charlie and Mustafa are based primarily in California, they are treated politely by these Arizonans, but as interlopers with little to contribute now that the ball has rolled across state lines. This suits them perfectly. Hours earlier, their prospects had seemed grim. But the enthusiasm with which this operation has been mounted and staffed puts all expectations on the shoulders of those in charge of it, leaving Charlie and Mustafa as bystanders who can, at the sad end of all this, file a report regretfully but solemnly noting the errors in the strategy behind it and the inadequacies of procedure.

As the two of them stand at the end of the buffet, eating in the shade, Mustafa says, "These roast beef sandwiches would be better if they contained sliced cornichons."

"I agree," Charlie says. "What do you think of the egg salad?"

"Too much yolk, Charles. And not enough chopped onion."

"Exactly. But the lettuce is crisp."

"Yes, and it is the only correct lettuce for such sandwiches."

"Romaine," Charlie agrees, "is the best of all lettuces."

9

After the three of them showered and dressed and loaded their luggage in the Terrain Denali, they reconvened in Vikram's room at 8:00 A.M. and sat at the small round table.

For the first time in weeks, Jane intended to venture into the world without a disguise. No wig. No colored contacts. No nose ring or fake mole attached with spirit gum.

"Well, if it isn't Alice Liddell," said Charlene. "How you been, girl?"

Although Vikram always wrapped himself in effusive, glittering personality and good cheer, within that foil was a tenderness and shyness that were the best of him. He regarded Jane now with the bashfulness of a boy and spoke with the awkward poetry of adolescent yearning. "It is such a gift to see you again as you really are."

The worry that oppressed Jane could not restrain her smile. "I've no reason to be someone else anymore. This either works or it doesn't. And if it doesn't, there's nothing else to do but run forever. I'm done with running. Are you ready?"

"No. Yes. Maybe." He nodded. "Let's do it."

"Play Manchurian with me."

"Yes, all right," he said.

"Go now into the whispering room and tell them where to come."

The nanoweb was powered by the electrical activity of the brain itself; however, incorporated in its design was also a microwave-rechargeable battery the size of half a pea to assure transmission capability. A closed-circuit shout-out to other adjusted people could carry as far as thirty miles in all directions.

After Vikram had spoken and simultaneously transmitted the words on which they had agreed, he said, "It's done."

"We better get moving. I'll leave you in a controlled state until this is finished. Are you okay?"

Rising from his chair, he said, "I'm terrified, but I'm all right. Replies are coming in, voices whispering in my head. It's so very strange."

His usual grace had not entirely deserted him, but he walked as if unsure of his balance, a man of two worlds with a foot in each.

Under a pale-blue sky, Phoenix thrust up in stark hard-edged Southwest splendor, a metropolis of light, brightness seeming to fall upon it from every direction at once, the shadows crisp and black and short-lived, the decorative greenery sparse and drought-tolerant and architectural, the benign thermonuclear nature of the sun more evident here than in other great cities.

Jane and Vikram sat together in the backseat of the Terrain Denali, neither of them speaking, while Charlene drove east on Van Buren Street. Traffic was light on a Sunday morning. They passed a complex of cemeteries to the north, the state capitol and associated buildings to the south, University Park to the north, heading toward the destruction of the Arcadians' utopia—or toward the end of the world as they had always known it.

10

They needed a venue where a crowd could gather without raising suspicion, a place near the heart of the city, where the first crowd might draw a second and perhaps larger throng that could insulate it from the easy assault of hostile forces.

The Phoenix Convention Center occupied two buildings. The first and smaller stood the width of the block between North Second Street and North Third. The second structure spanned the ground between North Third and North Fifth Streets.

Immediately behind the larger building, across from it on east Monroe Street, stood St. Mary's Basilica, a historic Roman Catholic church. With its twin bell towers and elevated entrance balcony with balustrade, which was approached by dual staircases, the basilica was beautiful and imposing. The extra-wide sidewalk in front formed a modest plaza, and to the west side lay a tree-shaded park in which were nestled the diocesan offices and residence.

One place where a gathering crowd might seem normal on a Sunday morning was in front of a church.

This was the final day of a large convention of manufacturers of home-improvement products. The doors of the Phoenix center would open in minutes. The nearby basilica stood at the intersection of Third and Monroe. Within a block or so were the Hyatt Regency Hotel, the Sheraton Grand, popular restaurants and shops, the University of Arizona College of Medicine—all sources for a potential audience.

Two of the metered parking spaces on the north side of Monroe weren't occupied. Charlene claimed one of them.

Already more than twenty people had gathered on the deep sidewalk in front of the basilica. None was in conversation with another, each isolate. About them hung a curious air of expectancy, but they didn't seem impatient as they surveyed the morning for an indication of what might happen next. Because their control programs had been engaged, they were not now themselves, but instead tools waiting to be used.

If Jane doubted these people were victims of the Arcadians, Vikram confirmed their nature. "They're all my kind."

The one difference between Vikram and these other adjusted people was that he had essentially taken control of them by a back door, by way of the whispering room. He was one of them, and yet he was for the moment their master.

"We'll wait for the crowd to get a little larger," Jane said.

They came quickly now, having parked their cars in public and hotel garages, at meters where available, to walk to the basilica as if for the nine o'clock mass. No vagrants were among them, no children, no teenagers, no one well past retirement. These were movers and shakers in Phoenix, ranging in age from about thirty to sixty-something, well dressed. In any other circumstance, they would have been more confident and assertive than they were at the moment.

By the microwave network that connected them through the whispering room, Vikram knew them, though he had never before met them. "She's a judge on the state supreme court. He's a major real-estate developer. He's the superintendent of schools."

Jane didn't expect all 286 of the adjusted people in the greater Phoenix area to respond to Vikram's summons. Some would be out of town on business or vacation. Others might be beyond the thirty-mile radius that was the limit of an unassisted whispering room broadcast.

In minutes, approximately a hundred had gathered along the front of the basilica, from the corner at Third and Monroe all the way to the diocesan park. Their silence and odd air of expectation began to inspire curiosity in some passing motorists who slowed to look them over. A few people across the street had stopped outside the convention center to stare in puzzlement at the gathering. A critical moment was approaching.

Jane said, "Let's go, Vikram."

"Me, too," said Charlene.

"You'll be safer here in the car," Jane objected.

"I once stepped back from life," Charlene said, "and that was a mistake. I won't step back from nothin' anymore. Besides, this here is history, and I'm a part of it."

They got out of the car and walked among the crowd, toward a point directly in front of the basilica, equidistant from each of the magnificent towers. As they moved, for Jane's and Charlene's benefit, Vikram identified some of those who had answered his call—the mayor, the founder and CEO of a major technology company listed on Nasdaq, the chancellor of the state university system, the president of the state senate. They all looked expectant, but none appeared anxious, for Vikram had counseled them against anxiety.

All eyes turned to him as he walked among the crowd. Some took notice of Jane and seemed to recognize her. No one spoke or shrank from her. She felt none of the menace she had known when, about two weeks earlier, she had made her way through a convocation of the hive that had assembled to stop her from leaving the town of Iron Furnace, Kentucky.

With Charlene, Jane and Vikram took up a position closer to the basilica than the street. At his direction, the throng closed ranks around them. The summoned were arriving more frequently by the minute, streaming in from surrounding streets, at least 150 strong.

Emblazoned with the call letters of an independent local station and complete with satellite dish, a local TV-news truck arrived and parked imperiously in the pickup zone in front of the convention center. "The head of their news division is adjusted," Vikram reported. In his summoning, he had called for those in the media to bring their cameras and broadcast what was soon to occur.

Not three minutes later, when the crowd had grown to at least two hundred, a second vehicle with satellite dish arrived. This one belonged to a station that was a network affiliate, where also the head of the news division had been injected, and it parked behind the first truck.

The incoming stream slowed, but there might have been nearly 250 adjusteds when the eight o'clock mass ended and scores of people exited the doors of the basilica, onto the elevated portico behind the streetside plaza. Unlike those below them, this group was animated and loquacious, assembling along the balustrade to marvel at the throng and the news trucks, calling down questions that none of the adjusted people answered, adding to the spectacle.

Now, as he and Jane had agreed, Vikram spoke softly aloud, and his words echoed not just within the minds of every member of the hive gathered here, but also, in theory, in the minds of all 16,910 of the adjusted people nationwide. There were two ways to broadcast from the whispering room: first, by direct microwave transmission to the adjusted within a thirty-mile radius; second, to the cellular-phone network of the nearest telecom provider, which would give him instant access to *every* telecom provider in the country through the cooperative arrangement that allowed them to provide their customers with universal service. Every nanoweb control mechanism shared the same electronic address at which it received messages from other members of the hive in a crisis. But Bertold Shenneck had intended that only Arcadian controllers would be able to order an adjusted person to use the whispering room and only for an approved purpose; he had not anticipated that the system could be backdoored.

Vikram told the many thousands that they would henceforth respond to only one key control sentence, not to any with which they had been previously programmed, and that sentence would be "We hold these truths to be self-evident, that all men are created equal."

He commanded them never to reveal this new sentence to anyone and to obey no other but him.

He commanded each of them, if possible, to recall the memory of his or her injection, which had been repressed: when and where it had occurred, who had done it.

For the many thousands, he recited the brief preamble to their revelations that he and Jane had composed, and he ordered them to repeat it six times before proceeding to reveal the details of their enslavement.

Finally, he said, "Speak now to the world."

A moment later, all around Jane, at least 250 voices rose as one. "I have been enslaved by a nanotech control mechanism that webs my brain. There are seventeen thousand of us living, more than nine thousand who killed themselves."

The unanimity of all those raised voices, the perfect chorus of horror brought sudden silence to the worshippers gathered along the balustrade above the street.

11

In a corner of the large command-center tent on the Wesley Bolin Memorial Plaza, Charlie and Mustafa are sitting on folding chairs, having coffee and discussing whether the finest polo shirt is indeed made by To the Nines.

Suddenly, elsewhere in the tent, Lambert Ash goes ballistic, shouting urgently. Agents scatter as if abandoning the search for Vikram Rangnekar to attend some other assignment.

As Charlie and Mustafa rise to their feet, Ash approaches them, his face so red and wrenched with anger that he looks as if he might suffer a cerebral aneurysm. "We got a report, he's like twenty damn blocks from here."

"Who is?" Charlie asks, for he can't get his head around the possibility that their quarry might actually be somewhere in Phoenix.

"*Rangnekar!*" Ash roars. "And Hawk may be with him. Something big is going down at the basilica."

A concert of sirens swells as FBI and Homeland vehicles break for the church.

"'Big'?" Mustafa asks Lambert Ash. "What big, how big?"

"I don't know. Something crazy big. How would I know when I'm wasting my time here, chasing your idiot intel?"

Ash kicks over the chair on which Mustafa had been sitting, and he hurries out of the tent.

12

" . . . **S**eventeen thousand of us living, more than nine thousand who killed themselves."

The synchronized voices had the haunting quality of Gregorian chant. As the crowd pressed around Jane and the sound washed over her, she shivered with emotion. Her heart pounded so hard that her vision pulsed in time with the rhythmic rush of blood. She felt exhilarated and terrified, because triumph and defeat seemed equally possible in this ledge walk on which they were engaged.

On-air talent with their microphones, followed by camera crews, had started toward the basilica when the crowd of well-recognized civic leaders abruptly launched into its shocking recitation. Startled, reporters and cameramen halted in the street, forcing eastbound and westbound traffic to come to a stop. Vehicles quickly clogged the intersections with Monroe at Third Street, and at Fifth. Sirens rose in the distance.

Vikram stood rigid, as though entranced, as if his mind were elsewhere—or in many elsewheres. As the throng swayed and shifted, Jane gripped his arm, concerned that they might be separated, and Charlene grabbed hold of Jane's sport coat.

The crowd completed the final recitation. Their sudden silence seemed to unnerve onlookers almost as much as had the moment when they'd first spoken as one. None of the people along the balustrade above shouted to those below, and for maybe ten seconds the TV crews stood frozen in the street.

Then the woman whom Vikram had identified as a state supreme court justice stepped into the street and spoke to the reporters. "I was injected on November sixth of last year, while attending a conference of judges in San Antonio. Sheila Draper-Cruxton, a justice on the ninth circuit court of appeals, invited me to have dinner in her suite, where I was overwhelmed by three men, bound, gagged, and injected."

13

The cable-news channel broadcast was live coast-to-coast when the co-anchor interrupted herself in the middle of a story about accusations of sexual misconduct against a congressman to say, "I have been enslaved by a nanotech control mechanism that webs my brain. There are seventeen thousand of us living, more than nine thousand who killed themselves."

In the control room, the astonished producer reached for the kill switch as the anchor finished the first sentence. But the network president, who happened to be present, stayed his hand as he, too, said, "I have been enslaved by a nanotech control mechanism that webs my brain. . . ."

—

The United States congressman, chairman of the House Committee on Natural Resources, was speaking at a brunch, before attendees at a convention of those engaged in the solar-power industry, when he seemed to forget his point and fell silent for a long moment, as though consulting his notes. Then he raised his voice to declare, "I have been enslaved by a nanotech—"

He might have gotten all the way through his two-sentence revelation before any of the bored attendees in the chamber realized that he'd gone off the rails. However, the ranking member of the minority party, also invited to address the gathering, began to repeat what the chairman said, speaking the words faster. When they began the second repetition, they did so in sync. By the time they were starting the fourth, all those in attendance had risen to their feet in alarmed bewilderment.

—

The archbishop of Boston, John Cardinal Hickney, an activist and figure of considerable political influence, scheduled to speak after lunch to four hundred business leaders and philanthropists in that city, was also there to provide the invocation prior to the serving of the first course. Standing at the podium on the dais, he had hardly begun when he interrupted himself to declare that he had been enslaved by a nanotech control mechanism.

Startled luncheon guests were further astonished when three of their own rose at various points in the large banquet room and began to affirm that they, too, had been enslaved.

As the cardinal and the three diners began their third recital of this revelation, six other attendees, at four different tables, rose in great agitation and bolted from the room, as if fleeing from an imminent threat. Moments later, John Cardinal Hickney named one of the six as the man who had overseen his restraint and injection fourteen months earlier.

14

Wainwright Hollister instructs one of the two rayshaws in the kitchen to strip off Tom Buckle's flannel shirt, baring his arm for the injection.

Restrained in his chair with zip-ties, the filmmaker tries to resist, but the rayshaw punches him in the face and then backhands him hard, nearly rendering him unconscious. Buckle slumps in his chair, as worthless as he proved to be throughout the hunt, when he'd been more mouse than man.

Hollister will have the pleasure of injecting the filmmaker himself. In little more than four hours, when the nanoweb is formed and interrogation begins, he will know the truth of the substance with which his food or drink was contaminated and will be able to take an antidote; he will then no longer hallucinate the brainless bitch with baby.

As he moves around the kitchen table with the rubber tubing that will serve as a tourniquet, the two rayshaws in the room, who usually speak only when spoken to, suddenly exclaim in unison, "I have been enslaved by a nanotech control mechanism that webs my brain. There are seventeen thousand of us living, more than nine thousand who killed themselves."

Amazement freezes Hollister. As they repeat what they have declared, his mind suddenly awakens to the unthought-of truths that no technology in history has been without flaw and that no attempt at making a utopia on earth has led to other than disaster. As they begin a third recitation, he orders the rayshaws to be silent. Both falter but then at once recover and continue. Thereafter, although he shouts at them to cease and desist, they will not. Indeed, they begin a fourth repetition of this impudent indictment, so that it seems as though they will follow him through all the days of his life, chanting their accusations. Born to power, Wainwright Warwick Hollister will not tolerate such insubordination from any man or woman, not even from presidents and kings, certainly not from these hollowed-out creatures who are mere meat machines. He draws his pistol with its extended magazine and opens fire, expending ten or twelve rounds, cutting them down and shooting them again, again, where they lie dead.

And yet one voice continues: "—enslaved by a nanotech control mechanism that webs my brain."

Assuming it is Thomas Buckle, not yet injected but mocking him, Hollister turns to the filmmaker trapped in the chair, intending to kill him as well, but realizes the error to which emotion and temper have led him. He should have ordered the rayshaws to commit suicide. He shouldn't have shot them himself, because these human equivalents of licensed-to-kill robots are programmed to respond to an attack against one of them as if it is an attack against all. Buckle sits in stunned silence, pale with fear. The remaining voice belongs to the third rayshaw in the house. Hollister pivots toward the hallway, but he is too late. In the open door stands his fate, its face as expressionless as that of a carved-stone god in some remote jungle temple unworshipped and undiscovered for thousands of years. Bullets rip the hero of the revolution, and all strength leaves him as all pain enters. He collapses to the floor as though he is just a man like any other.

He lies immobile on his left side, unable to move as much as a finger. He closes his eyes but sees things behind the lids that he does not like, and opens them again.

Naked, brainless, face fractured, Mai-Mai sits cross-legged on the floor, twelve or fifteen feet away. She is no longer cradling the dead infant. Smothered Diederick, gray-faced, his cataracted eyes as white as innocence, crawls toward his brother on his hands and knees.

Hollister cannot move the smallest finger, but he can roll his head and scream. Although a scream is unworthy of such a great man, he lets loose with it anyway. Relentlessly, little Diederick crosses the floor and comes face-to-face with his sibling. Frissons of horror shiver through Hollister's weakening heart and immobile bones. He turns his head away. Diederick leans closer, lowering his mouth toward his brother's, as though feeding on the increasingly feeble scream. The small cold mouth touches the billionaire's feverish lips, not in a brotherly kiss, but with a greedy, hungry sucking, drawing his breath from him and giving nothing back, until Hollister cannot breathe, cannot breathe, *cannot breathe.*

15

The basilica standing tall, serene, its towers hung with bells now ringing, and naught but chaos in the street below. Adjusted people clustering around reporters to accuse those who had enslaved them. The attendees from the eight o'clock mass on the elevated portico, the faithful arriving for the nine o'clock service, now delayed, crowding the dual staircases. Cars abandoned in the street, traffic hopelessly snarled for blocks along Monroe Street and Third and Fifth. Crowds of the curious, now far exceeding the number of adjusted people, pouring out of the convention center and the nearby

Hyatt Regency. A news helicopter overhead, a police helo at a lower altitude, their rotary wings seeming to chop the dazzling sunlight and fling it down in flickers.

Among that exuberant kaleidoscopic variety of humanity, the sudden incoming phalanxes of men in suits, all of a similar bleak demeanor, caught the attention of the adjusted, who had been warned by Vikram, through the whispering room, to be on the lookout for agents like these. The new arrivals acted with purpose and authority, pushing people out of their way, urgently seeking.

"Jane-ji," he said, "put your arm around my waist, hold fast, stay close. Charlene-ji, hold fast to Jane. My kind will make a wall around us."

"They already are a wall," Jane said, grateful that a fear of crowds did not afflict her.

"A tighter wall than this. And deeper." He cocked his head as though listening to a quiet voice in the cacophony, and then said, "The chief of police is here, he is one of us. He says a number of these newcomers are wearing unusual wraparound sunglasses fitted with cameras and carrying what he believes are facial-recognition devices."

16

Lambert Ash and five other Arcadians, two carrying facial-recognition gear, have located Jane Hawk in the sea of faces. They are moving through the multitudes now, with no intent to apprehend the bitch. She is too well insulated by the mob, beyond easy arrest.

Strangely, the crowd seems enchanted by her, here in defense of her, which must mean that something has happened to begin rehabilitating her reputation, though Ash cannot imagine what that might be. The best thing now is to kill her and later spin the story in the media so it is claimed that she opened fire first, necessitating a shootout in which numerous innocents were killed.

They are maybe thirty feet from her, aggressively wedging their way through the tumultuous crowd, when a famous actor, in Phoenix to shoot a film, looms in their path. Tall, muscular, known for roles in thoughtful TV dramas as well as in big-budget action films, he is an icon, especially to the young. He has one of the most dazzling smiles in the history of the movies, but he is not smiling now. He halts Ash by planting one large hand on his chest and saying, "Hold it right here, numbnuts. You're one of those who brain-scrubbed us."

Hearing this, others turn toward Ash and his men. He recognizes a justice of the state supreme court, the head of the state senate, the Phoenix chief of police.

He says, "Do you see the red queen?" which is the current sentence that opens the control program.

Instead of saying, "Yes, I see," the actor replies, "You're a damn Hawk hunter, but your license just got revoked," and he pulls back his fist to throw a punch.

17

Among these multitudes, there is little in the way of dress, jewelry, and fragrance of which Mustafa al-Yamani can approve. All around him swarm the common ruck and rabble who make him yearn for the quiet upper-class enclaves of Long Island. Why good taste and high style should elude so many of the hoi polloi is a mystery that he will never solve and doesn't care to investigate. Just being among so many of these regrettable people, enraptured by spectacle as they are, makes his skin crawl.

Mustafa and Charlie are standing in the bed of an abandoned pickup truck in the intersection of Third and Monroe, looking over the heads of the crowd, toward the TV crews that seem to be interviewing people in front of the basilica, about what he can only imagine. Whether he gazes south or north on Third, or east on Monroe, scores are hurrying in this direction. In this age of terrorism, people flee such scenes; they don't swarm toward them. There must be a thousand people in the immediate area, their numbers swelling fast. Evidently, something on television has excited them and given them the impression that it is safe to be here.

He says to Charlie, "What is happening, what does it mean?"

Even as he asks the question, before his mentor can respond, he hears the two words called out with excitement by some of the latest arrivals, who are pressing their way through the existing throng as if they must at any cost get closer to the center of the event: *"Jane Hawk . . . Jane Hawk . . . Jane Hawk . . ."*

Just then, four men come out of Monroe Street, moving against the tide, using fists and elbows to gouge through the crowd. The one in the lead is Lambert Ash, Arcadian and special agent in charge of the Phoenix office of the FBI. The three behind him, also Arcadians, are familiar from the command-center tent on Wesley Bolin Memorial Plaza near the state capitol. They seem to be in desperate flight.

Raising his voice, Mustafa asks again, "Charles, what does it mean?"

Charlie puts a hand on Mustafa's shoulder. "My friend, it means it is now every man for himself. Time for each of us to implement the escape plans he made if the worst should happen."

Bewildered, Mustafa says, "Escape plans? I have no such plans. When the revolution is won, I will at last have a mansion in East Egg village. That is my only plan."

Charlie's voice is deeply sad when he says, "My dear friend, I have not wanted to throw cold water on your dreams, but there is no such place as East Egg village or West Egg village."

"But of course there are. They are in the magnificent movie. I have read enough of the book to see they are in the book."

"The author, F. Scott Fitzgerald, invented them," Charlie insists. "They're fictional places. You'll find many nice towns on Long Island, but no East Egg or West Egg."

Charlie Weatherwax's voice remains profoundly sad. But there appears to be a sparkling delight in his eyes, the slightest curve in the right corner of his mouth that might be a mocking smile, as though he has long cherished the moment when he would be able to make this revelation.

"Good-bye," Charlie says. "I will never forget you."

Dazed and confused, Mustafa shakes the offered hand.

Charlie clambers over the tailgate, drops to the street, and makes his way outward through the hordes of incoming rabble, a tall and imposing figure, serene even in crisis.

"*Hawk . . . Jane Hawk . . . Jane . . . Jane Hawk . . .*"

The name reverberates like a canticle through the excited legions, as though they have always known the truth of her, have never bought the lies, and come now in celebration.

She may be a champion to them, but she is the destroyer of his future. Mustafa has no escape plans, no East Egg village anymore, no hope that he will be allowed to change his name to Tom Buchanan or Nick Carraway. He will never be welcomed into old-money society as if he were born to it.

Two men approach the pickup from Monroe Street, fleeing after Charlie, both wearing LLVision sunglasses and carrying a facial-recognition library the size of a hardcover book.

He shouts at them, flashes his FBI badge, and demands their devices. One of them gives him the finger and hurries on, but the other pauses to pass the gear up to him.

Wearing the glasses, Mustafa slowly turns his head this way and that, letting the cameras scan the crowd from his elevated position. Both Jane and Vikram are in the library. If he can find one, he will have found them both.

18

Through the roar of voices and the stutter of helo rotors, Jane heard her name, not once but repeatedly. The shouting voices of men and women rang with excitement, people calling out as might the fans at a rock concert eager for their idol to take the stage. The last thing she wanted, now or ever, was to be revered, to be held above other people as somehow exalted. She'd done only what circumstances had forced her to do, had fought for her life and the life of her child, and to clear her beloved husband's name. She was only one of the billions who struggled for happiness, such as they could find it, who passed from the earth little mourned, one of the billions that no one long remembered but friends and family, and only then for a generation or two. Her face and body were but the envelope in which she'd been sent into the world, no more to be venerated than anyone else's envelope. Her accomplishments, such as they might be, gave her personal satisfaction, but they were little enough when considered against the millennia of human history, the long climb from caves to a walk on the moon. She wanted only a chance at life as others lived it, home and hearth and child and friends.

"Jane Hawk . . . Hawk . . . Jane Hawk . . ."

Leaning close to her right ear, Vikram said, "Blame me, but don't hate me. I messaged the seventeen thousand, 'Jane Hawk is the architect of your liberation. Tell the world.' They're spreading the word everywhere they can. You're all over TV now, though not as a monster."

"But why?" she lamented. "Vikram, why?"

"A group of Arcadian assassins were closing fast on us, intent on killing you for pure spite, not yet willing to believe they'd lost it all. If we hadn't convinced them that this crowd might tear apart anyone who raised a hand against you, they would have killed others to get to you. But now they're fleeing."

Shaken, Jane held fast to him and to Charlene, listening to her name being called out louder, with greater frequency, with greater excitement, as if the growing crowd suddenly understood that she was not merely the force behind these events but was also present, here among them. Listening to them, she understood that she was now—and perhaps for some time to come—the most famous person in the nation, perhaps in the world, and that the experience and wisdom she had gained during her desperate crusade were all she had to help her cope with a very different set of challenges to come.

19

Efrata Sonenberg and her daughter Nophia brought the three from the secret basement by way of the hidden stairs—Bernie Riggowitz, Cornell Jasperson, and Travis. She ushered them into her family room, where the two dogs, Duke and Queenie, capered at the sight of them.

On the big-screen TV, network news anchors appeared dazed, as if the hammer of truth had rapped them smartly on their foreheads. Some of the very reporters who had bought into the demonization of Jane were now in the awkward position of offering a mea culpa and joining in not only the restoration of her reputation but also the construction of a heroic legend, for it was a tendency of the media to swing in extreme arcs.

The photographs broadcast of her were no longer chosen to suggest some wickedness in her heart. In fact, there seemed to be a competition among the networks to see who could present images that most dazzlingly celebrated her beauty.

A story came and went regarding the director of the FBI being arrested as he tried to board the private jet of an Internet mogul, bound for Venezuela. Events were unfolding on such a scale, with such rapidity, that what ordinarily would have been the biggest story of the year was a mere sidebar.

Seated in an armchair, Bernie held Travis on his lap. On the screen appeared a news-chopper shot of the multitudes gathered in the area of St. Mary's Basilica. When the news anchor identified it as a live feed from downtown Phoenix, Bernie said, "That's only a few miles from here, *bubeleh*."

"Is that where my mother is?"

"That's what they say."

"Who're all those people?"

"You might say they've come there to thank her."

"Does she have to shake all their hands?"

"Not all of them, no."

"'Cause she needs to come home."

"You'll see her soon," Bernie promised.

From a chair of his own, Cornell said, "This is the greatest day of my life, the greatest day, the greatest. It's like Mr. Paul Simon sang, *'Sail on silver girl . . . your time has come to shine.'*"

20

Two news choppers now, more reporters and cameramen humping on foot into the area from where they were forced to leave their vans and trucks, a few blocks away. People watching the news on their smartphones. A weird sense of history in the making combined with a freaky holiday vibe.

From his high perch, Mustafa has found her in the crowd. The facial-rec program confirms her ID. He takes off the sunglasses and drops them, with the library of faces, on the bed of the pickup.

He unknots his necktie and discards it, opens the top two buttons on his shirt. He unfastens his belt, strips the holster from it, and throws it away with the pistol. He shrugs out of his jacket. He rolls up his shirtsleeves.

He must not appear to be what he is. He must not look like an FBI agent or a Homeland agent, not like a government agent of any kind.

The switchblade in his pants pocket will do the job.

He climbs down from the truck, into the welter of obnoxious, sweating humanity. Politely, patiently, he makes his way through the ill-dressed mob, not one of whom is capable of recognizing that he is wearing Crockett & Jones shoes, handmade in England at a cost of six hundred dollars for the pair. He smiles affably, responding with a word or two when one of these cretins tells him what a wonderful day it is or how very excited they are. He hates them, every stupid, stinking, ignorant one of them. He would kill them all if he could, but he must settle for just her.

He does not approach her directly, but circles through the throng as a shark swims with no apparent agenda when in fact it is acutely aware of the source of the scent that whets its appetite.

21

"Jane . . . Jane . . . Jane Hawk . . ."

Whether in a violent encounter between two people or in a battle involving battalions, one of the moments most fraught with danger is the moment of triumph, when the other capitulates and the struggle seems to have come to its end at last. Exhausted, you want only rest, hard-earned peace. You have kept your guard up for so long that you feel as if you must let it down or perish of sheer weariness. At that penultimate moment, fortunes can be reversed in an instant.

Jane saw him pressing through the crowd, through the wall of adjusted people that had assembled around her but had begun to lose its coherence. He was a short man who smiled and nodded and spoke to everyone, as though he knew them. He never glanced at her, as if he didn't realize that she was cosseted in this part of the throng. He took a handkerchief from his pants to mop the perspiration from his face. He seemed harmless, and she looked away from him.

———

Mustafa is aware of her in his peripheral vision, her lithe form, her radiant golden hair.

"What a day, what a marvelous day, but so hot!" he declares to a woman whom he doesn't know. He wipes his sweat-sheathed face with a handkerchief and returns the handkerchief to his pants pocket and grips the folded switchblade that rests therein.

He dares to look at Hawk, and for a moment he is transfixed. He has seen photos and film of her, but they do not do her justice. In person she is more than he anticipated—more beautiful, her features more refined, her carriage more elegant than is that even of Daisy Buchanan in his dreams of East Egg village. She is lovelier and more exquisite than any Daisy in the movies, a woman for whom ill-fated Gatsby would have been right to sacrifice everything. If Mustafa can't have her in life, he will have her in death.

—

He seemed harmless, and she looked away as if indifferent to him, but only for an instant, for she had seen the A. Lange & Söhne wrist-watch. It cost north of fifty thousand dollars, identifying him not as some average Joe drawn into the street by all the hubbub, but per-haps as one of *them,* for they had an insatiable love of luxury.

When she looked at once back at him, he was staring at her, his expression dreamy yet intense. He'd returned the handkerchief to his pants.

As the assailant began to extract his hand from his pocket, Jane let go of Vikram, tore free of Charlene, pushed between two intervening people, surged straight at the bastard, and seized his wrist as the hand appeared. The blade flashed from the handle, and for an instant it seemed that all the sunlight of the day was concentrated in that thinness of steel. She kneed him in the crotch as she bent his wrist back. As usual, a good nut-cracking relaxed his grip enough for her to seize the weapon, slicing his thumb as she did so. He went to the pavement of the plaza in front of St. Mary's Basilica, and Jane jammed one foot hard on his neck to keep him down, where he writhed like a serpent, until others came to her assistance.

22

The pastures in the Texas high country were lush and green that spring when Jane turned twenty-eight. The horizon lay so far away and the sky arced so all-encompassing that sometimes it seemed as if the grassy plains were a sea on which she voyaged. She didn't feel adrift, but knew herself to be under sail with some purpose, some destination, that would in time become clear to her.

Her in-laws, Ancel and Clare Hawk, who had been in hiding, had come home in the aftermath of Phoenix, no longer under threat. She had arranged to stay with them at Hawk Ranch for as long as it might take for the world to decide that she did not walk on water and did not want adoration. The ranch hands and the county locals, with whom Nick had grown up, made an effort to treat her as they always had, as if she were no more than friend and family, which indeed was all she was or wanted.

She'd done one hour-long television interview before retreating to the ranch, just so it might be understood that she wanted nothing except a chance to live far outside the light of celebrity, as only another woman seeking happiness. She turned down unsolicited offers for a book deal. A young filmmaker named Thomas Buckle, who'd been present at the timely death of Wainwright Hollister, wanted to tell her story. She persuaded him to focus instead on the lives of Sanjay and Tanuja Shukla, Vikram's cousins, who had been on the Hamlet list and perished, for they'd had great promise as writers and had fallen victim to the Arcadians.

She spoke to Vikram twice a week. Toward the end of that day in Phoenix, he had commanded the 16,910 adjusted people to forget how to use the whispering room, thereby sparing them any worry that they might one day be accessed and controlled again by that back door. He'd become director of an advocacy agency created by the government to monitor the health of those with brain-spanning nanowebs, which might or might not lead to a greater number of cancers and other problems, and to compensate them and the families of those who had been on the Hamlet list. The rayshaws and the women who had been sex toys in the four Aspasia brothels, whose memories and personalities had been obliterated, were beyond rehabilitation and became wards of the state. All this work was in part financed by the billions seized from the Arcadians awaiting trial or, in other cases, after they committed suicide. Sometimes she called

Vikram *chotti batasha,* and he called her *bhenji.* Whether or not the love they had for each other might one day mature into more than the bond between honorary sister and brother, neither could say, and neither worried about it; the matter was one that only providence could sooner or later decide.

Bernie Riggowitz and Cornell Jasperson had bought a house of their own in Scottsdale, an odd-couple arrangement if ever there had been one. She talked to them frequently. They seemed to be cooking up some enterprise that they thought would intrigue her. But they knew she needed time to find her way back into the world.

Her friend and comrade in arms, Luther Tillman, a Minnesota sheriff who thought that he'd lost his family forever to nanoweb implants, was visiting at summer's end with his wife, Rebecca, and their daughters, Twyla and Jolie, to stay for a week at the ranch. Dougal Trahern was coming, too, and Charlene Dumont. It would be a week to celebrate triumph and freedom, but also to remember friends and others who had been murdered in the failed revolution.

The Arcadians who fled America found no refuge anywhere except in a few countries under totalitarian rule, where their lives would be blighted, especially because the United States was relentlessly tracking down every dollar they had squirreled abroad in expectation that their utopia might come to nothing.

On the afternoon of that eventful day in Phoenix, Vikram's cousin Harshad—armed with backup flash drives containing all the information obtained from the Diederick Deodatus Foundation, with Bertold Shenneck's research, and with certain DVDs that Jane had obtained from an Arcadian in Lake Tahoe earlier—emailed exhaustive files not just to numerous media operations in the United States but also to media around the world and, last of all, to WikiLeaks. The truth was too widespread ever to be contained or even censored.

She wasn't surprised that her father, Martin Duroc, famous pianist and secret murderer, had proved to be an Arcadian. He sat now in prison, awaiting one of the mass trials pending.

More days than not, she played the piano, everything from Chopin to Fats Domino. As it always did, music healed.

Travis proved to be resilient, the image of his father not merely in appearance, but also in mind and spirit, in the vastness of his heart. His Exmoor pony, Hannah, lived now in the Hawk Ranch stables, and Ancel diligently formed the boy into a better rider day by day. The pony, the dogs, Duke and Queenie, and a lot of time with his mother seemed to be all the therapy that Travis needed, and he was the only medicine that Jane required. They slept every night in the same room. She let him out of her sight only when he was with his grandfather, though she knew the day would come when she must trust the world with him.

Being here where Nick had grown up, she faced the temptation of living in the past. She resisted. Physicists claimed that time moved slower the farther you traveled toward the edge of the universe and that time also bent back upon itself, suggesting all that has ever been will repeat, perhaps endlessly. If so, there must also be a place along the continuum, at the end of one cycle and the start of the next, where the mouth and tail of time meet, where all that has been exists in a perfect timeless condition, where a husband and wife embrace in an endless kiss, where a father holds his child forever in his loving arms, where death has no dominion. She did not need to dwell excessively on the years with Nick, because they were already within her. She contained the precious past no less than she contained the shining future.

About the Type

This book was set in Palatino, a typeface designed by the German typographer Hermann Zapf (b. 1918). It was named after the Renaissance calligrapher Giovanbattista Palatino. Zapf designed it between 1948 and 1952, and it was his first typeface to be introduced in America. It is a face of unusual elegance.